JANET DAILEY

ASPEN GOLD

Little, Brown and Company

Boston   Toronto   London

Little, Brown and Company Edition

The characters and events in this book are fictitious. Any similarity to real persons, living or dead, is coincidental and not intended by the author.

Book design by H. Roberts
Cover design by Milton Charles
Cover illustration by Dan Osyczka
Hand lettering by Carl Dellacroce

Distributed by Warner Books.

Little, Brown and Company
Time-Life Building
Rockefeller Center
New York, NY 10020

Printed in the United States of America

Published simultaneously in Canada by Little, Brown and Company (Canada) Limited
This book was originally published in hardcover by Little, Brown and Company.
First LB Books mass market paperback edition: May 1992

10 9 8 7 6 5 4 3 2 1

PRAISE FOR

"Colorado mountains meets Hollywood glitz.
Aspen Gold is a . . . novel of
romance, glamour and power . . ."
—*Pittsburgh Press*

☆   ☆   ☆

"ASPEN GOLD is Dailey's latest . . .
extravaganza, set in the Aspen mountains and
crammed with factual history and lore of the
frontier town. . . Again, Dailey delivers."
—*The San Antonio Express-News*

☆   ☆   ☆

". . . Dailey wraps readers in a story filled
with glamour and style . . ."
—*The Ocala, FL Star-Banner*

☆   ☆   ☆

"Its scenic setting, interesting characters and
abundance of romance will make this . . . a hit
. . . Kit is . . . refreshingly alive . . . and the
glimpses of Aspen past and present are colorful
and invigorating."
—*The Richmond Times-Dispatch*

☆   ☆   ☆

". . . ripe with characters you love to love and
love to hate. A master storyteller of romantic
tales, Dailey weaves all the "musts" together to
create the perfect love story."
—*Leisure Magazine*

NOVELS BY JANET DAILEY

Touch the Wind
The Rogue
Ride the Thunder
Night Way
This Calder Sky
This Calder Range
Stands a Calder Man
Calder Born, Calder Bred
Silver Wings, Santiago Blue
The Pride of Hannah Wade
The Glory Game
The Great Alone
Heiress
Rivals
Masquerade
Aspen Gold
Tangled Vines

1

A Learjet streaked across the crisp autumn air, its nose tipped down in a slow but steady angle of descent. Below, the Rockies loomed, mighty upthrusts of granite bristling with spruce. It was a wild land, an ageless land, harsh and beautiful by turns. Its unbridled grandeur was limitless, constantly challenging the strong and mocking the weak—and always indifferent to man's attempts to tame it.

Here, where great herds of elk once grazed the high mountain meadow, five hundred head of crossbred Hereford and Black Angus cattle trailed across the autumn yellow grass, flanked by a half dozen riders. On the right, a river of aspen gold tumbled down the stony breast of a mountain slope, crashed through a black-green wall of pine, and spilled its bright yellow flood onto the meadow.

Sunlight glinted on the jet's polished surface. Old Tom Bannon caught the flash of metal and threw back his head, directing his gaze skyward, away from the cattle being driven to the winter pasture near the headquarters of Stone Creek Ranch.

The ancient Stetson hat on his head was brown and weatherbeaten like the eighty-two-year-old face it shaded. The big hands folded across the saddle horn were speckled with liver spots, and age had fleshed up his big-boned frame and shot his hair with gray.

His widely spaced and deep-set eyes looked out from beneath shaggy brows and searched the flawless October sky for the source of the light flash that had jarred him from his silent reminiscences of past autumn cattle drives. The sight of the sleek aircraft hurtling up the valley like a white arrow flying low—too low—brought his hard, square jaw together.

"Will you look at that blasted fool?" Old Tom flung a hand in the direction of the plane, directing the sharp-edged words at his son and namesake, Tom Bannon. "What in thunderation is going through his head to be flying that low? It's a damned fool stunt, that's what it is."

Following the line of his father's outstretched arm, Tom Bannon spotted the private jet. At thirty-six, he was a younger and leaner version of his father, with a face like the mountains, full of crags and hard surfaces, a face that wasn't handsome, yet one any woman would look at twice. Those who knew him well never called him Young Tom, or even Tom; he was simply Bannon. He'd been that from the first moment his father had set eyes on him and proclaimed, "He's a Bannon, right enough."

"What d'ya bet it's one of those idiots from Hollywood taking a scenic tour before landing in Aspen?" Old Tom challenged.

When Bannon saw the insignia of Olympic Pictures painted on the plane's white fuselage, he had an idea who was on board, but he didn't waste time on speculation. Instead his glance sliced to the cattle bunched in front of the open gate as the droning whine of the jet's engines began to make itself heard.

"Ned! Hank!" he shouted to the two riders on the flanks. "Push 'em through the gate!"

He spared one look to the rear of the herd, locating his nine-year-old daughter, Laura. She trailed behind, her head bobbing from side to side, her slim shoulders dipping and swaying, her fingers snapping to the beat of the rock music coming over her headset. Oblivious to everything but the song, she hadn't heard his shouted order.

Bannon whistled a shrill command to the two cow dogs trotting alongside her pinto. Like twin streaks, they shot after the herd, harrying them from the rear while Bannon pushed at the balking leaders, reluctant to leave the summer range. Ignoring their bawls of protest, he rode his buckskin against them, urging them forward with his voice and the slap of a coiled lariat against his thigh.

From the knoll, Old Tom watched as the first of the cows went through, stiff-legged and suspicious, heads lowered in distrust. But one look at the plane speeding through the sky and Old Tom knew they'd never get the rest of the herd through. The plane was so close he could see the pilot's dark aviator glasses and the faces pressed close to the cabin's porthole windows.

He yelled anyway: "Don't let 'em break. Don't let 'em break!"

The jet thundered by, a scant three hundred feet above the mountain's shoulder and the herd. The noise of its engines caught up with them, breaking across the cattle in a roar that vibrated the air and the ground. The aging red roan beneath Old Tom—a horse that never turned a hair at the blast of a thirty-ought-six between its ears—sank into a crouch, then spun in a half circle, joining the cattle that wheeled as one and bolted back across the meadow, their tufted tails raised high in panic.

For Old Tom, the sight of the stampeding herd and the racing riders was a patch from his youth, when half-wild cattle had run on the ranch. Caught up by the memory, he suddenly felt young again himself and spurred the roan after the herd.

Far ahead, Old Tom spotted his granddaughter sawing on the reins, regaining control of her frightened pinto. He took an instant pride in her skill. From her earliest talking days, he'd taught her to ride like that—loose and straight in the saddle yet always balanced, prepared for any sudden moves by her mount.

Then he saw the wall of aspens beyond, and she was forgotten. If the cattle made it into that dense timber, they'd scatter like leaves in the wind. It would take a day—maybe two—to gather them up again.

"Keep 'em in the meadow!" he shouted. "Don't let 'em get in those trees!"

But the fading rumble of the jet's engines and the loud drum of cloven and shod hooves drowned out his call. Then Old Tom saw that the warning had been needless. Bannon had seen the same thing, and had the buckskin stretched out flat, streaking to catch the leaders and turn them before they reached the timber.

Old Tom watched. There'd been a time when he and the old roan could have made a race of it, but no more. No more.

Inside the jet's lushly appointed cabin, Kit Masters sat on her knees, her shoes kicked off, her long legs tucked beneath her as she leaned across the back of the pewter velvet sofa to look out the window. A hand slid across her back, then settled with familiar ease on the rounded jut of a hipbone. Kit smiled, recognizing the touch of that hand. She glanced back, automatically tucking the loose tumble of honey blond hair behind an ear as John Travis folded his six-foot-two-inch frame onto the plump sofa cushion, angling his body toward hers.

He flashed her one of his trademark smiles—quick, crooked, and wicked—a smile that changed his face from merely sexy to dangerously charming.

"The pilot said we should be flying over your place shortly. Anything look familiar to you yet?" John Travis briefly peered out the window, the downward tip of his head bringing into view the sun-lightened streaks in his darkly gold hair.

"Nearly everything." Idly Kit studied his lean and faintly aristocratic face. It was a strong face, handsome with well-defined bones and a dimpled chin, a face made even more unique by its combination of charm and blatant sex appeal. A combination that had proved to be irresistible to the world at large ever since John Travis had burst onto the Hollywood scene fifteen years ago, soaring to almost instant stardom.

Looking at him, Kit was struck again by the illusory feeling that she'd known John Travis all her life, when, in fact, she'd met him for the first time just six short weeks before, at a party she'd attended only days before auditioning for the female lead in his new, yet-to-be-filmed movie, *White Lies*. A role she'd ultimately won, with the shooting scheduled to begin in a matter of weeks.

Kit turned back to the window, smiling when she recalled the crazy roller-coaster ride her life had taken these last six weeks—a ride full of heart-stopping speed and surprises. She'd loved every minute of it. Yet at the same time, she looked forward to the chance to finally catch her breath.

"If it's all so familiar to you, tell me where we are." John Travis arched a challenging look her way, a faintly ironic color to his blue-gray eyes.

"We're flying over Stone Creek," Kit replied easily, suppressing a slight twinge of pain, her nerves tensing at the sight of it.

"Stone Creek?" He peered out the window again. "I don't see any creek down there."

Her soft laugh drew a glance from Chip Freeman, the director and screenplay author of *White Lies*. But the instant his myopic eyes, aided by bottle-thick glasses, registered the blur of granite and gold mountains beyond the plane's windows, he turned back to the padded black-leather bar trimmed with chrome. The quick bobbing of his Adam's apple betrayed the fact he was a white-knuckle flier of the highest order.

Kit's agent, the stout and stubby Maury Rose, gave no indication that he'd heard her as he continued his nonstop hustling of publicist Yvonne Davis, determined to get Kit the lion's share of media attention at the charity dinner J. D. Lassiter, the billionaire owner of Olympic Pictures, was giving that evening.

Paula Grant was the Learjet's one remaining passenger, a veteran soap actress who possessed that exotic combination of flaming red hair, porcelain skin, and green eyes—a hard and sleek kind of beauty that matched the bitchy characters she portrayed so well. She listened with only half an ear to the byplay between Kit and John Travis as she gazed out the window, intent on the mountain scenery, her deep leather cabin chair swiveled in a conversational mode toward the sofa.

"Stone Creek," Kit explained, "is the ranch that adjoins ours."

Ours. She sobered at her choice of pronouns. Silverwood could no longer accurately be called *ours.* After the death of her father eight months ago, ownership of the four-hundred-acre family ranch had passed solely to her.

The image of her father—the dark and handsome Clint Masters—came readily to her mind. She had recognized long ago that she'd inherited his blood, his recklessness, and his insatiable love of life.

She hadn't been back to the ranch since the funeral—not by choice, but by circumstance. She tried and failed to imagine the ranch house without him in it, without his laughter to fill it.

"Look at all those cows running across the meadow," Paula Grant announced to no one in particular. "And those cowboys chasing them. Good Lord, Kit, don't tell me the Old West is still alive?"

Kit spotted the stampeding herd and groaned in dismay. "Oh, no, we've spooked the cattle. Old Tom's going to have my head when he finds out."

"I take it Old Tom owns the cattle." This close to her, John Travis noticed the sweep of her lashes, the faint freckling across her nose, and the curve of her mouth.

"He does," she replied, her smile radiating that breezy friendliness that had first attracted him to her.

On the surface, Kit Masters seemed typical of thousands of blond wannabes who possessed a kind of sunny and innocent California sexiness that had always had its place in Hollywood. Yet it was the unusual lake blue color of her eyes that lifted her out of the commonplace, eyes with a depth that suggested many things. He wondered if he'd ever uncover all her layers as he breathed in the warm, teasing fragrance of her perfume. It had been a long time since he'd more than indifferently wanted a woman. But there was nothing indifferent about his feelings toward Kit Masters.

"They're moving the cattle down from the summer range," Kit offered in absent explanation. "When I was growing up, Dad and I went over to Stone Creek every spring and helped with the branding and ear-tagging, the vaccinating, culling, and castrating, then drove the herd up to the high country for the summer. In the fall, we'd help bring them down," she recalled, and thought of Bannon, who was so inextricably woven into all her memories of the past. The thought of him revived the old hurt—and the thready tension. She pushed them to the back of her mind. After ten years of practice, she'd become quite skilled at that.

"I simply cannot picture you punching cows, Kit," Paula Grant stated with a bemused shake of her head.

John Travis couldn't help agreeing with Paula Grant's observation, especially when he glanced at Kit, seeing the confident and self-assured tilt of her head.

Kit laughed at her friend's remark and immediately adopted a thick drawl. "Well, Paula honey, I'm plumb sorry you can't see me punching cows, but I did it just the same." She abandoned the accent. "Daddy had me on a horse before I learned to coo—to my mother's horror, I might add. By the time I was two years old, I had a pony of my own. At three, he gave me a miniature lariat and I drove the dogs and chickens crazy trying to rope them. When I was six, I was riding a full-sized horse." Her smile widened. "Of course, my mother countered all that by enrolling me in ballet class, making sure I took piano lessons, and dragging me off to concerts in the Music Tent and performances at the Wheeler Opera House. If I was going to be a cowgirl, she was determined to make me an *urbane* one."

"*Very* urbane," John Travis agreed, taking in the drops of chunky gold that dangled from her earlobes and mixed with strands of long blond hair that ran faintly lawless back from her face. A trio of heavy gold bracelets circled her wrist and clashed with the bright coral jacket she wore over a grape-colored cashmere tunic and slacks. A gold flyaway coat, carelessly thrown over the arm of the sofa, completed the bold and thoroughly modern ensemble—an ensemble that few women had the flair to carry off with any degree of sophistication. Kit was one of them.

"Paula, John T. Look." She pressed closer to the window, her expression showing an excitement that made her appear much younger than thirty-two. "There's Silverwood. My home."

Picking up on the warmth in her voice, John Travis glanced out the window. Attachment to a place was something he'd never known growing up as he had on a succession of military bases scattered over half the globe. At seventeen, he'd run away to California rather than face another move to another base and another strange school. He'd taken up acting on a dare, trading one transient life for another.

With idle curiosity he studied the buildings nestled at the apex of a triangularly shaped valley, walled by two sprawling, snowcapped ridges of the Rocky Mountains. A picturesque barn, weathered gray by the elements, sat in the center with wood fences stretching to make square designs across the valley. In a grove of aspen trees stood a rambling, clapboard house with three gables and a porch that wrapped all four sides of the building.

"It looks positively rustic and quaint, Kit," Paula said on a note of rare approval.

"It does, doesn't it?" Kit murmured, caught up in the memories of the good times she'd had there—and the sad ones.

"It's the setting that does it," Paula stated. "The mountains rising behind it. The fabulous fall colors. I thought nothing could rival autumn in New England, but this"— she lifted a ringed hand to indicate the view from the jet's window—"this is incredible."

Kit's gaze wandered from her childhood home to the mountains that autumn had painted with distilled sunshine. Drifts of canary yellow gleamed between solid ranks of spruce marching up a granite slope. Farther on, still more masses of slender white trunks rose from the forest floor, waving their crowns of saffron, lemon, amber, and topaz.

"I told you how glorious it would be at this time of year, Paula, but you wouldn't believe me," Kit said with a light trace of smugness. "You're such a cynic. You should have been born in Missouri instead of Vermont."

"Cynicism is necessary for survival in this business," Paula replied. "When you've been in it as long as I have, you'll find that out for yourself."

"So you've said. But you know me—I'm an incurable optimist." Kit shrugged in unconcern.

"It's a pity you aren't shooting your movie now instead of waiting for winter, John," Paula Grant remarked. "This scenery is spectacular."

"Careful, Paula," John Travis mocked. "You're starting to sound like a tourist."

"After the charity benefit tonight, that's exactly what I'm going to be for an entire month," she declared, fairly gloating. "No more early-morning calls, no more long days, no more endless pages of dialogue to learn, no more working six days a week. You can't possibly know how ecstatic I was when the writers decided it was time to kill off Rachel—"

"—and the producers had to buy out your contract," John Travis inserted.

"That, too," Paula admitted in a purr. "But after seven years on *Winds of Destiny*, I think I've earned a long and highly paid vacation. Don't you?"

"Pay no attention to John T.," Kit said. "He's spent the last two hours with Chip thinking like a producer instead of an actor."

"It shows." Paula turned back to the window. Something caught her eye and she edged closer to the pane. "That mountain," she murmured. "It looks like it's made of solid gold."

"Considering the price of real estate in Aspen, it might as well be," John Travis observed dryly.

Paula gave an absent nod. "I've heard the cost of even a small place is sinfully high."

Privately Kit hoped they were right, then immediately banished the thought and its overtones of greed.

"That's Aspen coming up, isn't it?" Paula asked.

Through the window, Kit watched the town take shape, spilling across the narrow valley of the Roaring Fork River and onto the shoulders of the walling Rocky Mountains.

Ski runs snaked down the slopes of Aspen Mountain where one hundred years ago black-faced miners trudged wearily home from their shifts in the silver mines. Ultraluxe, ultra-modern mansions littered the mountainsides where once mining equipment stood guard over the entrances to the richest silver mines in the nation. Fashionable shops and trendy boutiques lined Durant Street, the former locale of Aspen's redlight district prior to the turn of the century. Here the rich and celebrated came to play where silver kings, railroad barons, and European royalty once visited.

Its tree-lined streets had known the rattle of horse-drawn streetcars, the rumble of freight wagons, the glitter of fancy carriages, the bleating of flocks of sheep, the tramp of ski-combat troops during the Second World War, the swish of skis, and the purr of Mercedes Benzes.

Kit smiled when she considered the uniqueness of her hometown—from rough mining camp to silver boomtown to near ghost town to world-class resort—a story Hollywood would have called *Cinderella Meets King Midas*. For once, they would have been accurate.

2

A bell chimed twice. John Travis picked up the receiver to the wall-mounted phone and pushed the lighted button, opening the direct line to the cockpit. He listened for a minute, then passed on the message.

"We've been cleared to land. The pilot wants us to buckle up."

Turning from the window, Kit uncurled her legs and searched for her shoes. Out of the corner of her eye, she saw Chip Freeman at the bar, bolting down the remaining juice in his glass. A smile ghosted across her mouth as she silently wondered if Chip had found a new source of Dutch courage.

She located her Bally flats and slipped them on while Chip made his way to the leather chair next to Paula's, his face pinched and white, his gaze fixed on his destination, looking neither to the left nor the right and missing the commiserating smile Kit sent him.

"Poor Chip," she murmured to John Travis as she felt along the back of the sofa cushion for the other half of her seat belt. "He looks like he needs a tranquilizer. You should have kept him talking about the film until we landed."

"We'll be on the ground soon." He cast an amused, but not unkind, glance Chip's way. "He'll make it. He's a big boy."

A particularly apt description, Kit thought. Charles "Chip" Freeman looked like an overgrown boy with his cowlicks and thin, gangly frame—something of a cross between the class genius and the class nerd with a little ninety-pound weakling thrown in. But in her estimation, he was more genius than anything else, both creative and intense.

Like her, after years of struggle, Chip was making his first major movie, complete with big-name stars and a fifty-million-dollar budget. The announcement naming him as director had stunned Hollywood. Granted, he'd written a brilliant screenplay in _White Lies_, incorporating both a compelling storyline and broad commercial appeal. But as a director, he was regarded as too experimental, too outré. True, his last few films had received great critical acclaim, but they'd died at the box office, an unpardonable sin in corporate Hollywood.

As far as Kit was concerned, her future in films couldn't be in better hands than Chip's. Of course, she had the advantage on the moneyheads at the studios. She knew his skill firsthand. Seven years ago, she'd worked under his direction in a local-theater production of _The Glass Menagerie_. The result had been pure drama and pure entertainment. By the end of the show's run, she'd been playing before sold-out crowds. He was good. With this film, he finally had the chance to prove to his multitude of detractors just how talented he was and receive the recognition he justly deserved. Kit was as happy for him as she was for herself.

A whirring hum vibrated through the cabin as the wing flaps were lowered. Chip blanched at the sound and dug his fingers into the ends of the chair's padded leather arms. Paula patted the hand nearest her reassuringly and Chip instantly grabbed it and hung on. Unable to free her fingers, Paula glanced at Kit and shook her head at the hopelessness of the man's terror.

But the action prompted Kit to wonder again at the relationship between Paula and Chip. Sometimes they squabbled like brother and sister; at others, they seemed more like good friends; yet a few times she'd suspected they were lovers. It was odd that she didn't know. She considered Paula her best friend in Hollywood. For the last three years, they'd worked together on the daytime drama *Winds of Destiny*.

John Travis leaned closer. "Will you hold my hand?"

"Why? Are you scared, too?" She smiled, knowing better.

"I could be," he replied, much too drolly.

"And pigs have wings." But she slid her hand in his just the same, fitting palm to palm and linking fingers, liking the warm and simple intimacy of holding hands with him.

At the table, Yvonne Davis shoved the last of her notes into her black crocodile case and clicked it shut. Maury Rose scooped some jelly beans out of the candy dish and settled back in his seat, his short legs barely long enough to let his feet touch the floor. A toupee of nut brown hair, sprinkled with gray to match the rest of his graying hair, covered the crown of his head. As usual, he wore a three-piece suit; he had a penchant for them, preferably made out of a fabric with a shine to it, like sharkskin. But the snug-fitting vest couldn't conceal that he was some thirty pounds overweight. Instead, it acted as a girdle, straining to hold in his spreading paunch.

"Don't forget to mark down that reporter from *People* magazine," Maury admonished, his rapid speech pattern and faint accent betraying his New York origins. "I don't want him mistaken for a paparazzo. You got that?"

"He's already on my press list, Mr. Rose." The Texas-born publicist peered at him over the top of the flame red frames of her half glasses, a thinly veiled irritation in her voice at his insinuation that she didn't know her job. "In fact, I believe I arranged for him to come tonight." But Maury was too thick-skinned for her cloying barb to register. Recognizing that, she turned toward Kit. "How long since you've been back to Aspen?" she asked, making an obvious bid to change the subject.

"If you mean for more than a long weekend, it's been years," Kit admitted. "I always planned to, but invariably, time, money, or circumstance worked against me."

"I know what you mean, honey." Yvonne nodded.

"When I left Houston, I thought I'd be back every year to visit my family in Tomball. And in the last sixteen years, I've been back maybe four times. You get so busy with your new life, you just seem to forget about your old one. I hate to think how many friends I've lost track of over the years. But it can't be helped, I guess." She set her case on the floor next to her chair.

"I guess it can't." Kit thought about Angie Martin, her best friend in high school, and felt a similar regret. Once they'd been notorious for their marathon phone conversations. They'd kept in touch off and on after Kit had moved to L.A., but lately it had been more off than on. Angie had attended the funeral for Kit's father, but they hadn't had time to exchange more than a few words. This time, this trip, it was going to be different. She and Angie were going to have one of their famous gabfests and bitch about Angie's horrible ex-husband, maybe even giggle over her new one. Good Lord, what was her last name now that she'd remarried? Kit couldn't think of it.

"Do you realize, Kit," Yvonne's voice broke into her thoughts, "that you are living everybody's dream—returning to your hometown a big success? Kit Masters, Hollywood's hottest new star."

Kit laughed. "That's very flattering, Yvonne, and *very* premature. We haven't even started shooting yet."

"That may be, but—honey—I've read the script and I've seen the screen test you did. You blew me away, Kit Masters." Tipping her head down, the publicist regarded Kit over the top of her glasses. "That's no hype either. When this movie hits the theaters, you're going to take off so fast nobody will see your smoke."

Kit stared, more than a little taken aback by that proclamation. She remembered John's producer, Nolan Walker, had said something similar after the screen test, but she'd shrugged it off as nothing more than normal enthusiasm for the project itself. She certainly hadn't taken him seriously.

Now, with Yvonne's statement reinforcing that one, she realized that no matter how trite or corny it sounded, this movie could make her a star. She waited to feel that first kernel of excitement at the thought, that first tingling thrill of elation. Nothing.

Granted, fame had never been her goal. She'd always pursued acting roles she wanted to play. Not stardom. Still, she remembered the excitement she'd felt when she first read the script.

She'd been at the studio, taping an episode of the hour-long *Winds of Destiny*, set in a fictional southern town outside Atlanta, Georgia, a place Kit had laughingly called a mix between Peyton Place, Twin Peaks, and Mandingo.

With another scene down and only one more to do before she was through for the day, Kit moved off the pillared gallery of the Great Oaks plantation set, past the pots of fake shrubbery to the floor of the soundstage. She carefully stepped over the cables in her path and headed for the exit, her thick blond hair tamed into a smooth, simple style that suited the quiet, genteel character she portrayed. A layer of makeup concealed the sprinkling of freckles across her nose and gave her complexion that pale, dewy soft look of a Southern woman.

As she passed the set for the Riverside Restaurant, the new center of all the clatter and confusion on the soundstage, one of the gaffers gave her a thumbs-up sign. "You looked great, Kit."

"Thanks." She flashed a smile.

"When are the writers going to let you get wise to that jerk?"

"Never, probably. But it wouldn't matter anyway. You know me—I'm Tess Trueheart." She lifted her hands in a hopeless shrug and continued on her way, sailing out the stage door.

She managed to ignore the temptations of the caterer's table and entered the maze of corridors beyond. Minutes later, Kit breezed into the dressing room she shared with Paula Grant. With few exceptions, shared dressing rooms were a common practice for most daytime-drama productions.

"You're up next," Kit announced and immediately stepped out of the high heels, kicking them out of the way. "Time to do your next dastardly deed."

"What fun," Paula drawled, lounging in the room's sole armchair, her script open on her lap.

Kit peeled off her character's requisite gloves and longed to shed the rest of her costume as well, but she had to wear it in her next scene. She dropped the gloves on the tweed sofa and began picking through the pile of clothes scattered over the back of it.

"Have you seen my smock?"

"On the floor behind the couch," Paula replied. "Don't you ever hang anything up, Kit?"

"Not often," she admitted, donning the sprigged cotton dress. "A lingering rebellion from being raised by a fastidious mother. The original neat freak. Everything was always put back in its proper place. Our floors were so clean you could literally eat off them." When Paula raised a skeptical eyebrow, Kit asserted, "I'm serious. She used a toothbrush to scrub around the floorboards. She even used to iron Dad's shorts. Which is probably why he switched to briefs." She walked over to their tiny, apartment-sized refrigerator for some apple juice and spotted the script on top of it. "What's this?"

"A screenplay Chip wrote."

"*White Lies*," Kit read the title. "This is the one John Travis bought, isn't it?"

Paula made an affirmative sound and rose from the chair to cross to the vanity mirror and check her makeup.

"Have you read it?"

"Yes." Paula fluffed her fiery auburn hair with the tips of her fingers. "There's absolutely nothing in there for me. What's the point of getting involved with a director who's a writer if he never writes a part for me in his scripts?"

"You like him, that's why." Kit smiled at that much-too-cynical remark.

"That has nothing to do with it." She surveyed her reflection. "This hair is a curse. In this town, a redhead is allowed to play either a hooker or a bitch. Do you know I have actually been to auditions, sat and waited my turn, watching brunettes and blondes go in to read. I walk in and the casting director stares for a full second, then accuses, 'My God, you're a redhead,' as if that automatically disqualified me for the part. I'll bet they never looked at a brunette and said 'My God, you're a brunette.' '' Paula leaned closer to the mirror and checked her teeth for lipstick smudges. Satisfied, she straightened. "I'm off."

"Do you mind if I read this?" Kit held up the script.

"Be Chip's guest." Paula waved a hand in permission and crossed to the door.

Alone, Kit settled into the armchair Paula had vacated, and opened the script. Within the first few pages it was obvious the female lead, Eden Fox, was a scheming blonde who had married a much older man for his money and position, then killed him to have them for herself. A few pages farther, Kit wasn't so sure. Another ten pages and she was completely captivated by this complex and fascinating character.

"She didn't do it," Kit murmured in astonishment, the closed script in her lap. "This isn't some jazzed-up rewrite of *Witness for the Prosecution*, *Body Heat*, or *Black Widow*."

She threw back her head and laughed at how thoroughly she'd been fooled. Why? Because the character of Eden was so believable, so full of contradictions. Paula walked into the dressing room and Kit bounded to her feet, excited by the story, the characters, everything.

"Why didn't you tell me how fabulous this is? My God, Paula, this script is gold. And Eden—she's far from being an angel, but she's not all bad either." She stopped, spinning in a circle. "God, I'd love to play this part. I'd kill for it."

Paula threw her a sideways look as she unfastened the rhinestone buttons on the cobalt blue cocktail dress she wore. "I always knew killing and loving could be very close together sometimes."

"Who's playing Eden? No—don't tell me." Kit waved off the question with her hand. "I don't want to know. It'll just make it worse knowing I can't have it."

"They haven't cast anyone in the part yet."

"They haven't! Are they still holding auditions?"

"The last I heard they were."

Kit didn't wait to hear more. She raced out of the dressing room and flew down the hall to the telephone. "Maury, you've got to get me an audition for the role of Eden in John Travis's new film *White Lies*,'' she rushed the minute he came on the line.

"Who's the casting director?"

"I don't know. I forgot to ask Paula."

"Travis, you say. It won't be hard to find out." He paused a moment. "That's moving into the big leagues, Kit."

"I'm going to get this part, Maury."

"Sure you are, Kit," he agreed absently. "If I'm not mistaken, Travis has a film deal with Olympic Pictures, Lassiter's company. He's throwing a big party, I heard. If I can get you an audition, I'll see if I can wangle an invitation to the party as well. You gotta work all the angles, Kit. Charm. Flirt. Whatever it takes."

"Just get me an audition and I'll take it from there." She hung up, still hugging the script.

Excitement. She'd felt tons of it. Now, faced with the possibility of stardom, she felt nothing—except maybe a little uneasiness.

The grinding whine of the jet's hydraulics signaled the lowering of the landing gear. A second later Kit felt the sudden drag on the plane, reducing its speed. Chip Freeman sucked in a breath and squeezed his eyes shut. Within minutes, the wheels skipped, then rolled onto the runway at Sardy Field, west of Aspen.

"I think it's safe to let go of my hand now, Chip," Paula murmured dryly. "We're on the ground."

"Right. Sorry." He released it and dragged in his first easy breath as the plane taxied off the runway toward flight-base operations. "God, I hate flying," he said to no one in particular.

"You're kidding." Paula gave him a deadpan look.

"Paula," Kit chided, biting back a smile.

"It wasn't your hand. Look, he snapped off a nail." She examined the damage. "Now I'll need a manicure before the party tonight."

"No problem," Maury inserted. "I've arranged for a hairdresser and manicurist to be at John's place at six to help Kit get ready for tonight's bash. When they're through with her, you can have the girl fix your nail.''

"You never said anything to me about this, Maury," Kit began. "I don't need—''

"Yes, you do. You're my star." He beamed at her, a warmth softening the usual shrewd look of his face. "I want you to look like a million dollars tonight—even if Travis refused to let his production company pay you that much," he added, sending a sly look at the man beside her.

John Travis coolly returned it. He didn't think much of Maury as an agent. He never had and he never tried to hide it. "We both know she isn't in a position to command that high a price."

Maury quickly qualified that by saying, "Yet."

"It's crass to talk about money." Chip was out of his seat the instant the plane came to a stop.

"If you think the movie business is about art, you'd better wise up, kid," Maury warned.

Chip swung back to face him. "You're right, Rose. You're dead right. For most of you, it's all about greed, grosses, and glory. But for some of us, it's still about the film. And without us, you'd be up shit creek."

"True," Maury agreed, not in the least offended.

The copilot chose that moment to emerge from the cockpit and crack the hatch door. Chip turned and went down the steps as soon as they were locked in place and the handrails were up. Paula followed him down. Maury waved for Yvonne Davis to go ahead of him and waited for Kit while she gathered up her purse and gold coat.

"That kid not only has a big ego, but he's got a short fuse, doesn't he?" Maury tilted his head back to meet her eyes. Even at five-six, she was still taller than he was.

"He does." She gave the end of his prominent nose a sharp but affectionate tap. "So behave yourself and stop lighting it."

"Me?" He drew back in mock innocence, then chuckled and headed for the open hatchway.

Kit shook her head. "He's impossible."

"Among other things," John Travis murmured, but didn't

elaborate. And Kit didn't pursue the remark. She already knew his opinion of Maury. It was old ground and she wasn't in the mood to quarrel.

Descending the steps, Kit emerged from the plane's shadow into the afternoon's brilliant sunshine. Automatically she lifted her eyes to the autumn-cloaked range of mountains, the blending of gentleness and grandeur reaching on and on, finally melting into the paint-box blue of the sky. Always a creature of the senses eager to absorb every sight, smell, and sound, Kit turned her face to the feathering breeze and drew in the invigorating freshness of the high mountain air. It seemed charged with ozone, alive with possibilities, a trace of pine resin giving it the smell of home.

When John Travis joined her, she turned, her glance skimming the parade of executive aircraft—Gulfstreams, Learjets, and Challengers—parked wingtip to wingtip outside Aspen Base Operations. With a nod of her head, she indicated the Boeing 727 that loomed over the other private jets. "It looks like J. D. has already arrived. There's his plane."

Paula overheard her remark. "You mean that one is Lassiter's personal jet?"

"What else?" Chip Freeman retorted somewhat caustically, leaving Kit with the impression he was still smarting from Maury's jibe. "The great man always has to have the biggest and the best in everything. It's a mania with him."

"That's hardly a crime, Chip." Paula sent him a half-amused glance, her expression showing a smooth and worldly wisdom.

His face took on a mutinous look. "The man's an autocratic ass. He thinks he can control everything and everyone."

"Now, where would he get an idea like that?" Paula mocked. "It couldn't be a little thing like power and money, could it?" When Chip clamped his mouth shut and looked away, she reached out in sudden sympathy and laid a hand on his arm. "Chip, it isn't smart to snap at the hand that feeds you . . . even if you do it behind his back."

"If he was here, I'd do it to his face."

"Careful, Chip," John Travis cautioned. "You're not exactly J. D.'s favorite person."

His head came around at that, the thick lenses in his glasses magnifying the glaring look of his brown eyes. "And he's not mine. That makes us even."

"Not quite." John's face was utterly smooth, but there was a touch of firmness in his tone. "It's still his fifty million that's funding the picture and his company that will be distributing the film."

"And you can bet he never lets anyone forget it," Chip muttered.

John smiled somewhat grimly. "Considering you were born without a filter between your brain and your mouth, do us all a favor, Chip, and keep your mouth shut around Lassiter tonight."

The resistance went out of him and he hung his head like a chastised schoolboy. "I'll try, John," he said. "So help me God, I'll try. But the man doesn't know a good movie from a bad one—let alone what makes a good script."

Two weeks ago Kit had heard a vague rumor that J. D. Lassiter was demanding some script changes. Was that what Chip was upset about? She knew Chip planned to do some fine-tuning on the screenplay as well as scout locations for the film while he was here in Aspen. Was Lassiter demanding more than that?

A man dressed in jeans and a windbreaker fastened at the waist approached the plane, his tanned, All-American face wreathed in a smile, his eyes singling out John Travis. "Welcome back to Aspen, Mr. Travis. It's good to see you again."

"Thanks, Dan." He stepped forward and shook hands with him, then turned back to the group, explaining, "This is Dan Somers. He handles security for me in Aspen. Dan and a couple of his men will be on hand tonight to make sure the fans—and the fanatics—stay at a safe distance."

Kit glanced at the bodyguard, aware that John Travis never made public appearances without at least one at his side. Three years ago he'd had his ribs broken after he'd been attacked at a premiere by a man wielding a baseball bat, a man who had stalked him for months. That, combined with the rash of attacks on other celebrities by deranged fans in recent years, had served to double his already heightened sense of caution.

Fame and fear had become almost synonymous; a sign of the times, Kit decided, a little soberly.

"Bert's bringing the limo up." Dan Somers motioned at the stretch Lincoln driving onto the concrete apron. "As soon as I check on your luggage, we'll be ready to roll."

"Sounds good."

With a saluting wave, the bodyguard moved toward the rear of the aircraft where two of the ground crew were off-loading their bags.

"I thought Abe and Nolan were going to meet us when we landed." Chip frowned absently. "I wanted to go over the preliminary shooting schedule with them. Nolan's got it way too tight."

"They probably got held up at the house." The limo came to a stop well clear of the aircraft. Taking Kit's arm, John guided her toward the car.

"Wait a sec, Kit," Maury called.

Looking back, Kit saw Maury, his short legs quick-step-ping to catch up with them. She disengaged herself from John's hand. "We'll be right there," she promised, then turned to wait for Maury.

He halted in front of her. Forced by his short stature to look up to nearly everyone, including Kit, Maury Rose had long ago adopted a tilt to his head that was blatantly aggressive, lifting his big, hooked nose in the air and allowing his deep-set eyes to fix their gaze on the person before him. It was that great beak of a nose combined with his New York accent and his tightfisted way with a dollar that had prompted people to believe he was Jewish.

Some years ago, he'd admitted to Kit that he was no more Jewish than Billy Graham. But shortly after coming to Hollywood, he'd discovered that actors liked the idea of their agent being Jewish, believing it meant he would bargain harder to get them a good deal. So, operating on P. T. Barnum's adage of "Give the people what they want," he'd stopped denying he was Jewish and started closing his office on Yom Kippur and Hanukkah, accepting invitations to bar mitzvahs for studio executives' and producers' sons, and eating his eggs and bacon at home and ordering lox and bagels in restaurants.

Without question, Maury Rose belonged in Hollywood.

"What is it, Maury?" Kit asked, her curiosity aroused by the determined expression he wore.

"It's about this bash tonight." He tucked his arm inside hers and headed in the general direction of the limo, his pace deliberately unhurried. "I want you to stay glued to Travis from the time you leave the house until you get back."

"Don't you think that could get a little awkward? Especially if he asks some other woman to dance or goes to the men's room?" she countered with a perfectly straight face.

"Be serious, Kit."

"Why?" She grinned. "You're serious enough for both of us." She could tell he was not amused. "Okay, I'm serious. You want me to be John's Siamese twin tonight."

"I do. *W* is covering the party tonight as well as *People*. If anybody takes a picture of Travis, I want you in the shot. Hang all over him if you have to, but make sure you're close enough that they can't crop you out."

"Right." She nodded, feeling more and more like a veteran of the publicity game—and not particularly liking it.

"Good." Maury rushed on, "Now, this Davis woman's getting some other interviews lined up for you. Mostly local stuff. 'Hometown girl makes good'—that sort of thing. We'll go over them once they're firmed up."

Kit sighed inwardly. She'd hoped that after tonight's charity benefit, she'd get a respite from all the interviews and photo sessions—at least for a few weeks until the filming actually started. The publicity blitz had started a month ago when she'd signed the contract to play the role of Eden in *White Lies*. At first, all the media attention had been fun and exciting. Now the pleasure had begun to wane. She wanted a break from it, but it seemed that wasn't to be.

John Travis stood beside the limo, watching their slow approach and feeling again an old run of irritation for that squat toad of an agent Maury Rose. A sound like a sigh came from Paula Grant. She was watching the pair, too.

Briefly she met his glance. "Why did he come along with us? I've never been clear on the reason."

"The next time you're close to him, take a deep breath," he suggested, cloaking his contempt of the man in amused disdain. "You'll smell two things: greed and fear. Kit is his ticket to the big time and the big money and he's terrified she'll dump him." He paused, then added, "I wish she would."

"He's been her agent from the very beginning." The slight lift of her shoulders seemed to indicate that settled the issue, but he could tell by her expression that Paula didn't disagree with him.

"You're Kit's friend. Convince her she needs to get rid of him and sign with some high-powered agency like Creative Artists or William Morris, one that can do her some good."

"I'd be wasting my breath. Kit's too loyal." Her smile turned wry and a little sad when she looked at him. "I believed in such things once. Didn't you?"

"I don't remember," he replied a little stiffly.

"Yeah, it's been that long ago for me, too." She turned and climbed into the limo.

Dan Somers came striding across the tarmac, arriving at the limo simultaneously with Kit and Maury. "Everything's taken care of," he said. "Ready?"

"Ready," John confirmed and offered an assisting hand to Kit as she slipped into the limousine.

3

The cattle milled in a tight circle, a black mass of bawling confusion after the silence of their run. Bannon reined the buckskin in alongside the lank and weathered Hank Gibbs.

"How many got away into the trees, Hank?" Bannon sat straight-legged in the saddle, one arm full length and the other lifted slightly with the reins. The afternoon sun gave his face a deep bronze cast and the shaggy edges of his hair showed a dark brown beneath his faded hat.

Hank's left cheek bulged with a wad of tobacco. He turned and spat a stream of yellow juice at the ground before answering. "Near as I can figure, about a dozen."

Bannon nodded. That had been his guess, too. "We'll come back tomorrow and round them up. Take the point, Hank. Let's get this herd lined out for home."

"Whatever you say, boss." Hank swung the sock-legged sorrel away from Bannon and pointed it toward the now-distant gate.

Once Hank was positioned between the herd and the gate, Bannon signaled to the other riders. Within minutes, the crossbred Angus and Hereford cows were strung in a loose line with Hank in the lead, a tobacco-chewing pied piper.

This time the cattle didn't have a chance to balk at the gate. Hank looped his rope around the neck of the lead cow and dragged it through. The rest followed as docile as shorn lambs. Bannon brought up the rear and closed the gate when the last one was through.

His daughter, Laura, waited for him on her flashy black-and-white pinto. She wore a boy's denim work jacket and a pair of snug jeans with the legs tucked inside small cowboy boots. Her black hair was plaited in a single braid down her back, the headset to her pocket tape player dangling forgotten around her neck.

"That was a real stampede, wasn't it, Dad?" Her gray eyes still held the excitement of it.

"It was a real one, all right," he confirmed with a half smile. Together they moved after the herd, putting their horses to a shuffling trot to catch up with it.

"It was awesome," Laura declared, then bit her lower lip in sudden delight. "I can hardly wait to tell Buffy. She's gonna die when she hears about it."

Bannon watched her giggle, seeing the liveliness in her eyes and the growing beauty in her face. Both came from her mother. It was something Bannon had watched for through the years. And yet, as much as he'd expected it, it was still unsettling to see in her the image of a woman who'd been dead for nine years. It was as if his wife—the beautiful and tempestuous Diana—was reaching out from the grave to remind him of that one brief, beautiful . . . and miserable year of their marriage.

"The Pie almost came unglued when the plane buzzed us. It was all I could do to hold him and keep him from bolting for the trees," Laura said, then reached forward and gave the pinto's arched neck a pat. "But you settled down for me right away, didn't you, boy?"

"He's a good horse." For all the piebald's showy color and showy ways, the gelding had a calm and steady disposition, making him the ideal mount for a young girl.

"He's the best," Laura replied matter-of-factly.

Old Tom Bannon caught that last statement as they joined him at the drag. "Who's the best?"

"The Pie, of course," she answered blithely.

"Humph." He cast a critical horseman's eye over the pinto's lathered sides and neck. "He's all sand and no bottom," he announced, picking out the animal's one major fault—lack of endurance. "Now, you take that buckskin your father's riding, he can go all day and still be as fresh at the end of it as when he started."

"Gramps, that's not fair."

"Fair or not, it's the truth."

She knew better than to argue. Instead she changed the subject. "Did you see the plane, Dad?" She tipped her head back to look at the sky, her expression all soft and dreamy. "Who do you think was in it?"

"Fools, that's who."

"Gramps." She flashed him an exasperated look, then resumed her idle musing. "Do you suppose it was Cher? Or maybe Melanie and Don Johnson? Or John Travis? Or that guy who played the Joker in *Batman*?"

"Jack Nicholson," Bannon supplied the actor's name, certain she'd been closer to the mark when she'd mentioned John Travis. And certain as well that Kit had been on board with him, making a triumphant return as the co-star of Travis's new film to be shot in Aspen. No one deserved success more than Kit. Bannon was glad for her. Yet the thought of her brought a nagging feeling of guilt and regret.

"I wish I was going to the party at the Jerome with you tonight," Laura said with a sigh. "It would be neat to see all the stars."

Bannon smiled at the wistfulness in her voice. "Look at it this way, Laura, in a few more years you'll be old enough to be my date."

"Get real, Dad." She threw him a sidelong look of admonishment. "Girls don't date their fathers."

"My mistake." He laughed and gave the front of her hat brim a tug, pulling it low on her forehead. She pushed her hat back to its former angle and laughed with him, making the moment something special between father and daughter, something to be stored away and remembered at a faraway time.

The shared laughter left a soft curve to his mouth as he cast a measuring glance at the sun, gauging the time by its position in the sky. "If we don't get these cattle moving, your granddad and I are going to be late for the party, and you're going to be late for supper with Buffy."

Immediately the three of them picked up the pace, pressing the ambling beasts in front of them into a trot.

"How many cows got away in the trees?" Old Tom wanted to know.

"About a dozen." Bannon slapped his coiled rope at a lagging cow that briefly considered making a break for it. "I thought we'd get them tomorrow."

"But that's Sunday, Dad," Laura protested. "Our youth choir is going to sing at church and I have a solo. Aunt Sondra's coming and everything. You've got to be there. We've been practicing for weeks and weeks."

"We can't miss that, can we?" he murmured and winked at his father. "Do you think we can leave them till after church?"

"I don't know." Old Tom pretended to give the matter serious consideration. "They could get so lost we'll never find them."

Laura knew she was being teased. "You can't fool me. I know you'll be there tomorrow," she said with complete conviction, then touched a heel to the pinto and sent it cantering ahead to assume a position on the flank.

Bannon watched her for a moment, then shook his head in bemusement. "I think she has our number."

Old Tom grunted an acknowledgment, then both men lapsed into silence. For a time Old Tom watched the black-rumped cows in front of them, their chunky hips rising and falling in rhythm with their shuffling gaits. But the old roan knew the job and the trail as well as he did. Soon Old Tom let his age-mottled hands settle onto the saddle horn and let his attention wander.

He lifted his gaze and surveyed the craggy sea of peaks, the light pure and the sky blue. A faint wind came off the peaks and rustled through the trees like the echoes of a distant waterfall. Across the years, he heard the voice of his wife—

his beloved Beauty—as clear as if she were riding beside him. "Only Mozart made music beautiful enough for a day like this, Tom." In his mind's eye, he saw the rapt look on her face as she gazed at the mountains aflame in a symphony of color.

Ahead, the broad trail opened into another meadow that made a tawny splash against the emerald solidness of the pines. The cattle, bred for the leanness of their beef, stretched in a wide, black line across it, flanked by outriders.

Facing this range that was his home, the only one he'd ever known, seeing its thick layer of fertility, its length and its breadth, its wildness and its beauty, Old Tom felt a strength in his chest and his muscles. With pride, he watched the cowboys working ahead of him, keeping the line steadily moving.

"Cowboying is a lousy job," Old Tom announced, breaking the silence. "Low pay for long hours of dirty, backbreaking work. There's nothing glamorous or romantic about it."

"The same can be said for ranching," Bannon said with a smile.

"Don't I know it." Old Tom snorted a laugh. "Been at this business better than sixty years and about all I got to show for it are bones that creak louder than this saddle. Hell, we're still just one step ahead of the bank."

"True." A faint smile lightened the assured and rather hard cast of his features.

"But it don't matter what you say against it. This is the way man was meant to live—close to the earth where you can watch the seasons change and feel the cycle of life." The roan horse splashed through a small stream, its clear waters muddied by the cattle's cloven hooves stirring up its bottom. "Out here, there's none of them newfangled computers or the stink of towns, no walls hemming you in. There's just weather, water, grass, and cattle—and man standing against the things the mountains put against a lone man. That's what stiffens his backbone and makes him view the world differently than other men."

"Could be."

"Could be? Hell, it is."

"Right." Again the smile showed.

Taught by the land to be watchful and aware of his surroundings, Bannon let his glance make a sweeping arc, pausing for a moment on the mountains to the north. Winter crouched somewhere beyond it. One day or one night, it would swirl in and turn the land white, shriveling every living thing exposed to it. He knew this land, and the feeling of being in it expanded his chest and sharpened his pleasure in the moment.

It was a country of extremes, of deep silences and howling winds, of incredibly lush greenness and high suns rent by boiling thunderheads unleashing jagged bolts of lightning to walk the rims and canyons amidst torrents of rain, of the drowsy crystalline peace of a winter dawn and the ominous roar of an avalanche somewhere high up. This was the Rockies, raw and primitive, beyond taming. It scoured the softness out of a man and put an expression in his eyes that never faded. And a claim on his heart that never lost its power.

The limo rolled to a quiet stop in front of a sprawling, multileveled house located in the exclusive, gate-guarded community of Starwood, Aspen's renowned luxury subdivision. Spread across the shoulder of a mountain overlooking the town, the contemporary structure was all wood and stone and soaring glass, strewn with sun decks, terraces, and balconies.

"Here we are." John Travis helped Kit out of the rear passenger seat. She paused beside him to stare at the house, her eye drawn by the striking counterpoint its geometric lines made to the natural beauty of the mountain rising behind it. He gestured at the house, presenting it to her with a lift of his hand. " 'Be it ever so humble.' "

"Not humble, John T.," Kit declared, her eyes alight with humor. "This house wouldn't know how to be humble."

"You could be right." The cleft in his chin deepened with his answering smile.

"I know I am." She turned back to the house. The land around it had a wild, natural look, the evergreens and shrubbery growing free, showing no traces of a gardener's shears—the sure sign of an expert's touch.

"Look at this view." Paula stood on the other side of the limo, facing the view the house commanded of the Roaring Fork Valley, the town of Aspen, and the Elk Mountain range. "You should be shooting your movie now, Chip," she said to the man beside her. "Think what an opening shot it would make with all this spectacular color."

"It wouldn't work," he said, not even trying to temper the curtness of his rejection. "*White Lies* needs the winter setting, Aspen blanketed in snow. I already know the opening shot I want." He held his hands, framing the shot for his mind's eye. "We'll be at the top of the ski run on that mountain overlooking Aspen. The focus will be on three gorgeous women, snowbunnies in tight, bright, spandex ski suits, their backs to the camera. We'll pull back a little." His voice had an intense pitch. "Then Eden will whoosh in from off camera, goggles covering her eyes, her blond hair loose and flying. Down the slope she'll go, the camera following her all the way to the bottom, where she'll spray to a stop and rip off her goggles. McCord's waiting for her." Chip paused, lowering his hands. "And there will be Aspen, all iced and glamorous," he ended softly in utter satisfaction.

"Yes," Kit nodded. "It's perfect, Chip. I love it."

He whirled to face her, his eyes round with sudden alarm. "I never asked—can you ski, Kit?"

She was tempted to tease him and say that she couldn't, but Chip Freeman didn't have the greatest sense of humor; in fact, it was almost nonexistent.

"It's been a few years since I spent much time on the slopes, but—yes, I can ski," she told him. "Although I'm better at cross-country than downhill."

"I planned on using a stunt double for the major portion of the run." Chip walked around the back of the car. "But I wanted *you* skiing into frame. The camera to see *your* face. If I have to splice something in the editing room, it would ruin the whole shot." Stopping beside her, he cocked his head to one side, the thick lenses in his glasses giving him an owlish look. "When you went in for your fittings last week, did Sofie show you her sketch for your ski outfit?"

"Yes." Sofie DeWitt was the costume designer for the film, a woman on her way to becoming a Hollywood legend.

"Forget what she showed you. I threw it out. The colors were all wrong." Chip took her by the arm and propelled her toward the series of steps leading to the front door. "I don't want Eden in blacks and yellows or those fake lizard-skin looks. She's too classy for that. But the outfit needs to be bright enough for her to stand out from the other skiers when she's going down the slope, yet unique. I see her in jewel tones. Sofie and I talked about using a rich shade of amethyst for the ski pants and a deep royal blue for the jacket . . . with a little iridescence in it to give a hint of purple."

"Sounds gorgeous." Kit stopped by the front door of hammered bronze, inset with swirled, opaque glass.

Maury halted at the top of the steps, laboring to get his breath. "That was some climb." He mopped the perspiration from his forehead, careful not to dislodge his toupee. "I'm out of shape."

"It's the altitude," Kit explained. "Aspen sits over eight thousand feet above sea level. Up here, it's probably closer to nine."

"They should pass out oxygen tanks," Maury puffed.

"You can say that again," Paula murmured.

Maury weakly shook his head. "I don't have the breath."

John made his way up to the front door and opened it. "Come on. You can collapse inside."

"Thank God," Paula muttered and followed Kit into the house. Four steps inside the dramatic entryway, she stopped and grabbed Kit's arm. "This is no mansion," she said in an undertone. "It's a snow palace."

"And *snow* is the operative word," Kit agreed.

The entryway was all in shades of white: the glazed walls, the marble floor, and the staircase. The enormous chandelier suspended from the ceiling resembled a modern ice sculpture done in gleaming silver and crystal. Its brilliance bleached the whiteness even more, dazzling the eyes.

More white shone from the room beyond the double doors to her left. Curious, Kit walked over and descended the two steps into a spacious, cathedral-ceilinged living room. This time the white of the walls and furniture was broken by the rich brown of oak flooring and the green of potted ficus trees. She barely glanced at the sunken conversation pit in the corner or its fireplace of white stone. The whole of her attention was caught by the sweep of glass and the mountain vista beyond it, the absence of color making the view the focal point of the room.

"It must be stunning in the winter when the mountains are white with snow." Kit turned, expecting to find Paula and discovering John beside her instead.

"It is, especially at night with the lights of Aspen glittering like clusters of ground stars." Reaching up, he let his fingers tangle lightly with the ends of her hair. "Of course, it's a view best seen from the balcony off the master suite." He brought his gaze back to her face. "I think you'd like it."

"I'd probably love it," she agreed easily.

"I meant the master suite."

"So did I," Kit admitted. This close to him, it was easy to remember the heat of his kisses, the taste of them, and the heady feelings they evoked.

"Then what's stopping you?" He moved closer, his low voice all bourbon warm and lazy, the sound of it making it even easier to imagine making love with him.

"The scars from old burns." She'd loved before—wholly, deeply, completely—the only way she knew to love. But that love had been rejected. She'd never forgotten the pain of that. Since then, she'd learned to be cautious of physical relationships. Not an easy thing for her to do considering she operated on emotion. "Besides, John T.," Kit said, keeping it light, "you're not exactly known for your constancy with women."

"True." His gaze traveled over her face, its look thoughtful and unexpectedly serious. "But I have a feeling it will be different with you. Very different."

Kit laughed and brushed a quick kiss across his cheek. "It's about time."

Before he could follow up on that kiss, Maury walked down the steps into the living room, the others drifting along

behind him. "This is some layout you've got here, Travis."
Maury took note of the full bar along one wall and ignored
the flicker of irritation in John's expression. "You got a
pool?" He padded over to the glass doors leading onto a
wood-decked balcony.

John lit a cigarette and blew out the smoke, his gaze following Kit as she wandered over to idly inspect a celadon vase.
"An indoor-outdoor pool, sauna, hot tub, exercise room, a
climate-controlled wine cellar, a billiard room, private studio
office—all the amenities."

"What? No bowling alley?" Maury joked.

"No." John swung toward Chip. "The media room is
equipped with a projector and screen. We'll be able to view
the dailies there."

"Great." His face lit up at the news.

"Forget the amenities. The house is still beautiful."
Yvonne Davis paused in the center of the room, running an
admiring glance over the elegant furnishings. "You must love
coming here, John."

"Actually, I'm hardly ever here. In fact, I'd planned to
sell it—"

"Why?" Kit frowned.

He glanced at her. "I bought it five years ago for a million
and a half. In today's market, it will sell for four and a half
to five million."

Maury whistled. "That's what I call a tidy profit."

"Yes, it is." John blew out a stream of cigarette smoke.

"I suppose you're going to rent the place to your production
company for the filming and rake in a few more bucks,"
Maury guessed.

"When you film on location, there are always lodging
costs," was his answer.

"But the accommodations aren't always so plush." Maury
grinned. "Are you gonna rent something like this for Kit?"

John ground his cigarette out in disgust. Didn't the fool
know that if he wanted special perks for his client, he should
have made them part of the contract?

"It isn't necessary, Maury," Kit inserted. "I'll stay at the
ranch."

John shot her a look, discovering he didn't like that idea at all.

"We'll see," he said, tabling the subject as Nolan Walker and Abe Zeigler came striding across the marbled entryway to the living room. Both men wore sweat suits; Nolan's was, naturally, a Bill Blass design, and Abe's was the sloppy YMCA variety intended for real workouts.

"We thought we heard voices." Nolan ran lightly down the two steps, looking trim, tanned, and remarkably fit.

Abe plodded down behind him, looking anything but. "Did you guys just get here? How was the flight?" He stuck out his meaty hand to Chip.

"Don't ask him," Paula inserted. "Chip had his eyes shut the whole time."

Chip ignored her. "Where have you two been? I thought you were going to meet us at the airport."

"We've been down in the gym working off some frustration," Nolan replied. "It seemed more productive than hanging around the airport waiting for your plane to land."

"Sorry to interrupt," Yvonne Davis broke in. "But could I persuade you to point me in the direction of my room, John? Or better yet, considering the size of this place, draw me a map? I still have a few last-minute things I need to get done."

"While you're at it, direct me to mine." Paula ran a hand through her red hair. "I need to freshen up."

"Rooms," Abe groaned. "Did you have to mention rooms?"

"Carla will show you to your rooms." With a nod of his head, John directed them to the woman standing quietly in the doorway, the black of her maid's uniform doing absolutely nothing to disguise her chunky figure.

"Why? What's the problem with the rooms?" Chip asked, following up on Abe's remark.

"Not the rooms here," Nolan explained. "Abe's pulling his hair out over the lodging for the filming."

"Yeah, it looks like we'll have to put the crew up in Basalt or Glenwood Springs . . . if we're lucky," Abe grumbled. "I hope you know what that means in additional transportation costs and travel time."

"You can't put them up in Aspen?" Chip frowned in disbelief.

"Not unless you want to play musical motel rooms. And believe me, you'd have one damned unhappy crew if they had to keep changing rooms every four or five days."

"This conversation sounds like the beginnings of a preproduction meeting to me," Kit said, smiling as she moved past John. "If you'll excuse me, I'll leave you to it and catch up with Carla."

John wanted to call her back. Or better yet, go after her. He did neither. Instead he watched her run lightly up the white staircase after the others.

He lit another cigarette and dragged deep on the smoke, irritated to discover she had him tied in knots. He didn't need that. He had enough problems, enough pressure in his life right now. He had to stop thinking about her and concentrate on the movie.

White Lies had to be a success. He needed it if he hoped to stay on top. After a string of megahits, his last two films had been flops. True, they had made money. But not nearly enough by Hollywood standards, where any film that fails to gross over one hundred million is considered a flop.

If *White Lies* didn't roll up those kind of numbers at the box office, he'd lose what power his name still had—and he'd lose control over his films. He'd be back in the fray, fighting for roles.

Christ, he might even find himself back in the grind of a television series, like Burt Reynolds.

Grim-lipped, he flicked the ash from his cigarette and listened to the voices of Chip, Nolan, and Abe in the background, the sound of them reminding him of the less-than-subtle pressure he'd been getting from Lassiter on every aspect of this film from casting to his choice of director, from script revisions to the decision to shoot it entirely on location.

Lassiter. John glanced at the stairs. He'd met Kit at the pseudosocial cocktail party Lassiter had thrown at his Bel Air estate—a party John had been commanded to attend. He'd gone grudgingly. . . .

* * *

Lights blazed from every window of the sumptuous Italian-style villa, located along one of Bel Air's typically twisting roads, hidden behind high walls and screened by even thicker hedges. John swung the Ferrari around the multitiered fountain in front of the house and stopped at the door. Stepping out, he surrendered the keys to a white-jacketed attendant. Rock music came from the pool area in the rear courtyard, the blare of it filtering above muted voices and laughter. He threw a glance at the villa's Juliet balconies in front and ignored the squeal of tires as the attendant roared off in his Ferrari. With a resigned sigh, he went inside.

Chip latched on to him the minute he walked in. Totally out of his element, he tagged along while John made the obligatory rounds. The party was exactly what he expected. Dress ranged from Saint Laurent to Salvation Army; the French doors to the loggia and courtyard beyond were open wide, allowing the warm night air and the party guests to circulate freely; the driving drumbeat from the rock band by the pool underlay the talk and the laughter, the falsely hearty greetings, and the bitchy whispers.

He found Nolan Walker at the bar. The three of them took their drinks and moved off to a relatively quiet corner in the spacious living room.

"I think Lassiter must have dumped a gallon of Georgio in the pool." Nolan waved a hand at the heavily scented breeze wafting through the French doors. "That stuff gives me a headache."

"How soon can we leave?" Chip grumbled.

John had been trying to calculate that himself. "Not yet." He spotted Lassiter moving toward them, working the crowd like a veteran politician. "Here comes J. D."

At sixty, J. D. Lassiter was tall and trim. He had a yachtsman's tan and a full head of dark hair, clipped close and neat with only a tracing of silver. As a young man he'd taken his family's small pharmaceutical company and turned it into one of the largest in the industry. From that, he moved into insurance, then computers, publishing, communications, oil, real estate, until he had more than one hundred companies under the Lasco umbrella, including Olympic Pictures. His detractors called him relentless, ruthless, dictatorial, cunning, and egotistical; his admirers claimed he was honest, benevolent, philanthropic, and charming. John suspected the truth was all of the above—depending on the situation and circumstance.

"I'm glad I found the three of you together." J. D. Lassiter stopped before them, his smile wide, his eyes cool. "Have you cast the female lead yet?"

"We're still auditioning," John replied evenly. "We haven't found the right actress for the part yet, but we will." Assuming she existed other than in Chip's mind.

"I have some good news for you," Lassiter announced.

"We could use some." He lifted his drink, toasting the comment.

"Kathleen Turner will be available through March—and she likes the script. We should be able to sign her up for—"

"In what part?" Chip frowned.

"The lead, of course."

"She can't play Eden." Chip shook his head in firm rejection. "She isn't right for the part."

"Not right for the part?!" The words practically exploded from Lassiter. "We're talking about Kathleen Turner, for God's sake."

"I don't care if you're talking about Kathleen Turner or the Queen of Sheba. She isn't right for the part," Chip insisted stubbornly. "Eden is a woman of mystery, of secrets and deep sensuality. We need an unknown for this role—not some actress the public has seen in a half dozen other roles, including feeding her husband pâté made from the liver of his pet dog."

"An unknown? You can have Kathleen Turner and you want an unknown?" Lassiter challenged, then swung toward John. "Have you explained the facts of life to him, Travis?"

"I've tried."

"You'd better try again. And while you're at it, remind him this is not one of his artsy-fartsy films." He took a step to leave, then stopped and pointed a finger at Chip, stabbing the air. "You have two weeks to find your Scarlet, then I'm signing Turner." He walked off.

"He can't do that," Chip muttered, red from the neck up. "He has no right—"

"You're wrong, Chip. He has fifty million of them." John downed a hefty swallow of Scotch.

Two years ago no one would have dared to issue an ultimatum like that to him, or to criticize his director. Today he had to stand there and take it. The knowledge stuck in his throat and the Scotch didn't dislodge it.

Chip shoved his drink glass onto the tray of a passing waiter and stalked off. John didn't try to stop him.

"There's no business like the movie business, is there?" Nolan swirled the cubes in his glass. "At least now I remember why I never liked tightrope acts when I was a kid."

"Especially the ones that don't have nets."

"Right." Nolan took a sip. "Are you about ready to leave?"

"I'll be damned if I'll go now," John stated. "Lassiter wanted me here and I'm staying."

Nolan chuckled. "I like your style, Travis." He clinked his glass against John's. "I truly do."

Smiling, John took another drink of his Scotch. Over the rim of the glass, he saw her walk in—a mane of honey blond hair flowing past her shoulders, a gold chain interspliced with pearls and crystals around her neck, a white silk blouse and pleated trousers draping her slim figure. She crossed the grand gallery with an easy and breezy stride, her heels clicking on the highly polished black granite floor. She scooped a glass of champagne off the tray of a waiter and made a spinning turn that was natural and graceful. He briefly wondered whose wife or lover she was. She had the look of the typical blond and beautiful hangers-on, without the talent or skill to make it in the business where people attached themselves to someone important so they could be part of the scene. She stopped and planted a kiss on the cheek of a young male actor, starring in his first television series, an actor touted to be this season's hunk.

". . . what do you think?"

John turned back to Nolan. "Sorry, I missed that. What do I think about what?"

"Our potential Scarlet over there."

"Which one?"

"The blonde who just walked in."

"She's an actress?" John took another look, this time watching for the self-conscious gestures, the affected poses, the body language that said "Notice me"—language used by every actress he'd ever known. But there was no indication, not even subtly, that she was "on." In fact he had yet to catch her looking around the room to see who was there. Curious, he thought, and wondered if she was that green or that confident. "Who is she?"

"Her name's Kit Masters. I glanced through her bio this afternoon. She's scheduled to read for us sometime next week." Nolan rattled the cubes in his glass. "For a change she looks like her photo."

"Any experience?" He reached for a cigarette, then remembered Lassiter didn't allow smoking and stuffed his hand in his pocket.

"The usual." Nolan shrugged. "A string of commercials, bit parts in some bad 'B' movies, a couple of horror flicks for Corman, and a few pilots the networks never picked up."

It was more than he'd expected. "How long has she been at it?" John continued to study her. She looked relaxed, natural, her manner fresh and free. Above the din of voices, he heard her laugh, not the sexy, throaty sound most actresses cultivated, but a laugh that was sunny and honest.

"I'm not sure. I think her credits went back about eight years."

"That long." If she had any talent at all, she should have made it by now. John decided she was another one of those who came to Hollywood believing that being blond and beautiful was enough.

"Do you think she can play Eden?" Nolan smiled even as he asked the question.

"With that face?" John gave a slow shake of his head. Her face was too open, too easily read. There was no mystery there, no hint of dark secrets, no smoldering sexuality, none of the things that were the core of Eden's character.

"I wonder why she isn't over here buttering you up and making her bid for the part," Nolan murmured curiously.

"Let's find out." John deposited his glass on a lacquered side table and started across the room.

The young actor spotted them first, and immediately stood a little straighter, unconsciously flexing his shoulder muscles in an attempt to assert his own importance.

"Hello, Mike." Nolan extended a hand in greeting. "We wanted to stop by and congratulate you on your new series."

"I hear it's a winner," John lied.

"Thanks." The actor preened a little and tried not to look too flattered. "Hopefully it will do for my career what *Vegas Heat* did for yours," he said, referring to the television series that had launched John Travis to stardom fourteen years ago.

"It can happen," he said, then let his glance stray to the blonde, silently prompting an introduction.

Taking the cue, the actor laid a hand on her shoulder. "Have you met Kit Masters? She and I go back a few years. We did a pilot together for Paramount."

"Miss Masters." He inclined his head to her.

"It's a pleasure to meet you, Mr. Travis." Kit lifted her champagne glass in acknowledgment, absently noting that John Travis in the flesh was not that much different from his screen image of a hard, polished diamond who didn't mind playing it rough. He exuded an aura that was a little aloof, a little arrogant, and devastatingly charming. She decided it was the fascinating bones and angles in his face, on the lean side and smoothly chiseled, with the merest suggestion of creases in his cheeks, nothing about it too perfect, nothing too handsome. "I've admired your work in films for years. You're very good."

It was truth, not flattery, although his acting ability had received little recognition within the industry. In the tradition of Jimmy Stewart, Clark Gable, Cary Grant, and more recently Paul Newman and Clint Eastwood, he was a behavioral actor, skillfully absorbing each role into his own persona and shaping the mannerisms, voice, and intelligence to blend with his own—and doing it all so smoothly that most didn't see it as acting but as simply playing himself. Kit didn't agree.

"Thank you." John paused a beat, expecting her to continue her campaign of flattery. When she didn't, he gestured to Nolan. "Nolan Walker. He heads up my production company."

"Which is another way of saying, I do the lion's share of the work." He bowed over her hand. "Ms. Masters."

"I've seen your name on the credits, Mr. Walker."

"That's some consolation."

"I'm glad." There was laughter in her eyes, and intelligence, too. They were an extraordinary color, John noticed, a deep shimmering blue—like a high mountain lake.

"I'm sorry, but I'm afraid I'm not familiar with your work, Miss Masters," John said, giving her another opening.

"Kit plays Marilee in the soap *Winds of Destiny*," the actor inserted, wanting back into the conversation.

Kit observed the flicker of disdain in that lean face, a reaction she'd encountered many times. She could be either amused or offended; as usual, she chose to be amused. "I never guessed you were a snob, Mr. Travis."

Nolan Walker choked on his drink and quickly retreated, coughing into his handkerchief. "Excuse me, I think I see my agent," the actor mumbled and escaped as well.

Alone with her, John tried to figure out whether this was some new tactic. She'd definitely gotten his attention. He couldn't make up his mind if he was irritated or intrigued. He certainly wasn't bored.

"I'm not exactly a snob, Miss Masters."

"Then what are you, exactly? Never mind." She laughed and waved off the question. "Maybe we'd better talk about something else. Did you hear that the Cubs won today?" She sipped her champagne. "The Cubs won today. I like saying it." She glanced at him. "I'll bet the Dodgers are your team."

"No."

"Oh, then you're an Angel fan. My dad had a soft spot for the Angels. He was a big Gene Autry fan when he was a kid." She saw his blank look and explained, "Gene Autry owns the California Angels franchise. You're not a baseball fan, are you?''

"No. What type of character do you play on the soap?''

"A modern Southern belle with a kind and gentle heart.'' She dipped a finger in her champagne, then delicately sucked the wine from it. "What do you think about the reunification of the two Germanies? I'm not sure they should be allowed to stand an army.''

"I'm more concerned about gun control in the States. How long have you been on the show?''

"Almost three years. Do you think the space program will actually try to put a man on Mars?''

He tipped his head to one side, his mouth quirking in a curious smile. "Why do I have the feeling that you don't want to talk about your role on the soap?''

"Maybe because I change the subject every time you bring it up?'' she suggested and sipped her champagne.

"Why?''

"Because you obviously have a low opinion of daytime drama and I'd feel honor bound to defend it. In which case, we'd end up arguing and my agent made me promise to be charming,'' she explained, her eyes dancing.

At last, she was coming to the point even if she had taken the long way getting to it. He smiled slowly, lazily. "Do you think you can succeed in charming me?''

"You?'' In all men there was a liberal streak of vanity and false pride; the streak was even wider in actors, making them easy targets for flattery. Yet Kit was certain it would be difficult, it not impossible, to reach John Travis through flattery. There was too much irony in his eyes—an irony that controlled his judgments of himself as well as other people. "I have the feeling you're probably immune to charm.''

"You could try.''

Smiling, she shook her head. "I don't fancy running into brick walls.'' She finished her champagne and idly twirled the empty glass. "You know I'm reading for the part of Eden next week.''

"I know.'' He could have told her she was wasting her

time, she wasn't right for the part. Instead he found himself toying with a strand of blond hair that had fallen across the front of her shoulder. She had touchable hair, soft and silky-feeling.

"Good. In that case, you may as well know I'm going to get it," she said with absolute confidence.

His gaze went from her gold hair to her slender feet and back up again, silently cataloging each slim curve. Belatedly he noticed the faint dusting of freckles across her nose and wondered where else she had freckles. "You are a very beautiful woman, Kit Masters," he murmured, turning up the voltage in his smile.

She saw what was coming. "And?" she challenged softly.

"And?" He frowned.

"That line invariably leads to another. I imagine you have a whole stock of them."

Undeterred, he held her gaze. "Which one do you want?"

"One you mean, but that's not likely to happen, is it? It would require an effort on your part and I think you've forgotten how. I wouldn't let it bother you, though. Lord knows, there are plenty of other blondes who would eagerly grab any line John Travis handed them." She handed him her empty champagne glass. "Good night, John T.," she said and walked off.

He stood there for several speechless seconds, her empty glass in his hand. Then he started to laugh. It was the first really good laugh he'd had in months.

The following week John made it a point to drop by his production company's office on the lot of Olympic Pictures and catch Kit's audition. Normally he didn't sit in on first readings; he left those to Chip and the casting director and involved himself only with the callbacks. Thus far there'd been only a handful of actresses called back for a second reading.

John stood at the window in Nolan's office, taking no part in the discussion going on among Nolan, Chip, and the casting director, Ronnie Long. He looked past the palm trees at the rounded roofline of Studio Four. There, spaceships, hotel lobbies, bordellos, and family living rooms were created out of backdrops, props, and ingenuity. The movie business was an industry of illusion. Phony trees, phony buildings, and phony emotions.

Behind him, the casting director said, "What about Ann Fletcher? I still think she gave us the best reading of any of them."

"She's too hard." Chip pushed out of his chair and paced over to Nolan's desk. "Eden has to have a hint of vulnerability."

Nolan rocked back in his leather chair and clasped his hands behind his head, breathing out heavily as he peered at the ceiling. "Kathleen Turner, here we come," he murmured.

The intercom buzzed, checking the outburst of denial forming on Chip's tongue. Nolan rocked forward to answer it. "Kit Masters is here for her reading," his secretary announced.

"Right." Nolan shifted through the papers on his desk until he found her composite. "Send her in."

John wandered over to Nolan's desk and hooked a leg over a corner of it, his eyes on the door when it opened and Kit walked in. She'd dressed very simply, he noticed, in a summery white dress in some loose-weave material, cinched at the waist with a wide, leopard-patterned belt. She colored the room, putting something into it, something like a faint charge of electricity. He took out a cigarette and lit it as she greeted the others.

Turning to him, she glanced at the cigarette. "Smoking those things will kill you, John T."

"So I've heard."

"It's your funeral." Her amused look held a touch of pity.

"Haven't you heard?" He raised an eyebrow in faint mockery. "Only the good die young."

She laughed at that, the sunniness of it lighting up the room. "And you are a bad, bad man, aren't you, John T.?"

"Totally wicked," he agreed. He was almost sorry she wasn't right for the part of Eden. He would have enjoyed matching wits with her on the set . . . among other places.

All business, Chip passed Kit a set of stapled sheets from the script. "We're using the confrontation scene in the bedroom. If you need some time to go over it—"

Kit skimmed the dialogue on the first sheet and shook her head. "No, I'm familiar with it." She was conscious of the tiny roiling knot in the pit of her stomach. Nerves, they always gave her that little edge, a tension that pushed her to her best.

"I'll cue you—" Chip broke off the sentence and swung toward John, frowning. "Or do you want to?"

He'd planned only to watch. There was enough pressure in auditions without adding the intimidation factor of reading with an established actor. But he knew the scene and the thought of doing it with Kit Masters was irresistible.

"Why not? I'm here." He crushed his cigarette in the ashtray on Nolan's desk and straightened from it, taking the excerpted pages from the script Chip handed him. "You don't mind, do you, Kit?"

Something in his attitude told her he expected her to give a lousy reading anyway. Good. She liked challenges; they made her sharper.

"I don't mind."

"Do you want a lead-in?"

"No." She took a deep, quiet breath and glanced through the scene. It was far from a simple one. It called for emotions ranging from ice to heat, from pride to anger, then passion. Each had to flow naturally into the other. Kit took a minute.

John watched her. She looked more like a bright-eyed ingenue than the sensuous, secretive woman the scene required. Then she turned toward him, a regal tilt to her head, her blue eyes icing over with a hauteur that took him by surprise.

"I don't recall inviting you to my bedroom." The small lift of an eyebrow echoed the cool challenge in her voice.

"An oversight, I'm sure." He delivered his line without consulting the script.

"You presume too much, McCord." She turned her back on him in dismissal.

"Drop the grieving-widow act, Eden. It doesn't suit you."

She went rigid, then visibly relaxed her body and slowly turned again to face him. "Oh? And what does suit me? You, perhaps?" She practically purred the words, suddenly all sultry and sexy, her eyes, her voice, her body smoldering with it and sending the temperature in the room soaring. "Is that why you came to my room tonight? To finish what we started on the mountain?" Moving closer to him, she tilted her head back, exposing the slender curve of her throat, her lips parting in invitation, growing fuller, heavier. "Aren't you going to kiss me, McCord?" she taunted as she slid her hands up the front of his shirt, spreading them over his chest. "Make love to me?"

He caught her wrists and pushed her hands from him. "What are you?" Her transformation to Eden was so complete, the words, the anger, the bewilderment came naturally to him.

Eden laughed, rather beautifully, and drew back from him. "Haven't you heard? I'm a murderess."

"Are you?"

Something flickered in her expression. Pain? Bitterness? Fear? It was gone too quickly for him to determine.

"That's what they're paying you to find out," she murmured.

"I want you to tell me."

"No, you want me to make your job easy for you and confess," she replied, then gave a challenging little toss of her head. "All right, I did it. I killed my husband. I married him for his money and killed him so I could have it all to myself." Her voice was flat but her eyes were angry. "Satisfied?"

"No."

"Too bad. That's all you're going to get."

"It isn't good enough."

"Go to hell," she flashed.

He smiled. "Ladies first."

Her hand arced toward his face. He caught her wrist, stopping her fingers short of their target. He stared into her face.

Her expression was angry, her eyes vulnerable. The climax of the scene called for him to haul her into his arms and kiss her.

"Good." Chip's voice intruded before John could put the script words into action. A pity, he thought, and released her wrist, all the impulses still rushing through him.

Kit threw back her head and released a long breath, feeling the tension and the character of Eden drain out of her, missing the look John Travis and Nolan Walker exchanged and the barely perceptible nod John gave in response to Nolan's unspoken question. Turning, she gave the pages from the script back to Chip, every instinct telling her she'd done well. Very well.

"Thanks. It's a great part." She flashed Chip a smile. "It really is."

Chip nodded his head and stared, saying nothing. Nolan Walker came out from behind his desk. "You did a good job, Ms. Masters."

"Thank you."

"Will you be available for a callback?"

"Of course." Inside, she was still soaring, still high from the adrenaline rush. She needed to get out, to feel the sun on her face and wallow in this feeling of near-victory. "I'll look forward to hearing from you," she said to all four.

Not even certain her feet were touching the floor, Kit walked out of the office, beamed a smile at Nolan Walker's secretary, and sailed down the flight of stairs to the first floor of the bungalow-style building. Before the reading, she hadn't let herself think about how much she wanted the role, how much she needed it, how much it could mean. Now, it just might be hers. Her lips were dry and her heart was pounding. It was all she could do to keep from hugging herself with glee. She didn't hear John Travis come up behind her as she approached the front door.

"I want to talk to you." He opened it.

"Sure." She walked into the sunlight, the air fragrant with the scent of bougainvillea spilling over a wall. She tossed her hair back, releasing another sigh, more of relief this time.

"Lord, but I'm glad that's over. My mouth is so dry I could start my own cotton factory."

"Let's grab a cup of coffee." He motioned in the direction of the commissary a block and a half away, more intrigued than ever by this bright-eyed actress who bore no resemblance at all to the bitter, pained, volatile character she had portrayed so convincingly moments ago.

"Do you mind if we go somewhere else? I'm too keyed up. I need to keep moving."

"Okay by me."

"Good. We can take my car." She dug her keys out of her purse as she crossed the grassy verge by the curb and walked around the hood of an older model MG Midget, a white convertible with red seats. It suited her.

She slipped into the driver's seat and deftly swung her legs in. John had to do a bit more maneuvering to get his long legs to fit in the small space.

"Are you too cramped?"

"Not if I cut my legs off at the knees."

Her eyes sparkled with laughter. "You have a sense of humor. I'm glad." She smiled and inserted the key in the ignition. "Your seat will go back a little more. The catch is underneath."

"Got it." He gained another two inches of much-needed room for his legs.

The engine sputtered hesitantly, then rumbled to life. He shifted slightly in the bucket seat, stretching one arm along the back of it and hooking the other along the window. He remained silent while she pulled away from the curb and onto the road. He waited until they had left the studio lot before he resumed the conversation.

"What are you doing on a soap?" In his opinion, she had too much talent for that. Considerably more than he'd given her credit for.

"That's easy." She smiled, enjoying the sensation of the wind blowing through her hair as the little MG zipped through traffic. "It's a well-written show and a steady job. At least, it was. I found out this week, my character is being written out. Which means I'll be back pounding the pavement and going to cattle calls." She spied a set of golden arches at the next corner. "Do you like French fries?"

"I guess so. Why?"

"I love them and McDonald's has the best. I can never make myself eat before an audition and I'm always starving afterward." She whipped the car into the lot and went to the drive-through, ordering a jumbo fry and two black coffees. She took a deep, appreciative smell of the aroma coming from the sack before she passed it to him. "It's enough to make your mouth water."

John wasn't sure he'd go that far, then tried to remember the last time he'd been to McDonald's as he wedged the sack in beside him on the bucket seat. They exited onto the street. Soon the little car was speeding through the traffic again.

"Who's your agent?"

"Maury Rose." She snagged a thick strand of hair the wind had whipped across her face and pushed it back.

"Maury Rose." John frowned. The name didn't mean anything to him. "What agency is he with?"

"The Maury Rose Agency." She sent him a quick, amused look.

"A one-man operation?" His eyebrows lifted.

"I think Joanna would resent that," Kit said, then explained, "She's his secretary and right arm. Maybe his left one, too."

"I know some people at William Morris and Creative Artists. I'll introduce you to them," he said as she swung the car onto one of the twisting, curving roads that wound into Hollywood Hills. "You've got a nobody for an agent. It's time you switched to a high-powered firm that can do some good."

"Thanks, but I'll stick with Maury. He's been my agent from the beginning."

"He hasn't gotten you very far after nine years, has he?"

"Maybe not. But he brought me to the dance. I'll go home with him."

"In this business, it's all business, Kit," he informed her. "There's no room for sentiment."

"To borrow a famous Kennedy phrase—'If not here, where? If not now, when?' "

"Noble but not realistic."

"And you're a diehard realist, aren't you?" she guessed.

"Guilty." The road climbed higher, the traffic noise fading.

"How did you get started in acting?" she asked curiously.

"On a dare. I made some comment about acting being easy and a buddy of mine challenged me to try out for a play a local theater group was putting on."

"Easy, eh?" She laughed. "How many times have you eaten those words?"

"Too many."

"I believe it." She slowed the car and pulled onto the shoulder, braking to a full stop. "Here we are."

When she switched off the engine, the silence hit him. Frowning, John looked around. They were high in the Hollywood Hills, the sprawling city of Los Angeles far below, veiled by a layer of smog that turned the sun into a hazy ball of fire.

"Don't forget the sack." She climbed out of the car and slammed the door, a jarring sound in the silence.

John crawled out of the low-slung car without opening the passenger door, vaulting over it, then reaching back for the sack with the fries and coffee. When he turned, he saw her standing a few feet away, her hands hidden in the slash pockets of her white dress, her legs braced slightly apart, the wind playing with the hem of her swinging skirt. With a twist of her shoulders, she looked back at him—the sun, the sky, and the city behind her. She suddenly seemed incredibly beautiful.

"Good. You remembered the sack." She turned and crossed the road, walking to the other side.

"I did." He took a step after her, then stopped, his focus widening to take in the row of towering letters. The Hollywood sign. He nearly laughed in amazement. He'd seen it thousands of times, so many he'd stopped noticing it.

At a distance, it looked big and white and inviolate. This close he saw the dirt and the gouges and the graffiti.

"A bit tawdry, isn't it?" Kit observed with a faintly puckish smile. "More Hollywood reality, right?"

"Right." Smiling, he followed her as she picked her way around a few rocks to the base of a fifty-foot-high *L*.

"Hollywood isn't a place anyway. It's a state of mind." She took the sack from him and handed back one of the containers of coffee, then brushed away the surface dirt on the letter and sat down, stretching her legs out full length and crossing them at the ankles, the hem of her dress barely brushing the ground.

"Do you know this is the first time I've ever been up here?" John peeled off the plastic lid on his coffee.

"The road's closed a lot. Probably to keep the kids from coming up here to party." She took a sip of her coffee and announced, "The same as the commissary's—bitter and black." She set the coffee container on a nearby rock and tore open a packet of salt for the fries. "I've actually learned to like the taste of it."

"Do you come up here a lot?"

"Whenever I get homesick for heights and I don't have the time or the gas money—or both—to drive up to Big Bear. Some days you can see a lot from here—downtown Los Angeles, that round building down there is Capitol Records near Hollywood and Vine, Century City." She studied the view a minute longer, then dumped the salt packet and coffee lid into the paper sack, using it for a trash bag.

"What makes you homesick for heights?"

"I'm a Colorado girl. I grew up on a ranch outside of Aspen."

"Really? I have a place there."

"Let me guess—in Starwood," Kit said, unable to picture him in one of the West End's fashionable Victorian mansions. Despite the aristocratic leanness of his features, there was nothing of the poet about him. There was too much strength in his face for that. She doubted that the frills and ornate bric-a-brac of the Victorian period would appeal to him. He needed a setting that was bold, sleek, and contemporary—like a lavishly modern house in Starwood.

"Naturally." He smiled, confirming it.

"Naturally." She grinned back. She liked it when he smiled like that, relaxed and easy, without that aloof detachment that so often tinged his expressions. But he looked relaxed and easy, she noticed, his sun-streaked hair a little rumpled from the convertible ride, the sleeves of his Armani shirt rolled back, showing the corded muscles in his tanned forearms. "Want some fries?" she offered when he reached for a cigarette.

"No thanks." He shook his head and lit the cigarette, then watched her through the raveling smoke as she took a bite of French fry and closed her eyes.

"Mmmm, ambrosia," she murmured and proceeded to chew it slowly as if savoring the taste of it. She consumed the next bite with the same slow relish. Until that moment, he hadn't guessed such sensual enjoyment could be derived from a French fry. She paused to lick the salt from her fingers and look at the view. "I like the quiet up here. The stillness. Just the sound of the wind in the brush—and sometimes the bark of a coyote. It always reminds me of home."

"When was the last time you were back?"

"Six months ago," she said, her tone changing. "For my father's funeral."

"I'm sorry." Oddly, he meant it, though he hardly knew her.

"Thanks." She sent him a small smile, then toyed with the fries in the giant cardboard pouch. "I think you would have liked my dad. Everybody did. He had this beautiful laugh—not loud, but full of genuine warmth that filled up your heart with the joy of life. He was always finding reasons to laugh, too. Nothing ever got him down, or kept him there. He was something, my dad."

He heard the affection in her voice and glanced at his coffee. "Is your mother still alive?"

She nodded. "She's here in Los Angeles." In a hospital, in a chronic-care ward, a victim of multiple sclerosis, but Kit didn't tell him that. It was her problem and her responsibility, something personal and private. "My parents divorced when I was sixteen."

"Is that when you came out here?"

"No. I stayed with Father. I didn't come out here until after college." She lifted her shoulders as if to shrug off the subject. "So, tell me—did you ever suffer pangs of homesickness when you first came to Hollywood?"

He blew out a stream of smoke. "For which home?"

"That's right—you were a military brat," Kit remembered. "I read that in a magazine somewhere."

"My father was a career Marine. About every two years, he was assigned to a new post." Unlike Kit, he didn't have any good memories of his boyhood or his parents. He'd hated that life—always fighting the military caste system, always fighting to be accepted in a new school, always fighting the strict discipline his father imposed and his insistence that John always had to be the best at everything.

"Are your parents still alive?" She carried another fry to her mouth.

"Yes. My father put in his thirty years with the Marines, took his military pension, and went to work for a defense contractor. He's still hauling my mother all over the country and she's still complaining."

"Still, they must be very proud of you."

"Hardly." He smiled without humor. "My father doesn't think acting is the kind of work a *man* should do. He wanted me to join the Marines. Follow in his footsteps. I didn't. I guess you could say I'm the black sheep of the family."

Kit eyed the burnished light in his hair and shook her head. "You're no black sheep. A golden ram, maybe, but not a black sheep."

He laughed warmly. It was the first time she'd heard him laugh other than in films. She liked it. "I'll take that as a compliment," he said.

"It was meant as one." She munched another fry. "Are you sure you don't want some? There are only a few left."

"I wouldn't want to deprive you." His smile teased.

"I love the taste of foods," she admitted with an engaging frankness. "Any kind of food. French fries, hot dogs at the ballpark, thick juicy steaks, caramel apples—especially the sticky, gooey ones, caviar—osetra's my favorite."

He raised an eyebrow. "Not beluga?"

"It's good, but I like the way the osetra eggs 'pop' when you press them against the roof of your mouth. As a rule, beluga caviar won't do that."

"Watching you finish off the last of the fries, I never would have guessed you were a connoisseur of caviar." Why? He wasn't sure. This woman had been surprising him every step of the way.

She laughed. "Another one of my many talents. Speaking of which"—she paused and stuffed the paper napkins and empty pouch into the sack, then stood up and shook any crumbs from her skirt before she finally faced him—"you said you wanted to talk to me and I'm the one who's been rambling on—as usual. I tend to do that when my nerves are all strung out."

"I noticed." He was amazed by how much he'd noticed about her, and how much more he wanted to find out.

"So?" She took a deep breath and smiled out a sigh. "What is it you wanted to talk about?"

"Your reading today." He dropped his cigarette and ground it into the rocky dirt underfoot.

Unable to stand the suspense or the silence, Kit said, "I know I did well." Her stomach was knotting again, making her conscious of the dryness in her throat. She tried to brace herself, but she didn't know which way it was going to go.

"You did better than well. You gave an excellent reading. We want you to do a screen test. If you come off on film as well as you did today, then—all other things being equal—you've got the part."

Kit tried to take the news calmly, to be professional about it. But her joy was too boundless. She had to release it. She had to share it. Laughing, she threw her arms around his neck and hugged him.

His arms automatically wound around her, then stayed to keep her there when he discovered how well she fit against him, their bodies perfectly aligned, the warmth of her breath on his cheek, a carelessly sexy scent radiating from her skin.

"You don't know how much I want this part, John T.," she declared earnestly, fervently. "It's such a wonderful part. Eden is such a challenge. There are so many layers to her, so many levels.'' She drew away, giving her head a dazed little shake, then throwing it back to laugh silently at the sky, her hands still linked behind his neck. ''I can't believe it. I've been waiting my whole life for a chance like this.''

''The part isn't yours yet,'' he reminded her. ''There's still the screen test.''

''I know. But I'm not going to blow it. I'm just not.'' She lifted her shoulders in an unconcerned shrug of supreme confidence.

He saw the dance of laughter in her eyes. Yet there was something else in them, too—a kind of inexpressible gravity that fascinated him as much as the laughter. Everything about her fascinated him.

''I believe you.'' His gaze shifted to her lips. The same impulses were back, the ones he'd felt at the reading. This time Chip wasn't around to call a halt to the action.

''Good. It's the truth.''

When he lowered his mouth to hers, she came up to meet it. After the first brief and warm pressure, she started to pull back. He tunneled a hand under her hair, cupping the back of her head to prevent her escape. He wanted no quick kiss of gratitude. Teasing and nibbling, he rubbed away that flicker of resistance, then explored the softness, seeking the passion the scene had called for, the passion she seemed to exude so naturally.

Taken by surprise, Kit had no time to prepare for the kiss— not that it would have made any difference. His mouth was mobile and warm, and he kissed with the skill and attention of a man who both knows what he's doing and enjoys doing it. Soft then demanding, giving then taking.

She responded out of pure pleasure, while some distant part of her mind recognized that the kiss between Eden and McCord would have been hard and bruising, erupting in full-blown desire. There wouldn't have been any of this warm kind of heat, this intimacy, this sudden kick of feeling.

Greedily she wanted to run with it, but she knew better. It was too soon, too sudden, too dangerous, and she was too vulnerable.

With practiced self-denial, she pulled back, resting her

hands against his chest and lowering her head, waiting a beat for the ground to feel solid beneath her feet again. Only then did she open her eyes and try to breathe normally.

"You come by your reputation honestly, don't you?" A faintly dazed, faintly dazzled smile took any sting out of the mild accusation.

"What reputation?" His hands moved to her waist, keeping her close. He hadn't expected to feel this need. Attraction and challenge, yes, but not this need. It wasn't what he had planned. He wasn't even sure if it was what he wanted. He backed away a step, releasing her.

"Your reputation as a lover of women, of course."

Of course. His public image was that of a womanizer, an image that had practically become carved in stone over the years. After one disastrous marriage and a dozen abortive affairs, there had been a subtle merging of his private life with his public one. There had been women. A lot of them. Most had wanted nothing from him but the thrill of making it with a big-name star. Something he'd never really understood.

But he chose not to deal with those facts. "Do you know how many affairs I've had with women I've barely spoken to? Not to mention the ones I've never met?"

"A lot, I imagine." She smiled. "But aren't celebrities required to have overactive libidos? I always heard it was part of the job."

"Maybe it is."

"Speaking of jobs, it's time I drove you back to the studio."

He glanced at his watch, surprised at the time. "Better make that the Beverly Wilshire instead. I have a tennis date in an hour and I need to change first."

"You're staying at a hotel?" Kit eyed him curiously as she retrieved the sack with her trash from the base of the *L*.

"I have an apartment there. That's where I live." He walked with her to the car.

"No house in Beverly Hills?" Somehow she'd thought a home would have been one of the first things he would have bought for himself, considering he hadn't had one growing

up. That's what she wanted—a home, family, children—
someday. At thirty-two, she was fast running out of some-
days.

"What would I want with one?" He stepped over the
passenger door of the low-slung sports car and lowered himself into the bucket seat. "I have all the room I want at the
Wilshire, plus privacy, valet and maid service, twenty-four-
hour security, room service, and all the rest of the hotel's
amenities."

"True." But she still didn't think it qualified as a home.

"Plus, it drives the paparazzi crazy."

"I'll bet." She flashed him a quick smile as she turned the
key in the ignition. "I've heard your photo is worth thirty
thousand."

"That depends on who I am with, and how many clothes
we have on," John replied and listened to her rich laugh.

The ride to the Beverly Wilshire went much too quickly
for him. When she pulled through the black iron gates of the
motor entrance, he wasn't ready to let it be the end.

"Have dinner with me tonight." He climbed out and leaned
both hands on the door.

"Sorry." Her smile indicated regret. "I already have other
plans."

"You can cancel them."

She shook her head, blond hair sweeping her shoulders. "I
don't do that."

Irritated by her refusal, he challenged. "I thought you
wanted the part." He knew it was the wrong thing to say the
minute the words were out. He wasn't even sure why he'd
said it unless it was a test to see if she really was a woman
of scruples.

Her chin came up, the angle proud and a little stiff, her
eyes going cool on him. "I want the part. And I'll give my
best performance to get it. But that's all." She reached for
the gearshift.

"Hey, it was only a joke. A bad one, maybe, but—"

"A very bad one." She shifted the transmission into gear,
but kept her foot on the clutch while she gave him a long,
considering look. "And you weren't joking, John T. Not

really. If that line would have gotten you what you wanted, you would have taken it."

Candor seemed called for. "Probably." So did an apology. "I'm sorry."

"Why? Because it didn't work?" She sighed and smiled rather ruefully. "I have no idea why I like you, John T.," she said. "At times, you're probably not a very nice person, although you could be if you tried." She gunned the motor. "Let my agent know about the screen test," she said and drove away.

The screen test went well. Better than well. When they showed it to Lassiter the following week, John sat slouched in his seat, a cigarette dangling from his fingers, the smoke wafting through the bright light from the projector. Nolan Walker sat behind him and Lassiter was in the row ahead of him.

By rights, John knew he should be watching Lassiter's reaction, but he couldn't take his eyes off Kit's image on the screen. Makeup concealed the freckles on her nose and highlighted the deep blue of her eyes. Her blond hair gleamed smooth and sleek; the satin peignoir of lavender ice gave evocative glimpses of her shapely form. The clothes, the makeup, the hair—she was Eden.

More than that, she seemed to fill the screen with her presence, making it impossible not to look at her.

Nolan leaned forward to whisper in his ear. "The camera loves her."

John nodded, aware something mystical and magical had happened in the developing room. She projected an inner radiance, an aura, that commanded attention.

He watched the scene unfold—the same scene they'd used in the reading. The chemistry between them was there—as he'd instinctively known it would be—the tension between them electrifying the screen, the sexual sparks flying, the passion exploding in the kiss.

The scene had called for him to be rough, and he'd been rough. John watched her fingers curl to rake him, then stay to dig, and remembered that moment of surrender when she'd become suddenly soft and boneless in his arms, the sensation filling him with a tenderness that had overwhelmed, leaving him shaken.

The flicker of empty frames flashed across the screen. "Thanks, Jonesy," Nolan called to the projectionist in the booth. "That's all we need."

The screen went dark and the lights went up. John started to take a drag on his cigarette and discovered it had burned all the way to the filter. He dropped the butt into the ashtray on the floor by his feet.

"She's good," Lassiter said from his seat in the next row, his attention still focused on the darkened screen.

"She's more than good, J. D.," John said. "She *is* Eden."

Lassiter turned in his seat. "Who is she?"

"Her name is Kit Masters." He lit another cigarette, ignoring Lassiter's pointed look. He needed it.

"Never heard of her. What has she done?"

"She's been a regular on one of the soaps for the last three years," Nolan volunteered.

Lassiter digested that information, then nodded thoughtfully. "Some top names have come out of daytime television. What kind of following does she have?"

"Almost none," Nolan admitted with a faint grimace. "She plays a minor character."

"Too bad." Lassiter stood up as if that ended the discussion.

John rolled to his feet as well. "She's perfect for the part, J. D."

He didn't argue the point. "Turner's better. She has a name."

"If it's a name you want," Nolan inserted, "Kit Masters can have one by the time this film is released."

Lassiter eyed him skeptically. "And how do you intend to accomplish that?"

"The old-fashioned way." Nolan smiled. "We'll hype the hell out of her. Kit Masters: a surprising new star; Kit Masters: John Travis's hot new love interest. Hell, J. D., she was even raised in Aspen, where we're shooting the movie. That's great human-interest stuff. We can milk the hell out of it.

And generate enormous interest in the film before it's ever in the can."

"A big publicity buildup," Lassiter mused with a thoughtful nod. "It hasn't been done in years. It might work."

"If it's handled properly, it will," Nolan added, but wisely didn't press.

"Who do you have in mind to handle it?"

Nolan shrugged. "Davis and Dunn are the best in the business."

Lassiter raised both eyebrows at that. "And expensive, too."

"Think what we'd have to pay Turner. We'll save a bundle using Kit Masters in the part. She has a small-time schmuck for an agent. We can sign her for fifty grand, easy. Maybe less."

Lassiter turned and glanced thoughtfully back at the screen. "She was good. In fact . . ." He eyed John, a smile edging the corners of his mouth. "She just might steal the movie from you the way she stole that scene."

John smiled, concealing the twinge of unease. "More power to her if she can do it." But he knew this film had to be *his* hit; he needed it to get back on top. To share the glory was one thing, but to have it stolen from him totally was another.

"It won't happen," Nolan stated. "This film will undoubtedly make a star out of Kit Masters, but it will get John an Oscar." He gave John a long, steady look. "I watched both of you in that scene. The anger, the confusion, the desire, the distrust, it was all there. You outdid yourself, my friend."

John didn't doubt that Nolan meant that. Honesty had long been the keystone of their relationship. They never blew smoke at each other. Yet he was uncomfortable with the praise and tried to laugh it off.

"In the words of the immortal Duke—'That'll be the day.' " John knew he didn't make the kind of movies that won awards. "Besides—"

"Besides, hell." Nolan chuckled. "You'd give anything to get that little golden statue and you know it."

He wanted to deny it. He wanted to pretend awards didn't mean anything to him—that he only wanted to make solid, entertaining films, films that were financially successful and long-lasting. That was enough.

But it wasn't. He wanted that damned Oscar.

"The role could get you the Oscar, John," Lassiter said, then added, "it's too bad you don't have a director who can get you one."

Behind him, John heard Chip arguing with Abe. "No, I am not doing the interiors in the soundstage. *White Lies* needs to be filmed entirely on location. All of it," he insisted angrily. "You can fake the look and feel of some places, but not Aspen."

"Okay, Chip." Nolan, ever the diplomat, stepped in. "Cool down. You've made your point."

John turned back to finally join the discussion, forcing Kit out of his mind—for the time being.

4

The guest bedroom, like the rest of the house, was decorated stunningly in shades of white with a few vivid slashes of blue for accent. Kit decided it was gorgeous and that she'd never want to live in it permanently. Not enough color.

Entering the room, she set her purse on a free-form glass table, discarded her gold coat on an ivory mohair chair, shrugged out of her coral jacket and gave it a toss onto the bed's plump duvet of white velvet, then crossed to the glass doors leading onto a private terrace and a spectacular view of the green and gold mountains beyond. For a moment she simply gazed at the craggy sea of peaks capped with snow, then pulled open the doors and breathed in the sharp mountain air. It was good to be back in Aspen for more than just two or three days—even if it meant facing Bannon again.

"Is there anything else I can do for you?" The maid waited in the doorway.

Turning, Kit smiled at her. "Nothing I can think of. Thanks, Carla."

With a nod, the woman left. Kit glanced at the suitcases lined up in a neat row on the cream white rug. She knew she should unpack but—first things first. Unconsciously she squared her shoulders and walked over to the telephone on the bedside table. She picked up the receiver and dialed from memory, then listened to the ringing on the other end while she ran a finger along the filmy edge of the white voile bed hangings, idly exploring their silken texture.

"Hello," a woman answered, somehow managing to make herself heard above the rock music blaring in the background.

"Hello, Maggie. It's me—Kit."

"Who? Wait a minute. I can't hear a thing," Maggie Peters grumbled, then shouted at her teenaged daughter, "Nicole Marie, I told you to turn it down! I'm on the phone." Hearing a muffled protest in the background, Kit smiled and sat down on the edge of the bed, stretching out the cord and kicking off her shoes, digging her toes into the rug's soft, thick nap. "Turn it down or you won't go anywhere for a month." The threat worked as the volume went down to a sane level. "Thank you." Maggie's voice reeked with sarcasm, then held a weary sigh. "Sorry. I'm back now. Is that you, Kit?"

"Yes. I'm in Aspen—"

"Then you made it safely. Good," she said and went on without a break. "In case you didn't guess, Nikki's grounded and I'm paying for it. Lord, it's such a relief to hear my own voice. I am so sick of those New Kids on the Block I could scream."

"You mean you haven't?" Kit teased her neighbor.

Maggie chuckled, recovering a portion of her sense of humor. "If the truth was told, about every five minutes. Don't ever be the mother of a teenager, Kit. That's how you get gray hairs, deaf, and grumpy," she declared. "Anyway, I'm glad you called. I stopped by the hospital and saw Elaine this morning."

"How was Mom today?" Kit held the phone a little closer and shifted back on the bed, drawing her legs up to sit cross-legged.

"The same. No, I take that back. Actually she was having one of her better days. We talked a little . . . about home . . . about you. I fixed her hair for her. I think she liked that."

"I'm sure she did," Kit murmured, her mouth curving in a faint smile that was both wistful and sad. "She was always concerned about her appearance, about looking nice."

"I know." Maggie's voice was just as sober and pensive as hers. "By the way, Dr. Evers stopped in while I was there."

"Did he have anything new to say about Mother? How he thinks she's doing?"

"No. But he did go on about all the publicity you've been getting. He was very impressed to see your name in the 'Out and About in Beverly Hills' column after you and John Travis were seen lunching at Spago's. Who knows? Maybe the good doctor is a closet actor or screenwriter and wants you to put him in touch with the 'right' people."

"Or he has a story idea that will make a blockbuster movie. Or he wants an autographed photo of John for his daughter or his wife," Kit said, adding to the list of common requests she'd received from all quarters lately. A similar thing happened after she had joined the cast of the soap three years ago, but on a much smaller scale. The number had increased in direct proportion to her change in status. Instead of playing a minor character in a daytime drama, she had a lead role in a major film playing opposite one of the biggest names in Hollywood.

"They've been crawling out of the woodwork, haven't they?" Maggie said sympathetically. "Do you have any idea how popular Nikki has become in school lately? Girls who wouldn't even speak to her before are coming over to the house, hoping to get a glimpse of you—or better yet, John Travis." There was a slight pause. "Not that I blame them. The guy is better looking in person than on the screen."

Kit readily agreed with that. "Speaking of John T., let me give you the phone number of his place here in Aspen in case there's an emergency and you need to reach me. Do you have a pencil and paper handy?"

"Got it."

She read the number off the phone to her, then added, "I'll be here through the weekend, then at the ranch."

"No problem," Maggie replied. "Just relax and have fun. Don't worry about anything on this end. I'll look in on Elaine from time to time."

"Thanks, Maggie," Kit said and meant it.

"What are neighbors for?" Maggie's poodle started yapping in the background. "Someone's at the door. I better go."

"Talk to you soon."

"Right. Have fun, Kit. Do what I would do if I was in Aspen with John Travis—*enjoy*," she said in a throaty growl, then laughed and hung up.

Smiling, Kit placed the receiver back in its cradle. But the smile faded as her thoughts turned from Maggie to her mother. So many feelings came rushing up—guilt, sadness, anger, love, resentment, but most of all, regret. Regret that they hadn't been closer, that they hadn't bridged their differences. Now they couldn't. Now they'd never even have the chance to try. Because of some stupid, horrible disease.

If only she'd known when she first moved out to L.A. nine years ago that the fatigue her mother complained about—the blurred vision and tingling in her left leg—if only she'd known those were early symptoms of multiple sclerosis, she could have made more of an effort to get to know her mother, to make peace with her. But it hadn't seemed serious, no cause for alarm, and she was busy building a new life of her own, working, going to auditions, landing a part now and then.

If only she'd known when her mother began having trouble walking over three years ago, requiring first a cane, then a walker, then a wheelchair and a live-in aide, that when the doctor said her mother was suffering from a viral infection of the brain, he meant multiple sclerosis. But she'd always thought her mother would get better, that there was time, that time would heal both her mother's sickness and their own strained relationship.

If only. Such a haunting phrase. Words that had echoed over and over again in her mind during her last visit to the hospital. . . .

* * *

It was relatively quiet on the floor, no wheelchairs or cane-driven gurneys wheeling down the corridors. The supper hour was over; most of the patients were back in their beds. Television sets played in the background, competing with each other; voices murmured in hushed tones; someone shouted the answer to the *Wheel of Fortune* puzzle; and from other beds came low moans. After nearly eight months, the sights, sounds, and smells of antiseptic, medicine, and sickness had become familiar to Kit. Enough, at least, that she had stopped being uncomfortable in the environment.

A privacy curtain separated her mother's bed from the other three patients who shared her room—a stroke victim, a quadriplegic, and another MS sufferer. The curtain was drawn when Kit entered.

She lifted it aside and paused, her glance running to the young nurse with short, dark hair by the bed. After a split second of hesitation, she recognized the woman. "Dottie. You cut your hair. I like it."

"Thanks." The nurse self-consciously touched a hand to her short locks. "Bobby insists he liked it better long."

"Most men do," Kit admitted with a small, dismissive lift of her shoulders.

"But they don't have to take care of it." She smoothed a final hand over the sheet, then turned from the bed, moving toward Kit.

Kit smiled an agreement, then asked, "How is she?"

The nurse paused beside her, then cast a glance over her shoulder toward the bed. "She's having one of her bad days, I'm afraid." Which meant her mother wasn't talking, or was responding only in monosyllables. On good days, she talked almost normally, but even then her mental deterioration was apparent in her vagueness about time, place, or circumstance.

Kit acknowledged the information with a nod and turned to the bed as the dark-haired nurse left. For a long moment, she simply looked at the figure in the bed, the sheets pulled up to the neck, the head canted at an angle and bobbing at a regular rhythm, the sightless, staring eyes fixed on nothing, the short cropped hair heavily salted with gray, the wisps of facial hair on the chin and upper-lip area, and the gaunt body beneath the sheets, straight now after three operations to sever tendons in the legs and free them from a permanent fetal curl.

Eight months and the reaction in her heart was still the same—this was not her mother; this was a grotesque imitation of her, a horribly cruel one. But her mind told her differently and Kit walked forward.

"Hello, Momma. It's me. Kit." Leaning over the side guard, she brushed a kiss over a pale cheek, careful to avoid the nasal tube that now fed her mother. "You missed a beautiful day today. Hardly any smog. In fact, you could actually tell the sky was blue."

No response. Nothing. She hadn't really expected any, yet . . .

Lightly she combed her fingers through the ends of her mother's coarse hair, the gray and dark all mixed together. Once it had been a shiny mink brown, always worn in a tidy French twist—with emphasis on the "tidy."

"Daddy always said you had the most beautiful hair. I always wanted to touch your hair and see if it was as soft as it looked. But we didn't touch each other very much, did we, Momma? I was always crawling onto Daddy's lap, always sitting on the arm of his chair, wasn't I? But his arms were always open." Just for an instant, her fingers stilled their petting of the short hair. "I was Daddy's girl. I was *his* daughter, that's what you said."

The phrase, the scene was indelibly etched in her memory, all the edges razor sharp. She could still see that moment when her mother had stood by the staircase of their ranch home outside Aspen and looked at her sixteen-year-old daughter. Kit had just informed her that she was going to stay with her father, that she wasn't going to move to Los Angeles with her mother after the divorce. It was one of the rare times when her mother had shown any strong emotion.

"I'm not surprised." Her voice had been cold and bitter and cutting. "You aren't my child. You've never been *my* daughter. You were always *his*."

Remembering it, Kit sighed and smiled sadly. "We never

had a chance after that, did we? I hurt you a lot by staying with Dad. But he needed me, and you never seemed to need anyone. And I wanted to hurt you because you were hurting us.''

She touched the smooth forehead, gazing into the sightless eyes that once had been so calm and direct. ''But you were right. We never had much in common. It was always hard for us to talk, to find something to talk about. And after the divorce, we became such careful strangers. Always choosing safe subjects, talking about the weather, plays, television shows, restaurants, neighbors. But who were you? What did you feel? What did you want? You must have had dreams, but I don't know what they were. You're my mother. I've known you all my life, yet I don't know you at all.'' Her voice dropped to a whisper. ''Worst of all, I never asked.''

If only. That was what haunted her. What would always haunt her.

''Flowers.'' Paula strolled into the guest bedroom, crossing to the elegant free-form glass table and touching a scarlet nail to the petal of a white tulip, one of a dozen artfully arranged in a cobalt blue vase. ''I'd ask how you rate a bouquet in your room when I don't have one. But I already know the answer to that.''

Kit looked at her blankly for an instant, then pushed off the bed, shaking off the memories as she went over to admire the hothouse blooms, wondering how she hadn't noticed them before.

''This is obviously John's doing.'' She cupped a hand around a white tulip and bent down, breathing in its faint, almost negligible fragrance. ''He knows I have a weakness for flowers.''

''And he's obviously developed a weakness for you,'' Paula observed with a knowing look.

Kit smiled. ''I know it's getting harder to keep both feet on the ground when I'm around him—especially when he keeps trying to sweep me off them.''

''So let him.''

''If I'm not mistaken''—Kit tipped her head to one side,

arching an eyebrow—"you're the one who warned about John's reputation for having affairs with his leading ladies, then dumping them when the film's finished."

"I only wanted to make sure you knew the score going in." Paula lifted one shoulder in an idle shrug.

"I think I always knew it." Suddenly restless, Kit circled the room, pausing to touch objects along the way. "I learned a long time ago that just because you love somebody, it doesn't mean he'll love you back." She stopped at the terrace doors, remembering Bannon and how much it had hurt when he'd jilted her ten years ago.

"My God, Kit, you make it sound as though you've had a whole string of lovers." Paula's amused tones came from the opposite side of the room. Turning, Kit saw the redhead lounging amid the blue satin pillows on the ivory chaise. "How many have you had in your life? Two? Three? It couldn't have been more than that," she said with certainty. "What working actress has time for a love life? We're up at four or five in the morning so we can be at the studio by six. Fourteen hours of rehearsals and tapings, then back home to memorize ten to thirty pages of dialogue for the next day and off to bed early so you don't have bags under your eyes. Becoming involved with someone on the set is infinitely practical."

"It may be practical," Kit conceded. "But I'm not emotionally equipped to handle a casual affair. And I'm not sure John is offering more than that."

"Casual affairs are often best—especially in our business."

"Maybe for some, but not for me." Moving away from the terrace doors, Kit crossed to the set of soft-sided luggage lined up in a neat row inside the door. "Have you unpacked already?"

"Carla offered to do it and I accepted . . . readily." Paula rose from the chaise with unhurried grace. "I think I'll pamper myself with a long, luscious soak. Let me know when the manicurist arrives."

"I will." Kit hauled the garment bag to the bed.

"Tell me something, Kit," Paula said from the doorway,

her tone unusually thoughtful and serious, "do you think Chip is good enough to direct this picture?"

She was stunned that such a question would be asked by her. It was almost traitorous. "I think Chip is the best person to direct it. John couldn't have made a better choice. Why would you ask that?"

"Curious." She made to leave.

"Paula." It was her turn to be curious. "Are you serious about Chip?"

Paula thrust a half-amused glance at Kit. It was a complete answer that didn't need any added definition. But in the hall, she paused and swung her shoulders slantingly at Kit. "How can you discourage a schnauzer?"

"That's cruel. Chip is nice."

Paula's face was utterly smooth, but her green eyes held a reluctant sadness. "The day will come when you'll be just as cruel, Kit. More cruel than I am now—because you're going higher than I can ever go."

5

*T*wilight flowed across the mountain valley as sunset's rosy hues gave way to indigo ripples, deepening the shadows of the ranch buildings. Somewhere from the depths of the mountains, a coyote's howl floated across the gathering stillness.

Leaving the barn and pole corral, Bannon headed across the ranch yard, traveling in the slow, swivel-hipped walk of a man who'd spent a lot of time in the saddle. The herd was scattered over the winter pasture, settling down for the night to browse on the rich, dry grass. The evening chores were done, the horses turned loose in the corral, enjoying a good roll in the dust. The satisfaction of a day's work done and another autumn drive complete eased his tiredness.

"It doesn't seem the same without Clint being here," Old Tom said. "About now he'd be slapping one of us on the back, giving us a big grin, and demanding to know when we were going to break out the beer." He paused and expelled a fragment of a chuckle. "Remember that time—what was it? Fifteen years ago, I think—we'd just started bringing the cattle down and the skies opened up. Poured, it rained so hard you couldn't hardly see the cattle. By the time we got back here to the house I was so full of water I was afraid to go near the fire for fear I'd warp clean out of shape. But there was that Clint—that big laugh of his just booming out, and Kit right along with him. It didn't faze either of them one bit." He shook his head. "Those were good times."

"They were that," Bannon nodded.

"Growing old isn't a simple thing, Bannon," Old Tom declared. "This contemporary scene is for the young. It's your world, not mine. Old men like me live in the bright past when we cut a high, wide trail. We're nothing but spectators now, pushed aside by fellows like you. It's lonesome business to see old friends die. I guess a little bit of me gets burned out with each one—and pushes my world farther back in the mist."

"You're gloomy as hell," Bannon joshed with a good-natured smile.

"Comes from getting old. The men and women of my time were bighearted and wide-handed people. We had a lot of fun out of living." Old Tom turned a searching, sideways glance on him. "More, I think, than your generation does. We were never afraid of our emotions and never troubled ourselves greatly over our sins."

His smile faded just a little. "Must have been nice."

Laura broke into their conversation. "I wish we had a swimming pool."

"We've got one," Old Tom asserted. "The best kind—"

"Not that hole down in the creek, Gramps," she said with exaggerated patience. "I'm talking about a real swimming pool, a heated one like Aunt Sondra's got. And Buffy, too. Then I could swim all year round."

"Swimming pools cost money," Bannon said.

"I know." She sighed. "I wish we were rich."

"Life is rough, isn't it, short stuff?" Bannon pushed at her hat, shoving it down on her head.

"Sometimes it's a bummer. A maximum bummer," she insisted, moving out of his reach.

Bannon let her complaint go without comment, an easy silence falling, marked by the differing rhythms of three sets of strides and the muted jangle of his spurs.

"I'll tell you one thing," Old Tom grumbled. "I don't feel

like going to that fancy dinner tonight. Never did like getting all duded up.''

"That's not true, Grandpa," Laura stated with conviction. "You like getting dressed up."

"Now how would you know?" he challenged with mock gruffness.

She sent him a knowing smile. "Because I've seen you standing in front of the mirror admiring the way you look."

Her words opened up a door to the past, and Old Tom saw his wife's reflection join his in the mirror, her look teasing as she said, "You think you're a fine figure of a man, don't you, Tom Bannon?" She turned him around and adjusted the knot of his black tie. "The truth is—you are." Just for a moment, he let himself think about his wife—and the malignant brain tumor that had taken her life with such swiftness years ago. The pain of losing her had dulled with time, leaving him free to treasure the memory of the years they'd had together.

As they approached the sprawling ranch house built of hand-hewn logs, Old Tom lifted his eyes to it. Set on a foundation of solid rock, it faced the valley and the range of mountains, its steep-slanted roof rising sharply like the peaks. A porch wrapped itself around three sides of the house, hooding its night-darkened windows and deepening its shadows.

At first glance, it looked like any other big log house, yet it gave evidence of care in its framing and fitting. His father, Elias Bannon, had built it a century ago, and he'd built it to stand for a hundred more. The logs were solid and fitted to one another without a crack or crevice. No chinking here, each log had been faced with an adz until it lay cheek to cheek against the other, creating a wall two feet thick or more.

Old Tom eyed it with pride. That big old house had withstood many a blizzard, winds howling around it like raging banshees. It had known its share of good times, when the surrounding mining towns had needed the beef, hay, and draft animals it raised. It had known its hard times, too, when the mines shut down and the town died. The Great Depression had been a lean time as well, but the house had weathered them all, the good times and the bad. And through it all, it had known many a rake of a cowboy's spur, many a swish of a pretty dress, many a tear and many a laugh.

This had been home from the time the first timber had been cut. His father had built a house in town, but it had never been more than a place to stay, a place to practice as a lawyer. This was where his heart was, right here in Stone Creek.

Old Tom knew it was the same for him. He'd been born in the bed he slept in. Forty-odd years later Beauty had delivered their son in it. The Good Lord willing, he'd die in it. The thought was a pleasing one.

"The phone's ringing." Laura broke into a run for the front door, charging up the stone steps and across the porch, her boots beating a rapid tattoo on the rough-planked floor.

The storm door banged shut behind her. She paused long enough to hit the light switch on the inside wall and throw a yellow track of light across the porch before racing off to grab the ringing phone.

Bannon mounted the steps ahead of his father and entered the house. Out of habit he took off his hat and hung it on a wall peg, automatically running fingers through his dark hair to comb away its flatness. The lodgelike living room sprawled before him, rustic and solid, a timbered stairway rising to a railed balcony circling three walls off which four doors opened.

Laura had the phone to her ear and both elbows on the oak table. Unbuckling his spurs, Bannon listened while Laura chattered away to the caller, recounting the day's adventures and expounding on the stampede, turning it into a moment fraught with danger.

"He's here." Laura swiveled on one elbow to look at him, then added in response to something the caller said, "Sure." Straightening, she held out the phone to him. "It's Aunt Sondra. She wants to talk to you."

Bannon hooked his spurs on a peg next to his hat, then walked over to take the phone from his daughter. "You'd better go clean up and get your things together," he told his daughter, cupping a hand over the receiver's mouthpiece. "And don't forget to pack your toothbrush."

"I won't." She headed for the stairway.

"And don't be all night in the shower," Old Tom called after her, then glanced at Bannon. "I'm gonna get me a beer. Do you want one?"

Refusing with a shake of his head, he uncovered the mouthpiece. "Hello, Sondra. What's the problem?"

"I'm still at the office." When she heard the rich timbre of his voice, tinged with a faint drawl, Sondra Hudson turned toward the framed photograph on her desk, her lips softening, losing much of their usual cool and sober curve. "I called to let you know I'm running late, but from what Laura just said, you will be, too."

"Not too late, I hope," Bannon said. "Laura is spending the night at the St. Clairs'. We'll drop her off first, then come by the house to pick you up."

We. That obviously meant his father was coming along. What with one thing and another, it had been more than a week since she and Bannon had been alone—to talk, to touch, to love. She had hoped that tonight, after the dinner, they could—but that wasn't to be. Not with his father along. She contained her annoyance.

"Sounds perfect," she lied. "I have one or two things to finish up here, then I'm going directly to the house. With luck, I'll be ready when you arrive."

"In roughly two hours I should hope so," he remarked dryly.

Sondra smiled. "It always takes a woman longer to dress than a man. Haven't you learned that by now, Bannon?"

"I guess I've forgotten." His voice had a smile in it.

"That comes from not having a woman in the house," she said, then instantly regretted the remark that, by inference, raised the spectre of her late sister. She hurried on without giving Bannon a chance to speak. "I'd better let you go or I'll be even later."

After she hung up, Sondra reached for the photo, an enlargement of a snapshot taken almost ten years ago. It showed a winter scene in the Aspen mall, a trademark street lamp and artful snowbanks forming a backdrop for the smiling threesome in the center of the shot.

Bannon stood in the middle, his features softer, smoother, younger, a cowboy hat raked to the back of his head. Sondra was on his left, her head tipped to rest on the point of his shoulder while she smiled at the camera with a self-contained poise. The paleness of her platinum dyed hair made her as fair as the girl on his right was dark. Her younger sister, Diana—with her ebony eyes and long black hair; spoiled, tempestuous Diana, thoughtless and selfish. She hadn't cared that Sondra had met Bannon first.

Diana had always been like that—just like their father, never caring about anybody but himself. He'd only cared about having a good time and living well, even if it was off somebody else.

The only thing Sondra had ever learned from her father was how to use charm and wiles on people. It had worked, because she'd been smart enough to make it work. She'd scrimped and saved to get enough money to buy a small wardrobe of the "right" clothes and have her mouse brown hair bleached to a champagne blond. As soon as she had obtained her real estate license, Sondra had left Denver for Aspen and her piece of its dream. She'd gone to work for an agency that had treated her like a mindless errand girl. But it had been a beginning.

Then Diana had called—she and some friends were in Aspen for the winter carnival. When she'd suggested Sondra meet them for drinks, Sondra wished now she'd refused. She wished she'd said she was too busy, that her boss wanted her to take a contract to some couple for their signature. Instead she'd agreed, then left the agency to drive up-valley to some godforsaken chalet-style home.

After she'd gotten the required signatures, she started back to town to meet Diana and her friends. . . .

It was dusk. Snow flurries danced in her headlight beams. She had promised to meet Diana at the J Bar for drinks at five. It was almost that now.

Speeding, Sondra rounded a curve and hit an icy patch. The car skidded out of control, sliding off the road and careening down a bank, plowing through drifts and sending a spray of blinding snow over the windshield. Gripping the steering wheel, Sondra slammed both feet on the brake pedal and braced herself for a crash.

The car slammed into something, throwing her against the wheel. Then everything stopped.

Shaking, she rested her forehead against the wheel and waited for her heart to stop pounding. At some point, she realized the engine was still running and switched it off. The silence was crushing. Suddenly she was angry—angry with herself for speeding, angry at the maintenance crew for not salting the curve better, angry at the client for living on this horrid road, and angry at her boss for sending her in the first place when it was *his* client.

But anger wasn't going to get her back to town. Sondra started the car again, flipped on the wipers to sweep the heavy coating of snow from the windshield, and shifted into reverse. The wheels spun uselessly.

Five minutes of trying and the car hadn't budged an inch in any direction. It was stuck, hopelessly and impossibly stuck.

Sondra pounded a gloved fist against the wheel in frustration, then yanked the key out of the ignition and grabbed her purse off the passenger seat. She pushed the door open and climbed out, slamming the door shut behind her, the sound magnified by the surrounding silence and the hush of softly falling snow. She glared at the fence post that jutted from the front of the car like an off-center hood ornament.

Turning, she faced the road and the snow-filled ditch she had to cross to reach it. With jaws clenched in temper, Sondra glanced at her stylish snow boots. Dainty and fur-trimmed with pointed heels, they were ideal for Denver's slush but totally unsuited for trudging through deep snow. One step and she'd be over the top of them.

The loud snort of an animal came from behind her. Sondra whirled around, half expecting to see some wild beast charging out of the snow. Instead she saw a horse and rider on the other side of the fence, looking like they'd ridden straight out of a Marlboro commercial—the horse stocky and brown with a shaggy winter coat, the man rugged-jawed and lean, dressed in a cowboy hat and a heavy sheepskin-lined parka.

"Are you all right, miss?" he said in a pleasant baritone voice.

"I'm fine. It's my car. I hit an icy patch."

He dismounted and waded through the snow to the front of her car. He crouched down to inspect the situation, then swung a long leg over the fence, briefly straddling the wire before crossing the rest of the way. After walking partway around her car, he came back to the driver's side.

His mouth curved in a gentle, commiserating smile. "I'm afraid you're going to need a wrecker."

She was tempted to say: Tell me something I don't know. But she discovered she was reluctant to sharpen her tongue on this man.

"I was afraid of that," she murmured instead.

"Our ranch house is a half mile from here. I'll be happy to give you a lift."

"A lift? You mean—on that horse?"

A glint of humor appeared in his dark eyes, his look softly teasing and giving Sondra the impression he was laughing *with* her, not at her. "He won't mind us riding double if you don't."

Sondra smiled back, a little surprised to discover how easy it was. She usually didn't like men, their arrogance, the way they looked at women like they were some dessert to be eaten. This one wasn't like that.

"I don't mind."

"Good. By the way, my name is Tom Bannon." He thrust out a leather-gloved hand to her, in the manner of an equal meeting an equal. "But I go by just plain Bannon."

"Sondra Hudson," she said as her slim, soft-gloved hand became lost in the large grip of his, the warmth and the strength of it flowing through like a current. "I go by just plain Sondra."

"Well, Sondra." He grinned. "Shall we mount up?"

Within minutes she was balanced crosswise in the saddle in front of him, his arms comfortably caging her, his chest offering more solid support.

"Warm enough?" His face was so close she could feel the heat of his breath on her cheek, like a caress.

"Yes." She felt very warm, but more than that, she felt safe, protected. It was a new feeling, one she had never realized she needed.

Sondra no longer remembered what they talked about during that short ride to his ranch house. She only remembered the light swirl of snowflakes in the air, the gathering darkness that enhanced the feeling that they were the only two people in the world. That, and the rhythmic swish of the horse's legs through the snow and the sensation of being in Bannon's arms, the lazy warmth of his voice near her ear, their breaths commingling into a single vaporous cloud, the solidity of his body.

When they reached the house, Bannon had called a wrecker service for her. The man informed him he was buried under with calls and it would be the next day before he could make it out. So Bannon had driven her into town. On the way she'd persuaded him to let her buy him a drink as a way of thanking him for his help.

They had gone to the bar at the Hotel Jerome. Bannon had taken one look at Diana and from that point on, Sondra had ceased to exist for him.

She stared at the picture of the three of them. Less than two months after it was taken, Bannon had married her sister. A year later Diana was dead. But not once in all these years had Bannon forgotten her. Sondra loved him for that—and she hated him for it, too.

Still, she knew she had gained his loyalty and his trust after she'd stood by him when all those questions were raised concerning the circumstances of her sister's death. If it wasn't for that nasty business, she was certain he would have forgotten about Diana long ago. In time, he would. In time, he'd belong solely to her.

Abruptly she set the framed photograph down and briefly laced her slender fingers tightly together. A second later, she reached over and pressed the intercom button, buzzing her secretary.

"Inform Warren I want to see him in my office."

"Yes, Miss Hudson."

With that done, Sondra rose from her chair and stepped away from her chinoiserie desk. She paused a moment, her glance traveling over the plush sitting area in her private office, the deep, overstuffed sofa and chairs, elegant but inviting. As always her eye was drawn to the Chinese painted panels on the wall and the pair of late-Qing jars on the Venetian table by the sofa—visible symbols of her change in status.

She now owned her own real estate company. More than that, Hudson Properties, Inc., was one of the largest, if not the largest, in Aspen. Her roster of clients read like a list of Who's Who in society, politics, science, industry, state, and screen. It was a list she guarded jealously and expanded constantly.

But it wasn't enough.

She crossed to the corner windows and the view they commanded of the Aspen mall below, its thoroughfares paved with wine-colored bricks and strewn with trees, signature iron lampposts and planter boxes brimming with autumn flowers. Slipping a hand partway into the pocket of her boxy wool suit jacket, she gazed at the collection of upscale boutiques, trendy galleries, and arty bookstores housed in buildings designed to resemble the old brick and stone edifices of Aspen's silver-rich past.

Idly she studied the people—a trim jogger in a designer sweat suit with a golden retriever at his side; a pretty blonde in stenciled suede pants and alligator boots from Smith's, no doubt; and a slender woman, easily forty, sporting a shopping bag from Nuages.

Money and power were the only things people respected. Jerome Wheeler had known that in the late 1880s when he'd arrived in Aspen and set about transforming the rough, raw mining camp with more prospects than prosperity into the richest silver-producing area in the world, bending the town to his will, creating a place of beauty and culture by planting trees to shade its streets, constructing an opera house and a luxury hotel to rival any west of the Mississippi, bringing not one railroad but two into Aspen, making it a town with a sophisticated urban outlook, complete with electricity, streetcars, and telephones, turning Aspen into a place for eastern capitalists, touring royalty, and visiting dignitaries.

A half a century later, in the mid 1940s, Walter Papecke had come to Aspen and repeated the process, taking the sleepy mountain ghost town littered with abandoned, broken-down buildings and transforming it into a fashionable ski resort in the winter and a center of cultural and intellectual pursuits in the summer, attracting the likes of Albert Schweitzer to speak at the issue-based conferences at the Aspen Institute for Humanistic Studies, Itzhak Perlman to play in the famed Music Tent at the Aspen Music Festival, and Ballet West to perform at the Aspen Dance Festival. Again, power and money had allowed Papecke to impose his rule.

Another fifty years had nearly passed. Time for another to emerge and rule.

A light rap intruded on her thoughts. Sondra turned to face the door as it opened and Warren Oakes walked through, a tall and tanned forty-year-old with the dark good looks of a fifties matinee idol—and all the surface charm of one, too. Unfortunately he lacked the class to make it in a world of high-rollers.

Still, he was useful to her, especially when she'd first started the agency almost ten years ago—a time when a sugar bowl of cocaine was almost a standard favor at Aspen parties and nearly every transaction included at least one glassine envelope of the white powder as part of the deal. Rather than personally involve herself in such activity, she'd left it entirely in Warren's hands.

A pipe bomb rigged to the Jeep of a local dealer in 1985 had marked the end of both the prominence and dominance of cocaine in the Aspen scene. But Warren still had his uses, both as a storehouse of potentially valuable information about the ''old'' days and as a man who was strong enough to carry out her orders, yet weak enough to take them.

''Hello, Sondra.'' He flashed his white teeth at her, all of them capped. ''I didn't expect you to be here yet. How did things go this afternoon with the Arkansas chicken king and his plump little wife?''

"You mean the Atchisons, I assume." She thought of the coarse, ruddy-cheeked millionaire who had somehow managed to make a sizable fortune out of processing chickens for supermarkets across the country. A small flicker of contempt passed over her expression. "The poor man is under the illusion know-how still counts in this world when it's really know-who. He'd never even heard of the Mosbachers. Fortunately for him, his wife is a little smarter." She moved away from the windows. "However, to answer your question, I think the afternoon will ultimately prove to be successful."

"Wonderful." Warren wandered over to the chair in front of her desk and sat down, crossing his legs and automatically smoothing the crease of his gray slacks.

"Did you get that copy of the guest list for tonight's party? I didn't find it on my desk."

"I have it right here." He reached inside his double-breasted blazer of navy wool and pulled out an envelope, then half rose from his chair to hand it to her.

Sondra removed the list from the envelope. "Get me the fact sheet on that commercial block in downtown. I want to dangle it in front of Lassiter tonight. I think it may be big enough to interest him, but I'll need some specifics to give him."

"Your copy is in here." He tapped a folder on her desk top.

When she went to pick it up, her intercom line buzzed. She punched the button instead. "Yes, what is it, Susan?"

Her secretary's voice came over the speaker. "Mr. Atchison is on line two. He insists on speaking with you."

She glanced impatiently at the gold Cartier watch on her wrist, conscious of time slipping away. "Very well," she said curtly, then paused a moment to suppress any hint of irritation from her voice before picking up the phone. "Mr. Atchison, I didn't expect to hear from you so soon," she said with studied pleasantness.

"Ida and I have been talking things over since we left you," he said, his tone brusque, his accent thick. "We said we'd get back with you tomorrow, but we've decided we're going to take a little drive over to Vail and take another look at the place we liked so much there.''

"I think that's a very sensible thing for you to do," Sondra replied smoothly through a tightly held jaw. "Buying a second home is a major decision, certainly one that shouldn't be made in haste. Vail does have a great deal to offer. After all, Jerry Ford goes there. Now Aspen, on the other hand, tends to be the playground for the Kennedys.''

There was a long pause on the other end. Sondra deliberately didn't attempt to fill the silence, letting all the subtle implications of her words sink in.

Warren Oakes sat silently, listening with amusement and grudging admiration. Sondra Hudson was a cool one. But for all her coolness, there was always an anger there, simmering below that smooth surface. He had a feeling it was that anger that fed her discontent—and her ambition.

"Ida did like that house you showed us on Red Mountain," he said finally. "You said the owner was asking three million five for it. Do you think he'd take an even three for it?''

Sondra smiled. "Possibly. That particular home has been on the market for a few months. If you like, I can draw up an offer for that amount.''

"Do that.''

"I'll do it immediately and have my vice president, Warren Oakes, bring it over to your hotel for your signature.'' It was never wise to allow a buyer, or a seller, to have too much time for second thoughts; deals could easily be lost that way. "I'd bring it myself, but unfortunately I have a dinner engagement tonight.''

"That's fine. We'll be expecting him.''

Sondra hung up and turned to Warren with a faintly satisfied air. "They're making an offer of three million on the Baxter place. Draw it up and run it over to their hotel. They're staying at the Little Nell.''

"Will do.'' He nodded, invisibly shaking his head at her self-containment. If he'd been on the verge of making a sale this size, he'd be grinning from ear to ear—and sweating out the time until closing. But not Sondra. Never Sondra.

6

The stylist deftly smoothed a stray strand of blond hair in place, then spritzed to keep it there. "You have gorgeous hair," she told Kit. "It has so much bulk and body you can do anything with it."

"I can thank my Swedish grandmother for that." Kit sat with her eyes half closed, relaxing while the stringy brunette arranged her hair in a soft and classic upsweep.

"And you can thank her for the color, too, I'll bet." The stylist stepped back to survey her work, then announced, "All done, I think. Take a look."

Opening her eyes, Kit studied her reflection in the brightly lit vanity mirror, ignoring the drab plastic cape that protected her gown. "It's perfect." She nodded in approval.

The brunette bent down to unfasten the cape, her reflection joining Kit's in the mirror. "If Beau saw you looking like this, he wouldn't be so quick to chase other women," she said, referring to Kit's longtime love interest in the soap. "I watch *Winds of Destiny* all the time." She removed the cape and began folding it to return it to her case. "Truthfully, I don't know why you put up with that conniving, two-timing creep."

"What can I do? I love him," Kit replied in character as she reached for the pair of antique ruby-and-diamond earrings. Edwardian in design, the delicate drops were on loan for the evening.

"You can dump him, that's what you can do," the brunette told her. "He's no good and you're not going to be able to change him."

"I guess not." Kit hid a smile and fastened the first earring to her lobe, aware that the episode marking her departure from the daytime drama would air next week. "Maybe I should break off with him—this time, for good."

"You'll be a lot happier in the long run. Believe me." The stylist gathered up her case and her oversize shoulder bag and headed for the door. "Have fun tonight."

"Thanks." She smiled at the brunette as she waved and sailed out the door.

Alone, Kit felt a tension work its way through her nerves, a tension caused by the certain knowledge Bannon would be at tonight's gala dinner. He and Old Tom had been ardent supporters of the American Cancer Society ever since a malignant tumor had taken the life of Bannon's mother. It was only logical he would attend.

In any case, it was inevitable she would see him while she was here, probably several times—not because he lived in Aspen, but because Bannon was the executor of her father's estate. Still, seeing him again would be difficult. It always was . . . even after ten years.

All wounds eventually healed, but sometimes, when a wound was deep enough, it left a lingering ache that could last a lifetime, making it impossible to forget the cause of it. Brooding over it never helped. On that mental reminder, she reached for the mate to the Edwardian drop on her lobe.

With the second earring in place, Kit rose from the velvet-cushioned stool and crossed to the bed. The full-length cape that matched her strapless gown lay across it, a shimmering river of pale gold. A pair of opera-length gloves rested beside it, her only accessory other than the earrings she wore.

As she pulled on the first glove, there was a knock at her door, followed by the sound of John Travis's voice: "May I come in, Kit?"

"Of course. Come ahead." She reached for the second glove and glanced at the crystal clock on the bed table, reassured to see she was ready a full ten minutes early.

When she heard the click of the door latch, she turned to face it. John walked in, the sight of him triggering an awareness, an attraction that seemed to get stronger each time she was with him. She smiled, her gaze taking him in, the formal black suit offering a striking contrast to the deep gold lights in his hair.

"You look splendid, John T.," she declared, smoothing the second glove over an elbow. "Formal dinner jackets and cummerbunds suit you perfectly."

"Thank you." He inclined his head briefly at the compliment, a smile touching the corners of his mouth. "I saw the hairdresser leave and hoped I'd be able to catch you alone."

"You probably hoped you'd catch me indecently clad," she mocked lightly. "But you're out of luck this time, John T. What do you think?" She rested a hand on her hip in a model's pose, and executed a slow pirouette to show him the gown, then stopped to stand before him, a slim column the pale shade of twenty-four carats. "Do you like it?"

She looked refined, elegant, almost untouchable. He stepped closer, seeing the dusting of golden freckles she hadn't bothered to conceal with makeup. They took her out of the realm of a goddess and made her back into a warm, vibrant woman.

He kept her waiting while he pretended to inspect her with a falsely critical eye before he said, "It doesn't look right. Something's missing."

"You can't be serious." Frowning, she turned to look at her reflection in the mirror. "The gown is beautiful; it fits perfectly. There's not a thing wro—"

"Yes, there is." He lifted her right hand. "You need this."

He wrapped the bracelet from his jacket pocket around her wrist and fastened the safety catch to secure it. For an instant, Kit stared at the delicate gold-and-platinum bracelet set with small white and yellow diamonds.

"It's beautiful," she murmured, turning her wrist and watching the way the stones caught the light.

"A gift from me to you," he said. She started to shake her head as if in refusal. "Please. Rare and beautiful things should be worn by a rare and beautiful woman."

She smiled and curved a hand to his cheek. "I don't care if you've said that to every woman you've ever known. I love it. And I love the present."

Rising up, she kissed him, her lips moving warmly against his. He caught her close and deepened it, not caring if he crushed her gown or mussed her makeup. He needed to hold her, to taste her, to feel her, to explore these emotions that flowed from her so unconditionally, a heady wine that he wanted to get drunk on.

A voice in the hallway outside her bedroom restored a degree of reason. He drew back to hold her loosely, watching her eyes slowly open to look at him.

"Do you have any idea how much I want to skip that damned dinner tonight?" he murmured, fully aware he had to attend. Lassiter had commanded it.

"It's tempting, isn't it?" she murmured back, her gaze lifting no higher than his mouth. "Very tempting." She studied the peach-colored smudge from her lipstick and recalled the power of his kiss, the way it had whipped through her, flaring with instant intimacy. It would be so easy to throw away caution and love him as fully and completely as she wanted to—so very easy. "But you're right." Kit sighed her regret. "We should be joining the others."

When she moved out of his arms, he made no attempt to stop her. "You'd better freshen your lipstick first."

She walked over to the vanity and plucked a tissue from the box. Turning, she offered it to him with laughing eyes. "And you'd better wipe yours off."

He touched his fingers to his lips, then looked at the smear of peach with a hint of drollness. The expression lingered as he crossed to her and took the tissue. He watched Kit apply a fresh coat of peach gloss to her lips while he scrubbed his away.

Something about this simple scene appealed to him—Kit sitting at the vanity, dressed for an evening out with him, repairing the damage to her makeup that he'd caused. Simply looking at her, he found himself relaxing, a crazy contentment running through him. At the same time, he could see himself going over to her, running his hands over her bare shoulders, and bending down to nibble at her neck. Nothing more than that. He must be losing his mind.

"There," she said, satisfied with the results the mirror showed her. Rising, she slipped the tube of gloss into a gold-mesh evening bag and crossed the room to gather her cape from the bed. "I hope they serve champagne at the dinner tonight. I'm in the mood for champagne. Champagne and moonlight."

"Moonlight is for adolescents," he said. "You and I are flesh-and-blood people, Kit. It's time we moved on to something more real than that."

She swung around at his words, paused, then released a long, slow breath, accompanying it with a faintly dazed shake of her head. "You do have a way with women, John T."

"Why are you always throwing that up at me?" he demanded, his mouth coming together in a grim line.

"To protect myself, I suppose." She saw the desire in his eyes and knew that he wanted her, that he needed her.

In this last month, she'd sensed the tension in him, the pressure he was under on this film. A man like him needed love; he needed the ease, the inner security, the laughter, that love could bring him. And she wanted very much to give it to him. But he wasn't ready to accept yet. Maybe he never would be. And she was afraid of having her love rejected again.

"Protect yourself from whom? Me?" He raised an eyebrow in challenge.

Kit picked up her cape and draped it over a gloved arm as she smiled at him in mock reproach. "Really, John T., are you trying to suggest that I would be the first woman to lose her head over you?"

"Maybe I'm suggesting that you're the first woman I could lose my head over." He resented that; she could see it.

"Life is full of risks, John T.," she said gently and slipped her arm under his. "That's what makes the rewards so wonderful. Shall we go?"

He saw the light of humor in her eyes and wanted to curse her. But that was impossible when the urge to kiss her again was much stronger. Sighing, he escorted her from the room.

Bannon stood in front of the dresser mirror in the log-walled bedroom and absently buttoned his white dress shirt. A patchwork quilt filled with goose down covered the double bed behind him, its once-bright colors faded with time, like the braided rug on the planked floor. A spindle-backed chair sat in the corner, angled toward the blackened maw of a much-used fireplace, at one time the only source of heat. It was a room of simple comforts, yet homey and solid.

"Hi." Laura wandered into the room and stopped next to the dresser, propping her elbows on it and resting her chin in her hands, her hair falling loose about her shoulders in a gleaming black curtain.

"Hi." Bannon smiled down at her, catching the lemony fragrance of her shampoo. "Are you all packed?"

"Yep. My toothbrush, too." She watched him fit a gold cuff link through its opening while she swayed on one foot, waggling the other behind her. "Are you almost ready?"

"Almost." He fastened it in place and reached for the other.

"Gramps is all dressed. I saw him admiring himself in the mirror when I went past his room," she said with an I-told-you-so look, then pushed off the dresser and strolled over to the bed.

"Did you fix yourself a sandwich?" Bannon watched her in the mirror, smiling at her bored, faintly impatient look.

"No." She plopped on his bed. "Buffy and I are going to fix pizza as soon as I get there."

Bannon tucked the shirttails inside the waistband of his trousers, listening to the protesting squeak of the bedsprings as Laura lightly bounced on it. Then the sound stopped and there was silence. Bannon glanced in the mirror and saw her sitting on the edge of the bed, gazing at the walnut-framed wedding picture next to the lamp on his night table. He paused in the act of reaching for the black tie, for a moment unable to move as she picked up the photograph to study it.

"Do you think I look like her, Daddy?"

"When you're nineteen, you'll look exactly like her." Dropping his glance from the mirror, Bannon bypassed the bow tie in favor of a wide ribbon tie of black silk, the one his father always called his Sunday-go-to-meeting tie. "That's how old she was when that picture was taken."

Laura sighed, a soft and wistful sound. "It would be nice to have a mother."

Her words hit him hard, filled as they were with her loneliness and longing for a mother. They sent his thoughts racing back to that long-ago night when he'd met Diana, when she'd smiled at him across the width of the table at the Jerome Bar, putting everything into her sparkling eyes. He'd been twenty-four and she'd been the kind of wild dark-eyed beauty men dreamed about.

He hadn't cared about the man beside her, the one who was supposed to be her boyfriend.

The bar was packed when Bannon walked in, filled with the usual raucous and rowdy crowd of ski bums, party seekers, ski groupies, and assorted hangers-on. Not his scene at all. One drink and he'd leave, he decided.

He followed Sondra to a table occupied by a noisy group. His glance fell on a dark-haired girl as she looked up, her lips red and full, provocation in every soft curve of her cheeks, and her eyes dark and alive to him. He felt like he'd come in contact with a bare electrical wire, that's how sharply the sight of her had jolted him.

He pulled up a chair, unable to take his eyes off her, and ignored the attempts by the males in her group—frat brothers all—to make him feel unwelcome. He recognized the type, sons of Denver's upper crust dressed in turtlenecks and cashmere sweaters, more interested in scoring and getting high than in getting high scores.

Bannon sat with his chair rocked back, indifferent to the brags about runs made and slopes conquered, his gaze seldom straying from Diana's face. Beside him, Sondra Hudson asked, "How long have you lived in Aspen, Bannon?"

"I was born here."

"A native," Diana observed, a provocative pair of dimples appearing near the corners of her mouth. "How unusual." She shook her hair back with a toss of her head and continued to eye him. "Did I hear my sister say your family owns a ranch here?"

"Stone Creek. East of here, toward the Divide." There were a hundred things he wanted to tell her about it, but not here, not in this room full of people, some of them half drunk, some of them half stoned, all of them loud.

"A ranch by whose standards?" her boyfriend, David Thornton, challenged, his lip curling in a faint sneer, an arm draped around Diana in an assertion of ownership. "I've seen some of the so-called ranches around Aspen. A measly five and ten acres. My uncle owns a two-thousand-acre spread along the Wyoming border. I spent my summers there when I was a kid."

Bannon smiled slowly into his pilsner glass before lifting his glance. "Stone Creek encompasses a measly four thousand acres."

His softly spoken comment earned him a glare from David Thornton and a laugh from Diana. "Shut up, Di," Thornton snarled.

"Why?" she taunted. "You walked right into that one."

One of their group sauntered back to the table after a trip to the john. "What's so funny? Did I miss something?" He looked around the table, his eyes unnaturally brilliant.

"Just you, Eddie," Thornton snapped.

"Yeah, I am a funny fellow," Eddie agreed with a ridiculous grin, then proceeded to pick up the pitcher of beer and down half of it to slake his coke-dry mouth.

"Jeezus, Eddie, why didn't you just spit in it?" one of the others complained.

"Hey, there's Andy Holmes," Thornton said and placed two fingers in his mouth to whistle at the skier, considered by many to have been America's best hope for a gold in the giant slalom at the last winter games, until an injury had eliminated him. "Andy!" he called, waving him over and rising to welcome him. "It's good to see you again. We met last year at the Halston party and shared a few lines together. David Thornton,'' he said to jog the skier's memory.

"David, right. How've you been?"

"Great. Sit down. Have a beer."

"Sorry, I'll have to take a rain check. I've—" He paused in midsentence, catching sight of Bannon. "Hey, man. Where've you been? I haven't seen you on the slopes this year."

"Been too busy."

"Let's get together and make a couple runs down Bell before you head back to crack the law books again."

"Okay." Bannon felt Diana's eyes on him, the sensation a magnet that drew his glance back to her. Again he felt a tightness in his chest, in his loins, when he met the dark glow of her gaze. She seemed immensely pleased about something.

The sound of Thornton's voice floated to him, but Bannon missed his words. Then Andy Holmes spoke, obviously in response to Thornton. "They're probably heading outside to catch the torchlight parade down the mountain."

"I want to see it, too." Diana was out of her chair before she'd finished the sentence.

"What the hell for? It's nothing but a bunch of skiers coming down the mountain with torches," Thornton scoffed. "It's strictly tourist stuff. Not worth losing our table over."

"Then you stay and keep it," she said, coming around the table. "Bannon will watch it with me."

Laughing at Thornton's surly look, she took Bannon's hand and drew him away. He followed her to the door, fully aware it wasn't the warmth of her hand he wanted to feel but the heat of her body.

"Thornton didn't look too happy about you coming out here with me," Bannon observed as they stepped outside.

"I don't care," she said with a blithe shrug of unconcern.

Bannon knew he should care, that he should feel some twinge of conscience for moving in on another man's girl. He hadn't been raised that way.

He steered her away from the crowd that had gathered outside, responding to the greetings that came his way with a nod or a wave, but never veering from the course he'd set. When he found a shadowy spot, empty of people, he stopped. "We should have a good view from here."

"Great. I love parades, any kind of parade." She tilted her head at a beguiling angle, the velvety darkness of her hair blending into the shadows and making a cameo of her face. "Don't you?"

Bannon found himself agreeing, and feeling bewitched by the dark and tantalizing beauty of her. She was like an evening breeze, filled with all its mystery and elusiveness, the very essence of a man's dreams, vibrant and alluring, seductive as the night.

With an effort, he lifted his gaze to the snow-covered mountain before them, looming pale and tall against the black of the sky. Far up the slope, he spotted a gleam of light.

"They're starting down," he said.

"Where?"

"There." He pointed to the light, but she shook her head, not seeing it, and moved directly in front of him to follow the angle of his upraised arm.

A second later, she whispered, "I see them."

He lowered his arm, his hands automatically settling onto her shoulders, drawing her back to lean against him, the perfumed scent of her hair stimulating his already-aroused senses.

"Isn't it beautiful?" she murmured.

He wanted to tell her she was beautiful, but he forced his eyes to look at the winding ribbon of flickering light making its serpentine course down the mountain, and forced his mind to dwell on something other than her nearness.

"One hundred years ago, back when all the silver mines on Aspen Mountain were in full operation, you would have seen a sight like this every night," he told her.

"Every night? Why?"

"Every night at eleven o'clock the mines changed shifts and hundreds of miners crisscrossed that slope, carrying lanterns to light their way. The glow from them probably didn't look much different than the light from the torches of the skiers."

"There were mines up there?"

So sensitive to her, Bannon could almost see her eyes searching the face of the mountain for some trace of them. "Quite a few—the Aspen Mine, the Emma, the Durant, the Homestake," he said, naming off the major producers. "Before the ski lifts, there were tramways to carry silver ore down the mountain. The one to the Aspen Mine was a mile long."

"Really?" she murmured in a marveling voice.

"Really." He paused, then said, "Of course, Aspen's most famous mine—some claim the richest, outproducing even the famous Comstock—was the Mollie Gibson over on Smuggler Mountain. But it was in the Smuggler Mine that they found a nugget weighing close to a ton in a cavern encrusted with silver. The nugget had to be cut in three pieces just to haul it out of the mine."

"A one-ton nugget." She shook her head at the incredulity of it. "It doesn't sound real."

"It was."

"What happened to all the mines?"

"When the United States adopted the gold standard, the bottom dropped out of the silver market. One by one, the mines shut down. Over the years, they've all been abandoned, the entrances to their shafts filled in or boarded shut, like the one on our ranch. But the whole area is still honeycombed with tunnels—the surrounding mountains, the town. . . . In fact, we could be standing over one right now."

She turned her startled gaze on him. "You're not serious, are you?"

Beyond her, he had a glimpse of the first of the skiers sweeping toward the bottom of the run, cutting a black silhouette against the white of the snow. But it was all blocked out by the sight of her upturned face and the glistening invitation of her lips. The last vestiges of his restraint broke.

His mouth came down, hot and heavy, and she turned into his arms. There'd been no hope for it, no stopping it. Their attraction was mutual and strong, and progressed rapidly, passionately, into something deeper and more intense. Overhead, fireworks exploded in dazzling bursts of reds and golds and whites to light up the sky, but it had been nothing next to the impact Diana made on him.

That night had been the start of it. From then on, he'd spent every free moment, every free hour, every free night with her, showing her Aspen—the slopes, the intimate restaurants, the crowded après-ski spots, the shops, even the quiet of a moonlight sleigh ride.

Then the week had ended. Bannon had gone back to Boulder to resume his studies at the university and Diana had gone back to Denver. But he hadn't been able to stop thinking about her, wanting her.

Within a matter of days, he'd started burning up the road between Boulder and Denver three and four times a week, and every weekend. He'd known it was madness, but he'd been powerless against the attraction this stormy girl held for him, always so tempestuously happy to see him and so terribly forlorn when he left.

Four weeks after they'd met, she had clung to him. "Don't go. I can't stand it when you leave. Don't you love me, Bannon?"

He hadn't left, and the next day they had eloped—to his father's dismay and her father's delight, elated to have another daughter off his hands.

A month later Diana was pregnant. Unable to cope with his studies and the morning sickness that left her wretched and weak, Bannon did the only thing he could—he took her home to the ranch and placed her in the care of his father and the housekeeper, Sadie Rawlins. Three months later, he joined her—with degree in hand.

By then, the bouts of morning sickness were over and she found herself stuck on a ranch a long way from town, from parties and friends and excitement. It was a kind of suffocation against which she fought.

Then one summer afternoon, David Thornton stopped by the ranch. Bannon was in the hay field near the house and saw him drive in. When he reached the house, he heard the sound of Diana's laughter mingling with that of Thornton's. It hit him how long it had been since he'd heard Diana laugh.

The laughter stopped the instant he stepped onto the porch.

Turning, Thornton jeered, "How come you're sticking so close to the house, Bannon? Don't you trust your wife?"

He laughed again and Bannon hit him. Diana screamed a protest, but he didn't listen and went at Thornton again.

The fight was brief, ending when Diana rushed to the fallen Thornton and turned her black and accusing eyes on Bannon, the loathing in them stopping him cold. He looked at Thornton's bloodied lip and bruised jaw. He'd won, yet he'd lost.

Bannon tried to change that during the months that followed, but shortly after the cesarean birth of their daughter, Diana looked up at him from her hospital bed, white and weak, her love gone.

"I was wrong to marry you. I should have married David." Her voice was barely more than a whisper. "You and I aren't alike at all." She paused, her eyes black with bitterness. "God, I hate you for this."

Those were her last words to him. A few hours later she died. The cause of death, never known. Some said he was to blame. Maybe he was.

"She was very beautiful, wasn't she?" Laura murmured, her fingers lightly caressing the woman in the picture.

With an effort Bannon pulled himself out of the past and turned to the present—their daughter. Looping the ribbon tie around his neck, he walked over and sat next to her, curving an arm around her small shoulders.

He didn't have to see inside her head to know she held a wonderful image of her mother, an image created out of a child's need. And, as in a fairy tale, that image always had to be bright and fair.

"She was beautiful, Laura. She was very beautiful—with long black hair that gleamed in the sunlight just like yours. She had your dark eyes, too. She loved you very much. She loved both of us very much," he lied.

Laura remained silent, drinking in his words and storing the description in her memory. With a soft, satisfied smile, she let him take the photograph and set it back on the night table. He knew he'd made her happy. Nothing else mattered.

"Why don't you get your things and take them out to the

truck? I'll be down in a minute." He stood up and slipped the black silk ribbon under the white collar of his shirt.

"Okay." She moved toward the door, still wearing that pleased look, still warmed by the dream he had given her.

Bannon turned to the mirror and tied the black silk into a bow, then reached for the formal jacket to his trousers. He remembered with sharp, stinging regret the kind of young man he had been, the endless zest he'd had for life, the hopes and tempers and formless dreams that had lifted him. He'd had faith then. Faith and enthusiasm.

7

The stretch limousine glided in and out of the pools of light cast by the street lamps. Fallen leaves from the towering cottonwood trees planted a century ago whirled giddily in the long car's wake.

Kit sat tensely in the rear passenger seat, her face turned to the window, the high, ruffled collar of her evening cape flaring in a circle around her neck. On the curved seat across from her, Paula languidly crossed a leg and asked in idle curiosity, "How many will be at this dinner tonight?"

"Probably around two hundred," John guessed.

"That many," Kit said with a hint of a groan.

John angled his head toward her, his mouth quirking in amusement. "I thought you liked parties."

"Parties, yes," she replied. "These lavish, high-style affairs where people stand around being rich together—no. I always feel like I should post guards around my tongue."

"Don't we all," Paula murmured, looking more exotic than ever in an ethnic-inspired gown by Armani. Beside her Chip arched his neck and tugged at the tight collar and snug bow tie.

"Yes, but unlike you, Paula," Kit threw her friend a smile, "I've never been able to acquire the knack of lying well."

"You will," she replied with a certainty that made Kit uneasy.

She shrugged off the feeling and the subject with an indifferent "Maybe," and glanced out the window.

The limousine left the tree-shadowed area and passed into the more brightly lit business district of downtown Aspen. Almost immediately Kit spotted the three-story-tall brick hotel that was their destination.

"There's the Jerome," she said, then mused absently, "It's hard to believe it was built when Chicago's first lowly skyscraper was still being engineered."

"Have you been in it since it's been completely renovated?" John snubbed his cigarette out in the armrest's ashtray.

"Only once. Dad and I had dinner in the Silver Queen about a year after it reopened," she said, then glanced at him. "Did you know Gary Cooper used to sit on the bench out front with the spit-and-whittle boys and watch the girls go by?"

"Gary Cooper?" Paula repeated skeptically.

Kit nodded. "Back in the forties and fifties, a lot of the big Hollywood stars used to come here. There are endless tales about Hedy Lamarr holding down a barstool for days at the Jerome Bar—and the Duke buying up old silver claims and getting into brawls. Norma Shearer stayed at the Jerome," she recalled. "And I saw a photo of Lana Turner with her then-husband Lex Barker dining at the Jerome." She paused a beat to grin a little impishly. "Naturally she was wearing a sweater." The smile stayed as she remembered something else. "According to Dad, after the swimming pool was built, they used to have pool parties there, and the guests would jump in—with or without clothes—long before the Kennedys made it the fashionable thing to do."

"Did you?" John asked, his sidelong glance bold and naughtily wicked.

"Sorry." She grinned. "Those parties were before my time."

"What was the Jerome like when you were growing up?" Chip leaned forward, his writer's curiosity aroused.

"Nothing like it is now. Sometime after World War II,

they painted all the brick white and trimmed the stone arches above the windows in blue. We used to call it the building with the blue eyebrows," she recalled with a smile. "It always looked dingy and a little run-down. Off and on they made stabs at restoring it. Through it all, the Jerome Bar was always one of the most popular après-ski spots in Aspen, *the* place to be seen. Preferably in the front room where the bar is. Lord help you if you ended up at a table in the Ladies' Ordinary. Still it was better than not being there at all."

"The Ladies' Ordinary? What's that?" Chip frowned, wrinkling his nose as he pushed his glasses higher up on the bridge of it.

"It's the side room off the bar. When the hotel was built back in the 1890s, the Ladies' Ordinary was where an unescorted lady could sit in public and have tea—or something stronger."

"How liberated," Paula drawled.

"It was then," Kit reminded her and looked out the window again at the old and elegant hotel. "There was always talk about tearing it down when I was growing up. I'm glad they didn't."

The layers of paint were gone, removed in the major restoration process. The building's original facade of terra-cotta brick and peach-glow sandstone was again exposed. And once again, the Hotel Jerome stood in stately dignity, reigning tall and proud over the corner of Mill and Main, no more merely a symbol of Aspen's rich past but a vital part of its present.

A steady succession of limousines, Mercedes, and the ubiquitous Range Rovers pulled up in front of the hotel's porticoed entrance, bringing guests to the exclusive charity dinner and attracting the curious. As their limousine pulled into line to await its turn, Kit imagined the scene at the start of the Mauve Decade when the Jerome had been modern and new, when its Eastlake decor had been the height of fashion, when its elevator, its electric lights, its hot and cold running water, its indoor plumbing, and its French chef were the talk of the town.

Guests, drawn from the ranks of Eastern capitalists, railroad barons, and silver kings with an occasional European marquis thrown in for color, would have arrived in brass-and-patent-leather-trimmed carriages, snappy broughams, and smart runabouts pulled by matched teams of high-stepping horses. Sidewalk gawkers would have stared at the gentlemen in their cutaway coats and top hats, and the ladies, laced breathless into tight corsets beneath gowns of silk and satin, their hands gloved and their shoulders bare.

The outward trappings had changed, but little else.

A liveried doorman stood by to hand Kit out of the gleaming black limousine. She took John's arm as the bodyguards closed in to hustle them inside.

"Hey, John!" someone shouted.

Kit glanced to her left and a flashbulb went off, the explosion of light burning its imprint onto her retina. She blinked trying to get rid of the bright spot. The paparazzi definitely added a new twist to the scene, she decided as one of the bodyguards intervened.

"Come on, John. Just one more of you and Miss Masters," the bearded photographer protested, still snapping away despite the bodyguard in front of him.

John ignored both the request and the photographer as he guided Kit into the hotel, the head of his security team running interference.

Inside, she paused and pressed a hand to her eyes. "I'm still seeing spots. The paparazzi are everywhere, aren't they? Even in Aspen."

He nodded. "Like litter on a sidewalk."

The corners of her mouth deepened in amusement. "That's rather a profound analogy."

"And apt, too." He flashed her one of his smiles as Chip and Paula joined them.

The ballroom, with its polished floors and gilt-papered walls, was already filled with people and music. All around was the gleam of damask-covered tables, the glint of champagne in crystal, the shimmer of gems, and the scents of perfume and flowers.

Pausing, John scanned the gathered throng. Black-coated

waiters, bronze gods who could have come straight from central casting, circulated among the guests, dispensing glasses of Haut Brion from their trays or ice-cold Stolichnaya for those who preferred the more traditional accompaniment to the miniature, beluga-topped potato pancakes on the hors d'oeuvre trays.

Wryness edged one corner of his mouth as he noted the number of other private bodyguards in attendance supplementing the hotel's security staff. Some were burly and obvious, some nondescript and not. Their presence was accepted, virtually taken for granted and ignored by the guests as if they were nothing more than an ordinary accessory . . . like cuff links. Necessary for some, status symbols for others, but definitely a sign of the times.

He turned his attention to the guests who had come to dine, dance, and be photographed, paying a thousand dollars a plate for the privilege. There were dozens of people he knew, dozens more he recognized—the Mosbachers, the Basses, the Murdochs, the Fields, Nicholson and friend, Fonda and Turner, an elite collection of the rich, the powerful, and the famous drawn from Aspen's regular glitz contingent, with a few locals thrown in for color. Members of the press circled among them, documenting every designer gown present.

"This is strictly the 'A' list, isn't it?" Paula murmured upon completing her own survey.

"Not entirely," John replied. "We're here."

"Speak for yourself," she replied, arching a cool but amused brow.

Kit paid no attention to either of them as she scanned the throng of guests, mentally bracing herself for the sight of Bannon. When she failed to see him, she relaxed a little and let her attention drift to the magnificently restored Grand Ballroom, its walls covered in gilded wallpaper in a variety of patterns and its wide windows draped in French damask.

"Wouldn't this be perfect for a period film, Chip?" she said, her imagination already painting the scene with waltzing couples, the men in tails and bat-wing collars, the ladies in bustled gowns of emerald satin, scarlet mousseline, and ivory peau de soie, the flutter of fans and scented hankies, the swish of watered silk and bombazine, the air awash with the fragrances of bay rum, rose water, and lemon verbena. "I wish we were making one."

Chip studied her for a critical second. "You would make an ideal Gibson girl."

Maury walked up. "She'd make an ideal anything. You name it—Kit can play the part."

"You don't have to sell me on Kit," Chip insisted. "I was sold before you had a chance."

"Do you see our host?" Paula asked.

"No." Looking at all the familiar faces, John realized that was one of the problems with these parties. The same people, the same conversations, the same underlying boredom. The thought prompted him to glance at Kit, a slender golden column standing beside him. Not boredom. Never in her company.

He neatly plucked two glasses of champagne from the tray of the passing waiter and handed one to Kit. "I believe you said you were in the mood for champagne."

"I did, and I am." She took a sip of the effervescent wine, her eyes warm and alive on him, showing a pleasure that he'd remembered.

"Are the guards posted?" He sipped indifferently at his own, more interested in watching her.

"The guards?"

"Around your tongue. This is the part in the social war games where we're supposed to mix and mingle."

Her laugh was quick and soft. "I'll order them out, but don't be surprised if they fall asleep at their posts."

"I hope so." Smiling, John cast a jaundiced eye at the array of beautiful people. "It might be the thing to liven up this party."

"That isn't nice." Amusement glittered behind her look of mock reproach.

"I know." He grinned and took her arm, letting them be drawn into the vortex of the charity gala.

Old Tom paused in the broad sweep of the Jerome's lobby, his burly chest and big shoulders firmly encased in black evening wear, complete with cummerbund and black tie. With his grizzled hair and craggy face, he looked like a throwback to the cattle barons of old as he drew back his head and cast an assessing eye over the warm, earth-toned lobby, its walls covered in a rich terra-cotta fabric, its gracefully curved chairs in solid dusty blues and striped blues and mauves, its potted palms and baby parlor grand, its great fireplace and silverdust mirror mantel and the deer heads that flanked it.

When Bannon and Sondra joined him, he turned. Bannon recognized that reminiscent gleam in his eyes before his father spoke. "I remember back during the war when some of the ski troops from the army's alpine division bivouacked right here on the floor." He paused and chortled to himself. "And I remember a time or two, when somebody was driving a flock of sheep through town, that a few of them managed to find their way into the lobby. Of course, I wouldn't be saying how that happened."

"It couldn't have been with some help, could it?" Bannon wondered, the corners of his mouth deepening with the suggestion of a smile.

"You never know," Old Tom said, the twinkle in his eye belying the shake of his head.

"Are we ready?" Sondra prompted coolly.

For an answer, Old Tom started walking in the direction of the ballroom, taking his time as he looked around. "This place brings back a lot of memories," he declared. "Back during the Depression, fifty cents could buy you one of the best chicken dinners you ever tasted. Practically the whole town turned out for it on Sunday nights. During prohibition, they turned the bar into a soda fountain."

His pace slowed even more as they traveled down one of the hotel's broad, arched corridors, its walls lined with old mining maps and photos of Aspen's past.

"This hotel is as grand as it was in my father's day," Old Tom said fondly. "He was one who could tell you some stories about this place and how it was when Jerome Wheeler himself walked these halls." He turned to Bannon. "Did I ever tell you about the time your granddad walked into

Wheeler's private dining room while Wheeler and his fellow silver tycoons were sipping cognac and smoking their after-dinner cigars? Right there, under those glittering crystal chandeliers, your granddad told Wheeler he was representing a miner's widow and that his client intended to sue—''

"I think you have told me that story," Bannon broke in gently.

"Endlessly," Sondra murmured under her breath, then smiled quickly at Bannon in a show of tolerance.

"I guess maybe I have," he conceded, then came to an abrupt stop and peered at an enlargement of an old photograph. "Well, I'll be . . . Would you look at this woman in the picture here? The buxom one with the big hat and parasol." He straightened, an odd smile on his face. "I wonder if they knew this was a picture of one of Aspen's most famous madams when they hung it. She ran a high-class establishment, catered strictly to the carriage trade."

Bannon frowned. "How would you know that? That was before your time."

Old Tom reddened slightly beneath his tan. "Your granddad told me. He—uh—had occasion to represent one of her girls a time or two." Then his expression took on a faintly sly look. "Got well paid for his services, too, I understand." He started walking again, ignoring the faint stiffness in the tilt of Sondra's head. "To be honest, I wouldn't mind knowing how a woman looks at a man with a lot of money in his pocket. If he threw a thousand-dollar bill in her lap, would she show him something he never saw before? Would he get something for a thousand that he wouldn't get for ten? And when he paid for it—I wonder if it would be worth it?" He fell silent, pondering the thought.

Thrusting a half-amused glance at Sondra, Bannon murmured, "He's in a philosophical mood tonight."

"I noticed." She returned his look, her eyes a deep, dark brown with a stillness to them that always made him wonder what she was thinking, what her eyes meant when she watched him. He was never sure, not even during the times when they'd made love.

His glance lingered on her a moment longer, traveling over the pale blond hair running smoothly away from her forehead and temples. Her lips lay together in a soft, sober line, slightly full at the centers, lips that could heat with the first touch of his.

In those rare moments when Bannon thought about his future, there was a sense of Sondra in it. The slow gesturing of her hands and the small swing of her shoulders never failed to capture his attention. She never asked anything of him, never made demands. She was simply there, waiting with that calm watchfulness.

At the cloakroom, Bannon helped Sondra out of her fur coat of dark Canadian fisher, then pocketed the claim chit and escorted her into the ballroom.

Together, John and Kit made the rounds, wending their way through the silks, the satins, and the velvets, the Ungaros, the Saint Laurents, and the Lacroixes, drifting from group to group, indulging in the obligatory cheek-brushing and air-kissing, flirting and flattering, lingering when pressed, moving on when not. Once duty was finally done, John edged them back to the fringes.

Taking advantage of the respite, Kit traded her glass of stale champagne for a fresh one. Snatches of conversation came to her, the topics ranging from health spas, plastic surgeons, planned travel jaunts, and Aspen's usual cause célèbre—clean air and the environment—to discussions concerning the economic fallout of a united Germany and a divided Canada.

"It's crazy," she murmured, her lips curving in a bemused smile against the glass's crystal rim.

"What is?" John arched her a curious look.

"All this gloom-and-doom talk. First everyone was worried that the Japanese were going to buy up America. Ten years ago, it was the petro-sheiks from the OPEC countries. Next it will probably be the Germans."

"True."

"I hope he's getting in some practice," Kit remarked as

her roaming glance came to a stop on the pianist in the corner, one of the musicians from the swing band scheduled to play later in the evening.

"Who?"

"The piano player. Nobody's listening to him."

"But everyone would if he stopped playing."

"Probably." She smiled, her attention diverted by a pair of late arrivals entering the ballroom. The man with the receding hairline, cool eyes, and hard face was easily recognizable as Wall Street's notorious takeover tycoon. "That's Simon Renquist, isn't it?" Kit identified him without hesitation, but not the young blonde on his arm. "Who's the blonde? Is that his daughter?"

"Girlfriend."

" 'Girl' is right. She doesn't look a day over nineteen." She studied the two of them over the rim of her glass, guessing there had to be at least thirty years difference in their ages. "What on earth would they find to talk about?"

John gave her a long look. "You are being droll, aren't you?"

She laughed at herself. "Not intentionally."

Smiling with her, he let his glance drift over the gathering, then lifted his wine glass, acknowledging a nod of recognition from Jack Nicholson. Continuing the movement, he raised the glass to his mouth and took a sip. "I'd love to have a cigarette right now," he muttered, all too conscious of the ballroom's smoke-free atmosphere.

"At a cancer benefit? Shame on you, John T." Her sidelong glance was full of reproach, the laughter in her eyes removing any sting from her words. "Personally, right now I'm craving food."

"That's easily remedied." John caught the attention of a circulating waiter balancing an hors d'oeuvre tray on an upraised palm. He motioned him over, then waved a hand in Kit's direction when the waiter reached him. "The lady's hungry."

"Ma'am." The sun-bronzed waiter offered her a choice from the half dozen caviar-topped delicacies on his tray.

Kit hesitated. "Why do mothers drum it into our heads that it isn't proper to eat with gloves on?"

Without saying a word, John selected one of the miniature potato pancakes from the tray and carried it to her lips, the impish twinkle in his blue-gray eyes confirming his intention to feed it to her. Feigning demure obedience, Kit opened her mouth, intending only to take a bite from it, but he popped the whole thing inside.

Caught off guard, Kit struggled to chew the mouthful. The laughter gurgling in her throat made the task all the more difficult. Somehow she managed to chew and swallow it without choking, but only barely.

"That wasn't nice," she accused, the laughter still in her voice as she dabbed at the corners of her mouth, certain some had escaped.

"But was it good?" He grinned, remorseless.

"Mmmm, delicious," Kit confirmed and licked at her lips, feeling the telltale roundness of roe somewhere on the lower one. "It was beluga. No pop."

"You missed a crumb."

"Where?"

She started another exploratory search with the tip of her tongue. John stopped her. "Let me get it."

When he crooked a finger under her chin, she automatically tipped her face to him. In the next second, his mouth was covering hers and she felt the velvet stroke of his tongue glide over her lips, licking away the crumbs and taking her breath as well. She swayed closer, feeling the pull of desire and unconsciously seeking to intensify it.

"Really, Travis. Necking in public?" a male voice taunted. John lifted his head, holding her gaze for an instant, observing with satisfaction the soft glow in her face, a glow he'd put there, before he turned to face Tony Akins, one of the jet set's more notorious hangers-on.

"Some things are irresistible, Tony," John replied, smiling coolly.

"Tut, tut, John. Now you're stealing my lines," he chided. The sarcastic curve to his mouth softened when he turned his darkly handsome face toward Kit. "Don't tell me this ravishing creature is your new leading lady I've been reading about in all the right gossip columns. Kit Masters, isn't it?"

"The one and only," Kit confirmed when John remained silent.

"*That* I believe." He took her hand and made a show of bowing over it and kissing the back of her gloved fingers. "A new bright star bursting over Hollywood's horizon."

"How very flattering, Mr.—" She gently but firmly disentangled her fingers from his grip.

"Akins. Tony Akins—"

"Where's Madelyn?" John interposed.

His glance flicked briefly to John before centering again on Kit. "He's referring to Madelyn St. James. You've heard of her, I'm sure."

"Yes." Madelyn St. James was the granddaughter and heiress to the Hoffstead billions.

"I'm one of the pieces of luggage she carries around. 'Miss St. James arrived in Aspen today, with four trunks, five suitcases, and Tony Akins.' "

Kit smiled in spite of herself at his self-deprecating humor. "I doubt that's totally true."

"Oh, but it is," he insisted, his smile widening. "I'm not complaining, mind you. In fact, I rather enjoy being a kept man. How else would I get invited to all the best parties and stay in all the best places?"

She wasn't sure whether to believe him or not. "You're outrageous."

"That's how I stay in the game," he replied smoothly, then went on without missing a beat. "Tell me, has anyone warned you about Hollywood's golden boy here?" He flicked a hand in John's direction. "The affairs he's had with his leading ladies are positively legendary. I've often wondered if this penchant of his is a case of proximity, convenience, or expediency."

"Maybe it's a simple case of excellent taste," Kit suggested.

"That was fielded very deftly, my dear." Tony Akins

arched a dark brow in approval. "There may be a future for you in Hollywood after all."

"Who will you sell that quote to, Tony?" John challenged, then addressed his next remark to Kit without his gaze leaving Tony. "You should know that Tony is often the 'reliable source' cited in various gossip columns and tabloids. Peddling newsworthy items is a lucrative sideline for him."

"Gathering dirt is a rotten job, but somebody has to do it." He continued to smile, not at all troubled that John had told her. "Luckily it pays well."

Kit tried not to be shocked by his callousness, but not even eight years in Hollywood had made her immune to it.

"John, darling." Madelyn St. James swooped toward him in a shimmer of silver brocade and kissed the air near his cheek, making sure a nearby photographer had a shot of her best side. "How are you? It's been ages," she gushed, drawing back. "When was the last time? I remember—that celebrity tennis tournament. Heavens, that was two years ago."

"Impossible." John smiled at the thrice-divorced brunette, ten years his senior. "You're looking younger than ever."

"I discovered the most marvelous spa in Switzerland," she replied as if that explained it all. "They pamper you with glorious facials and beauty packs—and starve you with berries and nuts. But the result is better than a facelift . . . and infinitely less painful."

"I'll take your word for it," John replied, then turned and introduced her to Kit.

"What an absolutely stunning gown." Madelyn skimmed her from head to foot. "Is that from Dior's fall collection?"

"No. It's from Sophie DeWitt, the costume designer for the new film. A preview of the clothes I'll be wearing."

"Oh." Madelyn lost interest immediately and turned to John, pursing her lips in a ridiculously petulant pout. "I'm still angry with you for not coming to my party last winter."

"It couldn't be helped. I had other commitments."

"I'll have you know that you missed one of my best. It was held the very evening Ivana and Donald had their little blowup on the slopes. I was at Bonnie's when it happened and saw it all." She smiled a little wickedly. "What a delicious little avalanche that started. Of course, I'm speaking as a woman who's found herself standing in the same shoes facing a two-timing husband."

"Not the same shoes, darling," Tony inserted. "Your feet are much daintier than hers."

"True." Madelyn preened a little, then took his hand and gave it a squeeze. "You see why I keep Tony around, don't you? He's so good for the ego."

"I hope I'm good for more than the ego." He raised her hand to his lips and pressed a kiss in her palm, his tongue darting out to add a suggestive lick.

Her throaty laugh had a purr to it. "Definitely more than that."

Kit knew her smile was getting stiff, and covered it by taking a slow sip of champagne. She lowered the glass, curling both hands around its fluted sides and calling on her skills as an actress to maintain a pleasant and interested expression.

"Now look what you've done," Madelyn chided Tony. "You distracted me so I completely forgot what I was talking about."

"Avalanches," John said in a tone that had Kit fighting a smile.

"Avalanches? Of course." She smiled away her initial blankness with the curve of her orange-red lips. "Lord knows how many avalanches have started in Aspen. Why, it was in this very hotel at Don Henley's New Year's Eve bash that Gary Hart met Donna Rice. That man is a story in himself. I mean, can you imagine a politician changing his name? I grant you Hartpence doesn't exactly have a memorable ring to it, but only actors can get away with that sort of thing."

Maury Rose chose that moment to join them, arriving at a fast walk. "So this is where you slipped off to, Kit. I've been looking everywhere for you. I was just talking to some people who know you. Forgot their names." Without drawing a breath, he turned to the others. "Sorry to interrupt. I'm Maury Rose, Kit's agent."

He pushed a stubby hand at Madelyn, forcing an introduction.

"Madelyn St. James." She gave him her limp fingers, reluctantly.

"To tell you the truth, Miss St. James, I knew who you were. And I have to say, your life story would make a terrific movie. My Kit here would be the perfect actress to play the part. You could search the world and never find anyone better. You mark my words—she'll be a bigger star than Elizabeth Taylor ever was. I knew it the first time I saw her," Maury boasted. "Kit has fire and laughter. She's loyal and straight. Why, she could feed chickens on a farm or stroll through Buckingham Palace and look right at home in either place."

Kit grew increasingly uncomfortable with the praise he continued to heap on her. When she heard someone call her name, she turned, welcoming the interruption. The welcome became a wholehearted one the instant she recognized the chestnut-haired woman gliding toward her, sleek and elegant in a gown of basic black. Chanel, of course.

"Angie," she cried in delight and embraced the woman who had been her best friend through grammar and high school. "I was hoping you'd be here tonight."

"Someone said they had seen you and I had to track you down." Angie drew back from the warm hug. "My God, don't you look marvelous? I can't believe it's really you."

"Thanks." Kit laughed at the backhanded compliment, then spared a glance at the audience to their reunion. "You'll have to forgive us. Angie and I go back a long way."

"Yes. We were Aspen's gruesome twosome when we were growing up," Angie acknowledged, her hazel eyes twinkling with memories of their mischief. "Remember?"

"Do I?" Kit laughed.

"It's been ages since I've seen you. I think the last time was—"

"Daddy's funeral."

"Yes." Angie's expression sobered as her hand tightened its grip on Kit's gloved fingers. "I don't know if I had a chance to tell you how sorry I was. I know how close you and your father were. I tried to call you the day after the funeral, but you'd already left."

"I couldn't stay. I had to fly back right away. Mother had

gotten worse—the doctor said it was the emotional shock of Daddy's death."

A shock that had caused a full twenty-four hours to go by before she'd learned the news. She'd been on location in Italy at the time, taping her segments for the soap. Then she'd had trouble getting a flight out of Rome, arriving in Aspen on the morning of the funeral. The next day she'd left for Los Angeles to take care of her mother. She remembered too well the numbness, the grief, the fatigue, the anxiety of those days—days she never wanted to live through again, and ones she definitely didn't want to dwell on.

Mentally shaking off the brief spate of melancholy, she smiled at Angie. "But tell me about you. How have you been? How's the new husband?"

"Mark thinks he's found his calling."

"Really?" The first name struck a familiar chord, then Kit remembered Angie had married Mark Richardson of the Denver Richardsons. His father was a heavyweight in Colorado's financial circle. "What is it?"

"He's thinking about running for the U.S. Senate in three years. And with Daddy Richardson's contacts, he shouldn't have any trouble building up his war chest. But can you picture me as a politician's wife?" she asked with a mild shudder.

"Who knows? You might surprise yourself."

"I suppose it's possible," Angie conceded, her gaze traveling over Kit. "I mean, look at you. Who would have thought our little Kit would be in Aspen to star in a movie with John Travis? We always thought you were the girl most likely to get married and have kids."

"So did I."

"Tell me—" Angie paused and threw a look at the others, then took Kit by the arm and discreetly drew her apart. "Is it true?" she asked, lowering her voice to a conspiratorial level.

"Is what true?"

"Is John Travis really as fabulous in bed as they say he is?"

For a split second, Kit was too stunned to speak. In the next, the question was reminiscent of a hundred others they'd exchanged as girls curious about sex. She burst out laughing. "Angie, you haven't changed a bit."

"Not about some things." She grinned naughtily. "So? Are you going to tell me or not?"

"I honestly wouldn't know," Kit replied, still amused by the turn the conversation had taken, finding it just like old times.

Angie shook her head and smiled. "You haven't changed either, have you, Kit? You never thought it was right to sleep and tell. But you can't blame me for being curious," she said, throwing another sidelong glance at John Travis. "He has a reputation of being the best fuck around. There has to be some truth in it—not a single one of his old loves has a bad word to say about him." She grinned suddenly and wickedly at Kit. "Do you see now why I'd be rotten as a politician's wife? I'd be as bad as Jimmy Carter; only in my case I'd be looking at other men with lusting thoughts."

Kit had to laugh, glad to discover that Angie was as frank and funny as ever. "Then you'd better learn from his mistake and keep your thoughts to yourself."

"Impossible."

"Probably."

A waiter stopped and Angie took a glass of Haut Brion from his tray, then turned to Kit, lifting it in a toast. "Here's to lusting thoughts." Their glasses touched with a crystal ring. As Angie sipped from hers, she let her glance wander over Kit's party. "Madelyn St. James looks fabulous, doesn't she?"

Kit nodded in agreement and lowered her glass. "She went to some spa in Switzerland and got the full beauty treatment."

"She got the full treatment, all right, but at a clinic, not a spa. She's had her thighs sucked, her tummy tucked, and God knows what else."

"Meow," Kit murmured, hiding her smile behind the fluted glass but not the twinkle in her eyes.

Angie grinned back at her. "But isn't it delicious fun?"

she countered, then paused and raised a forefinger as if to interrupt herself. "By the way, have you run into the Bannons tonight?"

"No. Are they here?" She automatically turned to scan the ballroom, stiffening slightly.

"Somewhere. I spoke to them earlier. They're here with Sondra. Naturally."

"Sondra?" Kit hesitated over the name for a split second. "Oh, you mean Bannon's sister-in-law."

"Believe me, she plans to be more than his sister-in-law. Lord only knows how ugly things could have gotten for Bannon if Sondra hadn't stood up for him when his wife died so mysteriously." Angie's voice dropped to a confiding level. "You weren't here then, but there was an investigation into her death. All very hush-hush, of course. Still, the whole town knew their marriage was hardly a happy one. His wife complained to anyone who would listen that Bannon kept her a prisoner on the ranch and refused to let her friends visit. And—he was the only one with her before she died. But the autopsy came up with nothing. I think heart failure was listed on the death certificate, although they don't know what caused it. According to Sondra, her sister had rheumatic fever as a child, which might have weakened her heart. Anyway, it was all dropped. But I shudder to think what would have happened if Sondra had pointed the finger at Bannon."

Kit had heard most of this before. As far as she was concerned, it was absurd then, and absurd now. Bannon had his faults, but he was not the kind of man who could knowingly cause his wife's death.

Anyway, his love life, past or present, was the last subject she wanted to discuss. Instead, she commented, "Sondra sells real estate here in Aspen, doesn't she?"

Angie looked at her askance. "My God, you are behind the times, aren't you? Sondra Hudson owns one of the largest real estate firms in Aspen. More than that, she's become one of the most influential social doyennes here. When word gets out she's having a party, everybody holds their breath to see if they receive an invitation. She has this uncanny knack of knowing who's 'in' and who's 'out.' And if your name isn't on her guest list, it's like the kiss of death.''

"Sondra Hudson?" Kit frowned, trying to equate this statement with the vague memory she had of the woman—most recently of the cool, slim blonde at her father's funeral who had led Bannon's daughter away from the graveside. "I admit I've only met her one or two times, but she never struck me as the social type. I always had the impression she was all business."

"Darling, her parties are business. What better place to meet future clients wanting either to buy or sell here in Aspen?" It was a question that didn't require an answer, and Angie didn't wait for one. "Men use golf courses, tennis courts, and ski runs to widen their contacts; Sondra uses her parties. It's really quite ingenious when you think about it. Of course, it isn't as simple as it sounds." Idly she surveyed the gathering. "This is a tight little clique. They don't let just anyone in."

"Then how in the world did Sondra manage it?" Kit wondered aloud, her curiosity aroused.

"Well, first of all, she's no social climber. She's not interested in belonging to the social scene, only in using it. Oddly enough, she's respected for that, even admired. Secondly, she started small." She paused and took a quick sip of her champagne. "I'm surprised you haven't heard the story before. It's become practically a legend in Aspen."

"Don't forget, counting college, I've been away for the better part of twelve years," Kit reminded her. "You lose touch with what's going on. And Dad was my main source of information. But you know how he was. If it didn't have to do with the ranch or hunting or fishing or his friends and drinking buddies, it didn't get passed along."

"That I can believe." Angie nodded in understanding. "Anyway, Sondra's first—shall we say, important—clients were Claud Miller and his wife . . . of the Denver Millers. They bought some acreage along Castle Creek through Sondra. When they flew in for the closing, she met them at the airport with a horse-drawn sleigh, then picked up the owners at their hotel and took them all out to this wooded parcel. Somehow she'd learned that Claud loved French cuisine, and had arranged for one of the local restaurants to cater a full dinner. Actually, a picnic.

"The setting, the atmosphere must have been marvelous. Snow was lightly falling, the trees were covered with it, a big bonfire was blazing away, a damask-covered table, fully set with china, crystal, and silver flatware, stood beneath an open-sided tent, and a magnum of champagne waited to celebrate the actual closing of the sale. All that by itself would have been enough to make the occasion memorable and unique, but on top of that, Sondra convinced a local furrier to loan her four full-length furs for each of the principals to wear, plus a mink throw for the sleigh. The whole thing probably cost her every dime of her commission from that sale. But it paid off. The Millers couldn't stop talking about it—or her. In a matter of weeks, days, she was getting calls from their friends and business associates. Then, when Claud Miller's wife bought the sable coat her husband had worn for a Christmas present, the merchants fell all over themselves, rushing to Sondra's door, hoping she might borrow something from them and drop their name in passing. Needless to say, there were more sales and more commissions.

"But Sondra was smart; not every client received the royal treatment, only the important ones. And each time, she tailored it to the individual tastes of that person. Catered lunches in art galleries, hot-air balloon rides to picnic sites, down-home Texas barbecues, clambakes along the Roaring Fork—the list is endless," Angie declared, waving a hand. "Then, about six years ago, she started giving intimate little get-togethers. Reunion dinners she called them, rarely inviting more than twelve and always making sure the parties were uniquely themed. An event not to be missed. No one did if they could help it." She raised her glass again. "As I said, her strategy was ingenious."

"Very," Kit murmured.

"Now she throws two or three big parties a year, and only rarely does one of her famous 'closing' celebrations. I'd love to know how much money she's made—especially these last few years when the price of real estate has gone into the stratosphere.''

"A great deal, I imagine." The talk of money raised the spectre of the hospital and doctor bills, something Kit preferred not to think about tonight.

"So tell me," Angie eyed her curiously, "how are you and Bannon getting along? I understand he's handling all the legal end of your father's estate.''

"And managing the ranch for me," Kit added, then shrugged. "Everything's fine. Too much time has gone by to hold any grudges." Holding grudges was alien to her nature and any bitterness had faded long ago. Only the old hurt remained. She'd learned to live with that.

"I suppose." Angie's black-clad shoulders lifted in an indifferent shrug, then she paused, catching sight of someone. "Mark is motioning to me. I think they're shooing everyone to their tables so they can start serving." She turned to Kit, laying a hand on her arm. "How long will you be in Aspen this trip?"

"I'll be here until the cameras start rolling and I won't be leaving until they stop."

"Wonderful. Look, I'll talk to you later and we'll fix a time to have lunch together.''

"That would be fun."

Angie increased the pressure of her hand. "It's been too long since we've had a really good natter.''

"Much too long." Kit nodded emphatically.

"Catch you later," Angie promised and was off, gliding through the crowd to her husband's side.

Kit watched her a moment, then skimmed the milling guests with a searching glance. As John came up, she turned.

"Still hungry?" he asked.

"Are you kidding? I'm famished," she declared and linked arms with him, feeling again that tug of attraction, sharp and very physical.

8

After dining on artichokes stuffed with shrimp, pepper-roasted duck with Georgia peaches, and a classic and light crème brûlée that still had everyone chatting its praise, the tables were cleared, and votive candles in crystal holders replaced centerpieces of orchids and lavender asters. The lights were lowered to create a more intimate setting, then the swing band struck up a lively tune.

Bannon watched from the sidelines as the first couples moved onto the dance floor. Sondra stirred on his left, the slight movement drawing his glance. Her pale blond hair made a soft line at the edge of her temples, the cluster of diamonds on her lobe catching the ballroom's light and throwing it back. The thin, sharp scent of perfume came to him, heightening his awareness of her.

"Would you like something to drink?"

Breaking off her perusal of the crowd, she turned her head to him, a smile edging the sober curve of her lips. "Perhaps later," she replied. "That was a delicious meal, wasn't it? The duck was wonderful, and a clever choice over the usual chicken that's served in so many guises at charity functions."

"It was good, all right." Old Tom spoke up. "There just wasn't enough of it to fill a man up."

Sondra glanced pointedly at his thickening middle, girded by a black cummerbund, then lifted her eyes to him with cool amusement. "You look full to me, Tom. Maybe even a little too full."

He drew himself up to his full six-foot height, unconsciously pushing out his chest and pulling in his stomach. "Just shows what you know about it. I weigh the same as I've weighed for forty years."

Bannon joined in to tease. "It's just distributed differently."

"So I noticed," she murmured, catching the glare Old Tom threw at her. She knew Old Tom didn't like her any better than he'd liked her sister. But the feeling was mutual, if—for the most part—concealed from Bannon.

"Careful, son. You're aging fast, too," Old Tom warned, the remark igniting a good-natured byplay between the two that Sondra ignored as she resumed her visual search of guests, seeking J. D. Lassiter among the chatting, laughing throng.

She noticed Helen Caldwell, shimmying on the dance floor, making a total spectacle of herself. She'd seen her earlier, before dinner, laughing too loudly and drinking too much. The cause for her display was across the room—industrialist hubby Evan Caldwell, who was flirting openly with a high-fashion model, the current rage of the runways, and finding numerous excuses to touch her and whisper in her ear.

On the dance floor, Helen Caldwell grabbed her embarrassed partner's lapels and dragged him closer. Sondra watched, irritated by the woman's behavior—by the reason for it, and by the man who was inevitably to blame.

Once again Sondra coolly surveyed the distinguished gathering of media moguls, takeover tycoons, and industrial giants, despising their superior attitudes, their condescending treatment of women in business, and the masks of politeness behind which they concealed their prejudice. She viewed them with contempt, aware that she possessed a sharper intellect and a keener business sense than most. But she knew that mattered little. Power and money were the only things these men respected; it spoke the only language they understood.

She spotted J. D. Lassiter near the ballroom's terrace doors, his head bent to catch a remark his wife was making, his expression hovering on boredom.

"Would you excuse me for a minute, Bannon?" She absently laid a hand on his arm, claiming his attention. "I need to speak to J. D."

Bannon knew she wasn't asking his permission, but he nodded just the same.

After she'd moved off, Old Tom said, "What she need to talk to Lassiter about?"

"Business, probably." Bannon idly let his gaze follow Sondra as she made her way through the crowd, pausing to exchange pleasantries with those she knew.

"If your mother was here, her toe would be tapping in time to the music and she'd be doing her darnedest to get me onto that dance floor. She loved music. Any kind of music. She enjoyed teaching it, too," Old Tom recalled, looking at the band and seeing something else. "Especially piano. I sure wish she could have had the chance to give our granddaughter piano lessons."

Bannon started to respond, then heard a familiar laugh and turned, recognizing the sunny sound of it. "There's Kit."

"Kit's here? Where?"

"Over there. The one in gold, next to John Travis." He recognized the actor, but not the other members in Kit's small party.

"I see her." Old Tom stared for a long second, drinking in the sight of her wide, laughing smile, a smile that naturally had him smiling, too. "Come on. Let's go say hello."

Bannon hesitated for a split second then fell in step with his father as he set an unswerving course straight for Kit.

Catching movement in her side vision, Kit turned, her glance skipping over Old Tom to fall on Bannon. For an instant, ten years could have been ten minutes. She threw off the feeling and focused on Old Tom, moving forward to seize both of his age-mottled hands in greeting.

"Don't you look handsome tonight," she declared with unfeigned affection as she stood before this big-chested man with grizzled white hair. "I'm surprised you don't have a horde of women hovering around you."

"You always were good medicine for an old man, Kit." The light from the wall sconces played over his cracked and weathered face. With a warmth and an ease that few men her own age could match, he carried her gloved hand to his lips and pressed his lips against the back of it, a gesture without flourish or flirtation. Smiling, Kit thought again that there was something about this old-time rancher that reminded her of opening an attic trunk and discovering crinoline and linsey-woolsey from a bygone age. "You've been gone too long," Old Tom stated, half chiding.

"I know." She nodded briefly, then turned, keeping her fingers curled around Old Tom's hand, and faced Bannon, fighting off the tension and noting—as she had done countless times in the past—the blunt honesty of his features and the warmth and humor lurking around his mouth and eyes. "Bannon."

"Hello, Kit." He nodded to her, a smile deepening the small weather wrinkles about his eyes. It was obvious to anyone, even more so to Kit, who'd known both men all her life, that Bannon and Old Tom were cut from the same pattern. Bannon had the same granite chin and brow, the same wide and deeply set eyes, the same roughly molded cheekbones.

She noticed the bow of silk ribbon he wore in place of a formal black tie and smiled. "You still don't follow the crowd, Bannon."

"Not hardly." Amusement glinted in his eyes.

"Aren't you going to introduce us, Kit?" Paula asked in a prompting tone.

"Sorry." Still holding Old Tom's hand, Kit swung around to stand between Bannon and Old Tom, her mood deliberately lighthearted and gay. "I want you to meet some of my friends from Los Angeles, Tom. This is John Travis, who really needs no introduction. The redhead is Paula Grant. She and I worked together on *Winds of Destiny*. Chip Freeman is the director of the movie we'll be filming here in Aspen, and that's my agent, Maury Rose." She paused and linked arms with the two men flanking her. "Everyone, I want you to meet Tom Bannon. He owns Stone Creek, the ranch next to mine. He's a tried and true cowman. And the gentleman on my left is his son, Bannon."

The usual round of handshakes and greetings followed the introductions. When it was over, Kit didn't allow the conversation to lag.

"I doubt if any of you noticed the distinction I made when I described Old Tom as a cowman, but in western lingo, that means he runs *she-stock*—cows, in other words—and raises his own cattle. Now, my father was a *steer-man*. He bought young steers and raised them for beef. There's an old saying on the range that 'steer-men go broke, but cowmen never do.' "

"There's some that would dispute that nowadays," Old Tom stated.

"Probably." She studied his craggy face, the face of a man who had spent a lifetime grappling with the elements. A host of warm feelings and good memories welled up inside. "I didn't expect to see you tonight. I talked to Angie before dinner and she told me you were here."

"We got here late. We drove the herd down to winter grass today and it took longer than it should. Some damned fool plane—"

Kit covered his mouth with her hand, stopping the outflow of words. "I have a confession to make. I was in that damned fool plane that spooked your cattle, Old Tom. It was my fault. You see, I wanted to fly over the ranch and the pilot obliged. I'm sorry." She lowered her hand.

"You should be sorry. It cost us a lotta time to round 'em back up again." Old Tom tried to hang on to his gruffness as he looked at her with narrowed eyes.

"Kit's been worried you'd be angry with her when you found out she was behind it," John interposed, subtly coming to her defense.

"I gotta right to be. It was a damned fool stunt—though I guess she couldn't know beforehand that we were moving the herd," he grumbled in concession.

She winked at John. "I think I've just been forgiven."

"Don't get sassy," Old Tom warned, but without heat.

Paula spoke up. "I'll be honest. When I saw those cows stampeding and the cowboys chasing them, I thought I'd been transported back to the wild and woolly West. Especially when I failed to see any film crew around."

"The West still lives, Miss Grant." Bannon tempered his assertion with a gentle smile.

Kit missed Paula's skeptical look, struck by the contrast their comments had underlined for her. Only that afternoon, Bannon had been one of those cowboys in boots and jeans and spurs, racing his horse to check the stampede. Tonight he was in formal dress, completely at ease in these sophisticated surroundings.

"From the air, you appeared to have some good-looking cattle, Mr. Bannon," John remarked, and Kit had to smile, seriously doubting that he had any knowledge at all about cattle.

"They oughta be," Old Tom stated. "According to the market, I'm paying for the privilege of raising them."

Maury frowned. "If that's the case, why don't you sell out?"

"Cattlemen don't change, Mr. Rose," Old Tom informed him. "They just die."

"Spoken in the best tradition of the romantic West," Paula murmured, her mouth quirking.

"You don't believe in the traditional West, do you, Miss Grant?" Bannon observed.

"Haven't you heard?" Paula lifted her wineglass, eyeing him over the rim of it. "It died with John Wayne. It's a lot of old-fashioned, sentimental nonsense. It isn't even good theater anymore."

"You youngsters are hard people." Old Tom shook his head in pity. "You don't believe in anything. Maybe my generation was a little too given to getting choked up when the band played 'God Bless America.' But we believed in our tears. You folks won't allow yourselves the luxury of honest emotion because you're afraid of it. Now you're all turning brittle and cold."

Paula let one hand flutter to her throat. "I do believe we've just had our knuckles rapped with a ruler."

Old Tom snorted at the irreverence in her tone. "And don't give me that hogwash about how realistic you are. You don't know the first thing about it. I'm from a generation that built a church and a school at one end of town, and a whorehouse at the other. That's realism."

Kit knew from experience that Old Tom was just warming up. Laughing, she threw up her hands. "Enough. We surrender." The band struck up a slow tune, and Kit took her cue from it. "Listen. They're playing our song, Old Tom."

"Our song?" A frown pleated his forehead.

"It's a waltz, isn't it?" she countered with mock innocence. "According to my dance card, the first waltz belongs to you. Your arm, sir?" She held up her own, the angle of her head saucy and challenging.

"You're doing this because you want me to stop offending your friends and shut up." Old Tom dared her to deny it.

"Right. And I want to dance, too."

"Two birds with one stone, eh?"

"Something like that." Kit smiled.

Old Tom chuckled at her candor and took her arm. "In that case, let's go show those folks how to waltz."

Bannon watched the two of them make their way onto the dance floor, then brought his attention back to Kit's party and the redhaired actress who was studying him in a curious and speculating way.

"Your father is . . . ." Paula searched for the right word.

"—a character?" Bannon suggested gently.

Her head dipped in approval. "That's a kind choice. Thank you, Mr. Bannon."

"You can drop the Mister and call me just plain Bannon." He looked once again to the dance floor and the couple gliding through the waltz steps with graceful swoops and turns. "As for my father, he always has his opinion and he's never been shy about voicing it."

"How true," Paula agreed in a faint, dry drawl. "Any moment I thought he was going to call us a bunch of young whippersnappers."

"How old is your father anyway?" Maury asked.

"Eighty-two."

"Really." Chip said in surprise. "He doesn't look it."

"Would that we could all carry our years as well when we're his age," Maury declared, then patted his protruding girth. "Not much chance of that, I'm afraid."

"Excuse me," John Travis broke in. "I think I'll slip out on the terrace and have a cigarette."

Maury nodded. "Sure. I'll tell Kit where you are when she comes back." His departure created a brief break in the conversation. Then Maury picked it up again. "I take it you've known Kit a long time," he said to Bannon.

"A long time," he confirmed, unconsciously glancing in Kit's direction. Remembering. "We grew up together."

Paula, who missed nothing, murmured, "It was like that, was it?"

He brought his glance back to her. "It was like that," he said simply, then looked again at the couple on the floor, this time observing the flush of exertion that reddened his father's cheeks. "Sorry, but I think I'd better rescue my father before he overdoes it."

On the dance floor, Old Tom guided Kit through a series of sweeping turns that had other couples on the floor moving out of their way. "You do realize that everyone's watching us, don't you?" Kit teased.

"Only because I'm dancing with the prettiest gal in the room. Why, if Beauty was here, she'd been jealous. No, that's not true," he amended quickly. "She never would have been jealous of you, Kit. You were like a daughter to her, she was that fond of you."

"I loved her, too."

"I miss her." For the first time since they'd taken to the floor, his steps faltered. He recovered, but the sureness was no longer there. Belatedly Kit noticed the beads of perspiration that had broken out along his brow.

"You look tired." She suddenly wished she hadn't asked him to dance.

Old Tom scoffed at that. "Bannons are like Saint Bernards.

We look old and tired from birth.'' He didn't give her a chance to pursue the subject.''How long are you going to stay this time? Is this another one of those trips where you fly in and fly back out?''

''This time I'm going to be here so long that you're going to get tired of seeing me.''

''Not these eyes, Kit. Never of you,'' he insisted in a voice gruff with sincerity.

A hand clamped onto Old Tom's shoulder and there stood Bannon, his smile warm and faintly challenging. ''My turn, I believe.''

With a little bow, Old Tom backed away, turning Kit over to Bannon with an alacrity that betrayed his previous disclaimer of fatigue. Bannon's arm circled the back of her waist and his hand came up, catching hers, its calluses snagging briefly at the fine fabric of her glove as his fingers closed around hers. The wedding band he wore stood out against the deep tan of his skin, a glaring reminder that he'd married someone else even though he'd said he loved her—obviously not as much as she had loved him.

She looked away, her eyes seeking Old Tom and watching as he paused on the edge of the dance floor and wiped the perspiration from his forehead and around his mouth. His hand trembled slightly when he returned the handkerchief to his pocket.

''I shouldn't have asked him to dance,'' she murmured.

''He enjoyed it.''

''Just the same, I'm glad you cut in.'' In that respect, she meant it.

''It seemed natural.'' Bannon smiled.''One more dance floor, one more dance—homecoming, the prom, Andre's disco. This goes back a long way. Dancing with you is a habit I can't seem to break.''

She tipped her head back. ''Do you remember so many of those dances, Bannon?'' She'd always wondered if he thought about her.

''When I'm dancing with you, I do.''

''That was a long time ago. More than ten years.'' Yet the firmness of his hand on her back was an incredibly familiar sensation—as was the pattern of his steps and the slope of muscle in his shoulder where she rested her hand. Only back then, they'd danced slower . . . and closer. Mentally shaking off that memory, Kit drew in a deep breath and smiled. "We had some good times, didn't we?" It was a perspective of the past she wished she could keep.

"We did, indeed," Bannon agreed, then mused idly, "Ten years." He cocked his head to one side and made a show out of peering intently at her nose. "I do believe you've acquired a few more freckles in that time."

"You used to tease me horribly about my freckles," Kit remembered. "You almost made me cry once. I went home and used lemon juice, Clorox, peroxide—I even tried sandpaper to get rid of them."

"I'm glad you didn't succeed. I like them."

"They give me a touch of character, don't you think?" With a tilt of her head, she pushed her nose up a little higher and struck a pose. Long ago, she'd learned it was easier if she kept the conversation light.

Bannon laughed. "As if you needed any more," he said, then recalled, "we never pulled our punches with each other, did we? We always talked straight, had our share of arguments, too."

Kit nodded thoughtfully. "Funny, but I can't remember what a single one of them was about." No longer smiling, she lifted her gaze to his face. "Can you?"

"Not anymore."

"I wonder why." She puzzled over that.

"Probably because we never argued about anything important."

"Then why did we argue at all?"

"Maybe because we were together so much. Because we had so damned much fun." He wasn't sure what it was he was trying to say. Kit Masters had been a strong, deep part of his life. There'd been a time when she was nearer to him than any other woman. Some of that old feeling remained so that, even now, as he danced with her, he felt at ease, comfortable, knowing there was nothing he had to explain to her, knowing she would understand. "We were young, Kit.

We knew each other well. We knew which buttons to push to set off the other. Once in a while, we pushed them out of sheer orneriness.''

"I suppose." Her expression became faintly grim.

"I never meant to hurt you, Kit." Yet he knew he had, even though she'd never said so.

She gave him a quick smile. "I know you didn't." But her warm smile was accompanied by a quick lift of her chin, an assertion of pride in its tilt—a pride that he'd hurt. "I forgave you long ago, Bannon."

Forgave, but she hadn't forgotten. Bannon understood that, just as he understood that beyond her breezy smile and laughter-loving nature was a woman of strong feelings and a strong will.

He didn't say anything, letting the waltz music carry the silence, something dreamy and wistful in its lilting tune. He watched her, conscious of the soft line of her lips and the steady return of her gaze. He felt some of the heat from those earlier days when he'd gone with her, danced with her, kissed her, and felt the half-giving, half-resisting strength of her body.

Kit turned her head, breaking the contact, an earring swinging with the abruptness of the movement, an abruptness she tried to disguise by smiling at a couple dancing past them, and wondering how she could have known what he was thinking after all this time—and been stirred herself by the exact same thoughts and memories. She must have imagined it.

She faced him again with a measure of her former composure. "I thought I'd drop by your office on Monday and pick up the ranch keys. It will probably be in the morning. Is that all right?"

"That's fine. In fact, it'll be a good time for us to go over some paperwork regarding Clint's estate."

"If you say so, but you should know by now, Bannon, that all that legal stuff is Greek to me."

"Don't you mean Latin?" He grinned.

Kit laughed, her bare shoulders lifting in a faint shrugging movement. "Latin, Greek—it doesn't matter. I still don't understand. Thank heaven Dad knew that and named you his executor.''

''You would have managed if you had to.'' Bannon deftly steered her between two couples.

''Barely.'' She thought about that for a minute, then added,''Although after all the forms and paperwork I've had to fill out on Mother, I should be an expert.''

''How is she?''

''The same. Stabilized. In remission. They tell me she could live another thirty years. But she'll never come home again.''

''Kit—''

She saw the sympathy, the pain and pity in his eyes. For her and for her mother. ''I don't want to talk about it. Not tonight, Bannon.'' She smiled quickly, firmly.

Bannon observed the determined set of her chin and nodded. ''Okay.'' Yet he couldn't help thinking of all that Kit had been forced to cope with these last nine months with her father's death, the sudden and rapid deterioration of her mother's health, and the demands of her career—and quietly marveled at the resiliency of her spirit.

Without meaning to, Bannon drew her closer and caught the soft, subtle fragrance of her perfume. It brought back every old memory and some of the old desire as they circled the dance floor, their steps matching with the ease of two people who had danced a lifetime together.

Sondra paused in front of the terrace doors, her lips thinning in irritation at the sight of New York financier George Greenbaum with J. D. Lassiter. She could guess at their conversation. George had been boring everyone this evening with his inside knowledge of all the political posturing in Washington over the S&L scandal. For the moment, J. D. appeared to listen with interest, which meant it would be the wrong time to break in.

Aware that she couldn't continue to stand there without conveying the impression she was waiting to gain an audience with J. D., Sondra searched for a diversion. The ballroom doors on her left opened directly onto the terrace with a softly lit fountain as its centerpiece. Silhouetted figures moved in the darkness, guests from the party, the telltale glow of cigarettes in their hands. Sondra instantly rejected the thought of joining them and turned back to the ballroom—just as John Travis approached, one hand already delving inside his jacket for a cigarette.

"John, how wonderful to see you again." Sondra forced the meeting, deliberately ignoring the initial flicker of annoyance in his glance.

"Sondra." His hand came out from inside his jacket, without the cigarette pack, as he stopped to brush a kiss across her cheek in greeting. "You look lovely, as usual." He stepped back, sweeping her with a look. "Black suits you. But how could it not when you have all that moonlight trapped in your hair?"

"I see you're still playing the charming rogue." She smiled at his flattery, coolly unmoved by it. "I wondered if you were here. You come to Aspen so seldom anymore. It did me no good at all to sell you that house in Starwood."

"You know how it goes—I've been busy." There was something about her that reminded him of a cat—a Siamese cat with manicured claws.

"Yes, everyone's buzzing about the new movie you'll be filming here this winter." Out of the corner of her eye, Sondra saw someone come up to speak to George Greenbaum. She turned slightly and pretended to notice J. D. for the first time. "There's J. D. Would you excuse me, John? I need to have a word with him."

"Of course." He took a step toward the terrace door. "If my agency can be of any help with lodging or locations, you call."

"Promise." Smiling, John reached for the handle and Sondra turned away, blocking him from her mind and focusing solely on Lassiter.

"J. D." She walked directly to him and smoothly extended her hand, forcing him to take it. "I want to congratulate you on throwing such a marvelous party. The atmosphere, the

food, the wine, the entertainment, the artful mix of people—
it's all perfect. Hardly anyone has left. I couldn't have done
better myself.''

"Coming from you, that's high praise, Sondra," he replied.

The patronizing tone of his voice set her teeth on edge, but
she managed a throaty laugh. "Now you are the one who's
being too kind, J. D.''

"Nonsense." But his smile said otherwise, although Sondra was careful not to notice that.

"By the way, I almost called you today, J. D.," she said.
"If I hadn't known I'd see you tonight, I probably would
have."

"Oh?" An eyebrow lifted in only mild interest.

"Yes, my company has obtained an exclusive listing on
an absolutely prime piece of property in downtown Aspen.
An entire block, in fact. Naturally I immediately thought of
you—"

He cut her off. "I'm not interested."

She hadn't expected that response—or the abruptness of
it. But she was too skilled at her business to let it show. She
simply smiled and shook her head as if amused by him.''You
will be when you hear the location," she said confidently.

"No, I won't." Both his voice and expression were indifferent.

She kept her smile and refused to accept his answer. "You
don't really mean that."

"Don't I?" he countered. "How many times have you
contacted me about buying some commercial property since
you sold me my home on Red Mountain, Sondra?"

"Several." She matched him, cool stare for cool stare.

"And each time I told you I wasn't interested. I should
have thought by now you would have gotten the message."

"But—"

He held up his hand. "Spare me the sales pitch, Sondra.
Save it for someone else. Marvin Davis or Trump might be
content to own a *block* of Aspen. I'm not. Only another Aspen
would satisfy me."

At that instant, Sondra realized she'd underestimated the size of his ego. "I'll keep that in mind, J. D.," she murmured.

"Do that," he said and folded his hands behind his back, a gesture that struck her as being somewhat kingly—like the way he tipped his head to peer along his nose at the couples on the dance floor. "That's Bannon dancing with the female lead in my new film, isn't it?"

Sondra followed the direction of his gaze all the way to Bannon. Her glance touched briefly on his blond partner, then went back to rest on Bannon's smiling face. She felt a sharp jolt of jealousy at the way he looked at the woman in his arms.

"Yes, that's Bannon."

"He seems quite taken with Kit."

"They've been friends since childhood." Sondra tried to dismiss his observation, only to remember the talk around town at the time of Bannon's marriage to Diana—the kind of talk that suggested Bannon and Kit Masters had once been considerably more than friends.

"Yes, she's originally from Aspen, isn't she?" Lassiter nodded absently. "John's been playing that up in the publicity he's been doing for her." His mouth twisted in a faint smirk. "John's ego won't let him romance a nobody."

Sondra wondered if J. D. realized how much his talk sounded like mud throwing, and mud throwers never have clean hands. The waltz ended, the final notes fading into the steady hum of conversation. A few of the dancers acknowledged the band's efforts with a show of applause while Bannon continued to hold Kit Masters for several beats after the music had stopped. Was he listening to something Kit was saying? Sondra couldn't see. At last they parted and joined the other couples drifting off the dance floor.

Watching them, Sondra glared at the faint smile on his lips and the hand placed possessively on Kit's back. She felt her teeth scrape together, her breath holding against an urge to scream.

No, it wasn't going to happen again. She wasn't going to lose him, not again.

She murmured some excuse to Lassiter and moved away, angling through the crowd to intercept them.

Scant seconds after Bannon had escorted Kit back to her friends, Sondra walked up, a mask of serene composure firmly fixed in place. Bannon nodded to her, but his hand remained on Kit's back—a fact that didn't escape Sondra's attention.

"You remember my sister-in-law, Sondra Hudson, don't you, Kit?"

"Of course, we've met before. Hello again, Miss Hudson." Her voice held a guarded warmth and there was more than a trace of reserve in her eyes and her smile.

"Sondra, please," Sondra insisted, her mouth curving in a polite smile.

"Sondra," Kit replied in acknowledgment, then proceeded to introduce her clutch of Hollywood friends whose names Sondra didn't even attempt to remember.

"It's nice to meet all of you," she murmured, then turned to Bannon. "Where's Old Tom?"

Bannon's head came up as he threw a look around. "I don't know."

"I think I saw him head for the bar," the red-haired actress volunteered.

"Maybe we should see," Sondra suggested. "It's getting late."

"Of course." Bannon nodded once, then glanced at Kit Masters. Sondra was quick to note the change in his expression, a warmth gentling all the hard angles of his rough-cut features. "I enjoyed our dance."

"So did I," Kit said as Sondra watched their interchange, conscious of the odd closeness that sprang between them, discernible in the private smiles and private words, their meanings wrapped up in an old memory only they shared. "We'll have to do it again sometime."

"Like I said—" Bannon's mouth slanted in a warm and lazy line. "Old habits die hard."

Her response was a soft, almost soundless laugh as Bannon moved to Sondra's side. "See you Monday."

"Right." He turned Sondra toward the bar. She stiffened

at the unbearably casual touch of his hand on her back, drawing his glance. Bannon caught the brief tightening of her lips and the very faint line of dissatisfaction between her brows. "Is something wrong, Sondra?"

"No." Her denial was quick, instant, like the glance she threw him, but not so quick that he missed seeing the flash in her eyes that was a bit of anger, a bit of desperation. "My talk with Lassiter didn't go well, that's all."

When she failed to elaborate, Bannon didn't delve further. The specifics were her business, not his. He dropped the subject and let his mind drift back to Kit.

❧❧ 9 ❧❧

Kit watched Bannon disappear into the crowd with Sondra. Somehow she hadn't expected dancing with Bannon would evoke so many old memories, so many old feelings. This ache of an old loss, yes—but not the rest.

"If that's his sister-in-law"—Paula stood next to her, studying the black cut of Bannon's shoulders over the rim of her wineglass—"where's his wife?"

"He's a widower."

"A widower—what an old-fashioned word," Paula said in amusement. "I haven't heard it in years."

"It suits Bannon." The band swung into an uptempo number and another set of dancers took to the floor, fingers snapping, shoulders dipping, and satin hips swaying to the faster rhythm. Kit thought she recognized Angie among them. Then the woman turned and it wasn't her. "I wonder where Angie disappeared to," she mused idly and scanned the faces around her.

"Angie Dickinson? Is she here?" Paula raised one eyebrow in surprise.

"No, Angie Richardson," she corrected, then realized the name meant nothing to Paula. "We were best friends. I ran into her before we sat down to dinner. We were supposed to get together afterward and set a date to have lunch, but I haven't seen her. I hope she hasn't left already.''

A pair of hands brushed the points of her shoulders, then glided firmly down her arms to the tops of her gloves. Kit caught the scent of John's cologne an instant before he bent his head and nipped lightly at the ridge of her shoulder.

"Were you looking for me?" he murmured.

With a turn of her head, she encountered the gleam in his eyes. "No."

He frowned in reproach. "Wrong line. This is where you say 'yes.' ''

"It is?" She feigned confusion. "But what's my motivation?"

"Maybe you missed me?"

"That would work, wouldn't it?" She couldn't honestly say she had missed him, but she was definitely glad he was back.

"Especially if you danced with me."

Laughing, Kit turned the rest of the way around. "I thought you'd never ask."

"Did you now?" he murmured and swept her onto the dance floor.

They laughed and talked, danced and flirted their way through song after song, never leaving the floor until the band took a break. While John went to fetch a drink, Kit slipped off to the ladies' lounge.

A socialite's wife, weighted down with a suite of diamonds and rubies, sat in front of a lighted vanity mirror fussing with her hair, a monogrammed silver brush in her hand, when Kit walked in. The woman glanced at Kit, then ignored her, the same way she ignored the lounge attendant standing nearby. Kit smiled at her anyway, chose an empty stall, and went inside.

Seconds later the door to the lounge opened, admitting a rush of sounds from the outer hall and a voice Kit recognized at once as Angie's. Hastily she smoothed the skirt of her gown over a hip and reached for the stall latch, a wide smile curving her lips.

"Don't be naive, Trula," Angie was saying. "Of course

Kit is sleeping with John Travis. How else do you think she landed a leading role in his new movie?''

Kit went motionless, too stunned to move.

"Did she tell you that?'' the other woman, obviously Trula, asked with an avidness that Kit found revolting.

"Oh, she denied it, of course,'' Angie replied. "Which didn't surprise me at all. Kit always acted so virtuous in school it was positively disgusting at times.''

There was more, but Kit shut it out as she struggled to understand why it hurt so much. Worse things had been said or insinuated in Hollywood. But she'd expected that kind of spiteful and malicious talk in Hollywood, where egos abounded and jealous claws were unsheathed on anyone who climbed a little higher. She'd always laughed off such snide remarks. But she couldn't laugh this time. This time it wasn't amusing. This time it was Angie, someone she'd always thought of as her best friend, who was accusing her of sleeping her way to stardom. This time it hurt. She felt betrayed.

She heard the tap-tapping of heels on the marble tiles, the click of stall doors latching, and the rustle of clothing. Intervening stall partitions gave Angie's voice a hollow sound.

"Damn, I just ran my stockings.''

Kit took advantage of the moment to slip out unnoticed. John was waiting for her with a glass of wine when she returned to the ballroom.

"Thanks.'' She took a sip and found it tasteless. She lowered the glass, her fingers tightening around it. She felt suddenly restless, impatient, irritated with everything—the wine, the music, the people, the party.

"Something wrong?'' John tipped his head at an inquiring angle, his glance probing.

She gave a vague shake of her head. "It just seems noisy and loud in here.''

"Doesn't it though?'' Paula murmured and pressed a hand to her temple. "It's given me a pounding headache.''

"Do you want to leave?''

"Please.'' Paula spoke up before Kit could respond.

"Do you mind?'' Kit glanced at John.

"Not at all. I've had my fill of the party scene, too."

"What about your old school chum, Kit?" Paula remembered. "The one you wanted to have lunch with?"

"I guess I must have lost her somewhere," Kit said and shrugged. "It doesn't matter."

But it did.

Back at John's Starwood mansion, Kit followed the others' lead and went straight to her room. But the white bed with its voile hangings looked anything but inviting. She ignored it and discarded her evening bag on the glass table, then crossed to the glass doors and stepped onto the private terrace, the sharpness of the mountain night washing over her.

Drifting aimlessly, she wandered beyond the pool of light from the bedroom to the edge of the flagstoned terrace. She tried but she could not put a name to this mood she was in. She felt restless, lonely, nagged by a feeling of melancholy over the loss of Angie's friendship—and Bannon's love.

Immediately she gave herself a hard mental shake. She was not going to indulge in a lot of what-might-have-been's and what-if's. That was old ground. She had a new life, a new direction—maybe even a new love. She lifted her gaze to the star-strewn sky, wishing.

"Is this private or may I join you?"

Kit swung around, her evening cape billowing with the movement in a satin whisper. She stared, unable to say a word, startled to discover her wish had become reality as John stood outside the terrace doors she'd left open.

"I saw your light was on," he said. "I knocked, but you obviously didn't hear me."

"No, but I was wishing you were here," she admitted, recklessly throwing caution aside.

"And here I thought I'd have to use all my powers of persuasion to convince you to have a nightcap with me." Glass glinted in his hand as he moved away from the doors. "Earlier tonight you said you were in the mood for champagne and moonlight. But, since there isn't much in the way of moonlight"—with a nod of his head, he indicated the silver crust of a new moon in the sky—"and there wasn't any champagne chilled, I hoped you might settle for brandy and starlight.''

"I think it's a perfect combination.'' Kit accepted the glass he offered, then added, recalling his remark earlier that moonlight was for adolescents, ''And much more adult.''

"I thought so.'' Smiling faintly, he touched his glass to hers.

She briefly swirled the brandy, then took a sip, aware it was as much the look in his eyes as the heat of the brandy that made her feel warm all the way to her toes. Definitely a pleasant feeling.

Idly she perused the midnight sky, strewn with thousands of stars. "It's a beautiful night, isn't it? Just look at all the stars,'' she murmured. "It's been ages since I've seen so many. And they look so close—as if you could reach out and touch them.''

"You're the kind of woman who makes a man want to pluck all the stars from the sky and present them to you in cupped hands just for the reward of your smile.''

"I do believe you're flirting with me, John T.,'' she teased.

"Not flirting.'' He grazed the back of a finger along her cheek, then ran it into her hair. "I'm making my move on you.''

"Is that right?'' She sounded slightly breathless, and knew it was from the familiar thrill of his touch.

"Nothing has ever felt more right.'' He brushed his mouth over the path his finger had taken.

"I do believe you have designs on my virtue, John T.'' Out of habit, Kit tried to keep it light even as she felt all her resistance melting because it did feel right. Tonight more than any other night, it seemed, she needed to love—she needed to be loved.

"I have designs on your virtue, your body, your lips, your heart.'' He rubbed his mouth near her ear. "I have designs on you, Kit.'' The low, husky whisper of her name was like a caress over her skin as he took the brandy glass, freeing her hands. She slid them over the front of his chest, but not in protest. "Do you know how much I've wanted you these past weeks?''

"No," she said softly, thinking only that she wanted to feel the pressure of his mouth on hers and the sensations it always evoked.

"Too much. Too damn much." His hands framed her face, his fingers threading into her hair, mussing its smooth upsweep. "It's gone past wanting and become needing," he declared and finally took her waiting lips.

The taste of him exploded on her tongue, sweeping through her until she was filled with it. Instantly everything seemed to quicken—her blood, her heart, her senses. She tipped her head back, inviting him to deepen the kiss. Seduction, she might have resisted; demand, she would have fought, but she was vulnerable to his need, and to her own.

When her hands curled around his neck, drawing him to her, his mouth came crushing down, sending them both reeling. He tugged at the silk-covered buttons of her evening cape, impatient to touch her skin. As they came loose, he pushed the satin fabric from her shoulders. It fell in a glistening pool at her feet. She shivered, first from the cold of night, then from the heat of his hands and his lips as they played over her skin, exploring her neck, throat, and shoulders.

All along he'd intended to end the evening in bed with Kit, but he hadn't expected to feel this urgency, this desperation. She touched something primitive in him. He fought to control it even as he scooped her up and carried her into the bedroom.

There, he set her down. For a moment, they were locked in each other's arms. His hands tunneled into her hair, scattering pins until it spilled onto her shoulders. He murmured something, his actions speaking louder as he plunged deep into her mouth again.

Hurriedly, impatiently, they began to undress each other. His fingers fumbled with the zipper of her gown. He swore. She laughed, definitely breathless. Then they were on the bed, flesh to flesh.

He could feel her nipples harden against his chest, and wanted to take her immediately. He banked the need, vowing to enjoy her slowly. From her brandy-flavored lips, he took a leisurely journey to the warmer taste of her throat. But his hands were already roaming demandingly. Kit moved under him with an uncontrollable urgency as his fingers found the peak of her breast, intensifying her pleasure. Skimming over her skin with his tongue, he moved down to her breast.

Kit arched beneath him, her hands digging in to press him down. His teasing kisses had her moaning in delighted frustration. His mouth lingered at the swell of her breast, sending more and more shivers of pleasure through her. His tongue flicked lightly over her nipple, then retreated to soft flesh. She murmured his name, urging him back. Slowly he circled it, his mouth on one breast, his hand on the other, driving her into mindless sounds and convulsive movements beneath him. Ending the torture, he captured a straining nipple between his teeth, then left it moist and wanting while he journeyed to her other breast to taste, to explore, and finally to devour.

She ran her fingers over him, tracing the taut muscles in his shoulders and down his strong back, then skimming over his narrow hips. Amid a haze of sensation, she felt him shudder at her touch as his own hands moved lower, exciting her as she had excited him.

He traveled down the valley between her breasts, her stomach quivering beneath his lips. As his mouth drifted lower, she arched to meet it—willing, wanting. His tongue was hard and greedy, shooting pleasure from the center of her out to her fingertips. Her body felt heavy with it, her head light.

Giving her no chance to recover, his mouth came swiftly back to hers, loving her not so much with tenderness as with thoroughness. He was one solid ache for her, yet he was aware of every changing, rippling thrill she felt if he exerted more pressure here, took a longer taste there. It gave him a wild sense of power, a power made more acute by the desire to see her without control. Aware his own was ebbing too quickly.

He could hear her breathing—quick and short. She moved under him with complete abandon. She was his. He needed to know that, though he didn't know why. Her fingers touched him and the blood raced fast and furious into his head. A second later, she took him and drew him inside her.

They moved together, a driving rhythm taking them, neither leading, both following, the pleasure building until all sensation centered into one, just as they were one. And together they found the perfection that can be achieved only rarely as they gave perfection to each other.

～❦❧ 10 ☙❦～

Morning sunlight streamed through the church's stained-glass windows, giving the reds, greens, and blues of the colored glass rich, jewel-bright hues. Minute particles of dust glistened in the shafts of light that spilled across the outer aisles and invaded the space between the polished oak pews.

Old Tom Bannon sat in the last row, close to the doors along with the other ushers for the morning service. Bannon sat near the front next to Sondra, his glance drifting over the small congregation. From the pulpit, the minister read the selected verses from the New Testament, then issued a call to prayer.

Bannon automatically bowed his head and listened to the somnolent drone of the minister's voice, his attention wandering as it had all morning. Around him there was a murmur of voices echoing an "Amen" and he lifted his head, his gaze shooting to the dozen members that comprised the children's choir as the organist began to play. He scanned their solemn and earnest faces until he saw Laura's, her dark eyes intent on the director.

Sondra touched his arm, momentarily distracting him and reminding him of her presence at his side. Then he focused again on his daughter and observed the faint, barely perceptible bob of her chin as she counted off the beats in the organ prelude. Bannon found himself mentally counting with her, his feet pressed hard against the floor, a fine tension lacing through him.

He saw the decisive nod she gave as her lips parted on the first word and a chorus of young voices lifted in song, filling the sanctuary with the hymn "This Is My Father's World." Bannon quickly picked out the pure, clear tones of Laura's voice from the others. She had a small solo in the second verse and he waited for it, knowing how anxious she'd been about it and trying to remember the words himself. The moment came and her voice rang out strong and sure.

"This is my Father's world," she sang. "He shines in all that's fair. In rustling grass I hear Him pass. He speaks to me everywhere."

The other voices joined hers for the final verse and Bannon released the breath he hadn't been aware of holding. She hadn't faltered over a single note or phrase. Smiling faintly, he unclenched his hands and ran damp palms over his trouser legs.

When the song ended, Sondra turned to him, smiling as she leaned close to whisper, "She was perfect."

Bannon nodded and thought of Diana . . . of how pleased and proud she would have been of their daughter this morning. Suddenly he felt old and tired as if he'd been beaten in a fight. He knew the feeling and it left him vaguely depressed.

After the service was over, he followed Sondra up the aisle and reclaimed his hat from the rack by the door, then stood in the short line to shake hands with the minister. Outside the church there was the usual dawdling of parishioners and the noisy chatter of children released from forced silence. With a hand at Sondra's elbow, Bannon descended the steps.

"Morning, Ed." He nodded to the balding, ruddy-cheeked physician chatting with a local broker, Frank Scott, near the base of the steps.

"Morning, Bannon," he responded with typical cheeriness. "Gorgeous weather we've been having, isn't it?"

"It is." Bannon gave a glance at the high blue sky overhead, and the lone marshmallow cloud drifting across it. "Better enjoy it while we can. It won't last much longer."

"I'm headed straight for the links to play a few rounds," he replied, then turned to the broker as Bannon continued past him. "Give Martin a call and we'll make it a foursome."

Halfway to the parking lot, Bannon moved to the outer edge of the sidewalk and paused. "We'd better wait for Laura," he said to Sondra. "It shouldn't take her long to change out of her choir robe."

Sondra smiled an acknowledgment and stood close beside him, nodding to those who passed by them, well aware that the sight of her with Bannon didn't draw a second look. She and Bannon had been coupled in the minds of these people for too long. In fact, now they'd be quicker to notice if they weren't together.

The thump of a cane signaled the approach of the white-haired and ramrod-straight Hetta Carstairs, who never ventured out of her Victorian home on the West End without her gloves and pillbox hat.

"Good morning, Mrs. Carstairs." Bannon touched his hat to the widow of the late Pitkin County judge, Arthur Carstairs.

She recognized him and stopped, leaning briefly on her cane. "Mr. Bannon. Miss Hudson." She acknowledged both, then focused on Bannon. "May I compliment you on your daughter, Mr. Bannon. She has a very sweet voice."

"Thank you—" he began, only to be brusquely cut off.

"Obviously she gets it from your mother. She had a lovely voice, too, but yours—yours always reminded me of a beagle Arthur once had. I was quite relieved when you dropped out of the choir as a lad."

"So was I, Mrs. Carstairs," he assured her with a barely concealed smile. Her thin lips twitched with amusement before she nodded to him and moved on, her cane thumping the sidewalk with every other step. "Speaks her mind, doesn't she?" Bannon murmured to Sondra.

"When you're eighty-five, you can get away with it." She gazed after the woman, thinking of the old woman's house with its wrap-around porch and the clutter of flowers around it, mentally calculating its value. The house itself was worth little, but the lot—its size and location—would sell for close to two million. If only the old woman would sell. Sondra shook off that thought and lifted her glance to Bannon's face, studying the harsh angles of his profile. "Mrs. Carstairs was right, though. Laura does have a lovely voice. You were nervous for her, weren't you?" she asked, remembering. "I saw the way you tightened up when she sang. What were you thinking about?"

"Diana—wishing she could have been there to hear her."

Sondra looked away, her lips coming together in a thin and bitter line. "You never forget, do you?" she murmured too low for him to hear.

"Looks like Dad found Laura."

Sondra saw Old Tom and Laura as they came around the corner of the church, hand in hand. Laura waved to them. Smiling, Sondra waved back. Laura immediately released her grandfather's hand and ran across the grass to greet them.

"You were wonderful, Laura," Sondra said when she reached them.

"Thank you, Aunt Sondra." The girl fairly beamed at the compliment.

Looking at Laura, Sondra saw a great deal of her sister. That was the hold Diana had on Bannon. That was Diana's power, her way of forever reminding Bannon of the past. Thinking of that, Sondra hated her sister with a secret and passionate fullness.

Old Tom joined them. "I told her none of the others sounded as good as she did."

"That's true," Sondra agreed. "We were all very proud of you."

Laura's smile grew even wider and she sank her teeth into her lower lip, trying to hold it back. Then she turned slightly. "Do you like my hair, Aunt Sondra? Buffy's mother fixed it in a French braid for me."

"It's lovely."

"Do you think if I slept on my stomach tonight it would still look nice for school tomorrow?"

"I have a better idea. Why don't you persuade your father to come by my house before he takes you to school in the morning and I'll fix it for you?"

"Can we, Dad?" Laura raised her dark eyes to him.

"It means you'd have to get up a half hour earlier," he warned.

"I don't mind."

"Okay," Bannon said, giving in to the silent appeal of those dark eyes.

"If we have that settled, how about some food?" Old Tom rubbed his hands together in obvious anticipation. "I don't know about the rest of you, but that pancake I had for breakfast is long gone."

"How does beef burgundy sound?" Sondra asked. "With some of Emily's homemade dinner rolls on the side?" She caught Bannon's expression. "You are coming to dinner, aren't you?"

"Not this time, I'm afraid. We have some strays to round up. We'll have to head straight back to the ranch. Thanks anyway."

"Another time then." She smiled stiffly.

In the parking lot, they separated and Sondra went to her car. When Bannon drove out, he turned in the opposite direction from the ranch. Sondra didn't have to wonder where he was going. She knew. Every Sunday after church, he took Laura to the cemetery to visit Diana's grave. It was a Sunday-morning ritual that never varied. Her fingers had a stranglehold on the steering wheel as she forced herself to drive slowly out of the lot.

John Travis refilled his cup with coffee from the silver urn on the dining room's long buffet table. Beside him, Nolan Walker lifted the domed lid on a serving dish, releasing the tantalizing aroma of bacon into the room. John ignored it and rejoined Kit at the white-lacquered table.

"Want some?" She offered him a bite of croissant slathered with strawberry jam.

"No thanks." He glanced at her plate. Not ten minutes earlier it had been mounded with bacon, sausage links, crisp hash browns, eggs scrambled with chopped chives, and the croissant. Only the croissant was left. "You have an insatiable appetite, don't you?"

"Look who's talking." Her eyes mocked him with the

memory of his own insatiable appetite last night. Warmed by the reminder, John smiled and watched as she took a bite of the croissant. "You're missing something delicious."

"I had something delicious," he murmured. "So delicious, I'm probably going to want seconds and thirds and fourths."

"Greedy." Some of the jam threatened to drip off the croissant. Smiling, Kit scooped it onto her finger, then licked it off.

Paula paused in the doorway, red hair tumbling about the shoulders of her dressing robe of green paisley silk. "Must all of you make so much noise," she complained. "Have some pity, please. My head feels like there's a full symphony orchestra inside playing the 'Anvil Chorus' over and over." She made her way to one of the empty chairs at the table and lowered herself onto its Peruvian patterned seat. "I've never had such a horrible hangover from drinking a measly five glasses of wine."

"You don't have a hangover." Kit cast a sympathetic glance in Paula's direction and spooned strawberry jam from its crystal dish onto her plate.

"Really? My head tells me differently," Paula countered in a voice as arid as the desert, then lifted a limp hand. "Chip, be a sweetheart and bring a cup of coffee. Black."

"You're probably suffering from altitude sickness." Kit broke off a bite of croissant and dipped it in the jam.

"Pardon?" Paula's head came up slowly.

"The symptoms range from shortness of breath to nausea, heart palpitations, insomnia, and headaches. Sometimes excruciating ones," she added, smiling sympathetically at Paula.

"Insomnia?" Nolan set his plate on the table and pulled out a chair. "Is that why I had such a tough time sleeping when we first got here? Usually my head touches the pillow and I'm out like a light."

"Probably. It's caused by the reduced humidity and oxygen content in the air here. Don't forget, Aspen is more than eight thousand feet above sea level. Sometimes it takes your body a couple of days to adjust to the change in altitude." Kit popped the bite of jam-dipped croissant into her mouth and chewed slowly.

"If that's true, why are you so disgustingly chipper?" Paula eyed her with a mixture of censure and envy.

Kit shrugged. "I've always been able to acclimatize quickly . . . maybe because I was raised here."

"So what's the cure?" Paula wanted to know. "Other than a whole bottle of Tylenol?"

"There isn't one, other than time, although I've heard it helps to drink plenty of fluids, stay away from alcohol, and not overdo it."

"Believe me, I have no intention of doing anything more strenuous than sprawling on the couch all day," Paula declared as Chip pushed a steaming cup of coffee in front of her. She wrapped both hands around it and took a slow, grateful sip of it.

"How about something to eat?" Chip suggested.

Paula shuddered expressively. "Please, my head is already in revolt. I don't want my stomach joining it."

"Poor kid," Kit murmured and finished the last of her croissant.

When the heavyset maid, Carla, padded into the dining room to check the contents of the chafing dishes, John said, "Bring Miss Grant some aspirin, Carla."

Chip raised his hand. "I'll take some, too."

"I guess I don't have to ask what everyone's plans are for today," Kit said when the maid left to fetch the aspirin. "It sounds like you're all going to lie around, taking it easy."

"What are your plans?" John set his cup down.

"I'm glad you asked." She folded her napkin and laid it beside her plate, her eyes gleaming with a warm humor. "Because I was hoping I could persuade you to let me borrow a car so I can drive into town."

"No problem. Where are you going?"

"To the cemetery. I want to visit my father's grave."

"I'll come with you."

"You don't have to," Kit told him.

"I want to. Unless you'd rather go alone."

"It isn't that."

"Then I'm ready when you are." He pushed his cup back.

* * *

Sunlight spilled through breaks in the trees' leafy canopy and gleamed on the shiny-smooth surface of the granite marker engraved with the phrase "Beloved Father." Beneath it was the name Clint Masters, followed by his date of birth and date of death. Kit knelt beside it, one knee balanced on the autumn yellow grass, a hand running lightly over the granite.

John Travis stood quietly to one side, deliberately not intruding on her private moment. But he watched her and noted the softness of her expression, the love in it, and the sorrow.

A breeze sprang up and stirred the fallen leaves, sending them chasing after one another in a tumbling game of tag. Kit scraped aside long strands of hair from her cheek, then lifted her face to John, something distant, almost faraway in the look she gave him.

"This is the first time I've seen the gravestone." She straightened to stand erect and slipped the ends of her fingers inside the slash pockets of her tobacco brown jeans.

"It's nice." They were mundane words, but he didn't know what else to say.

"Yes." She stared at it for a long minute. "Next time I'll pick some flowers to bring. There won't be any larkspur, Indian paintbrush, or columbine this late in the year, but I should be able to find some of the purple daisies and the golden tops from the rabbit brush. Dad loved wildflowers," she said in explanation, then swung her gaze to the surrounding mountains. "In the summer, he used to ride deep into the mountains just for the beauty of the wildflowers. He said it was like seeing miniature alpine gardens."

"It must have been beautiful."

"It was. It is," she amended, then took a long breath and smiled. "Ready to go?"

"If you are."

She nodded, then reached out one last time and ran tracing fingers over the rounded top of the stone, some of the sun's warmth beginning to penetrate it. She turned to leave, then paused when she saw they weren't alone in the cemetery. Several rows away Bannon stood at the foot of his wife's grave, his hat at his side and his daughter's hand in his. She stared at the girl, her black hair pulled smoothly back to make a dark frame for her face, dark eyes turned up to her father.

John touched her arm and she almost jumped. "What's the matter?" He studied her curiously, his eyes probing her expression. Then he joked, "You look like you've seen a ghost."

"It almost feels like it in a way," she admitted, then nodded in the direction of the father-daughter pair. "Bannon's daughter—she looks enough like Diana to startle me."

"Diana?"

"Bannon's wife. She died shortly after Laura was born. There were complications . . . ." She shrugged off the rest.

"Was she a friend of yours?"

"No. I never met her until after they were married. I was away at college." She could say the words now without tasting any of the bitterness they'd once held, but she could remember the shock, the pain she'd felt when she'd read that short letter from her father informing her of Bannon's marriage. "Shortly after graduation, I moved to Los Angeles so I really only saw her with Bannon a few times. She was very beautiful—long black hair and dark, almost black eyes, flawless skin."

"No freckles?"

She met the warm humor in his eyes and smiled. "No freckles."

He held her gaze for another second remembering last night, then glanced idly back at the pair. "I take it he's never remarried."

"No. He hasn't forgotten Diana." Kit watched as Bannon shoved his hat onto his head and smiled down at his daughter. Hand in hand, they turned and made their way toward the high-riding black pickup parked on the grassy verge of the cemetery's narrow lane. Old Tom stood beside it, the sunlight making his hair look even whiter. Like Bannon, he wore a dark, western-style suit and a string tie. "It looks like they've been to church," she observed. "I haven't attended Sunday worship service in ages. When I was growing up, we never missed a Sunday."

"Was your family religious?" The pickup pulled away.

"Religious?" Kit hesitated over that. "I don't think that's the right word—although it's impossible to live in the midst of the Rockies without feeling the presence of God. I don't know—going to church was just something you did on Sunday. At least in my family."

She noticed John had that withdrawn look and guessed it was an experience he didn't share. With his next words, he changed the subject. "Let's drive into town and have some coffee at one of the sidewalk cafés."

"All right." She glanced at the white Range Rover, then at the trees and the sky, feeling the breeze on her face and breathing the fresh, sharp scent of the air. "I feel like walking. Do you mind? It can't be much more than a dozen blocks to the downtown area."

He hesitated only a moment, then said, "Why not? We can always catch a cab if we don't feel like walking back."

"Lazy," she accused with a laugh.

"I'll remember you said that."

With smiles still lingering, they left the cemetery and followed the road to the highway, his arm lightly draped across her shoulders, their pace a leisurely one. On the bridge that spanned Castle Creek, they stopped and leaned on the rail to watch a man in waders, knee-deep in the center of the stream, cast his fish line across a patch of shallow riffles. Traffic rumbled over the bridge at a steady rate.

"You'd think he would have picked a quieter spot," John remarked. "With all this noise, he isn't likely to catch any fish."

"Maybe he doesn't care."

"Why go fishing if you don't want to catch fish?" He eyed her with challenge, the cleft in his chin deepening at the wry twist of his mouth. The breeze had rumpled his sun-streaked hair, sending strands falling carelessly across his forehead.

"Maybe he just likes fishing for the sake of fishing."

"That doesn't make sense."

"Not everything has to have a purpose, John T." But she could tell he didn't understand that reasoning. "You have a lot to learn about life's finer moments of pure pleasure."

"Such as?"

"Do you know what would taste good right now?"

"Coffee."

"No. Ice cream." Kit straightened from the bridge rail and reached for his hand. "Come on. I'll buy you a cone."

"What flavor?" He pretended to resist.

"Definitely not vanilla." She flashed him a grin and took his hand, giving it a tug to pull him along. "There's nothing remotely vanilla about an autumn day like this."

Chuckling, John let himself be dragged away.

Across the bridge, the highway curved to make its wide sweep down Main Street. Ignoring it, they went straight and followed Hallam Street, once known as Bullion Row, to stroll through the West End.

With the pickup pointed toward Stone Creek and home, Bannon increased its speed, the city limit sign behind them. The sun was high and bright, warming the wind that rushed through the truck's open windows. Yet Bannon could feel the sharp, cool eddies of coming winter in the air.

He glanced at Laura, sitting in the middle next to him, her gaze fixed on the road ahead of them. "You did fine today, Laura. I was very proud sitting there, listening to you."

Sometimes when he talked to her, he felt the absorbing attention she paid him. Other times, as now, her mind was away on its own thoughts, locking him out—as Diana had locked him out.

She turned her head to him, her eyes serious and dark. "Will you ever get married again, Dad?"

Momentarily he was thrown by her unexpected question. "Why would you ask that?"

"I just wondered." Still serious, still thoughtful, a faint frown line between her eyebrows, she turned back to stare at the road. "Maybe I could like another mother."

The tone of her voice troubled him. It wasn't like her. It was cautious, holding her thoughts away from him. There was something on her mind she didn't want to talk to him about, making him realize she was no longer a child.

At nine years old the world was no longer all colored and wonderful to her; her thoughts were no longer a child's simple black-and-white ones. Soon she'd be thinking as a woman thought—complex, something no man easily figured out. Soon she wouldn't be his little girl anymore. The thought sobered him.

Laughing, Kit emerged from the ice-cream shop on the mall, then swung back to wait for John, taking a quick lick of her double-dipped cone to check its melting drip. She eyed the single-dipped cone in his hand with mock disapproval.

"Twenty-eight flavors and you choose strawberry. Very tame, John T.," she chided.

"I like it." He took a disinterested lick, preferring to concentrate on her, watching as her lips closed around the top dip of green ice cream, a look of pure enjoyment in her expression, a sexuality and sensuality pouring from her like warm sunshine.

"Mmmm, but there's no surprises with strawberry," she declared, her eyes darting, absorbing everything around them.

"My palate isn't as sophisticated as yours." He matched her casually wandering pace, his glance going to the cone in her hand. "What is that you're eating? Pistachio and—?"

"Swiss chocolate almond. I like nuts in my ice cream. I like the cold and the crunch." Kit hurriedly licked away a trickle of melted ice cream running down the sugar cone, then drew back, frowning thoughtfully. "I forgot. When you mix green and brown together, what color do you get?"

"Yuk." He caught her in the middle of a bite, startling a laugh from her. Her hand came up quickly to wipe the ice cream from her chin and cover her mouth while she struggled to swallow the bite through the laughter in her throat.

Succeeding, she turned dancing eyes on him. "That was a terrible thing to say."

"I could have said worse."

"True." She examined the cone again. "And you're probably right. The only color green and brown make is yuk." Untroubled, she took another bite and crunched on a nut while she let her gaze wander, her eyes taking in the scattering of other strollers wandering along the landscaped thoroughfare. "It used to be that just about everyone you saw was eating ice cream. It was the favorite way to get rid of the dryness in your mouth after a line of coke. Or so I was told," she qualified as a running breeze kicked up some fallen leaves and chased them around an iron lamppost.

"Aspen had a reputation for being fairly open about drugs, especially cocaine, back when you lived here, didn't it?" John tossed his unfinished cone in a trash receptacle next to a brick planter mounded with sunny yellow mums.

Kit smiled. "Come to Aspen and have a good time—in the modern sense of the word. That's what they used to say. To a certain extent, it was true when I was in school."

"How did you manage to avoid being swept into that scene?" he asked, thinking how quick she was to embrace most things.

Her shoulders lifted in an idle shrug. "I never liked the idea of giving up control for a quick buzz. Besides, I've always been high on life. Who needs something artificial when you have the real thing?"

"True." John wondered why he hadn't guessed that as she bit into the cone.

"Fortunately, the craze over white powder has become a craze for the kind of white powder you ski on." Kit nodded at Aspen Mountain, called Ajax by the locals, standing tall before them, dominating the view as it dominated the town nestled at its base. Its famed ski runs cut wide, tan swaths down its broad slopes, weaving in and out among the stands of evergreens and autumn-burnished aspens.

John lit a cigarette, comfortable with the silence that fell between them as they strolled along. He'd never known another woman like Kit, so able to both soothe and stimulate him. Finished with her cone, she wrapped both arms around his arm, then sighed, something in the sound arousing his curiosity.

"What was that about?"

"I don't know. Sometimes I'm amazed by how much Aspen has changed. I know it happens in every city in the country, buildings go up, businesses change hands. But you don't really expect it to happen in your own hometown, I guess." She tipped her head to one side. "Do you realize that when I was a girl, Aspen had dirt streets. Only Main Street was paved because of the highway. There was a definite small-town feel to Aspen. Now the whole character of it has changed. I mean, just look.'' She waved a hand at the expensive shops lining the streets. "It's more like Rodeo Drive in the Rockies except all the buildings are designed to look like something from the turn of the century.'' She stopped and sighed again. "It isn't that I don't like it. I just miss the old Aspen.''

"A case of nostalgia will cause that, I've heard.''

She laughed. "And I think I have a severe case of it. But there is a cure for it.''

"Really?''

"Window-shopping,'' she said decisively, then grinned. "And don't tell me you don't do that. Men window-shop every time they look at a pretty girl.''

With Kit setting the pace, they drifted from window to window, inspecting the wares displayed in each. John spent more time watching her than he did looking in the windows. Her reactions were unguarded, expressive, her thoughts revealed not just in her face but her body language. She drew back, shaking her head and laughing at an antlered chair in the window of a specialty shop, then frowned in deep concentration at the abstract paintings in a gallery window. He observed the disinterest in her eyes and the failure to linger over a full-length sable coat in a furrier's window, the rapt study she gave to a display of Havilland, Limoges, and Cartier china settings, leaning close to the window, and the provocative smile she sent him when they paused before a lacy and racy lingerie display.

As they came to a store offering the ultimate in western wear, Kit grabbed his arm. "Look at those boots. They are wild,'' she declared, her mouth staying open in a look of incredulous delight. "Let's go inside.''

Without waiting for him, Kit pushed through the shop's leaded glass door and walked straight to the tall, fire red boots on a display shelf next to a heavily ornamented western saddle. She picked the right boot up and ran her hand over its gleaming side, feeling the broken texture of its lizard-skin hide.

"May I help you?"

"No thanks." Kit turned to the clerk. "I—Donna," she gasped in surprise when she saw the sandy-haired clerk was a former high school classmate. "My God, this is like old-home week. I just ran into Angie last night."

The boots were forgotten while Donna sketchily brought Kit up to date on her life: she and her husband lived in Glenwood Springs now; they had just the two girls and both were in school. When John joined them, Kit introduced him to Donna and immediately noticed the almost visible withdrawal of her former classmate and friend, her smile turning into the pleasant kind meant for customers.

"If you like those boots, wait until you see this coat we have," she said, moving away.

Kit waited until Donna was out of earshot before whispering to John, "I think she's self-conscious with you here."

"Get used to it," he murmured back. "It'll be your turn next, once your face gets splashed all over the big screen."

"I suppose." But she didn't particularly like the idea that people might stop acting natural around her the way they sometimes did around John. Idly she turned the boot up and saw the price. "Four thousand dollars?" She stared, then laughed faintly in amazement. "Rodeo Drive is right."

Donna came back with a beaded Indian blanket coat to show her, then a hat, a stenciled-suede top. The articles kept coming; Kit kept looking and admiring and shaking her head. Finally, out of guilt, she bought a scarf she thought Maggie would like. She started to leave, then remembered she'd left the sales receipt on the counter.

When she went back for it, Donna was by the cash register with another clerk, her back turned to the door. Kit started toward them.

"I can't believe it," Donna muttered to the clerk. "All she brought was that lousy scarf. I thought I had a huge sale when she walked in."

Donna had seen her as a sale? Suddenly Kit had the same sick feeling that she'd had last night with Angie. She turned and walked out with John, not bothering with the receipt.

11

*O*n Monday morning, Kit paused in front of the turn-of-the-century Victorian cottage on Main Street. She caught the tantalizing aroma of freshly brewed coffee and yeasty sweet rolls coming from the house to the left of the cottage, a combination bookstore and coffeehouse. The structure on the right had been converted into a boutique.

Kit paid no attention to either as she gazed at the cottage's familiar gabled front and the finials soaring from its peaks. Box hedges lined the sidewalk leading to a front porch adorned with airy latticework trim and flower boxes filled with red geraniums at the windows. It looked just as she remembered it when Mrs. Hatch lived there except for the sign suspended from the brackets on the post by the porch steps.

Ignoring the noisy squabbling of the magpies in the cottonwoods, Kit walked up the bricked path and stopped to read the sign. Black letters on a white board spelled out the words

Attorney at Law
Elias A. Bannon (deceased)
Thomas E. Bannon

A smile edged her mouth at the rightness of it, at the feeling of life coming full circle. Over one hundred years ago, a young Elias Bannon had arrived in the rough and raw mining camp of Aspen, his saddlebags packed with law books and a few belongings. He'd started his law practice first in a tent, then rented a four-by-six space on the second floor of a saloon on Durant where the miners gathered. Five years later, he'd built this modest cottage to serve as both his office and his town home. Now his grandson practiced law from the same building. Bannon had always said he would someday, Kit remembered.

But that thought recalled other memories that still hurt. With a quick lift of her chin, Kit climbed the steps and crossed to the front door of walnut and etched glass. It opened directly to the parlor. Only now the parlor had been converted to a combination office and reception area. A reed-thin woman with gray hair piled atop her head in a knot looked up from her computer screen when Kit walked in.

"Yes? May I help you?" The woman removed her steel-rimmed granny glasses and let them hang by their chain down the front of her navy suit.

"You must be Agnes Richards." Kit thrust a hand across the desk in greeting. "We've spoken a few times on the phone. I'm Kit Masters."

"Miss Masters, of course." Bannon's legal secretary rose from her chair, a smile filling out the gauntness of her cheeks. "Bannon said you'd be stopping by this morning. I'm sorry I didn't recognize you. I should have, after seeing your picture in today's paper." She glanced at the phone on her desk, missing Kit's look of surprise. "I think he's through with his long distance call. I'll let him know you're here."

As she reached for the receiver, a connecting door swung open and Bannon stepped out, dressed in a tan corduroy jacket with suede patches at the sleeves and jeans faded from numerous launderings rather than expensive acid-wash. He had a clutch of papers in his hand and a distracted frown on his face, and his brown hair showed the tracks of combing fingers. "What happened to the McIntire file, Aggie? I can't—Kit.'' He stopped, his look brightening to a faint smile.

Grinning, Kit cocked her head to one side and said, with a touch of whimsey, ''Once there was a man named Bannon. He lived in the mountains and never came out. I heard he grew a beard and started talking to himself. I wonder what ever happened to him?''

Bannon smiled crookedly. ''He became a lawyer. Now he spends half his time behind a desk and writes a twenty-five-thousand-word court motion and calls it a brief.''

She laughed, a little surprised at how easy it was to slip back into that old pattern of light, touch-and-go humor that had marked their relationship in the past. It had been a way to cover serious feelings—at least in her case.

Sobering slightly, Kit let a small smile remain in place as Bannon walked over and pushed the sheaf of papers at his secretary. ''Clean this up for me, Aggie.''

''I always do,'' she murmured and raised her glasses to inspect the document. ''By the way, Pete Ranovitch called while you were on the phone. He said he had to see you right away. It was urgent. I told him you would be free around eleven and to come by then. Is that all right?''

''Fine.''

''I suppose you'll want me to log this in as a pro bono case,'' she said in a voice dry with disapproval. When Bannon nodded affirmatively, she added, even more dryly, ''That's what I thought.''

Bannon ignored that and motioned toward his office. ''Come on in, Kit.''

She followed him into the room, absently observing the muscular ease of his walk and the width of his shoulders beneath the corduroy jacket. His boots, she noticed, bore the scars of spurs and stirrups and rough use. Justin boots probably, or Tony Lama's, but they definitely weren't in the luxe category of the four-thousand-dollar pair she'd seen yesterday. By the same token, Bannon wasn't a Coca-Cola cowboy; he was the real thing.

''You look more like a rancher than a lawyer, Bannon.''

"On court days, I go the suit-and-tie route. The judges like that." He walked over to a brown-stained coffee maker and lifted the glass pot, one third full. "Want a cup? It's strong," he warned.

"You haven't tasted coffee on the set after it's simmered in a giant urn for fourteen hours or more. *That* is strong."

The corners of his mouth indented, bringing into play the slashed lines in his cheeks. How many times had her fingertips traced those smile grooves? Disturbed by the wayward turn her mind had taken, Kit pulled herself up abruptly and turned to examine the room, in one glance taking in the patterned wool rug on the maple floor, the wainscoting of ash, and the glassed-in bookcase.

"This room was your grandfather's law office, wasn't it?" Kit deposited her purse on the leather seat of a straight-backed chair and wandered to the bookcase, made of ash with a walnut finish. She heard the clatter of cups and swung back to look at Bannon. "Now it's yours."

"Yes." He filled two ceramic mugs with coffee, draining the pot. Picking them up, he used one to gesture toward the heavy walnut desk. "I even dragged his old desk down from the attic. A couple of the drawers were warped, but Dad fixed them for me. I thought about refinishing it, then decided to leave all the scratches, gouges, and stains just as they were."

Kit nodded agreement. "They add character."

"And they encourage my clients to pay their bills so I can afford a better desk." He held out one of the mugs and she looked at his hands, large-sized yet deft, his fingers long and his nails neatly trimmed. Hands that were gentle enough to pick a fragile wildflower and tuck it behind her ear without bruising a petal, yet strong enough to lift a saddle with one hand and swing it onto a horse's back. She took the mug from him and immediately took a sip, nearly scalding her tongue.

"It's hot," he said.

"Very," she murmured and bit her lips together, waiting for her tongue to stop burning. "I think I'll let it cool awhile." She set the mug on his desk and noticed the manual type-writer, a black relic that had to be forty or fifty years old.

"Haven't you joined the computer age yet, Bannon?" She punched one of the keys, but not hard enough to make it strike the platen.

"I joined it, but I think better on this old Royal."

"No wonder Aggie has to clean up your paperwork." She continued around his desk, then paused when she caught sight of the large framed photograph on the wall directly above the fireplace. "That's a picture of your grandfather Elias Bannon." She walked over to stand in front of the ebonized Eastlake mantel and tilted her head back to study the grainy black-and-white photo. "I've seen this before. You had it at the ranch."

"I thought it belonged here."

"It does." She looked at the head-and-shoulders shot of a man in his late twenties. His brown hair was cut short and parted off center, and a mustache shadowed all but the curve of his lower lip. He had the look of a rugged New Englander, bones protruding under bronze skin, cheeks gaunt, and eyes set deep in the sockets. "I remember looking at his picture and thinking how fearsome he looked. I can readily imagine him standing up to the likes of Jerome Wheeler. Yet, other times, his eyes seemed warm and kind, full of understanding, and I knew why people turned to him when they were in trouble." She smiled in remembrance and glanced idly at Bannon. "Remember how we used to sit around and listen to Old Tom tell us stories about your grandfather, the old days in Aspen, the silver mines?"

Nodding, Bannon leaned a hip on the corner of his desk. "Once he got started, there was no stopping him."

"True. But the picture he painted of Aspen back in the late 1880s and early 1890s," Kit recalled with a wondering shake of her head, "a modern mining town with electricity, telephones, streetcars, a magnificent opera house, a grand hotel, Victorian houses with gingerbread trim, fancy barouches pulled by matched teams of high-stepping horses, men in top hats, elegant morning coats, and striped trousers, ladies in high-necked silk gowns with wagging bustles, shaded by lace parasols, and—"

"—the constant din of machinery running twenty-four

hours a day,'' Bannon inserted, ''smoke from the concentrators and smelting works hanging over the town like a pall, streams polluted with wastes from the mines and the sawmills, the surrounding mountains stripped bare of their forests to supply the mines with needed timber, dirt streets that were either clogged with dust, a quagmire of mud, drifted with snow, or jammed with freight wagons and pack trains, miners blackened and sweaty after an eight-hour shift, the gamblers and card sharks, the saloons and bawdy houses with their painted ladies—''

''Wait.'' Kit raised a hand in protest. ''Old Tom never told us anything about 'ladies of the evening' or bawdy houses.''

''Probably not.'' He dipped his head, conceding the point. ''But most of my grandfather's clients came from Aspen's— so-called—lower class. Miners, small merchants, prospectors with undeveloped claims, and labor unions—and few of them had the money to pay for legal services. Most prospectors gave him an interest in their claims in return for representing them. Occasionally that paid off. The rest he traded out when he could, and wrote off when he couldn't.''

''Didn't he own shares in the Smuggler or Mollie Gibson at one time?'' Kit frowned, trying to recall.

''The Mollie Gibson,'' Bannon confirmed between sips of his coffee.

''Yes, the Mollie.'' Nodding, Kit wandered back to the desk and retrieved her coffee mug. She wrapped both hands around the mug and carried it to her lips. The coffee had cooled to a drinkable temperature. ''I used to have nightmares about all those gruesome stories Old Tom told us about miners killed in accidents—especially the ones where a miner pushed a loaded ore cart to a shaft to be raised to the surface, not knowing the platform had been moved to another level. He'd push the cart into the empty shaft and get pulled in after it, falling hundreds of feet to his death. Old Tom used to scare me to death with those stories,'' she recalled with a shudder.

''He did it on purpose.''

Her head came up. ''Why?''

''To keep us from exploring that old mine on the ranch,'' Bannon replied with a faint smile.

"The Keyhole Mine," Kit remembered. "I'd forgotten all about it." She shook her head and laughed. "If that was your father's motive, it worked. You never could get me to go more than ten feet inside that mine."

"And I had to drag you to get you that far." Bannon grinned.

"You're darn right," she retorted, then sighed in bemusement. "I'm surprised I had the nerve to set even one foot inside that mine."

The entrance had been boarded up, but that hadn't stopped them, not with visions of finding a giant vein of silver ore to lead them on. Bannon had pried a couple boards loose, creating a hole wide enough for them to crawl through. She remembered the dank, musty odors of a fecund earth, the scurrying sounds in the darkness, the spiderwebs that caught at her arms, face, and hair, and the distant drip-drip of water. "That flashlight you had was almost worthless. I just knew the batteries were going to go out on it and we'd be trapped in that blackness. The walls were so rough and slimy, and the timbers—pieces of them crumbled in my hands. Do you realize how dangerous it was, Bannon?"

He answered with a slow nod, then soberly met her glance. "Especially now that I have a daughter who thinks that old mine is a great place to play."

Kit stiffened at the mention of his daughter. It was that old wound getting bumped again. She managed to smile, quite convincingly. "And do you fill her head with all those scary stories to keep her away from the mine?"

"I leave those to Dad." He grinned easily. "But Laura's not like you. You have such a vivid imagination you were always easy to scare." A devilish twinkle appeared in his eyes, one that Kit recognized too well. "Like the time during that snowstorm when we spent the night here with Mrs. Hatch, and I convinced you the howling and banging outside wasn't caused by the wind but by a wolf. Then I snuck up and grabbed you from behind, snarling and growling—you were so scared you wet your pants."

"Rat." She punched him hard in the shoulder. "Why do

you always have to bring that up? I was a mere eight years old.''

"That hurt." He rubbed his arm muscle, but a smile lingered around the edges of his mouth.

"It was supposed to. In case you don't know it, it's embarrassing to be reminded of that.''

"Embarrassing, eh?" One eyebrow arched slightly. "Try explaining to the guys how a mere slip of a girl gave me a black eye. Or have you forgotten that you hauled off and hit me that night, too?''

"I did, didn't I?" Kit remembered, her smile turning gleeful.

"You did. Even?" Bannon lifted his mug toward her, offering to toast a truce.

"Even," Kit agreed and clunked mugs. She drank down a swallow of lukewarm coffee, then drifted over to the chair with her purse. "We spent many stormy winter nights here with Mrs. Hatch when we were growing up."

"Our parents thought it was safer than risking the roads."

"It probably was," she remarked absently, then lifted her glance to the ceiling. "The bedrooms upstairs, do you use them for storage now?''

"No. I converted the upstairs into a small apartment. One of the teachers at school rents it."

She glanced back at her mug and smiled, suddenly recalling, "Remember the hot chocolate Mrs. Hatch used to make for us? And always from scratch. I can still taste it." She turned to Bannon. "And she always had a bag of marshmallows in the cupboard—"

"—and a fire in the fireplace so we could roast marshmallows over the flames," Bannon recalled. "You liked yours charred black on the outside."

"Of course. That way they were both crunchy *and* gooey." She grinned. "You had to have yours lightly golden."

"Mine weren't so messy either."

"Maybe, but they didn't taste nearly as good as mine." She paused and sighed. "I haven't roasted marshmallows in years. I wish I'd asked Paula to pick up a bag at the store.

She volunteered to do the grocery shopping and John volunteered to take her while I met with you." She glanced at her watch, conscious of the time she'd spent reminiscing about the past.

"I guess we'd better get down to business then, hadn't we?" His remark hung between them. Bannon regretted saying it; he regretted the vague tension now in the air. He pushed off the corner of the desk and walked behind it.

"Yes, you said you wanted to go over some papers with me." Kit picked up her purse and sat down in the chair facing the desk.

"Mainly the estate tax return we have to file with the IRS and the state of Colorado next week." The springs in the ancient office chair squeaked in a noisy protest when Bannon sat down. He opened a folder and handed Kit a copy from it.

She glanced at the multipaged form and murmured, "I hope you don't expect me to understand this. I have trouble filling out a W-4."

He smiled briefly. "This won't be that bad." He ignored her look of skepticism and focused on his copy of the return. "As I mentioned when we talked on the phone, you are entitled to receive six hundred thousand dollars, tax-free, so to speak. All amounts above that figure are assessed at the applicable estate tax rates. Naturally the first problem was coming up with the value of your father's estate."

"Which is?" Kit stared at the columns of figures, trying to figure out which line meant what.

"Let's start with the ranch itself," Bannon suggested. "The appraiser I hired valued the improvements on it—the house, barn, sheds, corrals, et cetera—at seventy thousand. In the past five years, ranch land has sold for as high as twelve hundred dollars an acre. Which brings the value of the land and the buildings to five hundred and fifty thousand. To that, we have to add the life insurance your father had, the livestock, the furnishings, and other personal belongings. Then we subtract the mortgage and any debts he had outstanding at the time of his death."

Kit had stopped listening when Bannon placed the value of the ranch at five hundred and fifty thousand dollars. Was

that all it was worth? She fought back the waves of disappointment. True, a half million dollars was a lot of money, but
she'd hoped it would be more. Her mother's hospital and
doctor bills already totaled close to one hundred thousand.
Barring complications, her mother could live another thirty
years. Until now, she'd thought selling the ranch would pro-
vide the funds for those future medical costs, but at this rate,
the money wouldn't last long. It would probably be wiser to
keep the ranch and use the income from it to offset some of
her mother's expenses. In a way, she was relieved. She hadn't
wanted to sell her home.

Unfortunately she still faced the problem of finding the
money to pay for her mother's care. Kit unconsciously
squared her shoulders.

". . . request an early audit. That way if the IRS questions
the valuation of the estate, we'll know about it immediately
and be able to handle it," Bannon concluded. "Any questions?"

Conscious of his eyes on her, Kit hurriedly skimmed the
tax form, reluctant to admit she hadn't paid attention. "How
much tax is owed?"

"Roughly ten thousand. Ten thousand one hundred and
fifty dollars, to be exact. The figure's on the last line."

"And that has to be paid next week?" With eyebrows
raised, she stared at the number. "I'll need to get a loan from
the bank."

"No, you won't." Bannon met her questioning glance with
a smile. "I sold your steers two weeks ago and managed to
catch the market when the prices were up. After taxes and all
bills are paid, you'll have about seven thousand dollars in
cash. Enough to carry the ranch into spring."

"Good." Letting out a sigh, Kit tossed the copy of the tax
form on his desk.

"The rest of this"—rising, Bannon picked up another
folder and came around the desk to her chair—"is fairly self-
explanatory. Copies of correspondence, the sales receipt on
the cattle, that kind of thing." Bending down, he opened the
folder and went through the papers one by one. This time Kit
paid attention and glanced through each one, conscious all

the while of his head close to hers and the subtle, spicy scent of his after-shave mingling with the smell of soap. "You can keep these for your records." He gave her the folder with the copies inside.

"Thanks . . . I think." Her glance followed him as he again retreated behind his desk.

"That's it"—from the center desk drawer, he took a ring of keys—"except for the keys." They jangled as he tossed them to her.

She caught them in the air, then closed her fingers around them. "Dad's Jeep—" she began.

"I had it serviced last week. It's in the shed. And Sadie cleaned the house, so you shouldn't have to do anything but unpack once you get there."

She tipped her head to one side, a little amazed at his thoroughness and thoughtfulness. "Is there anything you haven't taken care of?"

He dismissed her question with a shrugging lift of one shoulder. "Just being a good neighbor."

"I'd almost forgotten what that's like," she admitted ruefully. "In L.A., I barely knew my neighbors." She held the keys an instant longer, then slipped them into her purse, aware the blame was as much hers as it was her neighbors' and the impersonal life of a big city.

Bannon nodded with a kind of grim understanding. "There are times when it seems that bad in Aspen. Mostly because your neighbor spends only a few weeks here a year. The house sits empty the rest of the time."

"Like Silverwood has," she added and stood up.

"I'll walk you out."

She crossed to the door and waited for him to open it, then took a step into the outer office before turning back and holding out a hand to him. "Thanks, Bannon. For everything."

He glanced at her outstretched hand. Suddenly the moment felt incredibly awkward to Kit, somehow formal and distant. He lifted his gaze and looked directly into her eyes with an element of regret—or was that longing?

His fingers closed around her hand and she felt the strength of his grip, and the warmth of it. "Now that you're back in Aspen for a while, Kit, don't be a stranger."

"I won't." The assurance came easily as she reminded herself it was time she thought of Bannon as a friend. A dear friend, and nothing more. Yet, when she looked at his tanned and rawboned face—more intriguing than handsome—she felt the pull of old emotions. Emotions that didn't get their power just from memories. Somehow she'd have to find a way to deal with them.

Discovering she'd left her hand in his much longer than was necessary, she drew it free and flashed him a quick smile. When she turned to leave, she encountered the cool stare of Sondra Hudson. She stood by the secretary's desk, straight and tall, the epitome of a professional and fashion-conscious businesswoman in a beige, tunic-length jacket of cashmere over the restrained black of a silk blouse and wool gabardine skirt. Her hair was smoothly coiffed, not a single platinum strand out of place, and the simple gold clips at her ears were her only concession to jewelry.

Kit knew all about images and she knew this was one that had been cultivated and crafted as carefully and completely as any in Hollywood. So completely, in fact, that she had no sense of the woman beneath it. She marveled that anyone could exercise that much control over her feelings. Yet, that was the only impression she was picking up from Sondra Hudson—of emotions suppressed, restrained, utterly controlled. Kit knew she could never bottle her own up like that without going mad.

"Hello, Sondra." Kit nodded to her.

"Kit." Her lips curved in a warm line, but even that struck Kit as practiced. Then Sondra switched her attention to Bannon, her expression subtly changing, taking on an added warmth although her eyes kept their measuring look. "I dropped by on the off chance you might be free for a few minutes."

She spoke with the familiarity of one accustomed to dropping in unannounced and being welcomed. Rather like a wife, Kit thought, then doubted that the two of them were at all suited. But what did she know? Maybe Bannon had peeled through all those layers and found the woman beneath all that control.

"I'm expecting Pete Ranovitch," Bannon said with a glance at his watch. "But I'm free till he gets here."

"Wonderful."

"I won't keep you," Kit said quickly. "It was good to see you again, Sondra. Nice meeting you, Agnes," she added and headed for the door.

Sondra watched her walk out, tasting the jealousy that edged toward fury. She was overreacting and she knew it, but it didn't seem to matter. She resented any part of Bannon's past that didn't include her—and Kit Masters was part of that. A close part of it.

"What did you need to see me about, Sondra?"

She turned smoothly and smiled. "Laura."

Amused, he shook his head and stepped aside, letting her precede him into his office. "What is it this time? Not her hair again?"

"Clothes. She needs some new winter things, Bannon. She's outgrown practically everything from last year." Sondra detected traces of Kit's perfume in the air. A loathsome scent. "The jacket Laura was wearing this morning—the sleeves don't reach her wrists."

"Clothes, eh?" he said with a faint grimace. "I guess I need to take her shopping."

"Let me." She saw his hesitation and pressed her advantage. "You know you don't enjoy going from store to store and waiting while Laura tries on clothes. But I do. It would be fun for me. And for Laura, too. Two girls loose on a shopping spree—we'll have a great time."

"I suppose," he said, still hesitant.

"Good. Then I'll pick her up as soon as school lets out today and we'll hit the stores." A coffee mug sat on the edge of Bannon's desk opposite the padded leather chair. Sondra noticed the smudge of lipstick on the mug's rim, the same shade Kit Masters had been wearing. Had they had a cozy chat over coffee, reminiscing about the past before getting down to business? The possibility didn't please her at all. "Who knows how long it will take to find the various things

Laura will need? It would be best if she spent the night with me. That way we won't have to rush. We can take our time, grab a bite to eat somewhere, have a real girls' night out.''

Warily he raised an eyebrow. "How much is this spree going to set me back?"

She tipped her head back and laughed in her throat. "I promise we'll be kind to your budget.''

"I hope so," he murmured dryly.

She laid a hand on his arm. "This will be good for her, Bannon. Laura needs to do girl-things—like shopping for clothes, experimenting with hairstyles, or painting her toe-nails."

"I guess fathers aren't always good at that, are they?" His mouth slanted in a rueful line.

"Sometimes she needs a woman." Sondra kept her voice deliberately casual, content to merely plant the seed. "When bad weather comes this winter, I wish you'd let her stay with me. She has her own bedroom at my place, with all her things in it, and she'd be able to play with her other girlfriends."

"I'll think about it."

"Laura likes me, and you know I care a great deal about her. I think I'd be good for her." She paused a beat, then added, careful to keep her reproof mild, "You're raising her like a boy, Bannon. She's picking up your habits, your quietness. You don't want her to become too old and serious for her age. You want her to become a woman."

Bannon looked down at the hand that rested lightly on his arm, the slender fingers, the soft skin. He felt a growing loneliness, aware that a son would have grown along with him, but a daughter . . . Sooner or later the day would come when Laura would follow a different path, when she would be closer to Sondra than to him. That was life—part of the natural order of things. He couldn't prevent it even if he wanted to.

"You are good for Laura." He put his hand over hers. "I owe you a lot, Sondra. I'm grateful."

She pulled her hand back and looked at him, dark, cool, and quick. "I don't want gratitude from you, Bannon," she said with more heat than she'd intended, and instantly wiped it from her voice and eyes. "I'm only thinking of Laura. What's best for her."

He frowned, puzzled by that gust of intensity that had come from her. "You were angry just then. Why?"

"Because I don't want you to think I'm nice to Laura because she's your daughter. She's my niece, too. I care about her. It has nothing to do with you and me—our relationship."

"I know that."

"I hope so."

In the outer office, the front door shut with slamming force, the sound followed by quick-striding footsteps on the hardwood floor. Bannon lifted his head and glanced toward the connecting door. Sondra knew his attention was no longer on her, but on the client outside.

"I don't know why you waste your time with Ranovitch," she said critically. "The man's a loser."

His glance flicked to her. "I've known Pete a long time." That was all he said, then took her arm. "I'll walk you out."

Loyalty, Sondra thought, recognizing that unbendable streak in him. Bannon stood by his friends, good or bad, with a tenacity and faithfulness that never wavered. And no matter how she tried to twist that to her advantage, she never seemed to fully succeed. Not even today.

Gratitude. She despised that word.

The instant Bannon set foot in the outer office, Pete Ranovitch was on him. Haggard and hollow-eyed, a scruffy windbreaker over stained kitchen whites, he easily looked sixty although he was only nudging fifty. He waved a fistful of papers in Bannon's face, not giving him a chance to respond to Sondra's good-bye.

"Do you see this?" Ranovitch punched the paper in his hand, his voice rising to a shrill edge. "I got this in the mail this morning. The bastard Miller says I've got ten days to move out of my apartment. Can he do that, Bannon? I've still got another ten months on my lease. I suppose that doesn't mean shit."

"Take it easy, Pete." Bannon rescued the papers from the man's ever-tightening fingers and placed a hand on a narrow shoulder, guiding the man toward his office, feeling the tension and the tremors that had Ranovitch holding himself rigid. "Come on in and sit down. Give me a chance to see what you've got." Over his shoulder, he said, "Aggie, bring us some coffee. My pot's empty and I think Pete could use some."

"What I could use is a drink." Pete Ranovitch sank into the chair in front of Bannon's desk and rubbed a hand over his mouth, then caught Bannon's eye and waved off the look. "Don't worry. I'll settle for coffee. But it's shit like this that makes a man drink."

Withholding comment, Bannon smoothed the crumpled sheets and kicked back in his chair to read through them. Agnes came in with two cups of coffee and took the dirty mugs with her when she left, closing the connecting door on her way out. Pete dug in his pocket for a cigarette, then snapped his lighter repeatedly trying to get a flame.

"Jeezus, now my damned lighter won't work." He jerked the cigarette from his mouth in disgust, his fingers curling around it and the plastic lighter. "Got a light, Bannon?"

Bannon tossed him a book of matches from the center drawer. Two strikes and the match flared. Pete held the flame to the top of his cigarette with a trembling hand, then blew out a quick puff.

"Can he do it, Bannon? Can he throw me out?" He sat forward in his chair, turning the matchbook over and over in his fingers. "In that letter, he says *I* broke the lease. He says I was four days late with my rent money—"

"Were you?"

"Yes, but I'd called him. I'd told him I'd have it for him as soon as I got my paycheck. He said it was no problem. I paid it just like I said I would, then he does this!" He puffed jerkily on the cigarette, his head bowed.

Frowning, Bannon slipped the letter behind the accompanying sheets that had been stapled together. "Is this the lease?"

"Yeah, I thought you'd want to see it." He took another hasty drag on his cigarette, then tapped the ash from it into the bronze ashtray on Bannon's desk. "I leased the place from him over a year ago, and he's got his rent every damned month for it, too. Just how much is a guy supposed to take, Bannon? I've been busting my ass, working two jobs, tending bar nights and cooking days, thinking maybe now I'll be able to start putting money aside so I can finally get a restaurant of my own. I've been here in Aspen for thirty years. Hell, I was here before Harry Miller. I remember when he was nothing but a bookkeeper, doing tax work on the side. Then he started his own business—and started investing. Hell, I hate to think how many people I watched get rich along with Aspen. I saw them get all the breaks and I kept waiting and struggling, thinking it's gonna be my turn next. But it never is. Something like this always happens.'' He paused when he saw Bannon flip through the last page of the lease. "Well? Can he kick me out? I paid the damned rent.''

"I know.'' Bannon sighed grimly and glanced through the lease again, even though he already knew what it said. "I wish you had let me look at this lease before you signed it, Pete. According to this, he can evict you and sue for the remaining ten months' rent.''

"You're kidding.'' The cigarette dropped from his fingers. "For crissake, tell me you're kidding.''

"I wish I was—''

Pete flung his hands in the air, ash flying from the cigarette. "What the hell am I supposed to do? Where am I gonna go? You know there's nothing here in Aspen I can rent, and with my hours working two jobs, I can't be driving back and forth from Basalt or Glenwood Springs. I'd be better off sleeping in my car.'' He jabbed the cigarette out in the ashtray. "You know why he's doing this, don't you? He's made a deal with that motel on the highway. Instead of renting his crummy apartments for twelve hundred dollars a month, he can rent them for two, three, or four hundred dollars a night to those damned skiers. The greedy—''

"Hold it.'' Bannon held up his hand to shut off the flow. "I said—he *can* do it. But maybe we can persuade him that he doesn't *want* to.''

"Doesn't want to? Harry Miller, not want to collect three hundred dollars a night? Fat chance,'' Pete Ranovitch snorted as he pushed out of the chair.

"It's worth a try, isn't it?"

"Sure, but . . ." He frowned uncertainly.

Bannon motioned him back into the chair and reached for the phone. "Sit down and drink your coffee while I call and see if he's in." He dialed the number on the letterhead. "Harry and I have locked horns a couple of times in the past. We understand each other."

Pete studied the hard, almost stubborn set of Bannon's features and slowly sank back into the chair. "But if he's got the right—"

"Sometimes a man can be within his rights and still be wrong, Pete," Bannon said, then swung the mouthpiece up. "Is Harry in?" he said into it.

"Who's calling, please?"

"Bannon."

"One moment." Muzak played and Pete lit another cigarette, his gaze clinging to Bannon, his fingers never still, toying with the cigarette, the dead match, in a betrayal of nerves.

"Harry Miller here."

Bannon recognized the brusque voice even without the identification. "Harry, it's Bannon."

"I must say this is a surprise." He sounded a bit amused, and a bit curious.

"It shouldn't be. Pete Ranovitch came by my office to show me a letter he received from you."

"Ranovitch. I should have known he'd come to you. He always could count on you to bail him out of the tank, couldn't he? Well, I hope he brought along a copy of his lease."

"He did."

"Then you know I've acted in accordance with the terms and conditions of it."

"I'd like you to reconsider your position, Harry."

"What is this? A personal appeal, Bannon? Look, I know the man's had trouble. We all have. This is business. The letter stands. I want him out in ten days."

"Don't do it, Harry," Bannon said calmly.

"He violated the terms of the lease—"

"I disagree."

"You what?" Before he had sounded impatient, a little irritated; now there was anger choking his voice.

"As Pete explained the situation to me, he called to let you know he'd be late with his rent and you raised no objection—"

"I received no such call."

"I expected you to say that, Harry." Bannon smiled without humor.

"I tell you I didn't. Are you going to take the word of a drunk over mine?"

He ignored that. "Furthermore, Harry, by accepting the late payment on the rent, you waived your rights under the termination clause—"

"Read the damned lease," Harry snapped. "I was entitled to collect that money."

"Maybe we'll have to let a judge and jury decide that," Bannon suggested, then paused deliberately. "Do you have any idea how much it might cost you in legal fees to take your case before a jury, Harry? It could run anywhere from twenty-five to fifty thousand dollars. Maybe more, depending on how long it drags out before we actually go to court. And I promise you, I'll prolong it for at least ten months."

"I'd win," Miller insisted stiffly.

"Probably. But you're good with numbers, Harry. Would it be worth it?"

"This is blackmail, Bannon."

"Now the way I see it, Harry," he countered lazily, "I'm giving you a chance to make a business decision. The lease has ten more months to run. You can collect rent and save yourself some legal fees, or you can try to evict Pete and I'll get an injunction and string this thing out for ten months. It's up to you."

"Ranovitch can't afford to pay you for this. You're bluffing."

Bannon just shook his head and smiled. "You ought to know me better than that, Harry. Think it over and give me a call around noon tomorrow with your decision. That's about how long it will take me to draw up the necessary papers for Pete." With that, he hung up and met Pete's avid gaze.

"What you said to Miller"—Pete sat on the edge of the chair, his eyes round with apprehension and hope, a tower of ash building up on the cigarette between his fingers—"can you do it?"

Bannon nodded. "I can."

"But . . . if it costs twenty-five thousand to take it to court—I haven't got that kind of money to pay you, Bannon."

"I don't think it'll ever come to that. But one way or another, you've got a place to live for ten months."

Pete dropped his head. "I don't know what to say," he murmured in a tight, choked voice as the ash tumbled from the cigarette onto the leg of his kitchen whites.

"Just try to pay your rent on time from now on and don't give Miller any more openings." Rising, Bannon handed back the lease along with the letter.

"I won't." Hastily he put out his cigarette and took the papers. "And thanks."

Bannon shrugged it off. "That's what lawyers are for, Pete," he said, aware the victory was a small one. Ten months from now Pete would have to find someplace else to live, a place he could afford. And in Aspen, he almost stood a better chance of winning the lottery.

A young couple in blue jeans, hiking shoes, and backpacks stood in front of the display case outside the offices of Hudson Properties, looking at photographs of some of the company's more choice locations advertised for sale. The girl, her brown hair tied in a ponytail with a string of blue yarn, pointed to one of the pictures beneath the protective glass.

"Andy, did you see this house? The price is six *million* dollars."

"You think that's something. Look at this—a two-acre lot in Starwood for two million dollars. Two million dollars just for a lot."

"John Travis has a home in Starwood."

On other occasions such comments might have prompted Sondra to gloat a little over the knowledge that her company had an exclusive listing on those particular properties. But this morning, their voices were nothing more than an annoying buzz as she swept past them into the building.

Warren Oakes lounged on a corner of the secretary's desk. Not in the best of moods after her less-than-satisfactory meeting with Bannon, Sondra gave him a cold, smileless look.

"Don't you have something better to do than bother Mary, Warren?" She stopped at the desk and picked up her messages.

"We were just talking about Lassiter's party Saturday night while I was waiting for you." Warren took his time straightening from the desk while the brunette wisely made an attempt to look busy. "Must have been some affair."

His remark reminded her that nothing had gone right Saturday night, or Sunday, or today, but she gave a noncommittal nod and leafed through her messages, giving each barely more than a desultory glance.

"Did you express that video of the Carlsen house off to the Eastlakes, Mary?" She fired a quick look at the pale-cheeked woman.

"Finishing it up right now, Miss Hudson," she promised.

"I want it out this morning." The order was issued over her shoulder as Sondra pushed open the door to her private office.

Warren strolled in after her, sensing a nasty temper simmering under that icy expression, arousing his curiosity. With other women, a little stroking, a little teasing, and a little sympathy would invariably cajole them into revealing the cause. But with Sondra, those tactics were more likely to gain him a sample of that temper, generously laced with contempt.

"Your chicken king called while you were out to see if we had any response on his offer," he remarked as he absently ran a hand along the fold of the newspaper.

"Have we?" Sondra tossed the message slips on her desk, adding the only hint of clutter to its otherwise immaculate surface.

"Not yet."

"You faxed the offer to him?" She pinned him with an accusing look.

Warren nodded. "And followed it up with a phone call,

plus I sent the original by certified mail." He paused in front of the chinoiserie desk and watched her stow her purse in a lower drawer. "What about Lassiter? Did he snap at the commercial block when you dangled it in front of him Saturday night?"

"No." Her lips tightened fractionally, and Warren had a feeling he'd stumbled onto something.

"No?" He probed carefully, aware that Sondra had been confident—more than confident, really—that the sale to Lassiter was all but a done deal.

"No." Her answer was harder and flatter with still no explanation forthcoming. Which could only mean she'd struck out royally on this one.

"Too bad." He glanced at the paper in his hand, debating whether he should probe further or if it would be wiser to do some ego stroking. He decided on the latter. "Saturday night wasn't all in vain. You got a mention in today's paper for being there. And a free plug for the company." The newspaper was folded open to the small write-up on the charity affair. Turning the paper to face her, Warren laid it on her desk. "Good photo of Bannon dancing with Aspen's future star isn't it?"

Going rigid, Sondra stared at the picture taken at the precise instant when Bannon's smile was fading and his awareness of the woman in his arms was rising. The woman was Kit Masters.

Something snapped.

Warren saw the rage that blackened her eyes and pulled the blood from her face until it was dead white. She lifted her head and gave him a bitter, killing glance—hating him because he was the only thing around to receive her anger. He backed up a step, stunned by the change, by the fury that altered her until she was no longer beautiful, no longer admirable.

"Leave me alone."

He was gone before she had to tell him again.

She looked back at the photo and reached for the cloisonné-handled scissors, part of a matched set of desktop accessories. With thumb and fingers fitted tightly around the emerald handgrips, she began to cut—scissor blades slashing through the grainy news photo and closing with a *snap*. Slash, *snap*. Slash, *snap*. Over and over again.

When the scissors finally fell silent, she was breathing heavily and the picture was in shreds. The evidence that Bannon had ever looked at another woman the way he was meant to look at her, destroyed.

❧❧❦ 12 ❦❧❧

*L*ate morning swelled across the triangular valley in warm full waves of sunlight. An alpine white Range Rover, chased by its shadow, cut across it, following the narrow dirt lane, its wheels churning up a low cloud of red-ochre dust in its wake. Slowing, the vehicle rumbled over a wooden bridge spanning a stream, its current sluggish and its waters low without the snowmelt that had it tumbling full in spring.

Ahead, a ranch house sprawled amid a sheltering grove of white-barked aspens. Catching sight of it, Kit leaned forward in the passenger seat, a warm, coming-home feeling rising in her throat.

When John Travis slowed the Range Rover to a stop in front of the house, Kit pulled on the door handle and swung out. One foot touched the hard-packed ground and she planted the other firmly on it and faced the house. Sunlight dappled the white-painted front, three gables rising to form the second story. A window looked out from each of them, a hint of chintz curtains showing behind the gleam of glass panes. A pair of wooden rockers sat on the wraparound porch, keeping company with a swing that hung by chains from the ceiling.

She lifted her gaze to the massed spires of spruce climbing

the ridge behind the house and to the purple splendor of the mountains beyond, seeing the majesty of them, the power and strength of them that man could never subdue. Ancient and ageless, they stood as they had stood for millennia, ever changing and ever constant.

The slam of doors and crunch of footsteps broke the stillness. Half turning, Kit flashed a smile at Paula and John Travis as they joined her. "Welcome to Silverwood Ranch," she said.

With one hand shading her eyes from the sun, Paula looked around with undisguised pleasure. "This place is even more incredible than it looked from the air. The views are breathtaking, Kit."

Pleased by her reaction, Kit swung expectantly to John. He stood with his head thrown back, his eyes narrowed in thoughtful study of the scene, the sun shining on his hair and toasting it gold. "How big did you say your ranch is?"

"Four hundred acres. It extends to the other side of this ridge, then roughly halfway up that mountain and the ridge that juts out over there," she replied, pointing out the boundaries.

He gave her a considering look, an eyebrow quirking in mild curiosity. "Do you realize how much this land is probably worth?"

Kit nodded. "Roughly a half million."

His short laugh scoffed at the figure. "More like five million, you mean." He turned back to the view. "On second thought, with a setting like this only minutes from Aspen, you could probably get ten for it."

Stunned by his statement, Kit stared at him. "You're joking, of course." It was the only explanation that made sense.

"Why would I joke about it?" His smile was puzzled. "Any real estate agent in Aspen could tell you this ranch would be in the ten-million-dollar range. Who knows? The right buyer might pay more than that and never blink an eye."

"You're serious," she murmured when it became plain he believed it. Yet she knew it was impossible. Not an hour ago Bannon had told her Silverwood was worth roughly five hundred thousand dollars, a value he said was based on current prices. Why had he said that if it wasn't true? There wasn't any reason for him to lie. No reason for either of them to lie. Kit frowned, thoroughly confused.

"Of course I'm serious." A trace of dry amusement briefly glittered in his eyes as his smile deepened. "When you inherited this ranch, you became one very wealthy lady, Kit Masters."

"Ten million dollars," Paula mused. "I'd be content to have the interest on that much money. I never dreamed you were so rich, Kit."

"Neither did I." In truth, she still wasn't convinced she was, although she was at a loss to explain the huge discrepancy.

A horse whinnied from the barn area. Turning, Kit saw the chestnut gelding at the corral fence, its neck arched over the top rail and its blaze face pointed toward them.

"It's Sundance," Kit said, unable to keep the delight from her voice. "I raised him from a colt."

She struck out for the corral, aware that John followed her. The chestnut nickered again and rubbed its head against her shoulder.

"Remember me, do you, old fella?" Kit affectionately scratched the thick coat around the horse's ears, rumpling its forelock. "Well, I remember you, too. We were best buddies, huh?" She laughed when the horse nuzzled at her pockets, searching for a treat. "Sorry, Dance. No carrots this time."

John curved a shoulder against a corral post and lit a cigarette, watching her through the ravel of smoke. Without even asking, Kit knew by his faintly amused expression that he'd never had an animal for a pet, never felt that bond of affection. She thought again that his childhood must have been a lonely one.

"You seem surprised to find your horse here," he remarked.

"I thought he'd been sold with the rest of Dad's horses. Bannon must have kept him and not said anything." It sounded like something Bannon would do. "I broke him to ride myself."

"Really. How long have you had him?"

"Forever. At least it seems that way sometimes." She lifted the chestnut's head and stroked a hand over the softness of its graying muzzle. "I was ten when I got him." She did some fast subtraction in her head. "That makes Sundance twenty-two now."

"That's old for a horse, isn't it?"

She grinned. "He's definitely no spring chicken, but he's still got a few good years left in him. Don't you, fella?" she crooned to the horse, then laughed when the gelding tossed its head as if in confirmation. "See?" She sent a twinkling look at John. "Sundance agrees."

"If you say so," he replied, dubiously arching an eyebrow.

"I do." Smiling, she gave the horse one final pat. "I have to go, fella. Paula's waiting and we still have to get our things unloaded." The chestnut nickered a protest when she started to leave. "I know," she said. "I'd like to throw a saddle on you and go for a ride, too, but that will have to wait until later."

John gave her an amused look and fell in step, matching her casually swinging pace. "Have you always talked to animals like that?"

"Always," she replied with careless ease. "When I was growing up, there weren't any kids on the ranch for me to play with. The horses, Dad's hunting dogs, the chickens, they all became my playmates." She looked at the yard that had been her playground, memories stirring. "I used to people this yard with characters—from movies I'd seen or books I'd read, or simply from my own imagination—and I'd act out all the parts myself. Good training, eh?"

"The love scenes must have been difficult."

"Very." She grinned, laughter dancing in her eyes. "But considering some of the wooden actors I've kissed, it was good practice."

"You're not putting me in that category, I hope," he replied, and she laughed.

"Not you, John T., never you." Her glance rested a moment on his lips, so experienced, so expert at evoking emotion. Especially from her.

There was so much invitation in that look John almost

followed it up with action, but Paula was there. "Shall we start unloading?"

"Might as well." Kit nodded and fished the house key out of her purse.

Three trips later and all the luggage and groceries were out of the Range Rover and in the house. John walked into the pine-walled kitchen and set the last sack of groceries on the Formica countertop.

"That's all of it," he announced.

"Great." Kit stashed a gallon of skim milk in the refrigerator. "Paula's putting some coffee on—"

"Kit, where's the can opener?" Paula scanned the countertop, a new can of coffee in her hand.

"The second drawer to your right."

She opened the drawer. "My God, a manual one." She shoved the can opener and coffee into John's hands. "I'll break a nail. Now, where's the coffeepot?"

"On the stove."

"The stove." Paula stared at the old-fashioned range-top percolator and shook her head. "I can handle a Mr. Coffee, Kit, but not that. Tomorrow we go to town and buy an electric can opener and a coffee maker. For now, we'll forget the coffee and have tea instead."

"Think you can manage that?" John mocked.

The redhead flashed him a humorless smile. "In my sleep. There's nothing to it. Just fill the cups with water, pop them in the microwave—" She stopped and swung toward Kit. "You do have a microwave, don't you?"

Kit grinned at the look of dread on her friend's face. "Rest easy. We do. It's behind that sack of groceries next to the refrigerator. Dad bought it as a Christmas present to himself about five years ago."

"Thank God," Paula declared with typical dramatics. "I wasn't sure I could survive a month without a home-zapped meal."

When the can opener cut through the last centimeter of metal with a clicking finality, John pushed both away from him. "That's it. I'll leave you two to settle in and be on my way."

"You don't have to go yet," Kit protested and glanced at the wall clock. "It's almost lunchtime. Stay and have something to eat with us."

He lifted a brow. "You've forgotten I saw what Paula bought at the store. Lettuce, low-fat yogurt, and melba toast is not my idea of food."

"What can I say?" Paula raised her shoulders in a careless shrug. "When this little month's vacation is over, I still want to fit into my clothes. And I'd certainly never be able to do that if I continued eating the lavish meals at your house. Being a redhead is enough of a handicap in this business without being a plump one."

Kit cast an envisioning eye at her friend, slim-hipped and slender-curved in a cream silk blouse and khaki trousers cinched at the waist with a wide alligator belt. "I simply can't see you ever being plump, Paula."

"And you never will." She plucked a container of yogurt from one of the sacks and held it up. "My lunch."

When Kit started to respond to that, John interrupted. "Walk me out."

"Okay." Kit moved to his side and companionably hooked an arm around his waist when he curved an arm across her shoulders. "Be back shortly," she told Paula.

"She'll be back," John qualified her statement before steering her out of the small kitchen.

"What does that mean?" Her sideways glance was deliberately provocative.

"It means . . . I haven't been thanked properly for bringing you out here." They passed through the living room to the front door. John opened it and Kit ducked under his arm to walk out ahead of him. Once on the porch, he reclaimed possession. "And that could take some time."

"I thought you were in a rush to leave," she reminded him, a gleam of taunting humor in her eyes as they descended the steps.

"Not that big of a rush that I'd deny myself a little pleasure before business." When they reached the Range Rover, he pulled her around to face him, fitting her to the cradle of his hips.

"I think I know what the pleasure is." A small smile played across her lips as she settled comfortably against him and slipped her hands inside his light windbreaker, spreading them over the cotton knit of his polo shirt, feeling the hard, warm flesh beneath it and the even thud of his heart. "But what's the business?"

When she tipped her head back to look up at him, John brushed a kiss across her lips, then took advantage of the length of neck she exposed. "I have to check out some locations with Nolan and Abe this afternoon," he said between nibbles. "In the meantime I have to get together with Chip. Lassiter's getting impatient to see the script revisions and Chip's fighting me on them."

"He believes in the script as it's written." She closed her eyes to better savor the delicious little shivers dancing over her skin, her fingers creeping up higher, closer to his neck.

John lifted his head. "There's such a thing as compromise."

"True." Reluctantly she opened her eyes and rediscovered her fascination for the cleft in his chin, tracing the elusive dent with the point of a nail.

"Have dinner with me tonight. No chaperones. No Paula, no Chip. Just you and me."

"Sounds tempting." Idly she ran a finger along the patrician fineness of his cheekbone, following its chiseled ridge to his hairline, then toyed with a few short-clipped strands of dark blond hair near his ear, appreciating the silken texture of them, so unusual in a man. "Unfortunately"—she sighed her regret—"I'd better not. I have a thousand things to do and if I keep spending most of my time with you, I'll never get them done."

He didn't like her answer and it showed in the thinning line of his mouth. "Are they so urgent they can't be postponed?"

"Not urgent, just endless." She rubbed her lips over his mouth, teasing away its tightness. Before he could deepen it into a full-fledged kiss, she moved on, feathering kisses over his cheek, jaw, and chin. "I've got all my father's things to go through," she murmured against his skin. "The papers in his desk, the clothes in his closet and drawers, his stuff in the bathroom, and—all his hunting equipment," she remembered with a groan, burying her face in the side of his neck. "Plus all the food in the cupboards and pantry. Some of it's probably been there since before I moved to California." She drew back a little. "Not only do I have to go through everything, but I've got to figure out what to pitch, what to keep for myself, what to sell, what to give away and to whom—"

"I'm convinced." He silenced her with a quick, hard kiss, then softened it into something drugging and addictive.

When he finally let her surface for air, she was raw and trembling. But she liked the feeling. And she liked knowing there were things she could bring to his life that he needed, things like laughter and love, a sense of home and belonging, things he had no idea he was missing in his life.

He gazed at her through half-lidded eyes. "Dinner, tomorrow night." His voice had a husky rumble to it.

"You've got a date." She flicked his chin with her finger, then kissed him again, quick and light, and slipped out of his arms. "Off to work with you, or I'll never get anything done."

He felt a flicker of annoyance at the way she had slipped out of his grasp. In the next breath, he banished it. "You're right. I've got work to do," he said, aware that he had a tendency to forget that whenever he was around her.

Kit moved to the porch and waved as he drove away. She lingered a moment after the sound of the engine had died away, caught by a strange need to memorize the scene—the flawless blue of the sky, the strong scent of pine and rich upland grasses in the air, and the whisper of the wind through the medallion-like leaves of the aspen. Sights, sounds, and smells to carry with her when she left. But not yet. She wasn't leaving yet.

She turned and walked into the house.

Paula came from the kitchen carrying a circular metal tray. A blue-checked napkin covered the tray's Coca-Cola design and a teapot and two cups and saucers were balanced on top of it.

"The groceries are all put away." She set the tray on the

chunky-legged cocktail table in front of the living-room sofa. "The way my head's pounding, I decided I needed a break before I faced unpacking my suitcases again. Care to join me for a cup of herbal tea?"

"Thanks." Kit discovered she didn't feel like unpacking either—or doing one of the thousand things she'd just told John she needed to do. Instead she wandered the rest of the way into the living room, her glance taking in the oyster-glazed walls, the pine-planked ceiling, the rock fireplace, the rack of trophy antlers above it, and the decor she'd always labeled a cross between country and comfortable.

Paula poured tea into both cups, handed one to Kit, then moved aside the throw pillows on the sofa and sank onto its soft cushion, gracefully curving a leg beneath her. She sipped at her tea while casually running an assessing eye around the room.

"This is nice," she concluded. "Spacious but cozy." She paused and glanced dubiously at the trophy buck above the fireplace. "Although I'm not sure I like the idea of a dead animal staring down at me."

"Mother felt the same way," Kit remembered. "She wouldn't let Dad bring it in the house. He kept it in the barn for years." She stood behind his favorite chair, a big, overstuffed armchair covered in a masculine gray plaid fabric with an equally oversized ottoman in front of it, an afghan in shades of gray and wine draped across it. "Dad loved to hunt. Deer, elk, moose, sheep, turkey—it never mattered to him. The minute hunting season opened—bow or rifle—he was gone. He guided a lot of hunting parties. He used to laugh and marvel at the idea a man could get paid for doing something he loved. For him, it was never the kill, but the hunt."

She ran a hand over the white linen antimacassar that protected the back of the chair. The tatting around its edges had frayed in spots from years of laundering. The antimacassar had been her mother's doing; she'd been convinced his hair cream would leave a stain. After the divorce, his father had brought the trophy buck in from the barn, but he hadn't thrown out the antimacassar. Kit wasn't surprised. Both, in their own way, had been reminders of her mother.

Giving in to the need to feel close to him, she sat down in his favorite chair and let its bigness surround her, the same way his laughter and love had once surrounded her. She took a sip of tea, and simultaneously decided she was definitely keeping the chair.

"It's funny," Kit mused absently and balanced the cup and saucer on a wide, upholstered arm. "When I think of my father, I remember his laughter. With my mother, it's her silence. She was always so quiet, rarely ever smiled or laughed. I'm not sure she knew how to express emotion or affection."

"Maybe she was afraid of it," Paula suggested idly as she examined an old apothecary bottle on the wicker stand next to the sofa.

"Maybe." Kit lifted the cup and breathed in the tea's aromatic steam, then blew lightly at its hotness before taking a sip.

Paula noticed the small, gold-framed photograph next to the brown glass bottle and picked it up for a closer look. "This is a photo of your mother, isn't it?"

"Mmmm." Kit nodded and lowered the cup. "Dad loved that picture of her."

"He kept it sitting out?" Paula frowned. "He divorced her."

"She divorced him," Kit corrected. "He never stopped loving her, though." She thought about it a moment, then added, "As hard as Mother took his death, I'm not sure she stopped loving him."

"Then, why—?"

Kit shrugged with a touch of uncertainty. "In their case, I think loving each other just complicated their other problems."

Looking back, she suspected she'd probably always known things weren't right between her parents, that they had problems. But it had never entered her head that they might break up. Divorce happened to other people's parents. Not hers.

She'd learned how wrong she was that awful Saturday morning when she'd come home after spending Friday night at Angie's house. It had been October, too—a gray and cloudy October morning with winter's chill in the air. . . .

The heavy storm door banged shut behind her as Kit swept into the house. "Hi, Mom. Hi, Dad," she called out. The rush of outside air she'd let in turned her breath to a vapory stream. She barely glanced at either of her parents as she advanced into the living room, dropping her canvas bag on the floor, tossing her schoolbooks on the pine side table by the door, peeling off her muffler and throwing it over the back of a chair, dropping her mittens on the cushion—leaving her usual trail of clutter. "We had a riot last night. I'm not kidding. It—"

"Kit." Something in the tone of her father's voice stopped her. She looked at him, sitting in his chair, all slumped forward, his elbows propped on his knees, his hands hanging limp between them. He had trouble meeting her eyes. He looked pale, ashen almost, and red-eyed. She grimaced a little in silent sympathy, certain he'd had too many Friday-night beers and was paying for them this morning. "Sit down, Kit. Your mother and I have to talk to you."

"This sounds serious," she mocked and glanced at her mother. She sat on the sofa, as always very stiff and straight, her face expressionless like a porcelain doll with blue eyes and rich brown hair. Her lips were pressed in that firm line Kit knew so well, a look that invariably preceded a lecture in something. "Don't tell me." Kit plunked herself down on the chair with her mittens. "Mrs. Westcott called to complain—"

"This isn't about Mrs. Westcott," her father broke in again, that strange, terse edge in his voice startling her. This time Kit waited for him to explain what it was about. "Your mother's leaving. She's going to her cousin's in California."

"California! Mother, that's fabulous. When are you going? How long will you be gone? God, I'd love to go. It will be so sunny and warm there. When are you coming back?"

"I'm not."

Kit opened her mouth, but she was too stunned to get

anything to come out. "What do you mean you're not?" she finally protested in disbelief. "What are you talking about?"

She looked from one to the other, trying to figure out what was going on and refusing to let that little suspicion in the back of her mind take form.

"Your mother's . . . going to live there." Her father faltered and stared at his hands, linking his fingers together and curling them tight. "There's no easy way to say this, Kit—"

"For God's sake, Clint, just tell her," her mother said and rose to her feet.

"Tell me what?" Kit demanded, already afraid of the answer.

"Your father and I are getting a divorce," she replied.

"No," Kit whispered the word, then repeated it more stridently as she jumped to her feet, fighting back tears. "No, you can't. You can't do this. You can't leave!" But she saw her mother was deaf to her appeals and she swung around to her father. "Dad, talk to her. Make her change her mind. Make her stay."

"Kit, stop it," her mother said harshly. "Nothing can be said that will change my mind. Not by you or your father. This was not an easy decision, but it's made. Please try to accept it."

"No," she sobbed, then turned and ran blindly from the house.

She made it as far as the porch steps and leaned against the post, sobbing uncontrollably. It couldn't be true. It couldn't be happening. They couldn't get a divorce. They couldn't.

Her legs buckled and she sank to the steps, an arm wrapped around the post, her body shaking with the horrible pain of her crumbling world. She didn't hear the front door open and close, or the footsteps crossing the porch. But she felt the weight of a hand on her shoulder and looked up at her father's tear-streaked face, mirroring the anguish of her own.

"I'm sorry, kitten," he whispered and lowered himself onto the steps beside her.

"It's all my fault, isn't it?" She tried to sniffle back the tears.

"No. No, it isn't."

"Yes, it is." She pressed the heels of her hands against her eyes. "She didn't want me to quit dance class. The piano, I haven't been practicing the way I should. My room's always a mess. I'll sell Sundance. I'll help around the house, keep my room clean, do the dishes. I won't tie up the phone talking to Angie. I promise, I'll—"

"Don't, Kit. Don't do this to yourself." He dragged her to him and pressed her face against the wool of his shirt, his arms hugging her tight and rocking her against him. "It's not you. I swear this has nothing to do with you. It's a problem between your mother and me, one that started before you were even born."

"I don't understand," she protested. "There's got to be something you can do about it."

"We've tried, Kit. We've both tried."

She hated the defeat in his voice, and pulled back to glare at him. "Don't you love her anymore?"

His eyes filled up with tears. "Yes," he murmured thickly. "Yes, I love her. I love her so much it hurts." His hand trembled as it touched the tears on her cheeks. Then gently he brushed the hair back from her face.

"Then there's got to be something you can do," she insisted. "Some way to make her stay. Maybe if you'd promise to quit drinking, if you'd stop seeing Bonnie Blaisdell—"

He blanched. "You know about her?"

She looked down at the front of his shirt, feeling sick, ashamed, embarrassed. "When Bannon brought me home from the game last week, I saw your truck parked behind her house. I knew it wasn't the first time," she admitted, her voice tight. "Kids talk, Dad."

"Oh, God, I'm sorry, Kit." He turned his head away, his arms loosening.

"Why, Dad? Why do you see her if you love Mom so much?"

For a moment, he just shook his head as if there was no answer. Then he lifted it to look at her. "How old are you now—sixteen?" She nodded, although he didn't seem to notice. "I guess maybe you're old enough to understand."

He turned his gaze to the mountains and stared off into the distance. "Your mother is a beautiful woman, Kit. The most beautiful woman I've ever seen. When I was your age, our class went on a school trip. We went to a museum in Denver. There was a vase there. An incredibly beautiful vase, centuries old. The blues and greens and gold in it were so vivid, so rich," he murmured, as if seeing it again in his mind's eye. "They had it displayed in a case, enclosed in glass. You couldn't touch it. All you could do was look at it." He paused and glanced sideways at Kit. "That's never been enough for me. When I see something beautiful, I want to touch it, hold it in my hands—in my arms. Your mother . . . she never could stand that. She tried but . . ."

Awkwardly Kit wrapped her fingers around his hand, letting him know he didn't have to say any more; she understood now why he saw Bonnie Blaisdell. "Either way, Mom's hurt."

He didn't reply. He just squeezed her hand tightly and held on.

"Kit." Paula had repeated her name a second time before Kit heard her.

"Sorry." She blinked once to rid herself of those vivid recollections of the past, then met Paula's faintly amused gaze. "I wasn't listening. What did you say?"

"Nothing important really. I merely remarked that I thought it was unusual that you stayed with your father. Most daughters go with their mothers when their parents divorce."

"They left the choice to me. At the time, I thought my father needed me more. Maybe he did. I'm not sure anymore." She lifted her shoulders, indicating her uncertainty. "Anyway, Dad and I were so much alike I'd always been closer to him. And I think I blamed my mother for not being the kind of woman he needed—and for hurting him so much. I never considered that maybe she couldn't help it."

It was something she'd wondered about lately, since her father died. At sixteen, there'd been so much she didn't know. Maturity and experience now told her that counseling might have helped her mother overcome her aversion to sex, although Kit suspected Elaine Masters was too proud and too private a person to have sought help. Now it would never be known whether the cause was psychological or an early symptom of multiple sclerosis.

However, Kit did know that, like her father, she'd never be satisfied to love at a distance either. She needed to touch, to kiss, to hold, to *give* her love the same as he had.

And like him, she'd learned that love could bring immense joy—and it could bring immense pain. It could make you hurt so much that you started to believe it was possible for a heart to literally break.

The past. She was thinking too much about the past.

Paula's cup clinked in its saucer, providing a much-needed distraction. "What I wouldn't give for a maid to unpack those suitcases," she said on a sigh.

"Dream on." In one long swallow, Kit drained the tea from her cup, then set it and the saucer aside. "Unfortunately neither dreaming nor sitting here will accomplish that—or all the other things I have to do."

As she pushed out of the chair, her glance fell on the old rolltop desk in the corner next to her father's gun case. With the entire afternoon ahead of her, Kit decided that after she called Maggie to check on her mother, she'd make it her first project to go through all the papers and records in the desk. Hopefully she'd run across something that would give her a realistic idea of the ranch's worth. For the life of her, she didn't understand how John's figure and Bannon's could be so far apart.

～⌘ 13 ⌘～

The sun sank lower behind the mountains, tinting the high, thin clouds into gossamer veils of amethyst, fuschia, and vermillion. The chill of a high mountain night was already in the air when Kit carried her coffee onto the front porch. Paula strolled over to the swing and draped herself over the length of its seat in a graceful sprawl, making a sleek and elegant picture in her quilted lounging pajamas of dark cocoa velvet, the deep color contrasting perfectly with the vibrant red of her hair.

Delicately she smothered a yawn and took a sip of her coffee, then snuggled deeper in the swing. "I have a feeling I'll have absolutely no trouble at all sleeping tonight."

"You're becoming acclimatized to the high altitude," Kit observed, then gave in to a surging restlessness and moved to the porch rail. Perching on it, she hooked a denim-clad leg over the rail for balance and gazed across the valley's empty pastures.

"Maybe I am. My headache's almost gone." Sighing, Paula curled both hands around her cup and tilted her head back to rest it against the swing's chains. "It feels like it's been an incredibly long day."

"It was definitely a long afternoon." With a kick of her

198

leg, Kit swung off the rail and crossed to stand at the top of the steps. "After sitting at the desk, sorting through Dad's papers all afternoon, I know I could never stand to work in an office every day."

She felt some satisfaction in knowing she'd accomplished the task, even though she hadn't found anything that could give her a clearer idea of the ranch's value. But that didn't compensate for the feeling she'd been caged all day, left with a lot of excess energy and no outlet for it.

A breeze curled down from the mountains and rustled through the aspen grove, the leaves shimmering with this new movement of air. Paula shivered a little. "It's getting cold out."

Kit lifted her face to the invigorating bite of the breeze. "It feels good," she said, recalling that she'd never minded the cold.

"Your blood is obviously thicker than mine."

"Probably." She wandered over to one of the chairs and gave the back of it a push, sending it swaying to and fro on its rockers. It didn't help, and she turned, facing the barn. The chestnut gelding stood in the corral, contentedly munching on the hay that had been thrown out to him. In that instant, the thought formed in her head.

"As beautiful as the sunset is," Paula said, rising from the swing, "I'm going to drink the rest of my coffee inside— where it's warm. Are you coming?"

"No," she said, the decision made. "I'm going for a ride. Want to come? Sundance will carry double."

Paula stopped halfway to the front door and stared at her with widened eyes. "You're going to ride a horse? It's almost dark."

"I love riding at night. It's my favorite time."

"Not mine. In fact, I'm not that fond of horseback riding at any time. I'll just stay here and read or watch television," she said, then hesitated, concern rising in her expression. "You will be all right?"

"Of course." Kit grinned. "Leave the porch light on for me. I might be late."

"You're crazy."

Aware that when the sun went down so did the temperature, Kit grabbed a jacket and gloves from the house and headed for the barn.

The light had faded to a ruby char in the west when she rode the gelding out of the corral, leaving the gate open. The mountains cut a black, cardboard outline against the purpling sky. The gelding was fresh and eager to travel. At a canter, they crossed the ranch yard and Kit pointed the chestnut at the aspen grove and the narrow trail leading into the mountains.

The ermine-barked trunks of the aspen trees stood out like slender white poles amid the deepening shadows. Kit found the old game trail and swung the chestnut onto it, dry leaves crackling beneath its hooves. Recognizing the path, the gelding pulled eagerly at the bit. Kit knew the trail as well as her mount and let the horse travel along it at an unchecked pace.

Beyond the stand of aspens, the trail began to climb, winding up the ridge. Darkness swallowed them as they passed into the shadowed aisle walled by towering pines. Here, a carpet of pine needles, made by a hundred years of falling, muffled almost completely the sound of the chestnut's strides.

For a time Kit could hear only the gelding's snorting breaths, the jangle of bit and creak of saddle leather. Gradually her senses became attuned to the night and she caught the sigh of the wind in the trees, the fragmented murmurings of a distant stream, the whir of a bird's wings, and the rustling of night creatures in the brush.

Leaving the pines, the trail became rougher, steeper. She gave the surefooted gelding its head, letting it pick its own way and its own pace. Never once did she feel any apprehension, not of the trail or the cloaking darkness.

At the crest of the ridge, she pulled the chestnut in and let it have a good blow while she took in the view. A crescent moon cast a pale light at the earth, letting the deep indigo sky sparkle with its dusting of stars—stars that looked close enough to reach out and touch. She could make out the jagged peaks of the surrounding mountains, the valley below and the quicksilver gleam of a stream running through it.

She smiled. This view from the heights was her kind of country, and she loved it. The isolation, the long distances, and the mystery of the star-swept sky overhead, she'd been born into it and she could conceive no other land as satisfying. She felt the wildness of the mountains flow around her, seeping into her bones and her mind, easing her tension. In the night, there was a timeless swing, a vast rhythm that caught her and carried her away from the little things. In the night there was an undertone of life that was without pause, without end.

She breathed in the chill air, her sharpened senses savoring the wind's keen edge, the great silence of the mountains, and the deep, deep glitter of the stars. The chestnut gelding nickered softly and swung its head toward the trail, pricking its ears in the direction of the winks of light two miles distant, the ranch lights of Stone Creek. Smiling, Kit touched a heel to the horse and the gelding moved out eagerly toward them.

The cattle checked, the evening chores done, and supper eaten, Bannon sat on the front porch of the log ranch house. A mental and physical weariness loosened his long frame and the ease of the darkening night moved over him. With an indolent rhythm, he swayed the rocker across the planked floor and breathed the fragrance of his cigar.

The ranch hands had long since gone to their homes. Old Tom stirred in the house, grumbling at the television's snowy reception. On the porch, night crowded around Bannon until he felt thoroughly alone. The call of a whippoorwill ran through the silence and a small steady breeze, cool with the coming winter, brushed over his face.

There were two great hours in life, Bannon decided—the hour of morning's first gray light, when everything was fresh and sharp and keen, and this hour with its softness and mystery and time for reflection.

He located the Big Dipper and the North Star, a bright, unblinking point of light that reminded him of the constancy of all things, the changelessness and fidelity of the outer world. Man was the only impermanent thing.

Those were his thoughts, all pathways leading back to his early manhood and to Diana, the woman who had been his wife. He remembered how bright and clear that time had been, how much fun they'd had. Then the fun had gone, leaving him alone—almost beyond the power of laughter.

He kept remembering her eyes, how black they'd been with anger and reproach when she'd looked at him at the last— black with the thought that their unhappiness had been his fault. She had died hating him for taking her from the life she'd known, hating him for a marriage she had so soon found wrong.

That was always the clearest thing—the memory of her eyes. That memory had left him with one permanent, impossible wish—to live those days over again and give back to her that insatiable love of life she'd had when they first met. Not her love for him. That, they had both learned, had never existed.

He rolled the cigar between his fingers and took another puff, reliving those old moments. As he blew out a stream of blue smoke, he heard the distant drum of hoofbeats coming out of the foothills to the west. He lifted his head, the sound like an echo of an even older memory.

He waited as the drum of cantering hooves came closer. A horse and rider emerged from the black shadows of the ranch buildings. Bannon recognized the chestnut's blaze face and four white stockings and knew it was Kit in the saddle. She rode the horse in a way that was good to see, her shoulders swinging, her body full of grace.

At the porch, she reined in and dropped to the ground in one careless jump. Bannon rose from the rocker as she came up the stone steps.

"Hello, Bannon." She stood in front of him, stripping off her riding gloves, smiling and watching his answering smile break the healthy darkness of his face.

"Kit."

The ride had deepened her breathing and whipped her cheeks pink. He caught the fragrance of her hair, a familiar fragrance that took him back, reviving old things better not revived. But she'd brought it all with her and faced him now, her vitality and strong spirit touching him and lifting his impulses.

"Have you come to sit on my porch again?" he asked lightly.

She tensed for an instant, then smiled and said firmly, "I think we should stay away from that, Bannon."

He knew she was right. "I see Sundance still remembered the trail." He brought over another rocker.

"We both did." She sank gratefully into it and lay her head back. "It was a wonderful surprise to find him in the corral. I thought you'd sold him."

Her arm trailed over the rocker's arm, the leather fringe on her suede jacket sleeve falling loose, her face and hair a soft-shining blur in the dark. But he didn't need to see her. He remembered how gently her lips lay together, how half serious and half amused her eyes would be.

"Nobody wanted to pay more than a killer's price for him. They thought he was too old. So I kept him." His cigar was out. He struck another match to it. "Laura rides him sometimes."

"Where is Laura?" She lifted her head and glanced back at the lighted windows behind them, an odd dread surfacing.

"She's spending the night in town with Sondra. The two of them were going shopping to buy Laura some winter school clothes. She's grown out of last year's."

Kit looked down at the motionless shape of her hands, keeping her expression composed. "It's good you're letting her spend time with a woman. A girl needs that."

"So I am beginning to notice."

She let an interval of silence run, then stole a glance at his face. It was in shadows, the lights from the windows showing only the uneven traverse angles of his face, the smoldering tip of his cigar a dull red glow in the night.

"You were doing some sober thinking when I rode up, weren't you?" she observed.

He stirred. "How would you know?"

"I know." She looked at the cigar between his fingers. Bannon only smoked one when he was caught up in heavy thought. "So well," she added in a small, fugitive murmur. "Too well."

If he heard her, he didn't comment, nor did he press for an explanation of her certainty. Instead he asked, "Did you get settled in at the house?"

"More or less." She had intended to lead the conversation around to the ranch. Now Bannon had provided the opening. "John Travis was impressed with Silverwood when he saw it. In fact, he said I could probably get ten million for it if I sold it."

"I wouldn't be surprised."

His ready agreement startled her. "But you told me it was worth a half million this morning."

"In the eyes of the Internal Revenue," he said in qualification.

"But if it's worth ten million, why would they let me value it for less?" She frowned in confusion.

"Under the special-use provision of the estate tax code, as long as you continue to manage and operate Silverwood as a ranch, you're allowed to use comparable operations as a basis for valuation rather than the land's appreciated value due to commercial developments in the surrounding area. It's a way of allowing family farms and ranches to pass on to the next generation. Otherwise, if you had to pay estate tax on ten million dollars, you would be forced to sell the ranch to come up with the money." He paused. "We discussed this on the phone several months ago."

"We did?"

"We did, about a week or two after the funeral."

Which probably explained why she didn't remember it, Kit thought. She'd been going on little more than sheer nerves at the time, spending ten and twelve hours a day on the *Winds of Destiny* set, then racing to the hospital to be with her mother while emotionally trying to cope with her father's death and the sudden and swift advancement of the multiple sclerosis in her mother, brought on—the doctors had suspected—by the emotional shock over the news of her ex-husband's death.

In that month following her father's death, she remembered speaking with Bannon two or three times about various matters concerning the will, the ranch, and the disposition of the estate. But during that same period, she'd also had endless consultations with her mother's doctors, meetings with Hatcher Brooks, an L.A. attorney who had helped her obtain a legal appointment to handle her mother's affairs, and visits to hospitals in the area with facilities for long-term, chronic care of patients with incapacitating diseases or injuries, seeking one she'd feel secure placing her mother in.

Under the circumstances, Kit wasn't surprised she had blanked out his technical explanation about the machinations of inheritance tax laws. Understanding such things herself hadn't been high on her list of priorities at the time—not when she had so many other, more pressing, concerns on her mind.

"So, what happens if I sell the ranch?"

"If you sell it within a certain period of time, you're liable for the estate tax on the difference. Without checking, I can't say if that's one year or two. Why? You told me you wanted to keep the ranch." The statement bordered on a challenge.

"I know I did. But I had no idea it was worth so much. Ten million dollars is a lot of money, Bannon."

He flipped the cigar into the night. "Nobody pays that much money for land unless they're confident they can make it back twice over." His voice turned cool. "They won't do that by ranching, Kit."

"No." She recognized that.

Bannon had never made a secret of his opposition to more development in the Roaring Fork Valley and the Elk Mountain Range. That opposition would be even stronger if it occurred on land adjoining Stone Creek Ranch. She understood that, and, to an extent, she agreed with him. Which made her own decision that much harder.

Door hinges squeaked a warning as Old Tom stepped onto the porch. "Bannon." His voice searched the shadows. "I heard voices. Are you talking to yourself out here?"

Welcoming the interruption, Kit pushed out of the rocker. "No. He's talking to me," she said cheerfully.

"Kit." He peered at her face in surprise, then noticed the

chestnut standing hip-locked at the bottom of the steps, and scowled. "A girl like you has got no business ramming around these mountains at night alone."

She laughed and planted a kiss on his cheek, feeling the rasp of a day's growth of whiskers. "You said the same thing to me when I was sixteen."

"Sixteen or sixty, it would still be the truth," he grumbled in an effort to disguise his pleasure at her kiss.

But his comment caused Kit a sharp twinge of sadness. She wouldn't be ramming around these mountains at night when she was sixty. There was no chance of it, not once she sold the ranch. Yet, there had been a time when she thought she'd grow old and happy in these very mountains.

"How come you two are sitting out here? Don't you know it's cold? Come on inside." He waved them both toward the door. "The coffee's hot and Sadie baked a chocolate cake. It's a little on the dry side but a scoop of ice cream'll fix that."

Kit glanced at the log ranch house that had been like a second home to her when she was growing up. Going in would just stir up more old memories, and that didn't seem wise.

"I'd better not," she said with a faint shake of her head. "I left Paula at the house by herself. If I'm gone much longer, she might start wondering if something happened to me."

"And she'd be right to worry, too. Ride home with her, Bannon," he ordered, just as he had all those years ago.

Kit protested automatically. "It isn't necessary. I—"

"Give up, Kit," Bannon said, his long shape making a black silhouette in the shadows. "It's an argument you won't win." She closed her mouth, knowing he was right. "Give me a minute to catch up the buckskin."

"Sure." She watched him go down the steps and head for the corral, striding with an easy, masculine gait.

"Might as well go give him a hand," Old Tom said. "That's what you always used to do."

"I know." But she took her time crossing to the barn, leading the chestnut. When she reached it, Bannon was cinching the saddle on the black-maned buckskin.

"Ready?" He threw her a look.

"Ready." Kit nodded.

They mounted and cantered out of the yard into the night, riding abreast along the wide dirt track of a ranch road and following it all the way up to the summer pastures. In silence, they crossed the dun yellow surface of the high meadows, lit by the pale light of a sickle moon.

At a far corner of the meadow, they struck the game trail and traveled single file along the narrow, steepening path. The strike of iron-shod hooves on rock and the clatter of stones rang across the night's stillness. Then they passed into the cathedral-like silence of the pines, where all was hushed and muted.

Beyond the pines, the trail turned and rose sharply into a rocky defile. As both horses labored to make the climb, the chestnut slipped and scrambled to regain solid footing. Bannon turned in the saddle to check on the others.

"Okay?"

"Yes."

"We'll rest where the trail widens up here."

"Right."

After another hundred yards, they broke out of the rocks and the ground leveled out for a short stretch. Bannon pulled the buckskin in and swung out of the saddle, catching the chestnut's reins as Kit dismounted.

"I forgot how rough the climb is coming back." She hooked the stirrup over the saddle horn and loosened the cinch strap, watching while Bannon ran an exploring hand down the chestnut's front legs.

"It's a hard climb for any horse at any age." He straightened and gave the gelding a pat, dropping the reins to let the ends trail the ground. "But you're okay, aren't you, Dance?"

Kit followed when Bannon moved away from the horses. "Just the same, I'm glad it's not much farther." They had stopped in the shadow of the ridge top. Silverwood lay on the other side of it.

"No, it's not much farther," he agreed idly and paused, facing the rugged body of land they'd just traveled over.

His shoulders made a black cut against the night; the brim

of his hat shadowed much of his face. Standing there, he reminded her of the land itself. He had its same rugged and enduring qualities, its deep silences and harsh beauty.

Then he turned, his gaze seeking hers, the moonlight touching his face, burned by wind and sun and marked by fine lines radiating out from the corners of his eyes—lines left by a lifetime of gazing into long distances and bright sunlight undimmed by city smog. His smile was a slash of white.

"This is the way it should be, Kit. A lot of riding. A little fun. Something to remember when it's all over."

"Yes," she said faintly, then again with gathering conviction. "Yes, it is."

He swung away, throwing a glance at the horses. "We might as well rest ourselves, too." He crossed to a gnarled tree and settled himself at the base of it, then patted the ground. "Sit down."

Kit toed a rock out of the way, then dropped down near him, and folded her legs beneath her. She trailed a gloved hand over the ground, then lifted some of the loose earth and let it sift through her fingers.

"No explanation, no apologies. That's the way you've always been," she remarked idly, thinking out loud.

"What else can anybody do?"

"Nothing, I suppose." She shrugged. "But I imagine it makes it hard for people to understand you sometimes."

"You never had any trouble figuring me out," Bannon recalled.

"Ah, but I have a special gift that way. I know you through and through," she declared, silently laughing with him, influenced by that undercurrent that had always buoyed them when they were together.

Shifting position, she stretched fully out on the ground and pillowed her head with her hands, staring at the star-flung sky. "Nothing ever changes, Bannon. Not the mountains or the moonlight. Not the things I want, or you want."

"What do you want?" He eyed her curiously.

She turned her head, so close to him that he could see the blue flakes of color in her eyes—and the dance of laughter in them. "Bannon," she said with mock reproval. "Never ask a woman's age, and never ask her what she wants."

Grinning, he looked up at the sky. "I know what I want. A slice of apple pie with a big chunk of cheddar cheese melted on top of it."

She sat up and caught back a laugh. "Bannon, do you remember that night we drove to Basalt in the rain? We stopped at that bar and ate pizza and played poker until the place closed and the owner threw us out. Lord, it was dark in the mountains that night."

"What ever happened to that blue dress?"

"You still remember it?" she murmured in a wondering tone, then wrapped her arms around her upraised knees and lowered her chin onto them. "It's packed away somewhere along with all the other things I outgrew and put away to forget—and never quite forgot." Turning her head slightly, she glanced at him. "Would you want to go back to those times, Bannon?"

He picked up a rock and idly rolled it in his hands. "No," he said. "I guess not."

She thought about that a moment, then sighed. "I guess I wouldn't either. We'd do the same things, make the same mistakes. Nothing changes."

With a touch of humor, Kit turned to smile at him, but the look on his face and in his eyes sent the smile away. There wasn't any haunting sadness in his eyes, no lurking shadows of regret; they were clear and dark-shining with wanting, just as they once had been when he looked at her.

Held by that look, she suddenly knew they were remembering the same things. She felt touched by those memories, dangerously stirred by them. The old closeness came back, the old, reckless, wild feelings came back to shake her. For one long, heady moment of time, she was shocked alive by the things his nearness did to her.

As the past rushed up, Bannon saw Kit as he had once seen her—a girl pushing him back with a pert and saucy reproach even as her eyes pulled him to her. He saw the dusting of freckles across her nose, the curve of her eyebrows, the smooth texture of her skin, faintly golden from the sun—and the reflection of himself in her pupils.

Rising swiftly, she stepped away from him, then turned back and lifted her chin. As her expression tightened against that flare of excitement, she pushed her hands behind her back—just as she had done in the old days when she'd been afraid of what was to come. An action he remembered so well.

"I think," she said, a little shakily, "it's time to go, Bannon."

"Right." He rolled to his feet and went to the horses, retightening the cinches.

He held the reins of the chestnut while Kit mounted. Once astride the buckskin, Bannon reined it toward the trail over the ridge. They set out on it again, single file with Bannon in the lead.

The porch light was burning, throwing its bright track past the steps when they rode out of the aspen grove. "Somebody's still leaving a light on for you," Bannon observed.

"Paula." Kit smiled. "I asked her to."

They rode past the house straight to the corral. Kit didn't object when Bannon stepped up to unsaddle the gelding. Somehow she couldn't seem to break the old routines, the old patterns. A sigh slipped from her. She wasn't sure where it came from, or even what it meant. She unbuckled the bridle and slid it off the chestnut as Bannon dragged the saddle from the horse's back.

She handed the bridle to him and waited in the corral while he carried the tack into the barn. Absently she stroked the buckskin's nose and lifted her gaze to the sparkle of stars in the sky. One fell, a brief white scratch in the indigo sky.

She heard Bannon's soft footsteps in the dirt, signaling his return. "It's a beautiful night. Hear the coyote?" She caught its faraway bark.

Bannon paused beside her. "He smells winter. So do I." He slanted a brief smile in her direction, then took up the buckskin's reins and started toward the house. Kit fell in step beside him. "Of course, winter doesn't mean the same thing to him as it does to me."

"No. To a rancher in the high country, winter means hauling hay, chopping ice, half-frozen feet, and numb legs," Kit recalled, then remembered something else that she thought she'd forgotten. "The only four seasons a rancher knows are before haying, during haying, after haying, and winter."

"You've got it." They had reached the house and Bannon stopped. He fiddled with the reins for an instant, his glance bouncing off of her. "I'll be going now." He moved to the buckskin's side and stepped a boot into the stirrup.

Kit watched him swing aboard, conscious of the awkwardness, the tension that had sprung between them. She lifted her chin a little higher and smiled. "Tell Old Tom I made it home safely again."

"I will." He touched a finger to his hat brim and touched a heel to the buckskin.

She stayed there a minute, watching him ride off into the trees, then turned and climbed the steps to the front door.

In the living room, Paula lazed on the sofa, plump pillows supporting her back, an open book propped on her knees. She looked up when Kit walked in, a flicker of surprise crossing her face.

"You are back. I thought I heard you ride out again."

"That was Bannon." Kit killed the porch light, then started pulling off her gloves.

Paula gave her one of her wise, faintly amused looks. "Oh," she said, managing to put a wealth of meaning in that single sound.

"Oh?" Kit replied with deliberate lightness as she tucked her gloves in the pockets of her fringed jacket and wandered into the living room. "What's that supposed to mean?"

"It means"—Paula closed the book and swung her legs off the sofa to sit up—"I saw the way you two looked at each other when you were dancing the other night. You'll never convince me that at some time he wasn't more than just a neighbor and an old friend."

"He was," Kit admitted easily. "In fact, I always believed we'd get married after he finished law school and I graduated from college. We were never actually engaged," she added in quick qualification. "It was just something that was understood." Or so she thought.

"Then you broke up," Paula guessed.

"Not really." With her jacket half unbuttoned, Kit sank down on the ottoman in front of her father's chair, folding her legs beneath her to sit Indian-style. She looked down and idly toyed with the fringe on her sleeve. It had been years since she'd talked about Bannon. Suddenly she felt the need to. "If we had, maybe it wouldn't have hurt so much when he married someone else."

"You mean he married someone else and you didn't find out about it until afterward?" The redhead frowned in surprise. "Was she someone he met in college, or what?"

Kit shook her head. "No. He met Diana here in Aspen during the winter carnival. I wasn't here. I'd flown to California to spend my winter break with my mother. We'd argued about that. Bannon wanted me to come home and be with him for part of it, but—I hadn't been with Mother for Christmas in five years and it didn't seem right to go all the way out there for only a few days. It wasn't a serious quarrel. He wasn't angry. Neither was I. It was just a disagreement. A silly, meaningless disagreement." She breathed in deeply and let it out in a sigh. "After I got back, I had a couple letters from him. Short ones that didn't say much. But I knew the class load he was carrying plus holding down a full-time job at the same time. Then Dad wrote me the first of March to tell me Bannon was married."

"Did he have to? Was she pregnant?"

"No. Bannon's daughter wasn't born until ten months later," she said. "She could have been mine. And that hurt, too." She paused and smiled ruefully, sadly. "If I could have found someone—anyone—that I really liked back then, I would have married him to hurt Bannon as much as he hurt me. That's how bad it was, how bad I felt." Her mouth curved in a sober, knowing line as she met Paula's gaze. "Bannon knows how much he hurt me. That's one of the things you see in his eyes when he looks at me."

"I suppose it is," Paula murmured thoughtfully.

Uncurling her legs, Kit rose from the ottoman, impelled into movement by a strange restlessness, a vague feeling of confusion and melancholy. She paused in front of the fireplace and buried her hands in the pockets of her jacket, fingers curling around the gloves.

"It's funny"—she stared at the blackened hearth—"but all I ever wanted was to marry Bannon and have babies, do some acting in the local theater here, then—later on—teach drama after the kids were in school." She glanced back at Paula. "I never thought about an acting career, or Hollywood. That wasn't part of my dreams for the future. Now look at me."

Paula nodded. "Life takes funny turns sometimes."

"You can say that again." Kit smiled and tried to shake off this crazy mood. "Anyway, all that with Bannon is in the past. I've finally gotten over him."

"Oh, Kit, don't you know about first love?" Paula chided. "You may grow out of it, but you never get over it."

The words struck true, leaving Kit without a response.

Bannon and his buckskin cruised through the stand of pines that grew on Silverwood property. Bannon could almost feel the alien qualities of the soil come up through the legs of his horse—and knew the moment they crossed onto Stone Creek Ranch even though there was no fence to mark the boundary. The quality of home soil was that real to him. He'd been born on it and raised on it. No matter the distance he traveled from it, the primitive pull of Stone Creek land was there.

He crested the ridge and sent his mount down the trail on the other side. Where it widened before the rocky defile, he reined the buckskin in briefly and glanced at the ground at the base of the tree, replaying the scene with Kit in his mind. One powerful flash, like heat, had touched them both, disturbing them in a manner they had both recognized. He relived it—as he had relived so many others like it with Kit.

Swinging away from the sight, he heeled the buckskin into the rocks and remembered those days when he and Kit had been young, headstrong, and totally absorbed in each other. Yet, in the space of two months, he'd married Diana and changed the course of his life.

Looking back, from the distance of ten years, he couldn't say what had been in his head or his heart then. He couldn't be sure anymore of the reasons for his sudden act. It could have been rooted in his quarrel with Kit, or in the magical torch parade and fireworks of the winter carnival, or in the eyes and lips of Diana when she'd looked at him.

Sometimes there was no explanation for the things a young man did. He'd left his youth behind that night, and he'd left Kit behind. Whatever his feelings for her had been, he'd thrown them away. He'd never spoken of that time to her, and he'd never seen an emotion in her eyes that told him how she felt.

All this was the past that bound him with its eternal regret for having failed. The marriage had been a mistake, as Diana had soon told him. Even though he recognized it as a mistake, he couldn't stop thinking that if he'd made a greater effort or had possessed a better insight into Diana's heart, he might have been able to make her feel differently. In his moments of deep loneliness and restless need, the old reproach of her eyes came back to make him feel that it was his fault.

14

John Travis sipped the Pinot Noir the wine steward at the Caribou Club had recommended. Kit sat across from him, a classic silk jersey sheath draping her upper body and discreetly hinting at the slender ripeness of her breasts. The fabric's forest green color brought out the blond of her hair and the deep blue of her eyes. Lowering his glass, he watched as she took a bite of her entrée and held the morsel of garlic-roasted chicken in her mouth, closing her eyes for a savoring, decadent moment, then chewing slowly and appreciatively.

"Delicious," she pronounced.

"Every time I watch you eat, I start envying the food." He set the wine down and reached for his own knife and fork.

"What on earth for?" she asked, sending him a bemused and curious look.

"Because you obviously enjoy the taste of it. Would you enjoy the taste of me as much?"

She picked up her wine goblet and provocatively met his glance over the rim of it. "That would all depend on how you taste."

"Why don't you take a bite sometime and find out?" he challenged.

"I just might do that." The corners of her mouth deepened in a smile of teasing promise.

Looking at her, he felt a hunger that had nothing to do with food, a hunger that was just as gnawing, but this was neither the time nor the place to satisfy it. "I'll hold you to that," he vowed.

"Somehow I knew you'd say that." Her smile grew more pronounced as Kit admitted to herself that she liked to play these man-woman word games with him. In their own innocent way, they could be very stimulating.

"You did, eh?" He sliced into his medium-rare steak.

"I did." She sipped at her wine, then let her glance drift over the mahogany-paneled room. "This is nice."

"I'm glad you approve," he said, then turned a cynical eye on the dining room of the exclusive, members-only club that attracted a mix of locals, superrich and supersocial, to its door. Since joining, John had discovered that anyone who frequented Spago's or Le Cirque would recognize half the people in the room. "The Caribou Club has been touted as Aspen's answer to Annabel's in London and Castel's in Paris. At least here, we can enjoy a quiet evening away from the tourists."

"You mean—away from the prying cameras and gawking fans shoving cocktail napkins and blank deposit slips at you, begging for autographs," Kit corrected, remembering other occasions when they'd dined at public restaurants in Los Angeles.

"Maybe I do."

"Well, you're right. Here, I don't feel like we're on display." Something she'd found unnerving on those occasions. But that wasn't a subject she wanted to pursue. "They've done a remarkable job of fixing this place up. I remember when this used to be the basement of a hardware store."

"Really?" he countered on a bored note.

"Don't sound so interested, John T.," Kit mocked.

"Shall I feign some enthusiasm?" He grinned.

"Don't bother. Tell me what you've been doing these past two days instead. How's Chip coming on those revisions you wanted?"

John responded with a mock grimace. "The way he's acting, you'd think he'd been told to molest his child. Ask me about the locations we've picked out instead."

"Okay. What about the locations you've picked out?" she repeated obediently and cut into her chicken, unleashing another waft of garlic-scented steam.

"A few were obvious—the pedestrian-mall area in downtown, the Silver Queen gondola, the opera house. We have verbal agreements on those. Abe has started getting all the terms and conditions worked out and the permission reduced to writing on those. As for your husband's house in the film, Chip turned thumbs down on every one Abe and Nolan had picked out. We went up and down every block in the West End before Chip saw one he wanted. It's a big, old rambling affair with turrets, Palladian windows, and enough gingerbread to satisfy even Chip. The owner took us through it. Every room we went in—especially the tower room—Chip said, 'This is it. This is my 'painted lady.' I have a feeling the owner was convinced he was on something.''

"Not Chip. Never Chip," Kit declared with a laughing shake of her head.

"Anyway, the owner is willing to let us film there—for a price. A very steep price. And he's insisting on a large deposit to cover damages.''

"Do you get the feeling he's heard about movie crews and directors like Chip who want to knock down a wall to get the shot they want?''

John responded to her twinkling look with a smile. "Could be." He took another sip of wine. "Do you remember the log cabin scene between Eden and McCord in the mountains and snow?''

"Where she finds out he's been hired by her late husband's family to prove she killed him—I remember." She nodded and forked another bite of chicken to her mouth. "Have you found it?''

"I think so. We spotted it from the helicopter this afternoon. It looks perfect. Nothing but mountains in all directions. No power lines. No man-made obstructions of any kind. There's a logging road that comes within about a quarter mile of it. Abe thinks we'll be able to use it to get the trunks and equipment up there. He's going to check it out tomorrow.''

"Where is it?" She sampled the caramelized onion on her plate.

"Not far from the Maroon Bells. It's a shelter that was built for skiers on one of the cross-country trails.''

"I'll bet I know which one you're talking about. It sits on the edge of some trees facing a broad meadow and there's a stream with a small waterfall about fifty feet from it. Is that it?''

"Sounds like it.''

"You're right—it would be perfect. Wait until you see it when it's all white with snow. It's gorgeous.'' She started to take another bite of chicken, then abruptly lowered her fork. "Wait. What about the interior scene? The cabin's too small. By the time you put the camera, lighting, and sound equipment in there, you and I will be cramped in a corner. I know Chip's a stickler for authenticity, but won't he have to find some other place for the interior?''

"He says no. He thinks he can shoot the scene through the window and hang lights in the rafters.''

As John launched into a long explanation of how Chip planned to shoot the scene in such limited space, his words opened a door to familiar scenes. In her mind, she could see the scene being shot, the clutter of crew and equipment outside, the miles of cable strung through the snow like long black umbilical cords, the camera at the window, the cinematographer stepping back to let Chip check the shot, the grips, the gaffers, the best boys busy making their final checks. She could feel the glare of the 4Ks in the rafters, see the mike boom just out of frame, makeup standing by with powder and gloss, the stylist with brush and spray. She could hear the A.D. call for "quiet on the set,'' the tech man verifying they had speed, the clapper falling on the first take, Chip asking for "action.''

It was all back—the clatter and confusion of moviemaking, the jargon, the tense moments of action, the explosions of temperament, the little intrigues off camera, the smell of bitter black coffee and the taste of stale Danish, the sometimes lengthy delays between takes, the excitement and the tedium, the tough technical nuts and bolts side behind the creativity and the talent. The pull of it stirred through her.

She hadn't worked on a set in weeks. Listening to John made her realize she missed it.

For their after-dinner coffee and drinks, they moved to the club's Great Room with its coffer-beamed ceiling and walls covered in British racing green, lined with western art. John's hand rode warmly on the small of Kit's back as he steered her through the room's cozy groupings of couches and chairs, plump and overstuffed in the best English tradition with Indian blankets for throws, an unquestionably eclectic decor.

Along the way, John acknowledged greetings from those he knew with a nod or a raised hand, but he didn't stop until they reached a couch along the far wall, slightly secluded from the rest. Among the paintings by Bierstadt, Remington, and Nesbit on the wall above it, Kit recognized a Remington that had been a favorite of her father's, and paused to admire it.

"Coffee, cognac, or both?" John asked.

Turning, she saw the butler in black tie waiting for her order. "Just cognac for me."

"The same," John told him, then took a seat on the couch by the arm and shook out a cigarette.

Kit curled on the cushion next to him, angling toward him. She watched him light his cigarette, her glance idly traveling over the aristocratic bones in his face that the camera loved so well. The soft light from the antler-based lamp on the end table accented the leanness of his features and turned his hair the color of dark mountain honey.

"By the way, I'm glad I agreed to have dinner with you tonight," she said.

He blew out the smoke in a quick stream and arched an eyebrow in challenge. "That's a backhanded compliment if I ever heard one. Inherent in that remark is the implication that you thought you might be sorry."

"If it was, I promise it was purely unintentional. I never had any doubt I'd enjoy being with you, but I didn't realize how much I needed the movie talk. These last couple of days at the ranch, going through my father's things''—so immersed in the past, she could have added—''I started to lose perspective of who I am and where I'm going.'' She took one of the glasses of cognac from the butler's tray. ''Tonight you reminded me.''

John lifted the remaining glass in a saluting gesture and added his own ending to her last remark. ''You're an actress shooting to the top.''

''Being swept along to the top, you mean,'' Kit corrected, smiling faintly. ''It's hard to believe, especially when I remember that all I ever wanted was to make a living at something I enjoyed.''

''Who are you kidding?'' John mocked. ''You're just like all the rest of us. There isn't anyone in this business who doesn't dream of hitting it big.''

She hadn't. She started to tell him that, but one look at his face warned her that he wouldn't believe her. If she tried to argue the point, he'd probably think she was protesting too much.

Kit took the middle ground and shrugged. ''Maybe not.''

God knows, she couldn't think of a single other actor who hadn't at some time talked about landing the role that would make them a star. She'd always dreamed about landing a role that challenged her in some new way, made her explore other emotions, other attitudes. Truthfully she'd always been glad she didn't feel that desperate need to succeed that others did. Why didn't she have that ambitious streak? Was there something wrong with her?

It was true she wanted the role of Eden. She wanted the role so bad she could taste it. But she wanted it because Eden was such a complex character, so different from any she'd ever played. That's why she wanted it, not for what it might do for her career.

But she didn't know how to make John understand or accept any of that. As long as she did, maybe that was all that mattered.

''To the debut film of Hollywood's newest star?'' John suggested in toast.

"To *White Lies*," Kit replied as their glasses touched with a melodic clink.

The cognac's smooth heat had barely touched her throat when a voice gushed, "Kit! I didn't see you sitting over here." She glanced up as Angie swooped down on them. John started to rise and she waved him back onto the couch. "Don't get up," she insisted and immediately perched on a corner of the cocktail table in front of them. "I won't even ask what you two are doing sitting over here by yourselves."

She grinned knowingly and Kit's smile became a little stiffer. "Angie. This is a surprise." Not a particularly pleasant one either. Certainly not as pleasant as she wished it could be.

"A bunch of us came in for drinks and a natter." Her hand drifted in the general direction of her party, one of possibly a dozen in the room. "I'd ask you to join us but—"

"Maybe another time," John inserted.

She winked at Kit. "I knew he'd say that. God, you are so lucky, Kit." She tapped her on the knee and gave her a look of mock envy. Kit felt her teeth grating together, but she managed to incline her head as if she agreed. "Look, I'm not going to stay. I know you two want to be alone to talk and . . . things," she added suggestively. "I just came over to remind you that we still have to get together for lunch. Give me a call and we'll set a date. Okay?"

"Sure." But Kit doubted she would. The idea of spending over an hour with Angie, being pumped about her allegedly torrid affair with John Travis and listening to all her sly innuendos—and always with the thought of what Angie might later say behind her back—was more than Kit wanted to endure.

She hadn't been able to forget that remark she'd overheard when Angie claimed that Kit had landed her starring role by sleeping with John. It had hurt. Not just because Angie had believed it, but because she'd wanted to believe it about Kit. She wanted to believe Hollywood had changed Kit and corrupted her.

As she watched Angie walk away, she felt as if she should be mourning the passing of a friend. The Angie she remem-

bered didn't exist anymore. This new Angie was a stranger.
She had changed. Kit knew she herself hadn't, not in the
ways that counted.

"Want to bet she'll ask you to meet her at Gordon's?"
John challenged, a heavy dose of irony in his smile.

"Why Gordon's?"

"That's where all the ladies who lunch go," he said and
downed a quick swallow of cognac, then set the glass on the
end table and stabbed out his cigarette. "Let's dance." He
caught her hand and pulled her off the couch. "It's darker on
the dance floor. It'll make it harder for our audience to watch
me nibbling on your neck."

"You have that feeling, too," she murmured sadly.

"In spades," he replied in a low, curt voice, then flashed
her one of his dangerously sexy smiles. "Want to give them
something for their avid little tongues to wag about?"

"I don't like that look in your eye, John T." Kit drew
back, eyeing him warily.

His hand snaked out and hooked her waist, hauling her
against him. In one quick, striding spin, he whirled her onto
the dance floor. Her gasping laugh of surprise turned into a
whoop as he bent her backward over his arm in a low dip that
had Kit grabbing for him.

When he held her there, she protested, laughter bubbling
through her voice. "John T., let me up."

"Kiss me, you vixen," he growled theatrically.

"Oh, God, if that's your best Errol Flynn impression—"
She never got a chance to finish the rest of it as his mouth
crushed hers in a kiss of mock passion that had her laughing
against it.

Still kissing her, he lifted her upright and the texture of the
kiss changed into something warm and evocative before he
drew back. "What do you think they'll make of that?" he
asked and began swaying to a Cole Porter tune.

"That you're crazy."

"Is it any wonder?" he countered. "I can't get you out of
my head."

"But you've got me in your arms." She drifted closer.

They danced through song after song, sometimes talking,

sometimes not, but always touching, even in the up-tempo numbers, mostly by ignoring the beat.

When the music turned slow and dreamy, John slowed their steps until they were doing little more than swaying in place. "By now, they've probably taken away our cognac."

"Probably." She closed her eyes as he rubbed the corner of his mouth along her cheek.

"We could go to the bar and get another."

"We could." She slid the tips of her fingers into the hair at his neck, idly playing with the fineness of it.

"We're going to be accused of monopolizing the dance floor if we keep this up."

"I don't care."

"Neither do I." He drew back a little bit and smoothed the hair from her face, something heavy and disturbed in his eyes. "But I think we'd better start talking. It's getting harder to be satisfied just holding you."

"So, what do you want to talk about?"

"Tell me what you've been doing these last two days," he suggested.

"Sorting through my father's things. Thinking. Remembering. Making decisions. Big and little ones."

"And what *big* decision have you made?" he mocked lightly.

She took a deep, long breath, then let it out. "To sell the ranch." Saying it made her realize how much she hated the thought of parting with it. Silverwood had always been there. A place to come back to. A home to come back to. But she had her mother to think of, and sentiment seemed a luxury she couldn't afford. So she tipped her head to the side, striving for a lighter tone. "Care to recommend a good real estate agency?"

"In my book, there's only one in Aspen with the kind of connections you'll need. Hudson Properties. Sondra Hudson owns it. Maybe you know her."

Sondra. Bannon's sister-in-law. "Yes, I know her." She brought her hands down to his shoulders, some of her pleasure going out of the moment. "Why don't we get that drink from the bar?"

His arms tightened for an instant, then he gave her a lop-sided smile. "Maybe we'd better."

He dropped a quick kiss on her lips, then curved an arm around her shoulders and guided her off the dance floor. There was a crowd at the massive, masculine bar, standing and chatting in groups, some in jeans and sweaters, others less casually dressed. As they approached the bar, a tall, slender woman in a dressed-for-success charcoal suit shifted out of someone's way, her smooth blond hair gleaming platinum pale in the club's soft lighting.

"Speak of the devil," John murmured near Kit's ear, then lifted his voice in greeting. "Sondra. Hello."

The woman turned, her glance falling on John in bland recognition, her lips curving to a coolly composed smile Kit was beginning to associate with her. "Hello, John. Did you come here to escape your hordes of adoring fans?"

"Kit and I just had dinner."

"How nice." Her glance flicked to Kit. "Hello again, Kit."

Was it her imagination or had Sondra's smile turned a notch cooler? Or did she simply want to find a reason to dislike the woman?

Kit smiled and nodded. "Sondra."

"I believe you know Warren Oakes from my agency. And this is Jess and April Barnes from Oklahoma." With a graceful lift of her hand, Sondra indicated the others in her group.

After an exchange of hellos and handshakes, John asked, "Would you believe Kit and I were just talking about you, Sondra?"

"Something good, I hope." She smiled as if she'd made a joke. But like most of the smiles Kit had observed, it didn't reach those calculating eyes.

"I'll leave that to you to decide," John replied. "Kit's decided to sell her ranch and she asked the name of a good realtor."

"You're selling your father's ranch?" Sondra looked at her with some surprise—as much as she ever showed. "Bannon never mentioned you were considering selling it."

"He doesn't know." Kit tipped her chin a little higher.

He will, darling, Sondra thought. He will. And he isn't going to like it, not one bit. Aloud, she said, "Naturally I'm familiar with the location of your property, but I really know little else about it."

"It's a stunning piece," John inserted. "Water, mountains, valley, trees."

"Sounds beautiful. Why don't I come out tomorrow and you can show me around, give me all the particulars?"

Kit wanted to say no, but that was an emotional reaction, not a logical one. It wasn't Sondra's fault her sister had married Bannon, and it was none of Kit's business if Sondra was now seeing Bannon. It was time she stopped letting such things color her judgments. This should be a business decision, based on Sondra's qualifications, and Sondra definitely had a reputation for being aggressive, innovative, and successful.

Still, Kit heard herself stalling. "A reporter from *People* magazine is coming in the morning to interview me. I'm not sure how long that will take."

"Actually late afternoon is best for me. Say, around three o'clock?"

Kit tried her best to ignore that trapped feeling, and smiled a little stiffly. "That sounds fine."

With that settled, Sondra turned to John. "By the way, I'm having a Halloween party the end of the month. A costume affair. I'd love to have you and Kit come if you're both still in town then."

"We'll make a point to be," he promised, then glanced sideways at Kit. "You've never been to a party until you've been to one of Sondra's."

"So I've heard."

"I'll drop you an invitation with the date and the time."

"Do that." John spotted an opening at the bar. "Excuse us."

"Of course. See you tomorrow," she added to Kit.

Kit nodded and gladly let John draw her along with him to the bar.

15

The day was bleak and dreary, marked with leaden skies and a stiff wind that ripped through the trees, unleashing a rain of falling leaves, a day that warned of autumn's end and winter's beginning, a day that depressed the spirits and added to the general gloom Kit was already feeling.

She geared the Jeep down and pointed it at the creek's ford, then eased up on the brake and let it roll down the sloping bank into shallow water, barely making a splash. The urge was strong to floor it and send high sprays of water shooting into the air, but Kit resisted it, doubting it would get rid of the wretchedness she felt.

When the Jeep climbed the opposite bank, Kit shifted gears again and shot a glance at her passenger. But Sondra was looking out the side window, her face averted, leaving Kit with a view of the back of her head and the equestrian-patterned Gucci scarf knotted behind her neck to keep her smoothly coiffed hair from being blown in disarray by the wind.

The ranch buildings were just ahead. The tour, requested by Sondra, of the areas accessible by Jeep was almost over. Sondra had been silent through most of it. Other than to verify the location of a boundary line or the source of the stream, she had said nothing.

Kit was just as glad. After her lengthy interview with the reporter from *People*, she felt drained. Interviews, she'd discovered, were work, not fun. Like giving a performance, she always had to be "on." There was always the pressure, the stress, to be interesting and charming, to make good copy, to skillfully turn aside questions that were too personal, that probed too deeply into her personal life, and, above all, to avoid the trap of "confessing all."

Unlike a performance, there was no feeling of satisfaction when it was over—only an empty kind of relief.

This tour of the ranch had done nothing to improve her mood. She clenched and unclenched her fingers on the steering wheel as she looked at the mountain peak that loomed behind the house. She wasn't sure how to describe what she was feeling. Guilt. Regret. Loss. Or a strange combination of all three.

Talking about selling the ranch had been one thing, but taking Sondra around had given a finality to the decision. She knew it was the most logical, practical, sensible thing to do under the circumstances. She also knew it was going to leave a hole in her life.

The Jeep bounced across the rough pasture and rolled through the open gate. From there, it was smooth riding to the house. Kit pulled up beside Sondra's Mercedes and threw the Jeep into park.

"That's it outside." She switched off the engine. "We can go through the house—"

"That won't be necessary." Sondra opened her door and stepped out.

Kit sat back in her seat, feeling as if she'd just been hit. The meaning of that remark couldn't have been clearer; Sondra believed a developer would buy the ranch and the house would be razed. Kit bit back a protest and told herself it was just a house; it was just a bunch of wood and paint and stone.

The wind whipped at her as she climbed out of the Jeep. It felt colder, keener somehow. Or maybe it was just the influence of her own bleak mood.

Sondra stood near the Jeep's front fender, the collar of her heavy black cashmere jacket turned up against the burrowing wind, her gloved hands tucked in its big square pockets as she surveyed the site, studying its possibilities. She scanned the aspen grove, ignoring its golden shower of leaves, then lifted her gaze to the high ridge behind it and followed its jagged line to its intersection with the lofty mountain that formed the apex of the triangular valley. She glanced at the ridge that jutted out from the other side, then brought her attention back to the ranch clearing.

A tiny furrow of concentration invaded the smoothness of her brow. Gradually it smoothed away as a picture began to form in her mind. She could visualize the ridges and mountainsides scored with ski runs, chair lifts marching up their slopes, a village at the base of it, sprinkled with ultraluxe lodges and condominiums, fashionable shops, trendy bars and upscale restaurants, and a residential area with extravagant homes—all very Swiss, very continental in flavor, like Aspen. Another Aspen.

She breathed in sharply at the thought—oh, God, that was it. Another Aspen.

"Would you like to go inside, get out of this wind and have a hot cup of coffee?" Kit suggested after several minutes had passed without Sondra budging from her spot.

The woman turned sharply as if she'd forgotten Kit was there. One look at her face and Kit immediately recognized the triumphant gleam in Sondra's eyes, a gleam that said, "I know how to handle this. I know how to make it work." There had been times when Kit had been gripped by the same feeling. It usually came after she had struggled over a scene, searching for the right way to interpret a line of dialogue, the right way to deliver it, the tone and expression she'd need to convey what her character was feeling and thinking. Then there'd be that flash of intuition and she'd know the answer.

Unlike Sondra, she wouldn't have held the triumph and the excitement in, letting it show only in her eyes. She would have given rein to the sudden exuberance—laughed and danced or spun around in gleeful abandon.

Just the same, she felt a new respect for Sondra, seeing her as a sharp, intelligent woman who knew her business.

"Have you thought about how much you want for the ranch?" Sondra asked, ignoring Kit's previous remark, that is, assuming she'd heard it.

"As much as I can get." If she had to sell, she saw no point in taking less than that.

The line of Sondra's lips curved slightly. "Then I suggest putting a price of twelve million on it. That will allow room for negotiation."

"All right."

"I assume your terms will be cash."

"Yes."

"In that case—if it's agreeable to you—I'll draw up a listing agreement for you to sign."

"Fine." She felt like Judas Iscariot; only instead of thirty pieces of silver, she'd be receiving twelve million. Inflation.

"Why don't you drop by my office tomorrow and I'll have it ready for you?" Sondra handed her a business card. "I'll need a legal description of the property, too. Bring it along if you have one. Otherwise I'm sure I can get it from Bannon."

"I'll bring a copy." Kit briefly fingered the card, emblazoned with the name Hudson Properties, then slipped it into her jacket pocket.

"I'll see you then." Sondra crossed to her car and slid behind the wheel.

As the Mercedes pulled away, Kit watched it leave, the wind tangling her long hair, lashing strands across her face. The leaden gray of the skies seemed to close around her. She turned and walked into the house.

With the cow dogs to aid them, a pair of riders held the herd in a loose bunch against a corner of the pasture, black-coated cattle on autumn brown grass under a dull gray sky. The last six hours had been spent cutting out the weak, the crippled, the inferior, and the young stock destined for market. With less than an hour's worth of light left in the day, the sorting was almost finished.

Bannon quietly walked the short-coupled bay into the herd, his flat-crowned Stetson pulled low on his head to frustrate the brisk wind. He ran a practiced and critical eye over the cattle shifting out of the gelding's path. Spotting a husky calf born that spring, an ideal candidate for the feeder market, he pointed the nose of the bay at the calf. Working calmly and patiently, they drove the calf to the outer fringes of the gather.

The instant the calf found itself cut off from the rest, it wheeled to rejoin them. Bannon sat low and deep in the saddle as the quick-footed bay turned back every attempt—sinking low, switching directions on a dime, and coming around with the agility of a cat.

When Bannon and the bay horse had the calf separated from the herd, Hec Rawlins and Dusty Travers rode in from the flanks and pushed the animal into the pen with the others destined for market. Again Bannon rode back into the herd to make another sweep.

It was out of necessity that he was present. His decision and his alone determined which of the animals would be sold. But it was sheer pleasure and a satisfaction he found in the actual work that had him actively participating in the sort. The physical demands it required, the long hours in the saddle, the biting wind, and the dreary day didn't diminish that.

Completing his turn through the herd, Bannon nodded to the outriders. "That's it."

One of them whistled to the dogs, then reined his horse away from the herd. At a trot, Bannon rode over to the pens. He spotted his father perched on a top rail, his shoulders hunched to the wind, his hands buried in his pockets, and his weather-beaten hat pulled low. Bannon swung the bay toward him and halted parallel to the fence. Old Tom had a cold and tired look. Bannon knew better than to suggest he go to the house where it was warm. His father was too stubborn to admit there were some things he didn't have the stamina to endure anymore—like long hours out in a blustery wind.

"Hec." Bannon motioned to his foreman inside the pen, calling him over. The Texan lifted his horse into a trot and crossed to the fence. "There's about a dozen of the young stock that are on the light side. Cut those and the older stock out. We'll throw them on some grain for a couple weeks and get some weight on them. All the rest, drive into the loading pens.''

The lanky rider acknowledged the instructions with a dip of his head, then backed his horse from the fence before wheeling it toward the penned cattle.

"The semis will be here in the morning to load up," Bannon said to his father. "We'll ship the others out in a couple weeks. If the prices hold, we should make out all right.''

Old Tom grunted in response. Bannon hadn't expected anything more. Ever since his father had handed over the reins to Stone Creek Ranch, he'd never commented on a decision Bannon made, withholding both approval and criticism. If Bannon asked his opinion, he gave it. If not, he kept his mouth shut.

"Any coffee at the house?" Bannon watched a trio of riders begin the final sort, satisfied that his instructions were being carried out.

"If there ain't, then Laura drank it all when she got home from school.''

"The boys will finish up here." Bannon dismounted, feeling the stretch of muscles stiff and tired after a day in the saddle. Yet the ache felt good. "Why don't you go pour us a cup while I take care of my horse?''

"Sounds good.'' Old Tom eased his body off the fence.

Bannon gathered up the reins and headed for the barn, leading the bay. Halfway across the yard, he caught the soft sound of feminine voices. A turn of his head and he saw Sondra walking toward him. Laura skipped at her side, bareheaded, her coat unbuttoned and flapping open to reveal the wool plaid skirt, white blouse, and red sweater vest she'd worn to school. He slowed his steps, watching the two of them for a moment. Laura was talking, quite earnestly, to Sondra, no doubt reciting the little things that had happened at school that day. Sondra's head was tipped down in an attitude of interest.

Seeing them together like that, Bannon was reminded again that there was a good deal of affection between those two.

He frowned, conscious of a resentment he couldn't control. Laura had a need he couldn't fulfill—a child's love for her mother. Sondra was fulfilling it. But it was a love that belonged to Diana, not Sondra.

He continued to the barn, tiredness and that familiar depression sweeping over him. Inside the shadowed barn, he looped the reins through a wall ring and hooked a stirrup over the saddle horn to slip the cinch strap from its keeper.

"Hi, Dad." Laura's bright voice came from behind him. "Aunt Sondra's here."

Bannon glanced over his shoulder at the two of them. "So I see."

"We were just coming out to watch you sort cattle. Are you done?" Separating from Sondra, Laura approached the bay horse.

"Yup." He tugged the strap free of the cinch ring as Laura stroked the bay's nose. "How about your homework?"

She wrinkled her nose a little. "Almost," she replied, then said to Sondra, "This is Mighty Mouse. We call him that 'cause he's not very big, but he's fast and quick. He's got cow sense, too. Dad says there's no better horse for working cattle in the whole state than Mighty Mouse."

"I'm sure he's right," Sondra murmured, staying well clear.

As Bannon pulled the saddle and blanket pad off the horse, Laura asked, "Are you going to put him in one of the stalls or turn him out in the corral?"

"The corral." With the saddle and blanket pad in one hand, he opened the tack-room door with the other.

"Can I do it?"

"May I?" Sondra corrected.

"*May* I, Dad?" she called out when he disappeared inside the tack room.

"Bring the bridle back and hang it up."

"I will."

One-handed, Bannon heaved the western saddle onto its rack. The soft plod of hooves came from the barn's alleyway, accompanied by the croon of Laura's voice. A movement in the doorway drew his glance. Sondra stood in the opening, a dark figure in her flat-heeled boots, charcoal slacks, and black jacket. Her face was the one pale thing about her, framed by the silk scarf that hooded her head and hid the silver-ash of her hair.

His glance briefly touched the smooth, classic lines of her features before he brought it back to the task at hand and turned the damp saddle pad woolly-side up, laying it across the saddle. "What brings you out this way?"

"I was in the neighborhood and thought I'd drop by. I spoke with Agnes this morning and she told me you wouldn't be in the office today."

"I had work to do here."

"So I gathered." She stepped out of the doorway as Bannon walked back.

"Is somebody interested in buying the old Johnson place?" he asked curiously, aware Sondra wouldn't have been in the neighborhood unless business was involved.

"Not that I've heard," she replied, then paused a beat. "Kit Masters asked me to come out."

"Kit?" Bannon halted, a frown of surprise narrowing his eyes.

Sondra saw it and lowered her glance, concealing any smugness from his probing eyes. "Yes, she's decided to sell the ranch and wants to list it with me."

"That isn't true." His voice was harsh, angry, with just a trace of uncertainty.

"It shocked me, too. When she asked, I almost refused. I knew you'd be upset. But—she's determined to sell, and if I don't take the listing, some other realtor will."

"I don't believe you," he snapped in accusation. "She would have said something to me. Kit wouldn't sell Silverwood."

"Don't take my word for it. Ask her."

"You're damned right I will." Bannon left Sondra standing there, long strides carrying him out of the barn and across the ranch yard.

Laura came running up. "Where's Dad going?" She turned a bewildered look on Sondra.

"To see Kit Masters, I suspect." A small smile edged the

corners of her mouth, the tiniest gleam of satisfaction lighting her eyes as Sondra watched Bannon climb into his pickup.

"He sounded mad."

Sondra didn't bother to deny that as the pickup roared off. "He just found out she's going to sell the ranch her father left her."

"She and Dad danced together at that party. Buffy showed me a picture of them in the newspaper. Dad said she was a friend."

"She used to be." Sondra seriously doubted that they would be much longer. Nothing could have pleased her more.

"The paper said she was an actress."

"Yes."

"Gramps says the people from Hollywood are full of themselves."

"People often make a fuss over them. I suppose it's only natural that all the attention would go to their heads and make them think they were better than others."

"I guess."

"Are you going to walk me to my car? I have to get back to town."

"Sure." Laura reached for her hand, clasping it firmly.

A shiny new automatic coffee maker filled the counter space to the left of the sink. Kit wandered to the other side and hopped up on the counter to sit with her legs dangling. Idly she plucked a carrot stick from the tray of raw vegetables Paula was arranging. She bit off the tip and chewed disinterestedly.

"Try some of this vegetable dip. It's delicious." Paula paused in her task to dip a broccoli floret in the dill-flavored sauce. "Even if I did make it myself." She popped the coated vegetable into her mouth.

"No thanks." Kit toyed with her carrot stick.

"Kit Masters—refusing a tasty tidbit? My, we are in a mood, aren't we?"

"Don't," Kit protested with a faint flash of irritability and jumped down from the counter, giving the rest of the carrot a toss into the wastebasket.

"It's the weather. It would give anybody the glums," Paula said, watching as Kit wandered over to a side window and plunged her hands in the pockets of her brown jeans.

"It's not that." She stared out the window at the premature dusk settling on the ridge top. "I think I'm just angry that I have to sell the ranch."

And it bothered her that she'd started thinking it was her mother's fault. It was unfair to blame her. It certainly hadn't been her mother's choice to have multiple sclerosis. Which only made Kit that much more ashamed of this vague, niggling resentment she felt. Maybe if they'd been closer—she cut off the thought and sighed.

"Personally, I vote for building a roaring fire in the fireplace and spending the entire evening in front of it, sipping hot toddies and grousing about life."

"Air it all out—and all that jazz," Kit said without turning from the window.

"Something like that. Did somebody just drive in? I thought I heard a car."

"I don't know. I can't see from here." She thought she heard the faint, muffled slam of a door and frowned. "I wonder who that could be. I'll check."

"I'll bet it's Chip. He and John probably had another fight over the script and he's come to cry on my shoulder. I wish he'd stop being such a damn prima donna," she muttered, then called after Kit. "Tell him I'll be right there."

Kit had taken one step into the living room when the front door burst open. "Bannon." She stopped in surprise.

He pushed the door shut with a backward shove of his hand, the glass panes rattling at the impact. Kit noticed two things simultaneously: one, he didn't take off his hat; Bannon always took off his hat the minute he set foot in a house; and two, the look on his face—that granite-hard impassivity printed from cheekbone to cheekbone, the kind of expression made by muscles tightly set.

"What are you doing here? What's wrong?" She frowned.

"I'm here to find out if it's true," he replied in a voice that was too quiet, too controlled.

"If what's true?"

"That you're selling the ranch."

"You've talked to Sondra," she guessed and wondered why she hadn't anticipated that.

"Then it is true." If anything, his expression grew harder.

"Yes. I was going to tell you—"

"When? Before or after the bulldozers showed up?" he challenged.

"Before, of course." She curled her fingers into the palms of her hand, trying to hold on to her temper. She hated his quiet anger, an anger that lost none of its impact despite the quietness of it. She wished he would curse or shout at her. She could have handled that better because she could have thrown it back. But Bannon never had fought fair.

"Why, Kit?" he demanded. "You told me you didn't want to sell it."

"I don't! But I have to. I need the money."

"The talk we had on my porch the other night—the minute you heard this ranch could be worth ten million, you started seeing dollar signs." His dark eyes were black with accusation. No, it was harsher than that. It was condemnation she saw in them. Condemnation mingled with disgust.

"I don't want the money for myself. I need it for my mother." She moved into the room, too upset, too angry, too agitated to stand in one spot the way Bannon did. "You have no idea how expensive it is to keep her in that hospital," she said tightly, hurling the words over a shoulder. "She doesn't have any health insurance and the annuity of thirty thousand dollars a year her aunt left her doesn't even begin to pay all the costs."

"There are programs," he began.

"She doesn't qualify for any of them because her yearly income is too high. I know. I've applied to all of them. I've filled out so many forms and applications for this agency or that program, I think I could do it in my sleep. I even had a lawyer in L.A. see if there wasn't some way we could break my aunt's will, stop the annuity so my mother could qualify. We can't."

"There are other ways. Maybe if you worked—"

"What do you think I've been doing?" She picked up one

of the sofa's pillows and threw it back down, barely—just barely—stopping herself from throwing it at him. "What do you think I'm doing here? Do you think I came for the fun of it? I'm here to work—to film a movie."

"So why the urgency to sell the ranch? From what I've read, it's a movie everyone predicts will make you a star."

"But I'm not one yet, am I?" Kit argued. "And I may never be one. Even if I did hit it big, would it last? Would I make enough to take care of my mother for the rest of her life? Sure, you hear about Tom Cruise or Harrison Ford getting ten or fifteen million dollars for a picture. But what did Meryl Streep get for her last one? Or Glen Close, or any other top female star? You can bet they were lucky to get a tenth of what a top male star would get. Then their agent gets a chunk out of that. Plus, there's a manager, publicist, and secretaries who have to be paid. Don't forget Uncle Sam wants his share, too. And what if it doesn't last beyond one picture? There's no such thing as security in this business. When you're hot, everybody wants you, and when you're ice, they won't even put you in their drinks." She gripped the back of the couch. "There are too many ifs—*if* I make it, *if* I earn enough, *if* I can stay on top for five years or more. I can't risk it. It's too big a gamble."

"But selling the ranch, Kit," Bannon protested tightly. "My God, your father must be turning over in his grave."

"That's not true. If he was alive, he'd be doing just what I'm doing so he could take care of Mother." That was her one consolation in all this, knowing he would endorse her decision. "Damn it, Bannon, you don't understand. Her bills already total close to one hundred thousand dollars. The doctors have told me she could live for another thirty years, but she's never going to get better. She's never going to be able to leave that hospital. The bills will never stop coming in. The way medical costs are constantly rising, the bills are just going to get bigger and bigger. I have to sell the ranch. It's the only way I can be sure there will be enough money to take care of her."

Bannon tipped his head down for a silent moment, then lifted it. "Why didn't you tell me all this before, Kit?"

"Because it didn't concern you. It's my responsibility and my problem."

"But if I'd known about it, maybe I could have gotten the state or one of the environmentalist groups to buy it for a wildlife preserve. Not for ten million, but for one maybe or—"

"It's not enough," she cut him off. "I'm sorry for not telling you of my decision, but I *am* selling the ranch—and I don't care whether you like it or not."

His expression took on that tight, closed-in look again. "That's about as plain as you can put it." He turned and walked out the door.

Kit stood behind the sofa, not moving, listening to his footsteps, the slam of the truck door, the growl of the engine. She wrapped her arms around her middle, hurting for herself—and for him.

16

Sunlight streamed through a break in the clouds and spilled over the liver-colored brick that paved Aspen's open mall. From the window of her private, second-story office, Sondra watched as Kit Masters stepped out of the agency's entrance, then paused to slip a folded copy of the listing agreement inside her purse. With a slight toss of her head, Kit shook back the loose mass of honey blond hair and moved off, angling across the square, briefly disappearing behind the diamond sparkle of the fountain's spray.

Idly Sondra ran her fingers up and down the top edge of the original copy of the agreement, then glanced at the signature on the bottom that so clearly spelled out Kit Masters's name. There was a faint, almost feline quality to the sober curve of her lips, one that matched the gleam in her eyes.

Both vanished the instant she heard the clink of crystal in the room. In a fluid turn, she faced away from the window. Warren stood in front of the lacquered Chinese cabinet, a decanter of Courvoisier in his hand.

A carefully bleached eyebrow lifted in cool censure. "Helping yourself to my private stock, Warren?"

"A minor celebration is in order." He smiled with easy confidence and splashed portions of brandy into two glasses.

"This morning we received a solid nibble on that commercial block from a group of Denver investors with beautifully deep pockets. Then this plum parcel is handed to us on a silver tray. Such good fortune should be toasted."

"There's time enough for that later." Sondra crossed to her desk. "We have work to do."

Warren considered arguing the point, then shrugged. "Suit yourself." He tossed down the contents of her glass, then picked up the second one and sauntered over to her desk. "By the way." He sat down in a black-lacquered chair and crossed a leg, smoothing the precise crease in his trousers. "Dr. Adams is coming to Aspen for the weekend. I plan on taking her out to dinner Saturday evening. At company expense, of course."

"Of course," Sondra echoed dryly, laying the listing aside and reaching for her initialed notepad.

"It's a shame I'm not a member of the Caribou Club. It would be the perfect place to take her." He swirled the liquor in his glass and watched the light play on its moving surface.

"Sell that commercial block to Dr. Adams and her group of investors and I'll include a year's membership in the club with your commission check as a bonus."

Warren raised his glass. "I'll drink to that."

"Then do it so we can get down to business." Her glance was cool and quick.

"What business is that?"

"Call Ernest Gruber and tell him to go out to the Masters ranch immediately. I want that property shot from every conceivable angle while there's still some autumn color left." She began committing to writing the mental list she had been making. "You can also tell him that I expect the finished pictures to look like something in a *National Geographic* spread. And I want it yesterday."

"That's going to cost you," he warned. "You won't get him to do this one for free."

"I know." She went on to the next item. "I want a video of the property with that same quality look. Contact Bluelake Productions and Silver Sky Video. Whichever one can give

me the fastest turnaround, I'll take. I'll need an aerial view
of the property, a topo map, and a plat by five o'clock this
afternoon.''

"Five?!" Frowning, Warren uncrossed his legs and sat up.

"No later than five-thirty. I'm meeting Austin James for
drinks at six.''

"Austin James, the land planner?''

"The same," she replied without looking up from her
notes.

"What are you seeing him for? What's this all about?''

"It's about another Aspen.''

"Another Aspen." Warren stared at her, his drink forgotten.

"Yes, Silverwood Ranch is the ideal setting for one," she
said, then paused, her head lifting slightly. "Silverwood,"
she repeated in a musing tone, then picked up the telephone
receiver and buzzed her secretary.

"Yes, Miss Hudson?''

"Check the atlas. See if there's a Silverwood, Colorado,
listed," Sondra instructed and promptly hung up. "What was
the name of the graphic artist we used on the Cottonwood
Condominium project, Warren? Sam—something, I think.''

"Sid Parrish.''

"Parrish." She nodded and marked that down. "Call him.
I want to see some of his ideas for the name Silverwood.''
Her glance lifted to Warren. "Don't you think you should
get started on all this?" she challenged.

He looked at her for another long second, then gulped
down the last of his brandy and stood up. "I just wish I knew
what 'all this' is.''

"A little homework, Warren. A little homework.'' She
smiled faintly, a determined light entering her eyes as she
silently vowed to be thoroughly armed when she approached
J. D. Lassiter this time.

With no particular destination in mind, Kit strolled down
Hunter Street, idly passing time while Paula was at the salon
getting her hair done. She refused to think about the copies

of the listing agreement in her purse. She'd made her decision and taken the necessary steps to carry it out; there was nothing left to think about.

The sun was out. The sky was beginning to clear. She had some free time on her hands and she was going to enjoy it.

Crossing Main Street, she turned left to wander past the Pitkin County Courthouse, an imposing red sandstone and brick structure built a century ago. As she approached the front steps, Bannon walked out of the building, carrying a briefcase and wearing a western-cut navy suit and tie with his usual cowboy boots and hat.

Bannon paused when he saw her, his features taking on a faintly grim set. Kit hesitated, too, remembering—as he no doubt was—their harsh exchange the day before. But she halted at the bottom of the steps, forcing a meeting.

"I'm glad I ran into you." She opened her purse and took out one of the copies of the agreement with Hudson Properties. "Since you're handling the estate, I thought you should have a copy of the listing agreement I just signed with Sondra. I was going to mail it, but I might as well give it to you now."

"Right." He slipped the copy into his inside jacket pocket.

Kit plunged on before he could walk away. "I was angry and upset yesterday. Bannon, I want you to know that it isn't that I *don't* care whether you like it that I'm selling the ranch. It's that I *can't* care. Please try to understand it wasn't a decision I made lightly. I know how you feel—"

"Do you?" he challenged quietly and looked away. "I wonder."

Conscious that her temper was dangerously close to the flashpoint again, Kit took a slow, calming breath and tried to respond in a reasonable tone. "I know you're against more development in the valley—"

Bannon cut her off again. "You're wrong. I'm not against *more* development in the valley. I'm against the *kind* of development that's designed exclusively for the rich. And you can bet that's exactly what will be built on your land. But that's not your problem, is it? You won't even be here . . . unless you use some of the money from the sale to buy yourself an expensive second home in Aspen so you can visit one or two times a year like the rest of your Hollywood friends do.''

He spoke without heat, but that didn't lessen the sting of his words. Kit struggled again with her temper.

"Bannon, please," she protested curtly. "I don't want to argue with you."

He held her gaze for a long second, then shook his head with a vague kind of weariness. "I'm not trying to argue with you, and I'm not trying to change your mind." He looked away and sighed. "I'm not even angry—just frustrated."

Glimpsing the tiredness and regret that shadowed his roughly planed features, Kit smiled faintly. "I believe you."

There was a glimmer of warmth in his brown eyes when he turned back to her. A heavyset man brushed past Bannon to climb the courthouse steps.

Bannon shifted out of the way and cupped a hand to her elbow. "Let's walk," he said and guided her to the corner. "Remember when we were in school back in the seventies and Aspen was faced with runaway growth from the skiing craze that swept through America after the Winter Olympics in Squaw Valley were televised? They tightened the zoning regulations to keep Aspen from turning into a condominium city. It worked, slowing growth to a crawl," Bannon recalled as they waited at the corner for the traffic light to change. "But it backfired, too. Restricting the amount of land to be developed, reducing the supply but not the demand, land prices soared. The harder something is to get, the more people seem to want it." The light turned green and Bannon stepped off the curb with Kit beside him. "That hasn't changed, Kit. If anything, it's gotten worse. In the last three years alone, land prices have doubled."

"It's unfortunate, but it's still better than the alternative. At least Aspen has been able to retain the character that attracted people here in the first place."

"Has it?" They walked up Mill Street, Aspen Mountain rising in front of them. "In case you haven't noticed, Aspen is fast becoming an opulent ghost town of multimillion-dollar mansions that get visited by the owners two or three times a year." He glanced sideways at her, something challenging in the look, but this time in a friendly way. "How many familiar faces have you seen since you've been back?"

"Not many," she admitted. "But I haven't been in town much either."

"That doesn't matter. You still won't see many. And every year they become fewer and fewer."

"People are always moving to new towns. It's a national trend."

"But their reasons aren't the same," Bannon insisted. "The director at the Aspen Art Museum recently resigned when she couldn't find a two-bedroom home in Aspen that rented for less than two thousand dollars a month."

Kit had no response to that. They walked a few more paces in silence. Then Bannon said, "I don't blame you for worrying about how you're going to take care of your mother. I worry, too. About raising my daughter in a town where there's so much subtle emphasis on material possessions, where the stores sell one-hundred-thousand-dollar fur coats." He waved a hand at the full-length sable displayed in the window of a furrier across the street. "Or boots that cost four thousand dollars, or sweaters for six hundred and up. Where other girls her age have their own television sets, compact disc players, and heated pools to swim in. High times, high style, high living—that isn't the kind of small-town environment you want to raise your child in."

"No," Kit agreed quietly, sobered by the thought that she had no children to raise, no cause for the same concern. She couldn't help thinking how different it might have been if Bannon hadn't married Diana. But there was no point dwelling on a past she couldn't change.

"Most of the people who work in Aspen can't afford to live here. Most of them don't even shop here. It's too expensive. Which makes it hard to get help. Several restaurants don't even open for lunch anymore. What's going to happen when all the volunteer firemen move someplace else?" he asked, grimly rhetorical, then sighed. "I do what I can, but it's never enough."

"Like the rooms above your office that you rent to the

school-teacher and that man you represented on a pro bono basis,'' Kit recalled, eyeing Bannon with a quiet pride.

He smiled ruefully. ''Sometimes I feel like the little Dutch boy with his thumb plugging the hole in the dike. A stopgap that stems the flow but doesn't correct the problem. There's no easy solution. There's too much money in this town and money changes the way people think. When you're poor, you look at things one way. When you've got a million dollars in your pocket, you look at things differently. The money won't let you do anything else.''

''I don't accept that.''

''It's true. If a man spent ten dollars and built a lemonade stand out of scrap lumber, then charged three dollars for a small glass, he'd be condemned for it. But if that same man spent five million dollars and built apartment units, then rented them for three thousand dollars a month, he'd be forgiven because of the amount of money involved—even though it's the same sin.''

''It isn't right.'' Even to her own ears, that sounded terribly naive.

''No, it isn't.'' Lifting his hand, Bannon glanced across the street. ''Do you remember Max Davis?''

''The tyrant of the boards? Are you kidding?'' Kit grinned, instantly recalling the big, ruddy-faced man who'd been the director of the first play she'd done with the local repertory company. ''No one could forget Max. Is he still around?''

''Still around, still involved with the theater company. In fact, they're in rehearsals for a new musical over at the Wheeler.'' He nodded in the direction of the red-sandstone building on the corner. The opera house was an Aspen landmark built over one hundred years ago, when silver was king. At three stories it was still the tallest building in Aspen. ''Want to drop in?''

''I'd love to.'' She broke out of her strolling pace and grabbed at his arm, drawing him along as she headed across the street with quickened strides.

The house lights were down, the only illumination coming from the work lights on the bare stage of the old and elegant opera house. Gravitating toward the stage, Kit moved quietly down the shadowed center aisle, her gaze riveted on the six dancers in practice tights and faded leotards working out a routine.

"Five, six, seven, eight!" the choreographer called out the count, his hands clapping the beat.

A piano banged out boisterous notes, the music filling the empty house as twelve feet hit the wooden floor in unison, six bodies moving and twisting as one, arms sweeping out on signal, heads tilting, legs lifting, feet slicing through the air. Kit slipped into the fifth row and sank into the second seat, leaving the one on the aisle for Bannon.

"Ball change before the kick," the choreographer shouted the reminder, hands clapping. "Good. Show me some hip in that turn. Make it sharper. You're dance-hall girls, not ballerinas."

Kit sat forward, absorbing the scene. The thud of feet on the boards resounded from the stage, the echo stirring. The dancers advanced, shoulders shunting at provocative angles, hands twitching imaginary skirts, the bawdy tune from the piano filling in the rest. Hair flopped onto sweatbands already soaked while sweat rolled. The smell was theater.

The music built to a close and stopped, the dancers frozen in their final poses, knees bent, arms outflung, chins pointed at shoulders, torsos heaving in labored breaths. Caught up in the magic, Kit wanted to applaud.

But the choreographer's voice stayed the impulse. "Again. From the top."

There were a few grimaces but not a single groan. That required energy, and energy, like breath, needed to be conserved. The dancers broke and moved to their starting positions.

Kit leaned back in the seat and whispered to Bannon. "Can't you just see it? Low-cut dresses in red satin trimmed with naughty black lace, feathery plumes in their hair, and garters flashing on black stockings, a saloon set behind them."

Glancing sideways at him, she saw the amused look in his

eyes—and she saw it fade, his eyes darkening with longing and something more. In the same second, she discovered his arm was draped across the back of her seat, the ends of his fingers lightly touching her arm. She didn't want to remember all the other times they'd sat close like this in darkened places, sometimes innocently, sometimes not. His gaze drifted to her lips and she felt that old ache come back, just as intense, just as heady as before.

His hand lifted as if to touch her. She caught the glint of his wedding band, the one Diana had placed on his ring finger, and looked back to the stage. Her heart seemed to knock against her ribs for an instant. Then Bannon was withdrawing his arm from her seat back, raising it over her head, and lowering it to the armrest between them.

Conscious of his profile sharply etched in her side vision, Kit stared instead at the stage's red-velvet curtain and the gilded and curved cornice above it. The brass rails on the ornately embellished side boxes flanking the stage gleamed softly, reflecting the glow of the work lights, as did the multiarmed, brass- and silver-trimmed chandelier overhead. But the graceful curve of the auditorium's balcony remained in deep shadows.

To break the heavy tension she felt, Kit said, "Mother used to bring me here a lot. I always thought it was the most beautiful place in the world—and that was before it had this last four-and-a-half-million-dollar facelift," she added, then went back to her original thought. "Before the lights went down and the curtain went up, I'd sit and imagine how grand it must have looked to the people who came a hundred years ago. I'd close my eyes and pretend I was there—silk and taffeta gowns rustling around me, perfumed handkerchiefs fluttering and scenting the air with myriad fragrances, my hands clutching a white-satin program," she murmured, letting her voice trail off. "Then the curtain would go up and I'd dream that someday I would be one of those actors on the stage."

"Maybe it'll happen yet."

"Maybe," she echoed with a touch of old wistfulness,

then mused, "When you think of all the years the Wheeler stood empty, boarded up after fires gutted the stage area, it's a miracle no one ever tore it down."

"I hate to count how many times Dad has told me about my grandfather's efforts to help put out those two fires," Bannon remarked, punctuating it with a silent, laughing breath.

"Endless, right?" Kit flashed him a smile, relieved that they had again made the transition back to an easy camaraderie and away from that dangerous tension, charged with past feelings.

"Endless," he confirmed, then nodded at a silhouetted figure slumped in one of the front-row seats. "That's Max sitting there, isn't it?"

"I think so." The burly shoulders, the challenging tilt of his head, and the bushy shock of hair looked familiar, but Kit couldn't see enough of his profile to be sure. Then he used the point of a finger to push his chin up higher, the distinctive gesture removing all doubt. "Yup, that's Max," she declared softly, watching the chin come down and the point of his finger press in the tip of his nose.

The music stopped. A crushing silence swept from the stage. "Good," the choreographer pronounced and signaled the dancers to take five. They scattered, grabbing up towels and mopping perspiration from their faces, necks, and shoulders as they sagged to the floor in casual heaps, flexing and unflexing legs, massaging calf muscles, and drooping in exhaustion. The choreographer, a slim, wiry man, turned to face the man slouched in the front-row seat. "What do you think?"

As Max Davis started to rouse himself, Kit spoke up impishly, "Looked good to me."

Max turned in his seat and glared into the shadowed house. "Who's out there?"

"One of the few people who ever had the nerve to talk back to you," Kit replied, rising as Bannon shifted into the aisle to let her pass.

When he saw her moving toward him, Max almost broke into a smile, then caught himself and glowered in mock menace. "You mean the only one stupid enough to sass the director, don't you, Kit Masters?"

"Let's just say I was green," she offered in compromise.

"You were green all right, and you had more talent than you knew what to do with," he declared, then wrapped her in a bear hug before pushing her back to take a good look. "But you're wrong about that routine. It drags."

"It won't—not once they're in costume, the orchestra's playing, and the props and set are in place," she retorted.

His gaze narrowed sharply. "Haven't you learned not to argue with the director?"

"Not when the director is you." She planted a quick kiss on his ruddy cheek, then breathed in the familiar scent of his after-shave. "The grandkids are still buying you English Leather for Father's Day, aren't they?"

"And my birthday and Christmas." He nodded, his mouth forming a wry smile. "I probably have a lifetime supply by now." He spotted Bannon behind her and jerked his head in his direction. "I see you're still keeping good company." He winked.

"Do you think so?" She pretended to give the matter serious thought.

"I know so," Max replied in a decisive voice and pushed a chunky hand at Bannon. "Good to see you again, Bannon."

"Same here, Max." He stepped up to briefly grip the man's hand, then leaned against the brass-railed divider that separated the seats from the orchestra pit.

"I haven't had a chance to thank you, Bannon, for all the lobbying you did to get some affordable housing in the area," Max said.

"I wasn't the only one."

"No, but you did some damned effective arm-twisting," Max replied, then glanced at Kit. "I'll bet he didn't tell you about that."

"No," she admitted. "He only mentioned that housing had become a problem."

"That's an understatement," Max declared. "Last winter, the repertory company had to cancel its season because they couldn't find housing for the actors."

"I didn't know." Kit frowned, surprised by the news. "Dad never mentioned it."

"Now you have an idea just how critical the shortage has become," Max stated. "A lot of people were shocked when the season was canceled, but at least it woke everybody up to the problem. Now the town's taken over some housing units to rent out cheap to teachers and employees. Unfortunately, there're still over two hundred names on a waiting list." He paused, a twinkle entering his eyes. "While we're on depressing subjects, remember Garth Turner?"

"Of course." She smiled, instantly recalling the actor she'd worked with so many years ago. "How's he doing? The last I heard he'd gone to New York."

"He's back. In fact, he's backstage."

"You're kidding," Kit protested in a mixture of surprise and delight.

Max cupped a hand to his mouth and shouted at the choreographer, "Hey, Chris. Holler at Garth and tell him there's someone out here to see him."

He waved an acknowledgment and exited stage left. Bannon straightened from the rail. "Sounds like you're going to be having a reunion, and I've got some calls to make," he said, glancing at his watch.

"Good to see you, Bannon." Max lifted a hand in farewell.

"You, too," Bannon replied, then nodded to Kit.

"See you," she managed to say an instant before Garth Turner burst onto the stage, followed by a half dozen other members of the cast, mostly young.

"Looks like Chris dropped your name," Max observed when he saw the others. "There's nothing that gets an actor's juices up quicker than having a star in the house."

"I can't believe I'm hearing that from you," Kit chided. "The first foot of film isn't in the can."

"But you've got what it takes to make it." He paused and ran a measuring eye over her. "You're still a little too soft, a little too trusting, but you'll toughen up."

She didn't like the sound of that, and tried to laugh it away. "You know me, Max. I have the proverbial heart of gold."

"So does a hard-boiled egg," he countered.

She was saved from coming up with a reply to that as Garth descended on her, catching her hand and swinging her around to face him. "As I live and breathe, it is Kit Masters in the flesh. And what gorgeous flesh it is, too." The little-boy deviltry in his eyes diluted the leer of his look.

She laughed, then sighed. "God, it's been ages, Garth."

"It has." His fingers briefly tightened their grip on her hands. "Did you come slumming or what?"

"*This* is hardly slumming." She lifted her gaze to the lush interior of the richly gilded opera house.

"True." He grinned, then turned to the group hovering in the background. "I want you to meet some of our illustrious cast."

Shy, eager, wary, self-conscious, hopeful, reserved—Kit saw one or more expressions reflected on the faces of the four actors and two actresses Garth introduced to her, confusing everything by including the names of the characters they were playing. She gave up any hope of keeping them straight and simply smiled and shook hands with each in turn.

"Garth told us he did some summer theater with you," the last one said, an older man in his fifties. "We all thought he was just bragging again."

"It's no brag; it's a fact," Kit insisted, smiling at the sandy-haired actor. "We had a lot of fun, too."

"Yeah, it was a regular barrel of laughs working with her," Garth declared in a tone that suggested otherwise. "Or have you forgotten the dirty trick you pulled?"

"Are you by any chance referring to the time I switched all the lines of dialogue you'd taped on various props?" she asked in mock innocence.

"You know damned well I am."

"You should have been there. It was hilarious," Kit said to the others. "Garth didn't have his lines down for this scene in the third act, so he'd written them out and taped them inside book covers, on the bottom of ashtrays, inside vases, everywhere. Somehow he managed to convince Max that he interpreted his character as being an inquisitive sort, always examining things."

"And Max bought it, too," Garth inserted, flashing Max

one of his boyish grins. "Then Kit discovered what I was doing and hung around after rehearsal and mixed them all up. The next day we were doing a final run-through before dress rehearsal."

"I'll never forget the panicked look on his face when he opened a book and realized it was the wrong line inside. He ad-libbed something and started moving all over the set, trying to find the right one."

"You did some dandy ad-libbing, too," he accused, then inserted in a falsetto voice, " 'Darling, what's the matter? Are you at a loss for words?' I could have cheerfully killed you."

"Only because Max chose that moment to unleash the ripest stream of expletives anyone had ever heard," Kit said in an aside to the others.

"You can bet I had those lines memorized before dress rehearsal," Garth added, smiling now at the memory.

"Doris McElroy was in that play, wasn't she? Where is she now? Do you know?"

"I think she got married and moved to . . . Texas, I think it was. Remember Bill Grimes? He's a news anchor at some little station in Nebraska." They spent a few minutes catching up on news of others they'd worked with that summer, then Garth remarked, "You're the only one of our old bunch that's made it into the big time."

Taking that as a cue, one of the actresses—the ingenue type—asked, "When's the filming going to start on your movie?"

"Not for a few more weeks yet. I don't think a date's been set."

"Will they be holding local auditions?"

"I don't know. I would think so."

"I hope you told them what a terrific pool of talent there is here," Garth said lightly, almost jokingly, but the look in his eyes was serious and hungry.

"John comes to Aspen a lot. I'm sure he knows." Kit smiled in understanding.

"The next time you see him, whisper my name in his

ear,'' Garth said. "I'm versatile. I can be anything—a ski instructor, maître d', concierge, a rich man, a poor man—''

"Yeah, you'd be good at that, Garth,'' one of the actors joshed.

"Can you imagine how it would look on my credits if I could list a John Travis film?'' a handsome and eager young actor declared, then raised clenched fists. "God, I'd kill for that.''

"Talk to them, Kit. Tell them they've got to use us.''

"You're wrong if you think I have any influence there.'' The whole scene was a repeat of a dozen other encounters she'd had with actor friends and acquaintances in L.A., all of them hitting on her, hoping she could get them a part in the movie, small or large, anything just as long as they had lines. It was a situation she found more awkward than irritating.

"I'll bet John Travis would disagree with that.'' The young actress gave her a knowing look.

"Yeah, Kit. You don't want to forget your old friends,'' Garth chided. "You've got your big break. Now help us get ours.''

Max cut in. "All right, let's break up this conversation and get back to work. In case you've forgotten, we're here to rehearse, not stand around all day talking.''

With a grin, Garth jerked his head at Max. "Still the slave driver.''

"I noticed.'' Kit smiled.

"Hey, Garth!'' one of the dancers called to him from the stage. "Is that pizza party still on at your place tonight?''

"You bet. We serve from five until ten. Come anytime, just bring your own beer or wine.''

The word pizza sparked an instant memory. "Does Jenny still make that fabulous pizza with pepperoni and olives and sausage?'' That summer ten years ago Kit had stuffed herself on his wife's pizza.

"Are you kidding? It's better than ever.''

"Impossible.'' She waited expectantly for an invitation.

"It's true,'' he insisted, then moved off with a wave. "See you around, Kit.''

"Right." She kept her smile in place, but it was a little forced.

As Garth walked away, she heard the young actress hiss at him, "Why didn't you invite her tonight?"

"Get real, Annie," Garth muttered out of the corner of his mouth. "Kit's moved into the big leagues. She'll be making the scene at Gordon's or Pinons or Syzygy tonight."

"Yeah, Annie," someone else chimed in. "She's too big to party with peons like us."

"I'm never going to be that way when I make it," the girl declared.

Kit wanted to tell her that maybe she wouldn't have a choice. First you have to be asked. Briefly she toyed with the idea of inviting herself to Garth's place, but she had the distinct feeling it wouldn't be the same. They wouldn't let it be the same.

She told Max good-bye and left to meet Paula.

17

Sunlight bounced off the chrome bumper of the white Range Rover parked in front of the house, the brilliant flare of light blinding Kit for a fraction of a second as she swung the Jeep into the ranch yard. Instinctively she threw up a shielding hand to block the glare, but the angle was broken by then.

"You have company," Paula observed from the passenger seat.

"It's John." She smiled for the first time since they'd left town as she saw him run lightly down the porch steps to meet them.

He opened the driver's door before she had the Jeep's engine switched off.

"Marvelous timing, John," Paula called across to him. "You can help us carry all my packages in."

"Somehow, in less than three hours, Paula managed to have her hair done *and* buy out half the stores in Aspen." Kit slung her purse strap over her shoulder and climbed out of the Jeep. "I don't know how she managed it."

"Practice, my dear Kit. Sheer practice." Paula stepped out and reached back to gather up one of a half dozen shopping bags.

"I'd help you with those, Paula," John said as he cupped his hands over the rounded points of Kit's hips, his gaze moving lazily and possessively over her. "But I'm afraid my hands are full right now."

"Is that a fact?" Kit spread her hands over the front of his heather gray sweater and tipped her head back.

"A most enjoyable fact." He rubbed his mouth over her lips, then came back to take them while his hands glided onto her back, applying enough pressure to align her body with his.

The softness was there, and that unique strength and pliancy only a woman's body possesses. Her lips were warm against his, almost exotic in flavor, seductive in their willingness to merge with his. She twined her hands around his neck, drawing him closer, her lips parting to invite the meeting and tangling of tongues.

He wanted her. He felt that need expand into more than a mere possession of her body. He wanted to absorb that energy, that verve, that sunny zest for life. He wanted to uncover again that passion that was behind all of it.

Kit pressed closer to him, seeking more contact with the hard warmth of his body, and savoring every sharp sensation. It made her feel warm and loved.

When he drew away, she settled more comfortably against him. "I needed that, John T.," she whispered and brushed her lips over the taut muscle in his neck.

"So did I." Turning, he rubbed the side of his jaw along her hair, breathing in the fragrance she wore that smelled as soft and subtle as an evening breeze. "Nolan and I have to fly back to L.A. and pull together a few things on that end. Throw some things in a suitcase and come with me."

She drew back. "How long will you be gone?"

"Four or five days. A week at the outside."

"It's tempting." She brushed a strand of burnished blond hair off his forehead. "But I have some interviews scheduled and—"

Paula's voice cut in, "I hate to interrupt this intimate little scene, but you're wanted on the phone, Kit."

"Who is it?" John kept his hands locked behind her back.

"Maury."

"Kit will call him back."

"Tell him I'll be right there." She reproved John with a look and reached back to pull at his wrists and separate his hands.

"Forget Maury," John said as Paula went back inside. "Come to L.A. with me. I want to introduce you to Sid Graham with—"

"No." She kissed him hard and quick to shut him up. "Subject closed. Now let me go so I can find out what he wants." With deliberate reluctance, he released her. Kit took a step toward the house, then stopped when he didn't follow her. "Aren't you coming in?"

"Nolan's waiting for me at the airport." He turned abruptly and walked to the Range Rover. "I'll call you."

He knew he sounded angry. Damn it, he was angry. Her blind loyalty to that Rose character was stupid. Noble but stupid. Why wouldn't she listen to him? He was trying to help. Why couldn't she see that?

He threw the vehicle into reverse and jammed his foot on the accelerator, spinning tires and spraying gravel as he wheeled out of the ranch yard onto the lane.

Watching the dust and gravel fly when he pulled out, Kit pushed a hand through her hair, suddenly tired, irritated, and tense all at the same time. She didn't understand what had happened to all the pleasure she'd felt moments ago. She sighed and climbed the porch steps. At the moment she didn't really care what Maury wanted.

"Why haven't you called me? You could check in with me once in a while. Let me know what's going on. How did the interview with *People* go?"

"Fine." Kit sat down on the arm of the sofa.

"What kind of questions did they ask? Did they say when the piece would run?"

"I didn't think to ask," she admitted.

"I'll find out. Now don't forget you've got that reporter from the Denver paper coming out on Saturday and some gal with the Aspen—"

"I've got it all marked down, Maury. We went over it before you left. Remember?"

"I remember. I'm just making sure you do. All this publicity is starting to pay off, Kit. I'm getting scripts sent to me every day for you to read. I've got a bundle here ready to go out to you today. Mark my words, Kit, I'll have another movie deal sewed up for you before you start shooting this one. People are talking about you in this town. The *right* people."

"That's wonderful." She smiled automatically and twisted the telephone cord round and round her finger.

"You don't sound enthused," Maury accused.

"I am." She let go of the cord, letting it spring away. "Come on, Maury, you of all people know how much I love acting." That part, at least, was true. It was the rest—the press, the prejudice, the pushing and pulling, the politics— that she didn't like.

"And you're a natural at it, too. I've been telling everybody that and they're finally listening. But I knew we'd do it. I've believed in you all along the way." He rattled on for a few more minutes, then ended with, "I expect you to call me and let me know how those interviews go—and what you think of the scripts after you read them."

"I will."

"Got to go. Some guy from Paramount is on the other line. Didn't I tell you I'd make you a star?" he said and hung up.

During the next few days Kit managed to stay busy. Deliberately. She didn't want idle time to think—or time to delve into the reasons why she didn't.

Cross-legged, she sat on the floor in front of the oak gun cabinet and dragged out the magazines stuffed on the shelves, mixed in with boxes of ammunition, gun cleaning equipment, oily rags, hunting knives, and an assortment of unrelated items like empty gum wrappers. She briefly wondered how her father had ever found anything in this chaos. But others had wondered the same thing when they saw her closets.

She tossed a three-year-old copy of *Outdoor Life* onto the growing pile of magazines beside her. A pair of dirty socks fell out from between the pages.

"I'll bet he never even missed them," she murmured and

moved them to the mound of musty rags, taking care not to breathe in too deeply.

"What did you say?" Paula lounged on the sofa, a beauty mask hardening on her face, her hair wrapped turban-style in a towel, one shapely knee poking through the folds of her turquoise satin robe. She ran an emery board over the tip of a nail while her knee swayed to the slow tempo of a bluesy jazz song on the tape deck.

Deciding the socks were better forgotten, Kit said instead, "I was thinking I should bundle these magazines up and take them to a recycling center—if there is one locally. It looks like Dad saved every magazine for the last three years."

"Is there anything worth looking at there?"

"Not unless you're into *Field and Stream* or *Hunter's Digest*." Kit smiled at the incongruous image in her mind of Paula Grant leafing through the pages of a hunting magazine.

"Hardly," she murmured in a voice as dry as the stiffening mask on her face.

"Did Chip say where he was taking you to dinner tonight?" She tugged at a magazine jammed in a corner and a whole stack tumbled out. She wrinkled her nose at the new mess and said grimly, "Probably Gordon's or Pinons." In the next second she was irritated with herself for remembering the restaurants Garth had mentioned.

"No." Someone knocked at the door, the series of sharp raps drawing a gasp from Paula and a panicked "Oh my God, someone's here." She flew off the sofa and dashed madly for the stairs, one hand holding the towel on her head and the other clutching the front of her robe closed.

Kit rolled to her feet and stepped over the scattered piles on the floor, then waited a beat to let Paula slip out of sight before crossing to the door.

The man on the porch turned when she opened it, a stranger somewhere in his late thirties, dressed in dark khaki slacks, sneakers, and a flannel-backed jacket. His mouth curved in what passed for a pleasant smile, but the sweep of his glance was definitely appraising and analytical.

"You're Kit Masters," he said.

She glanced past him at the rental car parked in front of

the house, then back to him. "I am, yes." She smiled politely, then noticed the spiral-bound notebook sticking out of his jacket pocket and a bulge that looked suspiciously like a tape recorder.

"I'm Clancy Phillips."

"You're a reporter, aren't you?" She had a feeling she was rapidly getting to the point where she could smell them.

"Free-lance." He nodded, his eyes watching her closely, no doubt filing away details—like her mussed hair and minimum of makeup.

"Did Maury send you?" Kit frowned, certain there was nothing in her notes about this.

"Maury Rose is your agent, isn't he?"

"Yes—"

"Look—if I've caught you at a bad time, I can come back."

"No, that's okay." She shook her head, preferring to get the interview over with. "It's just that either Maury didn't mention anything to me or I forgot you were coming today." She opened the door wider and stepped back. "Please come in. And please excuse the mess."

"No problem."

Within minutes, Kit was curled up in her father's favorite chair, the tape recorder on the table beside her, and Clancy Phillips opposite her on the sofa. The interview began typically enough with general questions about her background, then progressed to the subject of the movie—and John Travis.

"Care to comment on your affair with John Travis?" he asked with a taunting gleam in his eyes.

Kit laughed quite convincingly. "So now we're having an affair, are we?"

"A hot one, from what I've heard."

"Do you always believe what you hear?" she mocked lightly.

"You have been out with him numerous times. Surely you aren't trying to deny that?"

"Of course not," she replied and left it at that.

"Tell me, what's it like to date a male sex symbol?"

"John thinks of himself as an actor."

"He may, but half the female population in this country think he's a hunk. Didn't Robin Leach call him 'America's hottest sex-throb?' "

"I think he did." She was becoming irritated with this whole line of questioning, but she was too skilled to let it show. Play the role—that was the key to interviews.

"Does it bother you when you're out with him and other women flirt and make various attempts to get his attention?"

"Why should it?"

"A lot of women would be jealous."

"I'm not a lot of women. I'm me."

"Then that's not the cause of your fight, I take it."

"Our fight?" Kit repeated in a blank voice. "What fight?"

"Are you saying you and John Travis aren't having any problems? That you haven't been fighting?"

"That's exactly what I'm saying." She dropped the role. "What ever made you think we were?"

He shrugged vaguely. "You did fly out here with Travis, stayed in his house, then . . . abruptly moved out here. Now he's in L.A. and you're not."

For an instant, she was speechless, astounded that he could draw that conclusion from such a flimsy set of circumstances. "John has business in L.A. I have interviews scheduled here."

"You could have done them out there."

"Not all of them. Some were local." She knew she was dangerously close to losing her temper, and struggled to control it. "Can we move on?"

"Did you know Travis met with Kathleen Turner on this trip?"

"And?" She didn't bother to keep the ice out of her voice.

"She wants your part in the film."

"Is that supposed to surprise me, Mr. Phillips?" she countered. "The role of Eden is a dream part. There isn't an actress around who wouldn't kill to get it."

"What did you do to get it?" His implication was obvious.

"Really, Mr. Phillips, the casting-couch angle is as old as the hills," she said in disgust.

"The same thing has been said about prostitution."

"And both subjects have lost their shock value." Little alarm bells started going off in her head. "What publication did you say you were writing this for?"

"I didn't say."

"As a matter of fact, I don't think you actually said you scheduled this interview through Maury. Did you?"

"No."

"What publication is buying this story, Mr. Phillips? Or should I start naming off various tabloids?"

"The *National Informer* has expressed interest in the piece," he admitted.

"Providing you can come up with a sensational angle. Right?"

"I wouldn't say that." He smiled a little too smoothly.

"But you don't deny it either. This interview is over, Mr. Phillips." She switched off the tape recorder and pushed out of the chair. "Please leave."

"You're not being very cooperative."

"That's your interpretation." She picked up the tape recorder and carried it with her to the door. Turning, she pulled the door open and held out the recorder.

"The *National Informer* has an enormous circulation. You can reach an awful lot of people who've never heard of you." He made slow work out of putting his tablet and pen away and getting up. "You should think about that."

"I have—every time I've read some story in a tabloid that's full of twisted facts, quotes used out of context, and innuendos presented as facts. Sadly, too many people believe what they read." She swung the door a little wider. "Goodbye, Mr. Phillips."

"I always heard you were very easy to work with, Miss Masters." He strolled toward the door. "One little taste of success and you start getting temperamental."

She ignored his baiting. "Your recorder."

He took it, gave her a long considering look, and walked out. Kit closed the door with painstaking quietness. She heard his car start up and discovered that her jaw was clenched so tightly it hurt. She swung away and recrossed the room. He had gotten to her. Why had she let him? Maybe because she had this ugly feeling all this was just a taste of what was ahead.

She stared at the cluttered gun cabinet and the piles on the floor around it. For once it didn't work to tell herself to concentrate on something else. The little devils of discontent wouldn't leave her alone. She curled up in her father's chair and hugged her knees to her chest. She was still there when Paula came down two hours later, dressed for her dinner date with Chip in a bottle green evening suit of silk velvet.

"That interview certainly didn't take long." Paula clipped a faux jewel-studded drop earring to her lobe as she wandered into the living room.

"No, it didn't." Kit saw no point in going into detail.

Her glance flicked to the mess around the gun cabinet. "You haven't made much progress."

"I've been thinking."

She sent Kit a droll look and sank gracefully onto the sofa. "Careful. Too much thinking can lead a person to a bad end." She crossed a leg, silk whispering against silk.

"Maybe I've already come to a bad end," Kit replied with rare cynicism.

"Ah, but sin can be such a comfort once you get to know it, Kit," Paula declared. When her jesting remark failed to elicit a smile, her eyes sharpened on Kit. "What's bothering you?"

Her shoulders lifted and fell. "Things."

"That covers a rather broad spectrum."

A surge of restless energy carried Kit out of the chair and over to the fireplace. "It's just that—when I was simply another actress on a soap, things were different. I was Kit Masters. I could do what I pleased, say what I pleased, act as I pleased without my every word and action being scrutinized or criticized. I was a normal person. Now, people treat me like I'm not."

"Didn't you see that coming?" Paula asked gently.

"No," she said with a quick, agitated shake of her head. "I was so busy working, chasing parts I wanted that I never gave it a thought. Overnight I've become Kit Masters, a possible star, and everything's changed—everyone's changed. It's like they're suddenly all ready to believe the worst about me.''

"Are you by any chance thinking of John Travis?" Paula asked in a faint, dry drawl.

Kit swung away from the fireplace and released a humorless breath. "And all the talk that I got the part only because I'm sleeping with him, you mean? Truthfully I expected that kind of mudslinging in Hollywood. I expected the pettiness, the jealousy, the viciousness. I think I even understood. Maybe that's why it never bothered me. I knew mud washes off; it doesn't scar.''

"Then what is it?"

"It's the way other people have changed toward me. Strangers and people I've known nearly all my life. They believe that *I* have changed, that *I* think I'm too good for them now, that *I* couldn't possibly enjoy doing the same things anymore, that I've somehow become morally corrupt—'' She stopped, not wholly satisfied with what she'd said. "It isn't that they believe it. It's that they *want* to believe all those things about me.''

"And that surprises you?"

"From them, yes," Kit replied with unusual sharpness.

"It shouldn't." Paula smiled. "What makes you think your friends are any different from the people you know in Hollywood? What makes you think strangers are any different? Egos, jealousy, resentment—such things are hardly unique to Hollywood, Kit.''

"I suppose not," Kit agreed hesitantly.

"It's human nature to root for someone on their way up, then try to tear them down once they get there. It isn't that they resent your success. It's that your success reminds them of their failure. You've made it and they haven't. They can't stand the thought that it might mean you're better than they are. Out of self-defense, they have to believe that you did something illegal, unethical, or immoral to get there. It's nothing personal.'' She paused. "I'm not saying it's right or fair. It's reality.''

"I still don't like it." With arms tightly crossed, she walked to the window and stared at the dusk purpling the sky.

"No one does. But you can't let it matter. You can't let yourself care what they say." Paula's response was abruptly impatient. "If you're going to succeed—if you're going to be a star—you have to believe in yourself totally. You have to be selfish, at times even cruel and calculating, or they will tear you down. It's all part of the price of fame."

"But that's not me. That's not who I am."

"Poor Kit," Paula murmured in an amused tone. "It's hard to see innocence get its first shock. But you'll become hardened to it."

"Should I?"

"We won't go into that." Headlights flashed over the windows as a car pulled into the ranch yard. "That must be Chip." Rising, Paula slung a coat over her shoulders and crossed to the door. She paused with it partway open and glanced fondly at Kit. "Don't sit and brood over this tonight. You can't change it."

～～❧ 18 ❧～～

A fire crackled in the massive fireplace of river stone, its cheery light almost lost in the cavernous living room of the log ranch house. Bannon stood in front of the fire, watching yellow flames crawl over the bark of a new log, one booted foot on the raised hearth, a hand braced on the mantel. The faint, soft scratch of pen on paper told him Laura was still busy with her homework. There was a stir of movement in the big chair, followed by the click of teeth biting down on a pipe stem, then the drag of it being removed.

"The Gregorys are selling out, then." Old Tom tapped the dead ash out of the bowl.

"House, business, everything," Bannon confirmed. "His wife's tired of the fight, tired of being chained to the clothing store because they can't find any help. And, she doesn't think it will ever change."

"It's the old story," his father grunted. "The strong think they're strong and the weak think they're weak. They beat themselves by thinking so."

"I guess."

"I figure Silverwood will be the next to change hands." Old Tom scraped at the black char in his pipe with the wooden end of a match. "Be sad to see that."

Laura piped up. "I think it's horrible."

"Makes you mad, does it?" Old Tom eyed the girl seated at the small pine desk he'd built three decades ago for his son to use.

"Yes."

"Don't see the mountains getting mad, do you?"

"Of course not. Mountains don't get angry, Gramps," she said with a trace of disgust at such a foolish question.

"That's right. The mountains don't get angry or struggle or cry. If man does, it's of his own making and his own foolishness. This land knows that nothing man destroys will remain destroyed. Beside every fallen tree that man cuts, you'll find seedlings to replace it. Walk down any street and you'll find grass growing in the cracks. Man builds his houses, his towns, and his roads over it, and the land lets him, but the fertility is still there, underneath it all. When man steps aside, the land will reclaim what he left and erase all marks of it. Look at that old mine shaft and the brush taking over its tailings, covering up the tracks the miners left. That's the power of the land. Remember that."

"Gramps, you don't know a lot about pollution, do you?" She gave him a pitying look. "Acid rain has killed whole forests. Our entire environment is threatened by toxic wastes—"

He stopped her. "But the land will come back. Maybe not in your lifetime or even your grandchildren's, but the day will come. Man can destroy man, but he can't kill the land. When the last human has disappeared from the face of it, the land will still be here. The power of the land is endless, its fertility indestructible." He paused to suck on his empty pipe, testing its draw. "All this talk about ozone layers, polluting the water and the air, it isn't about man's fear of what he's doing to the land, but what he's doing to himself. Man doesn't want to protect the land; he wants to protect his own existence. Man knows, somewhere deep down inside, that the land will take care of itself just fine."

Bannon studied the thoughtful frown Laura wore, wondering how much she had absorbed of that. Abruptly she shrugged and turned back to her homework. "Just the same,

I think it's awful Silverwood is being sold. Aunt Sondra says someone will probably build a resort on it with ski runs and shops and restaurants and big homes.'' She wagged her pen, tapping the end of it against a cheek. "Buffy thinks that will be great. Maybe she's right. It would be close enough I could ride over on the weekends and Buffy and I could go skiing. She wants me to get a hot pink ski suit like hers so we'd match. She's got boots and everything to go with it. It's really sharp.''

The wistfulness, the hint of envy in her voice had Bannon turning back to the fire. Things. Clothes. Boots. Skis. Weekends spent playing. How could he tell her not to want the things her friends had? How could he make her understand that possessions weren't important, that they couldn't take the place of the things that made life worthwhile—like the bone-deep satisfaction of a day's work done well, the pleasure of shared laughter, and the enveloping warmth of love. They were needs of the spirit money could never fulfill. Without that fulfillment there was only loneliness. He knew that.

"I think I'll call it a night." The pipe clattered to its resting place in the rack. A second later, Old Tom heaved himself out of the chair. "This old body of mine seems to need more rest than it used to.''

Laura glanced up, sending him a quick smile. "Good night, Gramps.''

"Good night, chickapea." He called her by the nickname he always used in moments of deep fondness. His route to the stairs took him by the fireplace. He paused next to Bannon and lay a big, mottled hand on his shoulder, drawing his side-glance. "You can't fool me, boy," he said quietly. "It ain't the Gregorys selling out that's got your head down. It's knowing that when Silverwood's sold, the last tie is cut.''

His eyes, soft and sad with understanding, held Bannon's gaze for an instant longer, then Old Tom drew his hand back and continued to the stairs.

Kit's name hadn't been spoken, but it hadn't needed to be. Bannon listened to his father's footsteps on the stairs and gazed at the flickering yellow flames.

For a moment he remembered the scene on the ridge and

a little of that tumult came back to him. Her features and her mannerisms were clearly before him—the infectious warmth of her smile, the vivid blue color of her eyes in anger, the pride that strengthened her voice. She had an outward beauty and an outward grace, but more than that, Kit was rich in the way a woman should be rich, at times laughing and reckless, at times showing him the dark mysterious glow of a softer mood.

Remembering these things, Bannon felt an old rankling hunger that he knew would never grow less and never be satisfied. He stared at the fire, his head bowed and his eyes fixed on the past, so vivid yet so everlastingly over.

From the second floor came the faint creak of bedsprings, then the dull thud of boots landing on the wood floor. After more vague stirrings, there was only the soft hiss of the fire and the occasional rustling of notebook paper from the desk area. Bannon never changed his stance or broke his absorption in the flames. The clump of footsteps on the porch came to him distantly. A hand pounded three times on the front door before he roused himself and left the fireside.

He opened the door to a blast of cold night air. Kit stood poised on the threshold, a striped stocking cap pulled down around her ears, her hands clasped high on her chest as if she'd been blowing on them for warmth.

"Hi." A vapory cloud of breath escaped with the word. "Would you share your fire with a cold traveler?" Her lips were almost too stiff with cold to form the words. She huddled deep in her jacket, shuddering.

"You little fool." Bannon pulled her inside and shut the door. "Do you realize how cold it is out there?"

"Do I ever," she murmured, then shivered uncontrollably. "But it was just nicely nippy when I left the ranch. I forgot how fast temperatures can drop in the mountains."

"It's supposed to get below freezing tonight." He wanted to shake her but she was already doing that without his help.

"I think it's already there." Her nose was runny from the cold. She sniffled. "Dance threw a shoe. I had to walk him the last two miles. I unsaddled him and put him in the corral with your horses. Is that all right?"

"Fine." Belatedly he noticed the rifle case she hugged in front of her. "What's that for?"

"You." Her teeth were threatening to chatter now that the room's warmth had started to seep in. "It's Dad's favorite rifle. He'd want you to have it." She held it out to him. "He got his trophy buck with this. He always called the Remington his lucky rifle."

"I remember." Bannon ran a stroking hand over the length of the case, then met her eyes with a soft look. "I'll take care of it."

"I know." She smiled, a little more naturally this time, and automatically rubbed at her arms to stimulate circulation.

"Get out of that jacket and over by the fire," he said. "I'll see if we still have some coffee hot in the kitchen."

"Sounds good."

Her glance lingered on the view of his tapering back when he moved away from her. Turning into the room, she pulled off her stocking cap and shook her hair loose. The cheery fire beckoned and she headed for it, tugging off her cold leather gloves. She faltered in midstride when she saw the young girl at the desk coolly watching her. A young girl with Diana's eyes and Diana's hair and Diana's face. Kit told herself this was Bannon's daughter but it didn't seem to help.

"Hello, Laura." The small movement of her mouth barely passed for a smile.

"Hello." The response was slow and cool.

Kit searched for something else to say, but the girl eliminated the need by turning her back to Kit and bending over the schoolbooks on the desk. Her action unleashed a tide of relief so intense Kit was almost ashamed. She crossed quickly to the fireplace, putting more distance between herself and the girl. She stood facing the gently blazing logs, burying her cap and gloves in a pocket and shrugging out of the fringed jacket that had done so little to protect her from the mountain's plummeting temperatures.

When Bannon returned with the coffee, Laura got up from her chair. "I'm going to my room," she informed him and gathered up her school things.

"Have you finished your homework?" He felt the tension

and recalled the silence that had greeted him when he first returned to the room.

"I have a history chapter to read. I'll do it upstairs," she replied in a precise voice, her hands locked across her books.

"All right." The instant he nodded, Laura started for the stairs. "Laura." Bannon frowned. "Tell Miss Masters good night."

Turning, she looked at Kit. "Good night, Miss Masters."

"Good night, Laura."

Bannon had learned the shaded meanings in Laura's various degrees of silence and politeness. He recognized the odd restraint in his daughter, a veiled resentment toward Kit. Had he inadvertently transmitted it to her with his talk about the sale of Silverwood? Or was the cause rooted in something more feminine—like the presence of a strange woman in her home? He couldn't be sure.

He watched Laura climb the steps to her room before he went on to the stone fireplace. "Sorry." He flicked a glance at the stairs. "Laura isn't normally that unfriendly."

"It's all right." Kit wrapped both hands around the mug and raised it to her lips.

"I laced it with Jack Daniels," he warned an instant before the whiskey burn choked her throat.

She coughed to clear it, then said a little hoarsely, "Just what I needed—some antifreeze in the carburetor."

"That's what I thought." He returned her quick smile and lifted his mug to take a cautious drink of his own doctored coffee.

When she took another hasty sip, he noticed her hands clenched around the cup, the knuckles white from the pressure of her grip. Tension? It wasn't a word he normally associated with Kit.

"Where's Old Tom?"

"He's called it a night."

"Have you told him about my decision?"

"Yes."

"I suppose I'm in his black book." There was a rueful pull on her mouth.

"When I first told him, he may have written your name

down. I think he's erased it since then." He studied her a moment, perceptive enough to see that behind that brightness and light voice, something was troubling her. And he didn't think it was his father's reaction.

"Old Tom's always been remarkably patient."

"The land taught him that. It slows us all down. We can't go faster than it goes."

"True." She took the poker and stabbed at the logs, sending up a shower of sparks. "What about you? Are you still angry with me?" Her quick smiling glance indicated she wasn't too concerned about his answer either.

Still he gave it to her. "I was never angry with you, Kit. Only with your decision."

"Right." She put the poker back and wandered over to the floor lamp next to his father's chair. He wanted to tell her to come back by the fire and keep warm, but in this mood, Bannon knew she could never stand still.

"What's bothering you, Kit?"

"Is it so obvious?" A wryness tugged at her mouth as she trailed a finger over the lamp's brass stand, then lightly touched its shade before moving on.

"In you—yes."

She paused beside a Remington bronze. "When you come to a blind jump and you don't know what lies beyond it, what do you do, Bannon?"

He frowned at her question. "Jump it."

"As easy as that?"

"If you have to make the jump, why stop and think about it?"

"What if you can jump or stay behind?" She continued her circle of the room.

His eyes narrowed on her. "You're not the kind to refuse a jump, Kit."

She stopped, cocking her head to the side. "Are you so sure of that, Bannon?"

"You're a strong-willed woman, Kit."

"I'm not sure that's a compliment." She wandered over to the spinet and plunked an ivory key.

"It's the truth." Bannon sipped his coffee and continued

to watch her over the mug's rim, letting the silence between them build for a time. When she didn't break it, he finally asked, "What's this jump you have to take and can't see beyond?"

She briefly met his glance, then shrugged. "Fame—of a sort."

"Is it what you want?"

"Maybe." She sat down on the end of the piano bench.

Bannon stared grimly into his cup, a muscle flexing along his jaw. "Then jump." He bolted down a hefty swallow.

"That's a bit brutal," she replied with more energy than she'd used previously.

"Probably. But I think you made this decision years ago when you went to Hollywood." It was just as well that he remembered that. Kit had now joined the crowd that came to Aspen to party and play. Her decision to sell Silverwood proved that.

"If I did, I seem to be having second thoughts." She sighed and swiveled on the bench seat to face the keyboard.

"Second thoughts or stage fright? You always had a bad case of nerves before you went on," Bannon reminded her.

"Always," Kit admitted with a quick smile and began picking at the keys with one finger, plinking out the tune to "Twinkle, Twinkle, Little Star." "That's the first song your mother taught me to play. I used to enjoy coming over here for my piano lessons three times a week. Of course, it wasn't the piano lessons I liked—it was coming over here."

When she opened a music book and began to struggle through the song, Bannon drifted over to the piano, drawn by the familiar sight of her slim form bent over the keys, the light sliding across the honey gold surface of her hair, and the look of intense concentration on her face. She stumbled through the piece, wincing in amusement at her mistakes. Bannon smiled along with her.

Finished, she dropped her hands to her lap, her shoulders sagging. "I haven't touched a piano in years."

"It shows." Bannon rested an arm atop the piano, facing her.

"Thanks a lot." Kit reached up and sifted through the

music books until she found one for beginners. "This is more my speed." When she flubbed the third note, she threw up her hands. "That's it. I quit."

"You did that a lot, too," he said with a faint grin.

"And I did it for good when I discovered practice does not make perfect, it makes tedium." She closed the beginners book, then paused and smoothed a hand over the cover, her expression sobering a little. "Does Laura take lessons?"

He nodded. "She started this year. Her teacher thinks she has some real talent."

"That's more than I had. But I was always a better listener than a pianist." She looked up at him. "Do you still play?"

"When I have time."

"You have time now," she challenged and scooted to the far end of the piano bench, taking her coffee with her. "Come on. Play something for me."

Bannon hesitated a moment, then set his cup on top of the piano and slid onto the bench beside her. Strong, blunt-tipped fingers ran over the keys in an exploring riff. "Any requests?"

"Something soft. Something soothing."

Nodding, he thought a moment, then started to play. Kit listened, trying to recognize the selection. Beethoven. An adagio movement from one of his piano sonatas. She couldn't remember which one.

She detected a minor mistake and ignored it. What Bannon lacked in technique, he made up for in feeling. The single notes the fingers on his right hand picked out had a lost and lonely sound without any music from his left to fill them. Yet the notes kept trying to build hope, searching, rising, and falling back with a touch of despair only to rise again. A sound so lost, yet so determined. So in tune with her own feelings.

How well he knew her. How very, very well. Yet without really knowing her at all. She lifted her gaze from the work-roughened fingers moving so sensitively over the keys, and let it travel over his irregular features. Emotions she'd tried so hard to bury came filtering back.

He glanced at her, his dark eyes crinkling at the corners,

a half smile on his lips. Kit felt the quick lift of her heart and looked away, afraid it would show, afraid nothing had changed.

She covered her averted glance with a quick sip of whiskey-laced coffee. "Don't stop," she whispered and slid off the bench, not stopping until she had some distance from him.

Back by the fireplace, Kit settled into a brick red armchair, hooked the toe of her boot under its padded footstool to draw it closer, then propped her feet on it, knees bent. Thus relaxed, she let the music flow over and through her.

Darkness closed tight around the windows, but all was cozy and warm in the lodgelike living room. Rustic and solid, its log walls gleamed softly in the fire's mellow glow. The Indian rugs on the floor fit the room as comfortably as the spinet piano where Bannon played. Mostly classical pieces, mostly Beethoven.

Kit drank the last of the coffee and held the mug against her legs, her muscles loosening, her tension fading, her body warmed by the whiskey and the fire. Tilting her head back, she closed her eyes and simply listened.

With hardly a break to mark the transition, the music changed as Bannon switched from Beethoven to Bacharach and an airy, spritely tune filled the room. Kit laughed softly when she recognized the song "Raindrops Keep Fallin' on My Head." A choice that somehow seemed singularly appropriate as well. Crying wasn't for her, either.

"Checking to see if you were awake over there." His voice held an undertone of amusement.

"I'm awake," she assured.

He finished the chorus and held the last note, bringing the song to an end. She opened her eyes when she heard his footsteps cross the pine floor.

"More coffee?"

She held out her mug. "Lighter on the whiskey this time."

"Can't hold your liquor?" he taunted gently.

"Not tonight. The day's been too long—too full."

"I know the feeling." He took her mug and headed for the kitchen.

Kit turned her head toward the fire. It had faded to a few

flames flickering here and there among the glowing embers. Bannon came back within moments carrying the refilled mugs. He set Kit's on the table beside her chair. She glanced at the steam billowing off the coffee's surface and left it sit there to cool.

Leaving his mug on the mantelpiece, Bannon poked the fire to life and threw on another log from the wood box. He remained by the hearth, watching the leap of flames. A soft, inadvertent sigh of contentment slipped from Kit, drawing his glance.

"Tired?"

She shook her head. "Actually I feel two things—safe and secure. It's this house," she decided and let her eyes drift over the room's tall, log-beamed ceiling. "It's so solid and sturdy, nothing penetrates it. Not howling winter winds, not the rain, not the world's turmoils, nothing. They all pass by and this big old log house just stands here." A smile pulled at one corner of her mouth. "I suppose you think I'm being overly romantic."

"No." His gaze made the same slow journey over the sturdy log structure. "This ranch has survived a lot of storms and a lot of trouble. A good many people have lived out their whole lives on Stone Creek. That feeling is soaked into the house."

"It's soaking into me, too," she mused. "Here, in this house, nothing in the outside world seems very important anymore."

Bannon saw the tension that had gripped her earlier was gone. The languor of fatigue now showed itself in her heavy lids and the higher color of her cheeks. She sat purely relaxed in the chair, her body graceful and careless, the glow of her spirit shining in her eyes—unsettling him.

"Maybe that's why I liked coming here so much," she said thoughtfully. "Even when I was a young girl, I think I knew things weren't right between my parents. I must have sensed the invisible friction between them. Or maybe it was my mother's cold silences that made me uncomfortable at home. I'm not sure anymore. But this house became my haven, my center. In some strange way, it gave me the stability I needed to balance my father's laughter and my mother's silence, and my own confusion and guilt."

He eyed her curiously. "It's odd to hear you talk about stability."

Kit pushed the footstool back and stood up. "Without something to center me, my life would probably whirl out of control." She slipped the tips of her fingers inside the hip pockets of her jeans and wandered over to the hearth.

"What's your center now?"

"I'm not sure I have one," she admitted in a deliberately careless voice, realizing it had always been here, it had always been Stone Creek—until Bannon had snapped the link and she'd gone reeling off to L.A. "Maybe that's my problem." She shrugged as if it didn't matter.

She glanced sideways at him, meeting his slanted gaze. Again Kit felt caught by the strong undercurrent of things long ago said and done. She saw him draw back from it, then turn his head and lift it slightly.

Following the new track of his glance, she noticed the framed photograph, of his late wife, sitting on the mantelpiece only inches from his fingers. Years ago, she'd conceded Diana was very beautiful, possessed of a dark allure that men dreamed about. Kit tried desperately to hate the face in the photograph, but there was a vulnerable quality in it that made it impossible.

"You think about her a lot, don't you?" Kit broached the subject they had never discussed in all this time. Bannon didn't like it; she sensed that immediately.

"I think about a lot of things." He pulled his hand from the mantel and stood a little straighter, a little stiffer.

"You think of her," she persisted stubbornly. "At night. When you're tired. When you're lonely."

"Kit." Impatience riddled his voice.

Ignoring it, she regarded him critically, for a moment separating her own feelings and striving for objectivity. He was a solid man, strong and physically alive, a man in his prime. He had a man's thoughts and a man's desires. The memory of his late wife, as clear as it might be to him and as near as it might be, wasn't enough. A pale shadow couldn't satisfy him.

"You should get married, Bannon."

He looked at her, surprise and anger in his expression. "I think that's my business." He clipped out the words, making it plain he didn't regard it as a subject for discussion.

"When has that ever stopped me from giving you my opinion?" They both knew the answer was "never." "You know I'm speaking the truth. Laura is getting to the age where she'll want a mother to talk to as she grows up." Kit recalled too well how many times she'd gone to her own mother with questions—and been given pamphlets to read. Facts hadn't helped her to understand her feelings.

"I know that," he said in the same brusque tone.

"Then do something about it," she insisted, then flicked a hand at Diana's picture. "That door is closed. You've got to stop watching it as if someday it'll open again. You've got to stop looking back. For a man like you, Bannon, an old lavender-and-lace memory is wrong." She believed it and she said it in a strong, even voice.

"Stop it, Kit." His temper flared as he swung to her, catching her by the arms. "Stop rummaging through me like this."

The contact was a mistake. Bannon knew it the instant he felt the firmness of her flesh beneath his hands. He saw in her eyes that she knew it, too. But it was too late. He felt that old pressure drawing him to her lips.

His vision was like the lens of a camera narrowing down until he saw only the full swell of her lips and their increasing heaviness. The pressure of his hands grew greater, pulling her in. His mouth covered hers, raw with need and rough with a trace of anger, seeking to bury the pain and the regret.

Kit strained into it, needing it, wanting it, her heart catching at the discovery that nothing had changed. It was there—the same wild sweetness, the same immense shock, the same feeling of a deep need satisfied. There was a feeling in her of richness, of fullness, of happiness.

He pulled away. For an instant, his callused hand cupped

her cheek with almost loving gentleness. His dark eyes raced over her face with a look in them that had Kit swaying back. He checked the movement, then stepped back and turned away, but not before Kit had glimpsed the shadow that had passed over his face—that pale shadow of Diana.

For an instant, everything inside her went still, the pain sharp and intense. The sting of tears was at the back of her eyes. She kept them there. Pride was a shallow thing, but it was all she had.

"Kit—" Bannon began in a voice that was much too serious and much too loaded.

"Let's just say our trip down memory lane went a little farther than either of us wanted and leave it at that, Bannon," Kit suggested calmly but firmly. "It's time I went home. Good night."

She grabbed up her jacket and headed for the door. Halfway to it, she stopped and swore, then gave up and laughed dryly at her foolish theatrics. "So much for a dramatic exit." Turning, she looked at Bannon. "Can I beg a lift? I forgot, my transportation is broken down in your corral."

As the humor of it touched him, too, the troubled light left his eyes and a slow smile touched his mouth. "Give me a minute to let Laura know where I'm going."

"Sure. I'll be outside."

As Bannon climbed the stairs to his daughter's room, Kit shrugged into her jacket and pulled on her stocking cap and gloves. She stepped out into the night's sharp cold, almost welcoming its chilling blast, and crossed the porch to wait at the top of the steps.

The moon hung halfway up the sky, the yellow of its rising gone and its face turned to scarred white ice. It was a winter moon. Gazing at it, Kit murmured softly to herself, "It seems we're both haunted by ghosts from the past, Bannon. The only difference is—yours is dead and mine is living."

The front door opened behind her, the sound sending Kit down the steps before Bannon could join her. The drive from Stone Creek to Silverwood was a short one, but she had a feeling it would seem very long tonight.

~~≈~ 19 ~≈~~

O n Red Mountain, the living-room lights in Sondra Hudson's slopeside home flicked off one by one. The English-born domestic, Emily Boggs, switched off the last lamp and paused to admire the glitter of Aspen's lights now clearly visible beyond the room's sweep of glass. A smug, self-satisfied smile briefly curved her lips and smoothed the fine age lines at the edges of them when she thought how impressed—how envious—her sister from Cornwall would be when she came to visit in January.

Touching the gilded back of a Hepplewhite chair, Emily Boggs decided that she and her sister would sit here, sip their sherry, and nibble on some delectable morsels from her employer's well-stocked kitchen while they watched the torch parade and fireworks spill over the mountain across the valley. Her smile strengthened with an awareness that there were very definite advantages to being a live-in domestic other than the handsome salary she was paid, especially when one had a craving for rich surroundings and neither the brains nor the beauty to acquire them oneself. There were also responsibilities, she recalled with a sigh and turned.

Her sensible, soft-soled shoes made almost no sound as she crossed the living room's black marble floor, the rubbing swish of legs encased in support hose whispering through the silence, accompanied by the faint rustle of her polyester uniform. She passed into the hallway and followed it to the master suite.

The door stood open, light bathing every corner of the black, red, and gold room. Emily Boggs paused in the opening, her lips thinning at the sight of her employer ensconced in the center of the queensized bed, papers and drawings spread all over the red and gold satin spread. With that absolutely gorgeous glass-and-marble-walled study just down the hall, she would never understand why her employer invariably brought her work to the bedroom. Beds were for sleeping or sharing with a man, not for using as a worktable. Although she didn't know why that surprised her. Her employer practically lived in the bedroom. The rest of the house could slide down the mountain for all the time she spent in it—unless she was having a party or her young niece came or Bannon was here.

Bannon. Within months after coming to work for Sondra Hudson, Emily Boggs had realized that the woman was out to get her dead sister's husband for her own. In all the seven years Emily had worked for her, that had never changed. If anything, failure to get him beyond her bed to the altar had made Sondra more determined to have him.

Something about that always reminded Emily of her baby brother, who had gotten hooked on heroin years ago. The doctors had given him another drug to get him off it. It hadn't worked. Nothing would satisfy him but the heroin. That addiction had finally killed Teddy.

The remembrance of his death automatically had Emily offering up a silent prayer for his poor soul. Then she shifted slightly and waited for her employer to look up from the notes she was making, never doubting for a moment that Sondra Hudson knew she was there. In any case, she wasn't about to invite the sharp slash of the woman's tongue by disturbing her concentration. She'd made that mistake once before, and learned from it.

In the best British tradition, Emily Boggs stood rigidly in place and silently regarded her employer, sitting in the middle of the bed, all sleek and elegant in her black satin kimono and silver blond hair.

"What is it you want, Miss Boggs?" Sondra Hudson looked up, but not at her. Instead she directed her gaze at the black lacquer-and-brass armoire that housed an entertainment center. Belatedly, Emily noticed the television was on although no sound came from it.

"Would you like me to take your tray away now, mum?" she inquired, thickening the accent that had helped her get fifty dollars more per week than was standard in Aspen.

"Yes." Sondra continued to scrutinize the stunning mountain-scapes and autumn images on the screen.

Advancing into the room, Emily crossed to the Oriental chest that served as a nightstand. Atop it was the meal she'd prepared nearly two hours earlier. Inroads had been made on the Italian shrimp salad with oranges and herbed orzo, but the chocolate-walnut torte had only one bite taken from it. She stared at the rich dessert, recalling the delicious taste of it she'd had earlier when she'd cleaned off the knife and licked the crumbs from her fingers.

"Shall I leave the torte? You've barely touched it, mum."

"I don't want it."

"Yes, mum." Emily Boggs picked up the tray, already thinking that a cup of tea would go nicely with the torte. She certainly wasn't about to throw it away.

"CeeCee Hunt will be by around ten tomorrow morning," Sondra informed her without taking her eyes from the screen. "He needs to recheck some measurements in the living room. Something to do with ceiling clearance for some decoration he has in mind for the Halloween party. He might bring someone with him. I'm not sure, but let them in."

"As you wish, mum." She crossed silently to the door, tray in hand, then paused. "Will you require anything else this evening?"

"Some coffee."

Emily suppressed a sigh. "The Colombian blend or—"

"That will be fine."

As the housekeeper departed, the television screen flickered and went to a fuzzy gray, signaling the end of the tape. Sondra picked up the VCR's remote control, stopped the tape and pressed the rewind button, then glanced through her notes. A few minor edits and the tape would be ready for Lassiter to view. She glanced down at the land plans and the accompanying sketches for the proposed development she called Silverwood. Nothing really major there either. The financial projections for the development were already finished. Which meant she should have everything ready to present to Lassiter by the end of the week.

There was no way he could reject this property, not once he saw the profit figures. The thought of the way his eyes would dilate when he saw the numbers had Sondra lying back against the bed's gilded headboard and raising her hands above her head in a feline stretch, a throaty little laugh of anticipation bubbling out. It was going to be sweet, the sweetest sight she'd ever seen. She caught up one of the embroidered throw pillows and hugged its feathery plumpness over her stomach.

The soft burr of the telephone intruded on her extremely satisfying reverie. Sighing, she reached out a hand and plucked the receiver from its cradle without shifting from her reclining position.

"Hello?" She nestled the receiver against her ear.

"Sondra. It's Warren."

"Warren—" She started to mention that she'd just reviewed the videotape, but he cut her off.

"Has your boyfriend told you what he's up to?"

"Bannon?" She frowned in bewilderment. "What are you talking about?"

"He's been burning up the telephone lines this past week, calling every major environmental group and foundation in the country, and pitching them on the idea of buying the Masters ranch."

"What?" Sondra sat up, still clutching the pillow.

"He didn't mention that to you, did he?"

"No." But it sounded exactly like something he would do. "Not that it matters. All those groups move with the speed of an arthritic snail, and few of them could come even close to meeting the asking price. I'll have it sold long before he gets a 'maybe' out of any of them.''

"You're probably right.''

"I know I am." But why hadn't Bannon mentioned any of this? Why hadn't he asked her to help? That bothered her a great deal more than his actions. "Is that all you wanted, Warren?"

"Yes—"

"Then I'll see you in the morning." She broke the connection, then immediately listened for a dial tone and called Bannon at the ranch.

After the fourth ring, Laura answered. "Stone Creek Ranch."

Sondra stifled an initial surge of irritation and said pleasantly, "Laura, I thought you'd be in bed by now. Haven't you finished your schoolwork yet?"

"I've just got a couple more pages to read in my history book."

"Well, I won't keep you from it. Let me speak to your father."

"He isn't here."

"He isn't?"

"No. He left to take *her* home." Laura stressed the word with whiny sarcasm.

Sondra knew intuitively whom she meant. "Kit Masters was there tonight? What did she want?"

"Who knows?" she grumbled. "I went up to my room. But I heard her ask him to play the piano for her. 'Something soft and soothing,' she said."

"Did he?" Her mouth was fixed in a taut curve, her fingers curling even deeper into the pillow on her lap.

"Yeah, a lot of dreamy Beethoven stuff. It was sickening."

"I can imagine," Sondra responded with a distasteful murmur.

"Did you want me to leave a note for Dad to call you when he gets home?"

"No. I'll—I'll talk to him tomorrow."

"He'll be sorry he missed you."

"Good night, Laura," she said in a very tightly controlled voice and hung up.

Leaving her own tea to steep in its pot, Emily Boggs carried the small serving tray with its porcelain coffeepot and attendant cup and saucer arranged on top. When she passed the gilded mirror in the hall, she glimpsed a telltale torte crumb near the corner of her mouth and quickly licked away the evidence of the bite she'd snitched before exiting the kitchen.

Before she reached the master suite, Sondra stalked out of it, her long legs slicing out from the fold of the black kimono.

"Clean up that mess," she snapped as she went past.

"What mess is that, mum?" Emily asked with some confusion.

When she failed to get a reply, she stepped into the bedroom and froze, her mouth dropping open. Feathers. Soft downy feathers were everywhere, but the biggest fluffy mound was on the bed—next to an embroidered pillow cover that looked as if it had been ripped apart.

"A mess indeed," Emily Boggs observed, then clamped her mouth shut and set about cleaning it up. Though Lord knew how she was going to accomplish it.

The track of the pickup's headlight beams picked out the road's twists and curves. Bannon kept his gaze on them, never letting it stray to Kit, but he was conscious of her, every stir of movement, every soft breath.

When they pulled into Silverwood's ranch yard, the truck's beams flashed over the white Range Rover parked in front of the house. "Looks like you have company."

"It's probably Paula and Chip. Or maybe John T. is back from Los Angeles." She reached for the door handle the instant the pickup rolled to a stop. "Thanks for the ride, Bannon."

He nodded a silent response, feeling the blast of cold air that swept into the heated cab when she climbed out. He sat for a minute, out of habit, and watched her walk swiftly toward the house. A man stepped from the porch shadows to meet her, moonlight glinting on burnished gold hair. Bannon whipped the steering wheel around and drove off without waiting to see whether Kit went into the man's arms.

She ran right into them. "Hi."

"Hi, yourself." John dropped a hard kiss on her upturned lips.

The instant Kit felt the heat of his breath on her cool skin, inhaled the expensive fragrance of his cologne, and discovered the differing texture of his body, she knew this embrace wasn't smart. She didn't want to consciously or subconsciously compare the two men. It wasn't fair to John, and it wasn't fair to herself. But she knew that's exactly what she'd do.

"Miss me?" He nuzzled the lobe of her ear.

She pulled back a little, wedging her arms against his chest to create some space. "Were you gone?" she asked in mock innocence, deliberately inserting lightness before the moment became too heavy.

His eyes glittered with humor, eliciting a little tremble of relief. "You'll pay for that."

"Inside, please. We'll turn into icicles out here," Kit warned and slipped the rest of the way free of his embrace to head for the door.

John was right behind her. "Don't you think I could make you warm enough?"

"Not and still keep my clothes on," she said over her shoulder and swept into the house.

"There's a tantalizing thought."

She laughed and whipped off her stocking cap, shaking her hair loose. "I knew you'd think so." She saw Paula near the foot of the stairs, her ebony-dyed mink draped over the newel post. "Hi. How was dinner?"

She felt another wave of relief. This was one night she didn't want to be in the house alone with John. She was afraid she'd turn to him out of need, not love. When they made love again, she wanted it to be all love.

"Fattening." Paula unclipped an earring and rubbed at her lobe. "Did I just hear a car drive out? Your note said you'd gone riding. Horseback."

"I did. But Dance threw a shoe. He was too sore-footed by the time I reached Stone Creek. So I left him there and Bannon gave me a lift home." Kit stripped off her gloves and jacket, carefully avoiding the speculating gleam in Paula's green eyes. Sometimes her eyes saw too much. She started to give her jacket a toss onto a nearby chair, then stopped when she saw the stack of long garment boxes piled on its seat. "What's all this?" She walked over to investigate.

"Costumes for Sondra's Halloween party," John explained. "While I was in L.A., I went by wardrobe and brought back a selection for you and Paula to choose from."

"What fun." Seizing on the diversion, Kit pried at the lid of the top box. "What all did you bring?"

"Everything from a flapper outfit to gypsy costume." Watching her, John thought she had all the eagerness of a child opening her presents on Christmas morning.

"A gypsy—that's you, Paula," she said without hesitation. "Tell me there's a witch's costume in here. That's what I'd like to go as."

"Sorry." His mouth crooked in an amused line. "It didn't occur to me how appropriate that would be."

"Appropriate?" Kit looked at him with narrowed eyes. "I'm not sure I like that remark."

"You should—considering you appear to have the power to cast spells."

"Aren't you the smooth talker tonight?" she chided as she set the lid aside.

"It's the spell you cast." John lit a cigarette.

"A likely story." The tissue rustled noisily when Kit pushed it out of the way to see the costume it protected. She smiled in sudden delight. "Paula, look at this. It's gorgeous." She lifted up an old-fashioned shirtwaist outfit, the long tapering skirt in a deep electric blue and the high-necked blouse in a spotted silk with long sleeves, puffed at the shoulders. A second later she saw the high-laced shoes in the same blue satin overlaid with black Chantilly lace. "There's even shoes to match, Paula." She turned her bright glance on John. "I love it."

He lowered his cigarette, studying her. "You could have been the original Gibson girl—very feminine yet something of a feminist."

"Do you get the feeling he's been drinking, Paula?" Kit eyed him askance, then returned the outfit to its box. "Keep him entertained while I put on some coffee to sober him up."

All the life and color seemed to go out of the room when she disappeared into the kitchen. John took another drag on his cigarette and glanced at Paula, who continued to gaze in the direction Kit had gone. "Kit's in high spirits tonight," he remarked to fill the silence.

"Look again," Paula suggested dryly and removed the other earring with a sharp snap of the clipped back. "She's a little too bright and a little too cheery if you ask me. You may have returned just in the nick of time, John."

He lifted his head. "Care to explain that?"

Paula removed a flat gold case from her evening bag and lit a rare cigarette. "Kit's starting to feel the backwash of the spotlight—the meanness of people and the drawing back due to their own feelings of inferiority or insecurity." She took a seat on the couch, lounging back and crossing her legs. "She doesn't like it."

"Who does? But after a while you become callused to it—the same as you do with anything that rubs you the wrong way." Crazily John discovered he didn't like the idea of Kit acquiring that hard shell you needed when you made it to the top, the layer upon layer you acquired until you became cynical and indifferent, not totally trusting anyone or caring too deeply, not letting anyone get too close or risking being hurt by them. He didn't want to see that happen to Kit. He didn't want to see her being swept into the power struggles that went on at the top, and the fight to dominate the old game of You want this, then do this. Hollywood had a dozen ways to screw you over besides the casting couch. This last trip to L.A. served as a very vivid reminder of that. A dozen times he'd wanted to tell Lassiter what he could do with his money, but he needed it—he needed this picture. He'd fought for what he could, and bowed to the rest.

He discovered he wanted to shield Kit from things like

that, he wanted to protect her. He had started to care, and with Kit, there was no halfway. She gave totally and completely and she demanded the same in return. He wasn't sure he had the ability to do that anymore.

He pulled on the cigarette, dragging the smoke deep into his lungs. But the taste was too pungent. In the next second John stabbed the cigarette out in an ashtray.

"She'll toughen up," Paula remarked, almost idly. "She'll have to; we both know that. Right now she's resisting the whole idea." She stared at the front door with a faraway look. "And that rancher Bannon is part of the reason. You may have some competition there, John."

"From that rancher?" He raised an eyebrow.

Paula's mouth curved in a droll smile. "Careful, John. Your ego is showing. Yes, that rancher. Kit thought they were going to be married once—until he married someone else. Now I have the feeling if he asked her, she'd marry him and give up everything. It would be a sin for her to throw away a chance like this for a bedtime story. Talent is rare, one of the few things that grows richer over the years. Love dies."

"Kit's right. You're too much of a cynic."

Paula laughed in her throat, adding, "So said the pot to the kettle."

"What's this about the pot and the kettle?" Kit walked in, bearing a tray laden with coffee and cups. "It's no fair telling stories when I'm out of the room."

"I wouldn't worry," John said. "The punch line was as funny as it got."

After drinking only one cup of coffee, John lingered a few minutes over a cigarette, then pleaded fatigue from the long flight back to Aspen. Kit walked him to the door, waited until she heard the Range Rover start up, then flipped off the porch light.

"Another cup?" Paula asked when Kit turned from the door.

"Why not?" Her shoulders lifted in an indifferent shrug as she wandered back into the living room. Taking the cup Paula had refilled, Kit breathed in its aromatic steam without finding any pleasure in it. Paula slipped off her heels, the thunk of them hitting the floor emphasizing the silence of the house. Kit didn't like it and resorted to small talk to fill it. "Did you enjoy your evening with Chip?"

Nodding, Paula rubbed at an aching arch. "Did you? Enjoy your evening with Bannon, I mean?"

For some inexplicable reason, Kit felt the need to defend her visit. "I went over to give him my father's favorite rifle. Dad would have wanted him to have it."

"That's all?"

"That's all." Uncomfortable with the subject, Kit walked over to her father's chair and ran her hand over the back of it.

"Kit, you're not still waiting for Bannon after all this time, are you?" Paula said with more than a touch of impatience.

"Not waiting." Kit shook her head at that. "A woman doesn't wait for things she can't have. You're a woman, Paula. You should know we're more practical than that." She offered Paula a very sober smile. "We've always been the realists. It's men who are the idealists, the romantics. When a man falls in love—deeply in love—then loses it, he never forgets, he holds on to the illusion of it. He may satisfy his needs with someone else or seek pleasure somewhere else, but his heart stays true to the one he lost." She trailed her hand over the antimacassar on the chair's headrest. "Like my father."

"And like Bannon?" Paula guessed.

Kit withheld comment on that. "We women, on the other hand," she began on a slightly lighter, and slightly wryer, note, "when we love and lose, we hurt, we wail, or we rage—then we go on with the business of living because that's what we have to do." She paused. "Does that answer your question?"

"Yes, although now I wonder what stage you are at. Are you wailing or raging?"

"I'm getting on with the business of living," Kit stated firmly.

Looking at her, Paula silently hoped so.

~∂⊙∂~ 20 ~∂⊙∂~

*L*asco Industries' executive jet rolled to a stop in front of flight-base operations at Aspen's Sardy Field, the whine of its engines dying as the ground crew slipped the wheel chocks in place. Within minutes J. D. Lassiter emerged from the plane, clad in a black cashmere topcoat. He took little notice of Sondra Hudson standing at the bottom of the steps, waiting to greet him as he paused and glanced around, like a politician on a campaign stump surveying his surroundings and verifying which stop this was.

A man joined him. Lassiter turned to briefly speak to him, the strong afternoon sunlight picking out the traces of silver that crusted his hair. With forced patience, Sondra kept her smooth smile in place and waited while he made a leisurely descent.

"Hello, Sondra."

"J. D."

"Lovely day," he remarked, his glance making an inspecting sweep of the high blue sky overhead. "Did you order it specially for me?"

"I assumed you did, J. D.," she returned.

He chuckled, a smile spreading over his suntanned and vigorous face, a smile that didn't lessen the shrewdness of his eyes. "Very good, Sondra," he murmured, then introduced her to the slim, sandy-haired man at his side, identifying him simply as Rob Hoeugh, but he had the look of an architect to Sondra. She felt a little rush of anticipation, certain the sale was all but consummated. "During the flight, I had an opportunity to again review the video you sent me— as well as projections for a development on the site. The property appears quite promising."

"Once I have a clear understanding of a buyer's requirements, I do my best to locate a property that will fulfill them. I think you will agree, J. D., that this parcel has the potential to become another Aspen or Snowmass."

"If I didn't think so, Sondra, I wouldn't have worked this stop into my schedule to tour the site for myself."

"Then shall we begin? I have a helicopter waiting." With an outward lift of her hand, she indicated the chopper sitting on the pad some distance from the jet, its rotors whirring in a slow chop-chop, its engine idling. "An aerial view will give you an excellent perspective of the property, both the way it lies and its location in relationship to the area."

"Let's go." Lassiter headed directly toward the motorized cart that waited to transport them to the helicopter.

As soon as they were buckled in, the pilot took off, swinging the enclosed chopper up-valley, overflying Aspen. Earlier in the day, Sondra had gone with the pilot and familiarized him with the ranch's property lines and the areas within its boundaries to which she wanted special attention given. The preparation allowed her to speak with authority when she showed the site to Lassiter, never once resorting to a "maybe" or "I think that's it."

After Lassiter had seen all he wanted from the air, Sondra tapped the pilot on the shoulder and signaled him to set the chopper down in an open area of the pasture where Warren Oakes waited with a Jeep Wagoneer to take him on a ground-level tour.

An hour later they all stood in the ranch yard, a survey map of the property spread out on the hood of the Wagoneer. Lassiter ignored it, his attention wandering instead to the grove of white-barked aspen nearly stripped bare of leaves.

His glance ran curiously to Sondra. "Who owns this property?"

"Kit Masters."

"Really?" His eyebrows lifted in a faint show of surprise.

"She inherited it following her father's death a few months ago."

"Is she here?" He glanced at the ranch house.

"No. She made some mention of a tennis match with Travis and the man who heads his production company. I expect she's at the club courts," Sondra replied, then added, "I've found it's usually awkward to have owners present when I'm showing their property to a prospective buyer."

"Of course."

For an instant Sondra thought he was going to take advantage of the opening she'd given him to reaffirm his initial interest in purchasing the property, but Rob Hoeugh picked that moment to call to him. "Can I have a word with you, J. D.?"

"Excuse me." Lassiter joined the man with a quickness that suggested he'd been waiting for Hoeugh's opinion of the site.

Sondra watched with sharpened interest while the two men conferred. Hoeugh did most of the talking, Lassiter most of the nodding. By reputation, J. D. Lassiter was a man who made quick, but not rash, decisions. Once he was wholly satisfied with the feasibility of a given venture, he acted. He never mulled anything over for long periods. Knowing that, Sondra tensed in anticipation when he turned back to her.

"According to this survey, this property extends better than halfway up the ridge on the left," he said.

"That's right." She was puzzled that he should seek clarification of that.

"What about the land on the other side?"

"That's Stone Creek Ranch."

"You get that rancher to sell off the ridge and I'll buy both properties. Without it, I'm not interested."

She was stunned, then angry. Somehow she managed to suppress both and bury her balled fists in the pockets of her coat. "May I ask why?"

"Rob tells me that the ridge affords the best skiing. The other slopes are merely adequate. Ski runs, ski resorts are his area of expertise. That's why I brought him along. If he says we need it, then we need it."

"I certainly wouldn't disagree with Mr. Hoeugh," Sondra replied carefully. "However, if you'll look over some of the proposed development schemes, I think you will see that the ridge area can be much more valuable to you if it's used for an exclusive subdivision, similar in scope to Starwood."

"Possibly," Rob Hoeugh conceded. "But why would anyone want to buy a multimillion-dollar second home in a winter resort that can't offer world-class ski trails? Without that, you have nothing to attract them to come in the first place."

"Fortunately that can be corrected by convincing the neighboring rancher to sell me that ridge," Lassiter inserted. "It can't be of much use to him anyway."

"Convincing him of that will be difficult, J. D." She tried to keep the grimness out of her voice without much success. "I can tell you right now he won't sell."

"That's your problem."

"You don't understand. Bannon owns it. I have a better chance of moving that mountain than I do persuading him to sell that ridge."

"Bannon," Lassiter repeated thoughtfully. "He will be a hard nut to crack."

"To put it mildly." She could see the sale slipping away. Her plans. Her dreams. She vibrated with resentment, with anger.

"Tell you what, Sondra. I want this property. I want this project. You talk Bannon into selling off that ridge and I'll make it worth your while. Not only will I give your agency a five-year exclusive contract to sell the various condominium, residential, and commercial sites, but I'll also give you an ownership interest in the whole development. Say—seven percent?"

A small part of her leapt at the offer that would be a realization of so many of her dreams. Yet she knew, too well, what an immovable object she faced. "That's a very generous incentive, J. D."

"It was meant to be."

She sensed the challenge in his voice and in his look. But it was the faintly superior gleam in his eyes that goaded her.

"I accept your offer." Sondra extended a hand to shake on it.

He gripped it, returning the firm pressure of her fingers. "I have every confidence in your persuasive abilities, Sondra. We both know there are ways to convince someone it's in their best interests to sell."

"True." But how? How could she convince Bannon? How could she reach him? There had to be a way. But what was it?

The same questions still raced through her mind two hours later when she drove into the ranch yard at Stone Creek. She stopped in front of the massive log ranch house, staring at its solidness and thinking bitterly of Bannon, his deep affinity for the land, his implacable will, his quiet strength and blind loyalty. Qualities she'd always admired in him. Qualities that were now her biggest obstacle.

She stepped out of the heated car into the crispening air, her glance running automatically to the rustic log porch, shadowed by the gathering dusk. The lowing of cattle and the soft whicker of a horse drifted from the outbuildings and pens, background noises to be ignored as she started for the steps, only to stop when she heard her name shouted.

Turning, she saw a small, lumpy figure in a boy's heavy jacket and clumsy rubber boots standing in front of the barn. Laura. The corners of her mouth curved upward in the smallest of smiles. If Bannon had any vulnerable point, it was his daughter. With eyes darkly gleaming, Sondra raised her hand, returning Laura's wave, and set off to meet her.

With the penned cattle fed, Bannon climbed the pole fence and vaulted lightly to the ground on the other side, feeling the stretch of muscles in his back, arms, and shoulders, the stretch that came from being used. He headed for the barn to see if Laura had finished graining the horses yet. Halfway there, he spotted her standing in the middle of the yard, talking to Sondra. He altered his course to join them.

"Did you get the horses fed?" He dragged off his heavy

leather work gloves and rumpled the top of Laura's hair in playful affection, then sent a smile at Sondra, acknowledging her presence.

"Yeah." Laura ducked out from beneath his hand. "Aunt Sondra's been telling me about all the decorations and music and games she's going to have at her Halloween party next week. Her costume's going to be really neat, too. She wanted to know what yours is. What kind of costume are you going to wear, Dad?"

"It's a surprise." He smiled, then lifted an amused glance to Sondra, catching the watchful stillness of her gaze on him before she tipped her head toward Laura.

"As soon as you find out what he's wearing, you can tell me."

"Okay." Laura grinned with ready conspiracy, then sighed wistfully. "It's going to be so much fun. I wish I was going. I'll be glad when I'm finally grown up and I can go to parties."

"You'll grow up soon enough." Bannon gave her a little push toward the house. "Go wash up and help Sadie get supper on the table."

She swung around, hands on hips. "How come I get all the grown-up work and none of the grown-up fun? It's not fair."

"You'll have fun at Buffy's party."

"It's not the same."

"Then stay home with your granddad."

Laura whirled around, flinging her arms in the air. "Fathers," she muttered in disgust and stalked off toward the house.

"Kids," he murmured to Sondra, more amused by Laura's protest than anything else.

But Sondra didn't respond in kind; instead she gazed thoughtfully after Laura. "Remember how Diana loved parties and fun, bright lights and laughter. Laura's starting to sound just like her."

"All kids go through that," he said, no longer amused as he struck out for the house, then shortened his brisk stride so Sondra could keep pace. "What brings you out this way?"

"Business, I'm afraid."

"Afraid?" He shot her a side-glance, curious at her choice of words.

"Yes." Her eyes measured him briefly. "You aren't going to like this."

"What?"

"I have a client who wants me to find out if you're willing to sell that ridge area that adjoins Silverwood."

"I'm not."

"You haven't even heard his offer, Bannon," she reproved mildly.

"It doesn't matter. It isn't for sale at any price."

His tone was flat and final.

"I told him you'd say that."

"Good. Then we can consider the subject closed."

Covertly she studied the sharp angles of his profile, so unyielding and hard. "I wish you'd think about the offer, Bannon."

"There's nothing to think about." The curtness was expected.

"There's Laura."

He stopped and came around, cutting a high shape against the violet eddies of twilight. "What does Laura have to do with this?"

"She's growing up, Bannon. She's already worrying about clothes and fixing her hair. That's just the beginning. It won't be long before she'll want her own car to drive back and forth to school. There'll be boys and prom dresses and college . . ." Sondra paused deliberately. "All expensive, Bannon."

"I'll manage."

"Maybe." She read the telltale signs in his expression that warned of quiet anger behind the terseness—the tightness at the edges of his mouth, the way his eyes showed darkness below the straight black line of his brows. "But wouldn't it be a lot better if you didn't have to *manage*? If you already had the money tucked away? How much land would that ridge area encompass, Bannon? One hundred acres? Two hundred? What's two hundred acres when you have four thousand? What good is it to you? You can't graze cattle on it, and you don't run sheep. What could be the harm in selling that one chunk?''

"One chunk. That's the way the ranchers down-valley started, by selling their land off one chunk at a time. No thanks.''

Just for an instant, impatience broke through. "You could practically name your own price, Bannon. One million. Two. Think what you could do with that much money. And I don't just mean for Laura. Look at the improvements you could make in the rest of the ranch—the new barns, better breeding stock. You could finally afford to fix up that drafty old house. Or better yet, tear it down and build a new one.''

"With a swimming pool and a tennis court?'' His challenge was cool and hard.

Sondra realized she'd pushed too much. She waited a beat, then said quietly, "Laura would like that. I know you don't want to hear that, but it's the truth.'' She went on, without giving him a chance to respond. "Think about the offer, Bannon. That's all I'm saying. I know how much this land means to you. I admire that. But—be realistic. What will happen to the ranch when you're gone? Do you think Laura will keep it? Do you think she'll be able to *afford* to keep it? Isn't it more likely she'll sell it—just as Kit Masters is selling her father's ranch?''

Her words had unsettled him. For now that was enough. With a soft "Good night,'' she kissed him and left, eyes gleaming.

21

Giant jack-o'-lanterns carved in gap-toothed grins and grotesque smiles lined the driveway and sidewalks of the house on Red Mountain, sharing the paths with black cats peering out of shocks of cornstalks and scarecrows perched on bales of straw. Holographic ghosts haunted the lawn and shrubbery, materializing and dematerializing at preset intervals. Near the pool pavilion, glow-in-the-dark skeletons danced to the rhythm of the night wind while a five-piece band pounded out a calypso beat by torchlight and a blonde in a Cat-Woman suit arched low to make it under a limbo pole held by a vampire and a cowboy in wool chaps and a ten-gallon hat.

On the sundeck, ringed like the pool area with radiant heaters to ward off the cool temperatures, a motley group of witches and warlocks, caped crusaders and fairy princesses, buckskin-garbed Indians and Cleopatras gathered around a raised wooden barrel filled with water, a layer of shiny red apples floating on its surface. Kit bent low over the tub, her long blond hair swept atop her head in a pompadour style. She ignored the advice hooted at her from all sides as she tried to sink her teeth into the slick skin of an elusive apple and wound up with a mouthful of water instead.

"It's cold," she protested on a laugh and wiped the icy droplets from her nose before trying again.

"No fair using your hands." John looked on, garbed in the black suit, ruffled shirt, and brocade vest of a riverboat gambler, complete with a diamond stickpin in his silk cravat and a wide-brimmed, flat-crowned hat.

"Show them how it's done, Kit." Paula clapped in encouragement, gypsy bracelets jangling on her arms, large gold hoops swaying from her lobes.

Bannon watched from a distance, a thumb hooked through the belt loop of his well-worn Levi's and a hip leaning against the deck rail. A gap in the crowd afforded him a clear view as Kit primly folded her hands behind a waist that looked wasp slim. Again she took an open-mouthed aim on an apple. Admiration and something more tugged at him as he watched her abandon herself to this child's game of bobbing for apples—without seeming less of a woman.

Scarlet silk rippled in his side vision, the splash of brilliant color drawing his glance. Sondra stood in front of the glass doors to the living room, a pillar of red flame in her long cheongsam gown, her platinum hair pulled back in a sleek coil at the nape, her attention focused on the apple barrel.

A cheer went up. Bannon looked back as Kit straightened, water dripping from her chin and a red apple clamped firmly between her teeth. She plucked the apple from her mouth and held it triumphantly aloft, wiping the water from her chin with her other hand.

"Who's next?" she challenged.

A banker in a Robin Hood suit stepped forward to more applause, doffing his peaked hat in a gallant flourish as Kit spun over to John's side and finished taking the bite out of her apple.

"Mmmm, it's delicious," she said between crunches and swiped at the juice that tried to dribble from the corner of her mouth. "Have a bite," she urged, offering it up to him.

"What is this? Eve tempting Adam with the apple of knowledge?" He drew back in mock wariness.

"I didn't taste any knowledge, only cold, crisp and juicy,"

she replied, her eyes alight with humor. "Are you sure you don't want to try it?"

His gaze went to the shiny moistness of her lips. "Maybe I will after all."

He slipped an arm around her waist and pulled her closer as he tipped his head and kissed her, tasting all the apple sweetness on her mouth, lips, and tongue to the whistles and hoots of approval from the onlooking guests.

But not Bannon. Sondra saw the leap of muscle along his jaw a second before he wheeled away and walked into the house, his mouth pressed in a narrow line, his spurs making an angry jangle with each stride. Her glance went back to Kit and John Travis as Kit pushed him back, breaking the contact, a high color in her cheeks. Whether from the cool air, embarrassment, or pleasure, Sondra couldn't tell. Nor did she care.

Bannon's reaction was another matter. She hadn't liked it. She hadn't liked it at all. She followed him into the living room strung with gossamer-fine cobwebs and lit by an array of candelabras. In a shadowed corner, a pseudo-seance was being held, visited by a ribald spirit, judging by the hoots of laughter coming from the participants. Sondra paid scant attention to it or to the costumed guests who spoke to her as she continued straight to the sunken bar where Bannon had posted himself.

He didn't hear her come up until she spoke, the sound of her voice drawing him half around. "That little scene upset you. You don't hide it well, Bannon."

He pushed the pilsner glass back to the bartender and picked up the bottle of Coors, not answering.

"It's common knowledge they've been having an affair. Surely you heard that—or did you choose not to believe it?" she guessed, her eyes narrowing as he took a swig of beer. "John Travis always romances his leading ladies, Bannon. How do you think they get to be his leading ladies?"

His hand tightened around the bottle's slick sides, his gaze fixed on it. "Sondra," he began in a grating voice.

"You don't like the implications of that, do you?" she said, suddenly impatient. "Do you think men are the only ones who make bargains and compromises to get to the top? Women aren't any different. She spent nine years in Hollywood, working in soaps and bad horror movies. John Travis gave her a chance to do something more and she took it.'' She paused an instant. ''You live too much in the past, Bannon. It's gone. Let it go.''

Her voice choking in anger on the last, she swung away and walked off before she said Diana's name. She brushed past the Joker and headed blindly toward the dining room and its lavish buffet, but her way was blocked by a harlequin chatting with a rhinestone-studded cowgirl and a pirate.

As Sondra walked around a tall pedestal table bearing a giant jack-o'-lantern, she inadvertently triggered a motion sensor. A sudden, wild cackle filled the room as a witch on a broom swooped from its box mounted high in the room's cathedral ceiling.

Sondra jumped at the sound of the insanely shrill laughter, straight into a gossamer curtain of draping webs. She batted at it wildly, then curled her fingers into it and yanked it from its hangings. She stood there for an instant, breathing hard, her head pounding, the edges of her vision blurring as she looked at the silken cloth in her hand.

She darted a quick look around, but no one had seen. No one had noticed. Their heads were all tipped up to watch the flying witch complete her circle of the room and return to her box high in the darkly shadowed ceiling. She wadded the webbing into a ball and tucked it in a marble planter, then paused and glanced back at the sunken bar. Bannon wasn't there.

He couldn't have left—not this early. All her muscles tightened, a rage rushing through her again. Then she caught a glimpse of his back, the familiar set of his square shoulders beneath the short denim jacket, as he wandered onto the darkened empty deck off the far end of the living room. Immediately she forced the tension from her muscles and continued to the dining room to check on the caterers.

Laughing, Kit led the way back into the expansive living room, transformed by the multitude of flickering candle flames into a cavernous room of eerie, dancing shadows, an effect that not even the overstuffed sofas and sumptuous furnishings could negate. As her glance swept over it, she declared, "Hollywood couldn't have done this better."

"She must have used a professional set designer." Chip pushed his glasses back onto the bridge of his nose and peered curiously around him. "I wonder who she got?"

"Enjoy, Chip. Don't scrutinize," Paula admonished in a despairing tone.

"He can't help it," Kit informed her. "It's that mad-genius costume asserting itself."

"The 'mad' part might be right," John murmured near her ear, not loud enough for anyone else to hear.

Her over-the-shoulder smile faded when she saw John wasn't joking. The pull of his mouth was much too grim. It softened when he noticed her glance, but it came too late to make light of his remark.

When the pressure of his hand firmed on her back, signaling her to continue forward, Kit complied and tried to ignore the troubling implications of his comment, telling herself it meant nothing more than the usual clash of temperaments on a film project.

Away from the congestion around the doors to the sundeck, Kit paused. "What next?" she asked the others. "Dancing by the pool?"

"Look at this." Chip bent close to an open sarcophagus, propped in the corner, its mummy inside. "An electric eye of some kind." He pointed to a small black object mounted on the wall near it, then waved a hand in front of it, breaking the field. Ghostly emanations came from the sarcophagus as the mummy's eyes popped open and a hand lifted. "Isn't that something?"

"It's something, all right," Paula murmured. "This party has almost as many tricks as treats."

"Sondra's parties are always highly imaginative," John remarked as he ducked to avoid snagging a trailing cobweb on his hat.

"Do you realize that my vacation in Aspen began with a party, and now it's ending with one?" Paula said on a marveling note.

"You're leaving?" John glanced at her in surprise.

"Yes, I'm flying back to L.A. the day after tomorrow." She adjusted the gold bangles around her wrist. "It's a few days earlier than I planned, but my agent called. He's arranged for me to meet with the producers on *Days*. They're changing their storyline and introducing a host of new characters. They want me to be one of them. Right now they're talking the right number of digits. Plus I'll have some input on my character."

"Another villainess, of course," John guessed dryly.

"What else?" She lifted a shoulder, the scooped neckline of her peasant blouse slipping to expose much of its creamy whiteness.

"Paula has a talent for playing bad, good." Kit grinned.

"That I can believe." But his glance was on Kit, his eyes warm and bold, a blatantly sexual look. "So you're going to be staying alone at the ranch. That gives me some very stimulating ideas."

"Liar," she said, as always finding it easy to tease him. "You've had *those* ideas from the beginning."

"So I have," he admitted, his hand rubbing over her back in an idle caress.

"Speaking of ideas, treats, and what's next," Paula spoke up. "Let's see what goodies await us at the buffet table."

"Sounds good to me," Chip said, finally breaking off his inspection of the animated mummy.

Kit shook her head. "I think I'll pass. I'm still full from dinner."

"And the apple," John reminded her.

"That too."

"How about a drink?" he asked when Paula and Chip set off for the dining area.

"Please. Make it something nonalcoholic," Kit requested.

"Not champagne?" He raised an eyebrow.

"It isn't a champagne night." At some point the evening had gone flat; Kit wasn't sure when. "Halloween is mulled wine or hot chocolate with a splash of peppermint schnapps."

"I'll remember that," he said and moved off, the diamond-studded stickpin winking in the flaring light of a candle flame.

Alone in the shadowy corner, Kit wandered over to the sarcophagus and trailed a finger along the edge of its gilded lid. A breeze filtered through the open doors onto a side sundeck, its freshness scenting air redolent with the odor of hot candle wax. More restless than curious, Kit strolled over to the open doors.

Bannon lounged against the rail, his hands braced on the top of it, his long legs stretched out at an angle. A beer bottle sat on the rail next to him and his head was tipped down as if he were contemplating the scuff marks on the toes of his boots. Kit hesitated, but pride wouldn't let her back away— just as it had never allowed her to confront Bannon with the truth of how deeply she'd been hurt when he married Diana. Yet it was something else that kept her from admitting to herself that he still had the power to hurt her.

She stepped onto the deck, her long skirts swishing in a soft rustle of fabric. His head came up, the brim of his hat shading his eyes, but she could feel them on her.

"I suppose you call that outfit a costume," she said lightly, her glance running over him. The sun-faded jeans and denim jacket, the boots with the run-down heels and blunt-tipped spurs, the worn-soft chambray work shirt, and the weather-stained cowboy hat on his head, all were the clothes of a working cowboy, typical of the dress Bannon wore on the ranch.

"I can guarantee it's authentic." He drew one foot back, a spur musically rattling, but he didn't rise. The words were friendly enough but not the coolness in his voice.

He'd been on the front sundeck when John had kissed her. Kit had glimpsed the hard, closed look on his face before he'd walked off. Part of her had been annoyed by it. He had no right to be jealous; he'd given that up when he married someone else. Yet another part of her had taken perverse satisfaction out of knowing she could still make him jealous. It was this bewildering mixture of feelings that kept pushing and pulling at her, unsettling her, never totally letting her go.

"It's definitely authentic," she agreed and walked past him to the rail.

She paused there, facing the night, a nearby radiant heater

giving off a toasty warmth and the breeze cool and fresh on her cheeks. The band by the pool struck up a hard, driving rock song, the level of laughing, chatting voices rising and falling. Yet the feeling was one of quiet and stillness, a dusting of stars in the sky, visible beyond the soft glow of Aspen's lights, the surrounding black mountain masses cutting jagged chunks out of the sky.

"It's a beautiful night, isn't it?"

"Yep."

That one-word answer pulled her around, forcing her to acknowledge the tension in the stillness, the strong crosscurrents in the air, the heavy undertow of feeling.

"Spoken in the best tradition of the strong-and-silent type," Kit mocked, half serious and half in jest. "Gary Cooper couldn't have delivered it better."

"I guess you'd know about that." Bannon's glance bounced off her as he tipped the bottle to his mouth and poured the last of the beer down.

"Did Sondra mention to you that she has someone interested in buying Silverwood?" Kit asked, deliberately changing the subject.

"She mentioned it." He set the empty bottle back on the rail beside him.

"She brought some people out last week to show them around. She thinks that they may be making an offer soon." She tried to sound very matter-of-fact, but she couldn't keep the regret that she had to sell out of her voice. Her glance drifted over the contemporary stone-and-glass house in front of her. "I hate to think of houses like this being built along the ridge trail," she said with more vehemence than she intended.

Bannon pushed off the rail to stand up, a spur briefly raking across the wood decking. "Why waste the energy? You'll be going in a few months, back to a world that suits you better."

"Does it?" Lately she hadn't been sure of that and his remark reminded her of it.

"It's a little late to be asking yourself that question now, isn't it?"

"I guess it is." She rubbed a hand over her arm, the silk

sleeve of her spotted shirtwaist cool to the touch, a coolness that had begun to penetrate. "I think it's getting colder out."

Once that comment would have prompted Bannon to put his arms around her and warm her up. Now he said, "You'd better go inside where it's warmer."

"I think I'll take your advice."

As she crossed to the doors, Kit heard the music of his spurs moving away toward the laughter and the voices at the other end of the deck.

The warmth of the house washed over her the minute she stepped inside, the heat producing an involuntary shiver. She rubbed again at her arms, then paused when she saw Paula with the hostess. All her life Kit had made a habit out of observing people, their expressions, their mannerisms, their reactions. Looking at Sondra, she was suddenly struck by the smooth inscrutable mask she wore to conceal her thoughts. It made her choice of an Oriental costume singularly appropriate.

Continuing forward, Kit said, "It's beginning to feel cold outside without a coat."

"We'll have to start getting used to that," Sondra replied. "The forecast calls for snow the first of the week."

"John and Chip will be glad to hear that," Kit said, then realized neither of them was with Paula. "Where are they?"

"Lassiter cornered them." Paula searched through the finger food on her plate before selecting a salmon roulade.

"I didn't know he was here." Kit automatically lifted her glance to the throng of costumed party guests in the dimly lit living room.

"He arrived late. About twenty minutes ago," Sondra explained as a waiter caught her eye and motioned for her. "Excuse me."

Paula watched her as she moved off. "I'd watch yourself around her, Kit."

Kit turned to look at her, amused and puzzled by the remark. "Where did that come from?"

"From watching her watch you when you were out on the deck with Bannon. There was pure venom in her eyes." She continued her thoughtful study of their scarlet-gowned hostess, then glanced at Kit with equal attention. "She can be a vengeful woman when she's crossed."

Kit shook her head in bemused astonishment. "How can you say that? You don't even know her."

"I don't have to know her. I've played her kind for so long I recognize the type." She idly stirred a blackened shrimp in its honeyed sauce. "Believe me, that woman is capable of anything."

Kit shrugged, thinking of Bannon and his relationship with Sondra. "Everyone has their dark side. A breaking point."

"But in some, it's darker than others." Paula nibbled on the shrimp.

"I suppose." She spotted John moving slowly in their direction, two drink glasses in his hands, held carefully in front of him. His head was turned toward the person with him, giving her a view of his smoothly chiseled profile beneath the brim of his sleek black gambler's hat.

A shifting of guests revealed J. D. Lassiter walking between John and Chip, looking benevolently crisp and professional in a pharmacist's jacket emblazoned with the emblem of his family's pharmaceutical company. Responding to a remark from Lassiter, John flashed a familiar smile that successfully mixed arrogance with charm. Obviously Lassiter had said something to please him. Chip, too, for that matter, judging by the look he exchanged with John.

Maybe she'd misread that murmured comment John had made about Chip. If there was any trouble between them, it certainly wasn't apparent now. Kit was glad. It was never fun working on a set where there was a lot of friction.

"By the way"—Lassiter rested a hand firmly on John's shoulder in comradely fashion—"I had a chance to read through that last set of changes in the script. I think we have a winner now. So does everyone else back at the studio. Good job," he said to Chip.

"I'm glad you approve." There was just enough dryness in Chip's voice to insert a trace of sarcasm in his response.

To John's relief, Lassiter either didn't detect it with all the party noise around them, or chose to ignore it.

"Now that we have a final script, what's your start date?"

"The end of November, right after the Thanksgiving weekend," John replied, then smiled. "Assuming Old Man Winter cooperates and gives Aspen a solid coating of snow."

"There's such a thing as snow-making machines," Lassiter stated.

"We'll use them if we have to, and we have interiors we can cover with, so I'm not worried about any change in the start date," he assured him. "Believe me, we won't be the only ones crying if there isn't snow before the Thanksgiving holiday to kick off the winter ski season."

"True." Lassiter nodded, then craned his neck, spotting someone in the crowd. "I believe I see our hostess. If you gentlemen will excuse me, I need to have a word with her."

"Go right ahead, Mr. Lassiter," Chip insisted, a little too readily. "We won't keep you."

Lassiter pinned him with a sharp look. "Again, that was a good job on the script, Freeman. If nothing else, you're a helluva writer."

"I'm a helluva director, too." His chin lifted at an aggressive angle.

"That remains to be seen, doesn't it?"

With the verbal slap administered, Lassiter moved off at an easy pace. He'd never met a director yet who didn't think he was king. A few were, but that boy was still a knave. He hadn't liked him from the beginning. Travis was high on him, but what did actors know?

Nearing Sondra, he switched thoughts as effortlessly as walking from one room to another. When she saw him, she murmured something to the couple with her, then turned to meet him.

"Marvelous party, Sondra." His glance made an idle sweep of the artfully staged scene. "I'm surprised someone from Disney isn't running around making notes."

"Why should they? I stole it all from them."

He responded with the expected laugh, then came to the point, the obligatory pleasantries dispensed with. "Have you talked to Bannon again?"

"Not yet," she replied easily and smoothly. "Bannon isn't

a man to be pushed. After he's had a few more days to think about it, I'll speak to him again.''

''And if he still refuses to sell, what then?'' he asked, but didn't allow her time to answer. ''I'm not a patient man, Sondra. I don't like deals that drag out.''

Sondra stiffened imperceptibly. ''You made no mention of a time limit before. Are you placing one on me now, J. D.?''

He considered that for a long second. ''Sixty days.''

With a forced show of calm, she looked down at her lightly clasped fingers, suppressing an urge to scream at him. Slowly she lifted her head again. ''You have to admit that is not much time when you expect mountains moved,'' she said in an attempt to gain more.

''Sixty days. If you haven't convinced him by then, chances are you won't. In which case, you'll be wasting my time as well as your own. There are always other deals.''

For him, but maybe not for her. Not one of this size, this scope. She let none of her tension show as she inclined her head in agreement. ''Very well. Sixty days it is.''

''Keep me informed of your progress.''

''Naturally.''

The minute she was alone, Sondra felt the rising panic. Sixty days. It was hardly enough time. Her first impulse was to seek out Bannon, talk to him, reason with him. No. Not here. Not at the party. She had to wait. It was a mistake to let this new pressure change her original plan. She had to give Bannon a few more days before she talked to him again.

22

*B*annon sat at the desk in the lodgelike living room, his pen poised over a yellow legal pad, his gaze fixed on the deposition before him, his attention straying from it again. Sighing in irritation, he combed a hand through his hair and tried to block out the melody Laura picked out on the piano keys—stumbling over the notes the way Kit had. It didn't work.

He dropped the pen in disgust and pushed out of the chair. Old Tom lowered his newspaper. "If you're heading for the kitchen, bring me back a couple antacid tablets." The paper crackled as he shook it stiff, mumbling to himself, "I don't know why I eat that chili stew of Sadie's. Damned stuff always gives me a sour stomach." When Bannon swung toward the kitchen, Old Tom lifted his voice, "See if it's still snowing while you're up, too. Paper's calling for flurries. Looked to me like those clouds had a good six inches in them."

Six inches meant they'd have to haul hay to the cattle in the morning. Bannon sighed and continued toward the kitchen, restless and tense. Winter was barely here and he was already getting cabin fever.

The phone rang as he reached the kitchen doorway. The

harsh sound grated across his nerves like chalk on a black-board.

"I'll get it!" Laura bounded off the piano bench and raced to answer it. She snatched up the receiver in the middle of the second ring. "Stone Creek Ranch, Laura speaking." Swiveling, she looked at Bannon, the phone to her ear, the line of her mouth pulling crooked in a resigned grimness. "He's here. Just a minute. It's for you, Dad." She laid the receiver down and started back to the piano with a definite lack of eagerness.

"Who is it?" Bannon recrossed the room to the oak table and the phone.

"Pete somebody. He sounded mad or drunk or something." She flopped onto the piano bench.

"Hold up practicing while I'm on the phone."

"Gladly."

When Bannon picked up the phone, he heard a familiar voice shouting at someone on the other end: "—you be telling me shit. I know my goddamn rights." The words, the belligerent tone, were a rerun of the two years before Peter Ranovitch had given up drinking. Hearing it, he swore softly under his breath, knowing what this meant.

"Pete." He broke in. "It's Bannon."

"Bannon? Bannon, you gotta do something. You gotta get me outa here. Goddamn it, it isn't right."

"You've been drinking."

"One beer. One lousy goddamn beer! Not even enough to make their goddamn Breathalyzers light up. They can't keep me here for that. Damn it, it's not right. I said I'd pay for the goddamn damages, but that bastard insists on pressing charges—"

"What damages? What happened, Pete?"

"I broke my goddamn hand, that's what happened. I broke my hand and I can't work. And if I can't work . . ." He stopped. When he spoke again, there was no more anger in his voice, only defeat. "I broke some glasses and a chair—maybe more than that, I don't know. It was Harry's. I was standing at the bar, wondering what the hell I was going to do. There was some dirty glasses sitting there, and I just swept them off onto the floor. It felt so good when they crashed. I picked up a chair and . . . I've had it, Bannon. I've had it with this town and everything in it. I can't make it here. I've just been kidding myself. I'm never going to have a restaurant of my own. I'm never gonna have shit. Bannon, can you come and get me out of this?''

"I'll be right there, Pete." Hanging up, Bannon swung away from the table.

Old Tom lowered his newspaper again. "Ranovitch on the sauce again?''

"Not exactly, but it sounds like he did some busting up at Harry's." Bannon took his hat from the wall peg and pushed it on his head, then reached for his sheepskin-lined parka. "I'm going in and see if I can persuade the manager not to press charges—or arrange bail. I'll probably be gone awhile.''

"The road could be slick," his father warned.

"Right." He shrugged into the parka and reached for the door.

"Bye, Dad," Laura called.

"Bye." He sent her a smile and wink, then pointed at the piano. "Practice.''

She wrinkled her nose, making a face at him as he went out the door.

Snow fell soft and steady, a diaphanous white curtain with no wind to stir it. From the secluded terrace of John Travis's Starwood estate, the lights of Aspen were an indistinct gleam somewhere in the distance, a gleam made even more indistinct by the steam billowing above the heated, churning water in the hot tub.

Deftly, centimeter by centimeter, John worked the cork from the magnum of champagne until it was out with the softest of pops. Kit applauded.

"Well done." She took the fluted glasses from the shelf attached to the side of the hot tub, and held them out for John to fill, water dripping from her outstretched arms and more bubbling around the top of her blue two-piece swimsuit, one of many John kept for guests.

"Practice." He filled both glasses, then turned, the sheen of moisture on his bronze skin revealing the ripple of muscle along his arm and chest as he partially buried the champagne bottle in its bucket of ice, placed conveniently close to the tub.

"You've had a lot of practice, too, haven't you?" Kit taunted playfully, handing him a glass.

"Experience has its advantages." He touched his glass to hers, a glint of amusement in his eyes as his gaze traveled with deliberate boldness over her face and down to the visible swell of her breasts above the waterline. "And its rewards—on both sides."

His words evoked images, sensations of his hands, his lips, his body moving over her, kissing, loving, demanding, needing, satisfying. The sudden knotting heat she felt had absolutely nothing to do with the temperature of the water.

"That's a tantalizing thought." She lifted the fluted glass to her lips.

"Maybe even arousing," John suggested, the glint in his eyes turning to a wicked twinkle.

"That, too," Kit admitted, a tiny, pleased smile touching the corners of her lips when she saw the way his eyes immediately darkened on her, knowing her answer had aroused him. "Turnabout is fair play, isn't it?" she murmured.

He lifted his glass in a salute of touché. When Kit tipped her head to drink from her own, she felt the faint cool kiss of snowflakes on her skin. She lifted her face to the falling snow, the sip of icy cold wine sliding down her throat and the crystalline flakes melting on her eyelids and cheeks. She reveled in the contrasting sensations of the water's heat and the air's snow-sprinkled crispness, sensations that both relaxed and sensitized.

"I'm glad you suggested this, John T.," she said in a sighing voice, then straightened her head to look at him. "The hot tub, the snow, the champagne—it's all deliciously decadent. I love it."

"I hoped you would." Seeing the soft radiance in her face, John realized that he'd never derived this much pleasure out of pleasing someone else. It felt good. Just looking at her felt good.

"Do you know what this reminds me of?" she said softly, suddenly conscious of the exquisite silence that surrounded them, that blocked out all but the frothing tumble of water in the tub. "One of those globes of glass with a miniature winter scene inside that you shake to make the snow dance inside it. Right now, it's like you and I are in that enchanted world."

Her chin level once more, she met his gaze, the glow in her eyes more than he could resist. He pushed his champagne glass onto the shelf and caught the hand floating idly on the water's roiling surface, simultaneously taking her glass and setting it aside, pulling her toward him.

"Then enchant me," he whispered against her mouth.

He nibbled at her lower lip and Kit returned his tiny, biting kisses as his arms encircled her under the water. When she caught his lower lip between hers and moistened its contours with the tip of her tongue, she felt the subtle change in his breathing.

"Enchanted yet?" Teasingly, she rubbed her parted lips over his mouth.

"Try harder." He rubbed them back and Kit smiled, fully aware she was playing with fire and not caring. Every playful kiss sent more languid waves of warmth licking through her, waves as warm as the heated water swirling around both of them.

His mouth covered hers with a questing urgency and the warmth began to center, deeply and explicitly. He tasted of champagne and heat, the silk of his tongue sliding between her lips. She heard a faint, breath-caught moan and realized it was her own as his tongue sank deeply into the recesses of her mouth. It was a sensually powerful kiss that precisely underlined the reputation of the man behind it.

She kissed him back with the same urgency, relishing the physical sensations of his taste, his scent, his touch as his hand caressed her back, the flare of a hip, then up to cup her breast. He rubbed his palm lightly and rhythmically over the taut nipple. Suddenly she found it impossible to breathe, a familiar tingly heat settling between her thighs. He pressed his hand more firmly against her, increasing the friction of the bikini top's fabric against her highly sensitized flesh.

Aching all over, Kit arched closer, their legs briefly tangling in the water. Then his arm was curving, lifting, drawing her up to straddle his thigh, sitting high out of water. He started kissing her throat and shoulder, then ran his tongue along the swell of her breast flowing out of the swimsuit bra. Suddenly, he lowered his mouth and sucked at the taut nipple through the wet fabric. She arched her back, her fingers sliding into the firmness of his dark blond hair.

Then his lips made the climb back to her throat, his teeth grazing the side of it while his fingers tugged at the top's ribbon tie. She felt the material go slack. Another tug and the turbulent water swept it away.

"Have you ever felt the snow on your breasts, Kit?" he whispered against her ear, then nipped at the lobe with his teeth. "Have you ever felt their icy touch, felt them melt?"

"No," she whispered back, her voice thick.

His arms tightened around her, pulling her with him when he pushed up, water sluicing from their bodies, the cold night air washing over their heated skin. John sank back against the rim of the tub, feet braced, his hands firm on the slick skin over her hipbones.

"Feel it?" He looked at her, his eyes heavy-lidded and hungry. "Feel the snow."

White flakes drifted between them and on them. Crystalline drops glistened in his hair. Locking her gaze with his, she arched her back slightly, feeling the snow's icy kisses on her skin.

The motion lifted her pale breasts, her nipples dark and pointy in the dim light. He brushed them with his fingertip, feeling her start slightly. Drawing her nearer, he traced a moist circle around a nipple with his tongue, then felt her convulsive shudder when he took it into his mouth.

He caressed her hip, then ran a hand down her thigh and back up, across her stomach, then down again to caress her with coaxing fingers. She stiffened and started to say something, but he silenced her with a deep kiss.

This wasn't the place. When they made love, he wanted plenty of comfort, plenty of room, and plenty of time. But he couldn't keep his hands off her. He wanted to stroke, caress, touch, and feel her writhe with need. He wanted to bury himself inside her, deep inside and make her a part of him. Lightly, he drew his fingers along the soft fold between her thighs, feeling the heat through the bikini's thin fabric.

She breathed in sharply and moved against his hand. He knew from the way she strained, the way she trembled, that she'd be moist and hot, ready to take him in one long thrust of his body.

He resisted the urge to slide his fingers inside the bikini bottom and slip his fingers into her, finding that sensitive place and rubbing it until she was wild with need, then satisfying it, taking her over that last edge, hearing the love sounds torn from her throat, seeing the intense pleasure on her face, then entering her and finding that same release for himself.

"Not like this," he said huskily, rubbing the center of his mouth over her cheek and breathing into her ear. "I want you naked in my bed, Kit. I want to be deep inside you with your long legs wrapped around me. I want to watch you while we make love. I want you to watch me. I want you to tell me what you want, how you want it. Fast. Slow. Wild. Tender. I want you to scream if you feel like screaming. I want you, Kit. I want it all."

His words had her imagination vivid, the wildness, the sweetness, the hunger. She could feel herself trembling. When his mouth moved onto hers, she drove into it rashly, recklessly. Her skin hot. Her body hot. She was hot.

A discreet cough sounded, then came again, louder, more insistent. When John dragged his mouth away, Kit rested her forehead on his shoulder and laughed softly, shakily.

Nolan Walker stood between the tall hedges that screened the heated walk between the private terrace and the house, his back turned to the hot tub. John glared just the same.

"What is it, Nolan?"

"Lassiter wants you. He's on the phone."

John swore softly, ripely, his hands unconsciously moving with longing over the bareness of her shoulder blades. "Kit—" he began, his voice low and oddly gruff.

She pressed the ends of her fingers onto his lips, silencing him. "It's okay," she murmured, a faint curve to her mouth, rather liking the idea that he was concerned that she wouldn't understand.

A gentleness, a warmth she'd never seen before, entered his eyes. A second later, he said to Nolan, "Tell Lassiter I'll be right there."

The hush of falling snow magnified the sound of Nolan's retreating footsteps, making Kit even more aware of how absorbed she had been in John's embrace. His hands shifted to her rib cage and set her back from him while he straightened to climb out of the tub.

His hand reached back for her. "This could take a while," he warned. "You'd better come in, too." He helped her out, then leaned back over the tub and scooped her top out of the tumbling water. "It seems you may have a need for this after all." His mouth curved in an amused line.

Kit took the top, but she didn't bother to put the sodden bit of cloth back on. Instead, she donned the plush terry robe of Egyptian cotton she'd worn from the house. John slipped into a shorter version, with a monogrammed pocket.

With arms hooked around each other's waist, they padded barefoot along the heated stone path to the house, entering through the lower level and passing through the fully equipped gym and sauna area, then climbing the white stairs to the second floor. Kit walked with him as far as the study door.

He pressed a kiss to her temple. "Want me to have Carla bring you coffee? Cocoa?"

She shook her head. "I'm fine. Go." She gave him a tiny push toward the study door.

When the door closed behind him, she turned indecisively. The game room was directly opposite the study, its doors open wide. Accepting the invitation, Kit wandered in, her bare feet quickly sinking into the thick alpaca rug on the floor. One glance and it was obvious that Nolan, Chip, or Abe had taken over half of the room for an office area. The poker table was covered with a careless array of memos, schedules, and other important-looking paperwork. More was stacked on the chairs around it.

Wisely, Kit aimed for the billiard table and the pair of plump chairs upholstered in creamy corduroy that faced the brown marble fireplace beyond it. As she started to give the cue ball a roll across the green slate top, she noticed a script lying on the mahogany edge near the middle pocket. A yellow Post-it was taped to the cover. The words "Revised draft approved by Olympic" were scrawled across it and dated four days ago.

The revised script for *White Lies*. She hadn't received her copy yet.

"I wonder what changes Chip made." Curious, she fanned through the first few pages, then shrugged and picked it up.

She curled up in one of the chairs by the fireplace and began to skim through the script. Twenty pages in, she pressed her lips together. The more she read, the more tightly she pressed them, the pull of the corners growing grimmer and grimmer.

When she finished it, she swung out of the chair and crossed to the window. She stood stiffly in front of it, staring at the steady fall of white powder, her hands gripping the script. She was still there when John walked in.

He came up behind her, his hands moving onto the rounded points of her shoulders as he bent to nuzzle her neck. "Sorry."

She spun around to face him, holding out the script. "Is this the draft we'll be shooting from?" she asked in a tightly controlled voice.

John glanced at the cover note and nodded. "The approval came in a few days ago—"

"How could you do it?" Kit exploded. "How could Chip do it? You've destroyed the story. You've destroyed everything that made it unique and—"

"You're overreacting, Kit."

"Overreacting? You've turned Eden into a murderess. You have her killing her husband. She's a cliché. This story is a cliché—a rehash of a dozen other films."

"It's a formula that works." He turned away, digging into the pocket of his robe for his pack of cigarettes, needing one.

"But this isn't the script you bought," she argued, pacing over to the billiard table. "This isn't the story that excited you enough to buy it."

"Maybe not, but it's the story Olympic wants." He snapped the lighter to his cigarette and drew a quick deep puff on it. "They're paying for it, they're distributing it, and they're calling the shots. They decided the original script was too risky; they wanted a proven formula, and they got it."

"That's it. That's all you can say." Her hand made an angry sweep through the air. "The story goes to hell, but so what? Is that it?"

After a twenty-minute session with Lassiter, he had no more patience left. "Grow up, Kit," he snapped. "In this business, when it comes to a choice between the bottom line and the storyline, the storyline is always going to suffer."

She threw the script down. "Grow up? Don't you mean 'give up'? Just forget that I believed in the story and bow my head in acceptance the way you have."

"Damn it, Kit. I had no choice."

"No choice?" She stormed across the room. "You could have told them to take their money, their distribution, their bottom line, and go to hell."

"You don't understand, Kit." He fought to get a grip on his temper. "I need this picture."

"Olympic isn't the only studio in town."

"What the hell makes you think any other studio would want that script?" he shouted back. "Chip peddled it over half the town before I saw it. What the hell does that tell you?"

"That tells me you never tried."

"Damn it, my picture deal is with Olympic. Even if I could take the script somewhere else—" He stopped, dragging in a deep breath and forcing his voice down. "I'm in no position to dictate terms or conditions. John Travis may be a big star in the public's eye, but I'm on damned shaky ground in Hollywood. I need a hit. A big hit. I get that and I'm back in control. I can tell Lassiter to go to hell and make him like it. Until then, I have to play the game by his rules, just like you and everyone else."

She stood before him, her arms rigid at her sides and her hands clenched in tight fists, a definite snap to her eyes. "I don't think much of your game or the way it's played."

"Then leave the table," he shot back.

Her face went cool, her eyebrows arching. "Now, there's a thought."

Turning on her heel, she walked out of the room. In the guest room, she changed back into her sweater and slacks, grabbed her purse and coat, and headed for the front door. John was there when she reached it. His narrowed gaze centered briefly on the coat she'd thrown over her arm.

"You're not leaving, Kit."

Temper was licking its way to the surface again. She coated it with hot ice. "Wanna bet?"

He blocked her when she tried to move past him to the door. "Look." He tried to force some reason into his own angry voice. "I know you're disappointed with the change in Eden—"

"Disappointed doesn't begin to cover it. In fact, I'm in the mood to start throwing things and you would make a lovely target. So get out of the way."

This time, John didn't try to stop her.

The Jeep charged through the three inches of powder that covered the streets. Instinct guided the hands at the wheel to make all the right turns as Kit left Starwood, her eyes on the road and the steady fall of snow in the Jeep's headlight beams, her thoughts still on her argument with John.

"At least now I understand why Chip was giving John such a problem over the script's changes," she muttered, continuing the steady stream of conversation she'd carried on with herself ever since she'd driven away from John's house. "God. How could Chip butcher his own story like that? Whatever made him do it?"

She tightened her grip on the steering wheel and tried to give it a hard shake, wishing it was Chip she had by the shoulders so she could shake some sense into him. Then it hit her.

"Chip's a director first and a writer second. If he was given an ultimatum—change the story or forget about directing the film—he would have changed it.'' Kit sighed with a mixture of tiredness, frustration, and defeat. ''He would have kicked and screamed and dragged his feet all the way, but he would sacrifice it before he would give up the chance to direct a major film. Oh, Chip,'' she murmured sadly and swung the Jeep onto the highway.

Snowplows had already scraped away all but a dusting of freshly fallen flakes from the highway that cut through Aspen. Kit drove along it, falling silent. The traffic light ahead turned red. She slowed the Jeep to a stop and waited, her attention finally straying to her surroundings.

The Hotel Jerome rose tall and proud through the veil of snow, lavishly restored and refurbished to once again reign over the corner of Mill and Main as it had one hundred years earlier. Yet, so different from the Jerome she remembered as a girl, its blue eyebrows no longer raised at the goings-on around it.

On impulse, not even certain of her reason, Kit turned right onto Mill and drove until her way was blocked by the start of the pedestrian mall. She shifted into park and let the engine idle, her hands sliding together at the top of the steering wheel. Leaning forward, she rested her chin against them and gazed at the scene before her.

Snow blanketed the bricked thoroughfare and frosted the trees scattered along it. The white of their branches glistened. More flakes drifted down, creating a setting that was iced and glamorous, a winter wonderland that didn't seem quite real.

As her gaze wandered to the lighted shop windows that faced the mall, she tried to remember what the area had been like when she was growing up and the streets had still been dirt. But, too much had changed, too many new buildings replaced old ones—new buildings designed to look old and ageless like the Jerome and the Wheeler Opera House.

Aspen had changed, yet it still looked like the ideal place to live. Except it wasn't ideal. Bannon had shown her that. He'd shown her it was only ideal if you could afford to live here.

She remembered, too, his efforts to change that. Bucking

the tide, fighting the system, refusing to regard it as inevitable, refusing to give in, to give up. When he believed in something, there was no compromise in him. He stood by it to the last.

Not like John.

Bannon was like the boy with his thumb in the hole in the dike, trying to hold back the flood until help arrived.

Only this wasn't Hollywood, even though it looked like a Hollywood set. No cavalry would come charging in to save the day. It was the real world.

John would have been quick to remind her of that.

A bright light flashed its glare into her eyes. Blinking against its harshness, Kit glanced out the driver's-side window. A patrol car was alongside her Jeep. The officer on the passenger side signaled for her to roll down her window. Hastily, she complied.

"Are you waiting for someone, miss?" He played the light over her face.

"No. No, I'm not." She held up a hand to partially shield her eyes from its brightness. "I was just looking at the mall—and the snow."

"You're blocking the street. You'll have to move along."

"Of course." She nodded and shifted gears, driving off under their watchful eyes and making the swing back onto the highway and home.

23

A dusting of snow collected on the crown and rolled brim of Bannon's Stetson. He walked along the lighted street at a slow and easy gait, his lined parka unbuttoned to the still night air that felt pleasantly cool rather than cold. Beside him, Pete Ranovitch took a quick drag of his cigarette, one of a string he'd chain-smoked over the course of the evening. His bare head was bowed, the collar of his coat turned up to ward off the falling snow. His left arm was in a sling, a plaster cast covering it from the thumb to above the bend of his elbow.

"Need a lift, Pete?" Only lengthy negotiations, Pete's personal check for three hundred dollars, and a promise from Bannon to make the check good himself if it bounced had persuaded the owner of the bar not to press charges.

"No. My Bronco's parked a couple of blocks from here," he said, then expelled a fragment of a humorless laugh. "Assuming it hasn't been stolen or towed off. That'd be just my luck, wouldn't it?" He puffed on the cigarette again, then lowered it with a cupping hand. "I meant it, Bannon. I'm through trying. I'm leaving. When I get back to that apartment, I'm throwing my things in the back end of the Bronco and pulling out tonight. It's no use kidding myself anymore that I'm ever gonna have a restaurant of my own. I'm not. Not in this lifetime. That dream's over for me. I'm tired, Bannon. I'm just flat-assed tired."

Part of him wanted to argue with Pete to hold on a little longer. But he respected his decision, recognizing that Pete was the one who had to live with it. "Where will you go?"

"I got a friend working in a restaurant down in Telluride. I'll probably go visit him for a couple of days, then . . . find myself a job somewhere once I get this cast off."

Bannon's pickup was parked at the curb, its black color hidden by a coating of snow. He stopped and held out a hand to Pete. "Good luck, Pete. If you decide to come back this way, I'll buy you a cup of coffee."

"You're the one damned thing about this town I'm going to miss. I owe you a helluva lot, Bannon." His fingers closed around Bannon's hand with a fierce grip.

"Send the recipe for your barbecue sauce."

"I'll do it," he promised and jaywalked to the other side of the street.

Bannon watched him for a minute, then climbed into the pickup's cab and fished the keys out of his jacket pocket. He started the engine up, let it idle a minute, then pulled away from the curb, windshield wipers flapping at the snow blowing off the truck's hood.

With the lights of the town behind him, he thought about Pete and some of the others he'd known. He'd watched the dreams of so many die a little bit at a time, bled away by successive failures, bad luck, or the fading of spirit. For a time they'd repeat the old words of faith, of hope, until finally one day the words would be empty.

Maybe Aspen was harder on dreams than some places. But he couldn't blame it for the death of Pete's dream. It was life.

A pair of red lights rapidly flashed on and off a half mile ahead of him. Bannon slowed the pickup when he saw the vehicle with its hazard lights on. It looked like a Jeep pulled off on the shoulder. The road ahead looked clear, which left an accident or engine trouble. He'd already started to pull over when he saw Kit standing on the side of the road, waving her arms. He braked to a stop next to the Jeep.

"What happened?" he asked when Kit pulled the passenger door open.

"I ran out of gas." She threw her shoulder purse onto the seat and piled in after it.

"You—"

"Shut up, Bannon." She raised her hands, palms out, fingers spread, as if to ward off whatever was coming. "Please—just shut up and take me home."

Her emotion-charged voice sounded close to temper or tears and he was not in the mood to deal with either one— not from her, not tonight. He held his silence. Kit turned her face to the side window, propping an elbow on its ledge and her chin on her hand.

They rode the few miles to her house in silence. When he parked in front of it, she immediately climbed out of the truck, dragging her purse after her. "Thanks," she said as she closed the door.

He watched her dash through the snow and onto the porch. He waited until a light went on inside, then drove off, back down the lane.

Kit leaned against the front door, and let out a long sigh, then pushed away from it in a burst of restlessness and impatience. She threw her purse onto a chair and dragged off her coat, giving it a toss as well.

The phone rang. She whirled around and stopped, staring at it as it jangled again. It was John, calling to apologize— or argue with her some more.

"I don't want to talk to you." She crossed her arms tightly, her fingers kneading at her arms through the sleeves of her bulky, oversized sweater, all the agitation, confusion, anger, and uncertainty coming back stronger than before.

It rang a third time. What if it wasn't John? What if it was the hospital calling about her mother? Or Maggie Peters, her neighbor?

In two strides, she reached the phone and picked up the receiver. "Hello?"

"Kit. Where the hell have you been? I've been trying to

reach you for three hours.'' Maury's cranky voice came over the line. ''I ask you to keep in touch, but do you? No.''

''I went to John's for dinner.'' She sank onto the chair, clutching the phone with both hands. ''I'm glad you called, Maury. I just saw the changes that have been made to the script.'' The instant the words were out, she tilted her head back to stare at the ceiling. ''Changes. My God, what am I saying? They didn't change it. They ruined it.''

''I'm sure it's not that bad—''

''Maury.'' She stood up. ''They cut the heart out of my character.''

''They cut your part?''

''No. They cut the things that gave her depth and dimension. Now she's just an ordinary cruel, conniving witch. A stereotype of a dozen others. I tried arguing with John, but . . . Olympic insisted on the changes and he won't go against them.''

''If that's what Olympic wants . . .'' Maury let the shrug in his voice finish the sentence. ''I wouldn't worry about it, Kit. You'll make the role memorable. Everybody will sit up and take notice of you. You'll see. For that matter they already are. I—''

''I don't care if anybody notices me.'' She walked to the end of the cord and started back again, pacing like an animal on a chain.

''That's a strange thing to say—''

''Why?'' Kit demanded. ''Why is it so strange that I don't care whether I make this movie? I don't like the things that are happening to me. I don't like the things that *will* happen if I make it—''

''Kit,'' he cut her off. ''Kit, you're upset. Now you're not thinking. You're not being realistic.''

''My God, you sound just like John.'' She pushed a hand through her blond hair and threw her head back in disgust. ''And for your information, I have been doing a lot of thinking.''

''Then you are not thinking clearly about this.'' Maury began to speak slowly and very precisely, making an obvious effort not to sound impatient or irritated. "You can't quit this film simply because you are unhappy with some changes that have been made in the script."

"Why can't I? If that's what I want to do, why can't I do it?" she argued, suddenly fighting tears.

"For one thing, you signed a contract—"

"Then I'll break it. They can murder the script but they can't hold a gun to my head and make me do the film. That's illegal."

"Do you still have the money they paid you when you signed the contract? They'd demand it back, Kit."

She'd forgotten about that. "No, I don't have it. You know I used it to pay some of my mother's bills. But I'll find a way to pay it back. I don't know how, but . . ." She pressed her fingers to her forehead, feeling the beginnings of a headache.

"I can't believe you're saying this. I can't believe you would quit three weeks before this film is scheduled to start shooting. You've got a key role, Kit. Don't you realize how many people are depending on you to do your job and do it well? Sure, they can find another actress to replace you, but how far will that set the filming back? What about wardrobe, all the fittings you've had? What about the crew—the cinematographer, the grips, the gaffers, the assistant director? They've probably passed up other projects to work on this movie. Don't you realize the kind of problems you'd create? Is that fair, Kit?" He hammered at her. "My God, you talk like you've never played in a rotten film before. When did you suddenly get too good to do a bad script?"

"It isn't that, Maury," she said in frustration.

"Then what the hell is it?"

"I'm just confused." She sat back down, sighing over this feeling she was caught in a trap.

"You'd better get *un*confused. You're on your way up, Kit. You've got a big career ahead of you. For God's sake, don't blow it," he declared forcefully, then added, for good measure, "Do you hear?"

"I hear, Maury." Some of the nameless anger got into her voice.

"Good. Now, you take that script and make the best that you can out of it. That's what you're getting paid for. This is just the beginning, Kit. There will be other roles, better roles. You keep that in mind."

"I will." She told him good-bye and hung up, then sat there for several long seconds, holding the phone in her lap.

Maury made her sound like a spoiled child. Or a temperamental actress. But it wasn't that. Damn it, it wasn't that.

Giving in to the sudden wave of angry frustration, Kit roughly shoved the phone back onto the table and ignored the protesting jingle it made. She stalked out to the kitchen and slammed through the cupboards until she found the aspirin bottle, then slammed through them again for a water glass. She turned the cold-water tap on full force to fill it.

After she washed the aspirin down, she stood in front of the sink and gripped the sides of it. "Calm down," she told herself angrily, but that was impossible. She had to use up all this anger, all this excess energy.

Cocoa. She'd make cocoa. From scratch, the way Mrs. Hatch used to.

With immense pleasure, Kit rattled through the pots, pans, and skillets before banging a saucepan down on a burner, then slammed through the cupboards again, gathering all the ingredients listed on the Hershey's Cocoa can. She stalked to the refrigerator and yanked the door open, jerked the container of milk from the shelf, rammed the door shut, then turned.

Bannon stood in the doorway to the living room, melting snow dripping off the brim of the hat he held in front of him. "When I got to the end of the lane, I discovered your billfold on the seat. It must have fallen out of your purse," he said, tossing it on the counter. "I knocked, but I guess you were making too much noise to hear me."

"I'm mad, hurt, confused." Suddenly it all seemed to drain out of her and she let out a long sigh, dragging a hand through her hair and sending him a wan smile. "I'm making some cocoa. Take your coat off and have a cup with me." When he hesitated, she added, "There's nothing better to warm you on a snowy night."

Looking at her, Bannon remembered a few things that were better. It was almost enough to make him turn around and walk out. Almost.

"A cup of cocoa would taste good." He crossed the kitchen and hung his hat and coat on the hall tree by the back door, then pulled out one of the curved-back wooden chairs at the table and sat down.

A silence fell between them, an easy silence, as Kit measured ingredients into a pan and poured milk into another with none of her previous clang and clatter. He watched her moving about, stirring, mixing, tasting, all with the careless confidence of one accustomed to puttering about the kitchen. The simple, homey scene tugged at him again with the what-might-have-beens in his life.

"What brought you out on this wintry night, Bannon? Business or pleasure?" Kit asked as she stirred the combined cocoa concoction to keep it from scorching.

"I guess you'd call it business. A friend got into trouble, busted up some stuff." He leaned his arms on the table and moved the sugar bowl from side to side between his hands. "I managed to talk the bar owner into letting him pay the damages and not press charges."

"I take it your friend had been drinking."

"Not this time. No, he was just frustrated and upset. He was just letting it out—the way you were doing earlier."

"I was making a bit of a racket, wasn't I?" She pulled a rueful smile as she took two cups down from a cupboard shelf.

"A bit."

She filled both cups with cocoa and brought them to the table. "You always stick by your friends, don't you, Bannon? Right or wrong?"

"I'm a lawyer."

"Lawyer or not, you still would." She pushed one of the cups to him, then sat down in the opposite chair. "That's the way you are."

"I guess." The wedding band glinted on his fingers, catching her eye as he raised the cup and lightly blew on the cocoa's steaming surface. It suddenly didn't bother Kit to see it on his finger, at last seeing it as a symbol of his steadfast nature, standing by people whether they were around to know or not. After more than eight years in Hollywood, she recognized how very rare that was. But the thought reminded her of John and Maury and all the other things that were troubling her.

She took a testing sip of her cocoa. "It still doesn't taste as good as Mrs. Hatch's. Maybe she used something other than vanilla for flavoring. Next time I think I'll try a little almond extract and see if that's it."

Bannon tasted his. "Personally I think all that banging and slamming added a little extra something to it." His smile had a familiar touch of recklessness to it that warmed and teased. "Next time you run out of gas, remind me to drive on by."

"Running out of gas was only the final disaster to my evening." She swirled the cocoa in her cup and watched the miniature eddy the motion made. "John and I had a big fight tonight over the changes in the script."

"Oh."

Absorbed again by her thought, she missed the coolness in that sound. She glanced up when Bannon rose from his chair and wandered over to the window, looking out as if to see whether it was still snowing.

She regarded his back thoughtfully. "Now I'm not even sure why I got so angry over them. I know it hurt to see the changes they'd made in my character. I was disappointed, upset. But actors never have any control over things like that. You can protest, but it rarely does any good. You're stuck with what they give you. Artistic control only comes when you're so big that they don't dare say no to you." She paused, considering that for a moment. "Maybe, deep down, that's what I was reacting to—the kind of person you have to become to get that big, the bargains and compromises you have to make along the way, the way people will treat you and the way you'll treat them."

"That doesn't say a lot for Travis," Bannon remarked a little harshly.

"No, it doesn't, I suppose," she admitted. "But when people are so quick to use you, so quick to criticize, to judge, and condemn—fairly or unfairly—you have to become hard and cynical. You have to become a little ruthless, too. I never wanted to see that. I never wanted to believe that was true." She stared at her cocoa. "Remember what you told me about money changing the way people think, that the money won't let them think any other way? It's the same with fame. Fame is power, money, and glory all rolled into one." In a surge of restlessness, Kit got up and wandered over to the window by Bannon. Sighing, she gazed at the white flicker of snowflakes beyond the darkened pane.

"I don't like the things that are happening to me now, Bannon. I don't like the kind of person I'll become if I keep going. And I have to change to survive." Otherwise it would break her. It would tear her apart—the way it was tearing her apart now.

"What about the bargains you've already made?" Bannon's voice had a hard edge to it. "If you quit now, it means you've made them for nothing."

The events of these last few weeks made it incredibly easy for her to read between the lines of his remark. "Are you by any chance referring to John Travis and the dirty gossip that's been flying around that I slept with him to get this part?" The lift of his head and stiffening of his jaw provided all the answer she needed. "Not you, too, Bannon," she hurled, her voice vibrating with anger and hurt. "Damn you." She saw his startled frown and spun away, walking stiffly to the counter and slamming the cup down, cocoa sloshing over the sides. "Don't you see that's just what I've been talking about? The way people judge me, assume things. People who should know me better!"

"Kit, I . . . I was out of line—"

"You're damned right you were out of line," she declared, her chin quivering as she whirled back to face him, almost surprised by the confusion and regret she saw in his eyes. "For your information, I have gone to bed with him, but that's not what got me the part. I got it because I'm good. Because I'm damned good. It was only afterward that John and I—" She stopped and pressed a hand to her forehead. "God, why am I telling you this? It's none of your business."

She lowered her hand to look at him, fighting tears and a whole host of old emotions. "I wish we could kill whatever romantic illusion there still is between us."

Too many hot bitter tears blurred her eyes. She didn't see him move. Suddenly he was in front of her, his hands gripping her upper arms.

"I've wished it, too, Kit. But you don't kill things like that," he said in a low voice, then almost angrily hauled her to him, his mouth coming down to cover hers with a pressure that was hard and wanting. She found herself returning it without reservation, straining for a greater closeness, needing it.

John had kissed her with more finesse; he had made her feel more sexually alive. Yet the simple roughness of Bannon's kiss called up feelings much more basic, much more ageless—feelings that made a woman want a man for reasons that went beyond sex. It dazzled her and it made her want to cry, too.

Bannon drew back a little, his callused hands framing her face, his breathing more than a little ragged. His eyes moved over her, a dark and troubled light shining from them, the sight of it making her ache.

He kissed her again, this time like a man forcing himself to gently savor the taste of water after being starved for it. With the same restraint, he folded her to him, his mouth rummaging lightly through her hair.

"How can you taste better than I remember?" he murmured thickly. "How can I want you more than I did before?"

She closed her eyes against his words, trembling inside, unable to breathe and hurting because of it, her hands rigid on his waist. "Don't, Bannon," she whispered tightly. "I can't go through it again. To be as close as we were—and to lose it. As much as I want you right now, I can't go through that again."

"I can't defend the past, Kit. I can't explain it, not even to myself," he admitted. "I know the man I was with you; I know the man I am now. But the man I was for those three months, I don't know him. When I looked at her, did I feel the lure of something forbidden? Was it because she was dark like the night with all its mysterious promises and you were bright and fresh like a summer day? Was it because she was there and you were gone? Or was she someone new and different? Maybe it was all those things. I don't know, Kit.'' The pain that rumbled through his voice was an echo of her own. ''I can't change the past. It will always be with us.''

A strange and wonderful peace came over her. Despite— or maybe because of—his inability to explain, she suddenly understood. She didn't know how or why, but—it was all right now.

''Bannon,'' she whispered and let her arms slide around him again.

It was true the past would always be with them, and there would be a part of him that would always belong to Diana. She had been the mother of his daughter; she would always have that claim on him, and his daughter would always be there to remind him of it. Kit believed she could finally accept that.

He stiffened slightly. ''I want you, Kit. But you deserve more than I can give you.''

''Just give me all you can. That will be enough.'' It had to be.

A gusty sigh broke from him as his weight pressed her back against the counter with a suddenness that had her hanging on for balance. His mouth closed onto hers, driving and tonguing in its need, without control, without patience, his hands tight around her. His hips trapping her against it.

Kit responded with equal force. She'd stopped questioning the right or wrong of this minutes before; she'd stopped thinking about the chance she might be hurt again. There was a time for thinking and another for feeling, a time to be practical and a time to love. She'd convinced herself of all that and now she sought to show Bannon the truth of it.

He drew back an inch, his heated breath fanning her lips, his body heavy against her. His hands tunneled into her hair, caging her head. ''I want you, but not here—not like this, not like a couple teenagers making out in the kitchen. I want you in bed, your hair spread over a pillow, making a golden frame for your face.''

''Yes,'' she whispered.

Without preliminaries, he scooped her up into the cradle of his arms. She wrapped her arms around his neck, then ran her fingers through his hair while she explored his ear, chewing at its lobe.

He carried her up the steps and into her bedroom, then kicked the door shut behind him. With the world shut out, Bannon lowered her legs to the floor, letting her slide down his muscled thigh, her loose-fitting sweater bunching up under his arms, his work-roughened hands gliding onto her bare skin.

His mouth came back to claim hers and he tasted of cocoa and heat and desire, an addictive combination. When he stripped off her sweater, she pushed at his shirt, forcing it off his wide shoulders. He shrugged out of it, then impatiently came back to run his hands over her skin. She felt the rasp of them, sensed the snag of callus on the lacy fabric of her bra when he sought its clasp.

In minutes they were twined together on the bed, their clothes stripped with a haste that would have staggered Kit if she'd taken the time to think about it. But she hadn't; the haste had been her doing as much as Bannon's. They had ten years to make up for, ten long years. It was part of the desperation that drove both of them, that made enough never enough.

Her hair spilled over the pillow the way he had dreamed about. Now the dream was coming to life. She was here, with him. He gathered her hair in his hand, drawing her head back to expose the long pale line of her throat. The faintly blue vein pulsed wildly as he traced his tongue over it. Her hands glided over his chest, then lower, and his stomach muscles quivered under her touch.

When he slipped inside her, there was a low murmur. From him? From her? Kit didn't know. All that mattered was this joining, this life-validating union. She moved beneath him, wanting more, always wanting more. Instantly his hands were at her hips, digging in to stop her.

"Don't," he warned. "Honey, if you so much as twitch a muscle this will be over before it's started. That's how bad I want you. That's how long I've wanted you."

She let her eyelids drift open so she could see him poised above her. She saw the pain of control in his face, a control exercised for her sake.

Reaching up, she smoothed a hand over his cheek. "The night is young, Bannon. Especially if you spend all of it with me."

"All of it," he murmured the promise into her mouth, releasing her hips to let them rise and meet the plunge of his. The race began, the rhythm hot and reckless, sensation slamming into sensation. In this haze, she saw his face above her, saw it tense on the edge of release, tiny beads of sweat breaking out on his skin, his features twisting with the pain of pleasure. Because of her.

Then his full weight was on her. But only for an instant as he rolled onto his back, pulling her with him to lie on top. Her long hair fell forward and she combed it to one side with her fingers. He caught her hand and carried it to his lips, rubbing it over them and lightly nibbling at the pad of her thumb, his eyes still clouded and dark from a need freshly satisfied.

"Now it's your turn," he said huskily, then lowered his gaze to the hanging weight of her breasts, their hardened tips barely brushing his chest. "Or is it mine again?"

He kissed her fingers, the front of them, the back of them, drawing each into his mouth. He moved to the palm of her hand, his tongue tracing a lazy circle in its center. His teeth raked over the hill of her hand and his lips discovered the fast-beating vein in her wrist. They followed it to the crook of her elbow and lingered there to nuzzle its hollow before continuing up her arm to her shoulder. He nibbled his way along its ridge, then began a slow and leisurely exploration of her neck and throat with his mouth, his teeth, and his tongue.

For Kit, it was like sinking into a dream, too impossibly beautiful to be real, because he made her feel loved.

Even as his mouth continued its downward journey, his hands moved to her rib cage and lifted her higher on his body. He cupped a hand around her left breast and lightly, so very lightly, rubbed his lips over a nipple, teasing it until it was taut and aching. A protest against this torment formed on her lips, then dissolved in a sigh when his mouth closed around it, flexing in languid, sucking motions. It was death and life all rolled into one. She dug her fingers into his hair, trembling when he shifted to her other breast and laved it with his tongue and mouth, too.

With a slight turn of his body, he slid Kit off him and onto her side, then continued his downward travels, intent on carpeting every inch of her with his moist kisses, from her navel to the curve of her hip, down her long thigh to the point of her knee, along her calf to the break of her ankle, over the sensitive skin of her arch to her instep, from her toes to her heel, leaving her alone in the darkness, adrift in the sensation of it, unsure how she came to be on her stomach while he made his way up the back to nuzzle the hollow behind her knee, trail kisses over her bottom, linger at the dip at the base of her spine, then follow her backbone up to her shoulder blades. He scraped her hair aside, exposing the back of her neck and kissing every cord and muscle in it.

Never, never had she felt so loved, so cherished. *Cherished*. That was the word. She felt cherished by him, something to be treasured, to be treated with loving care and deep tenderness.

He turned her into his arms, at last seeking her lips. She lengthened the kiss, needing him, wanting him. She hadn't known she could feel so weak yet so strong, so limp yet so excited. Dear God, but she wanted this moment to last into forever.

She drew back. "Let me touch you, Bannon."

He hesitated, then let his hands trail off her arms, and rolled his shoulders back onto the mattress. "I want you to."

For an instant she simply stared at him, the long, lean length of his body, the muscles coiled under darkly tanned skin. Rangy and loose-limbed, his body had been toughened by physical work, bronzed by the elements into something sleek and powerful.

"I like the way you look." She stroked a hand over the long ropes of muscles in his chest. "I like the way you feel."

Lowering her head, she brushed her lips over his shoulders—shoulders wide enough for her to lean on if she wanted to, but not so wide they overwhelmed her. The muscles in his arms were strong and hard, strong enough to protect her if she wanted to be protected, yet she knew they'd never try to dominate her. And his hands—she picked one up and pressed it to her face—they'd never hold her back; they were the kind that would always be there to reach out and welcome her.

She pressed a kiss in the center of his palm, her mouth opening to breathe in the scent of him, her tongue darting out to lick the salty flavor of his skin. "I like the way you taste."

His fingers closed around her chin. "Come here."

She leaned down, pausing just short of his lips and smiling. "And I definitely like the way you think."

As he kissed her, his hands shifted her on top of him, their bodies matching, fitting, and again he was inside her. "Ride me, Kit," he growled the words in his throat. "Ride me hard."

She did, and her hands braced on his shoulders, his hands on her hips, his body urging her relentlessly on. There was madness here; she knew it. It was impossible to feel so much and still need more, impossible for the pleasure to keep building and not explode. Impossible.

When she was on the edge of going over, he flipped her onto her back, his hands sliding up her forearms, his palms covering hers, his fingers linking tightly with her own. His face was inches above her, his eyes not letting her look at anything else but him. She thought he whispered her name, but she was beyond hearing, beyond thinking as she wrapped her legs around him, discovering pleasure alone was a mild thing, but pleasure combined with love was all.

∞⚬∾ 24 ∾⚬∞

*T*he soft pearling gray of dawn glowed outside the bedroom window, the hint of light making itself felt on her closed eyes. Kit stirred and instantly became aware of the tight bands that held her, trapped her—and the block of heat pressed against her, running from shoulder to toe.

Bannon. She smiled at the discovery she was nestled against him, their bodies molded together spoon-fashion, his arm encircling the front of her rib cage to keep her close to him, its tickling of hairs barely brushing the soft undersides of her breasts. With growing awareness, she became conscious of his warm, moist breath near her ear, the faint bristle of his night beard snagging her hair, and the male scent of him that always reminded her of deep forests and high mountains, a scent earthy and fresh with an indefinable tang to it. She snuggled closer and felt the imprint of his morning hardness against her bottom. She pushed against it and his arm immediately tightened.

"You'd better be awake," he murmured, a deep throaty sound still gravelly with sleep.

"More or less," she whispered back.

A second later she was consumed by the need to see him, to see his face, the granite chin and brow, the sometimes impenetrable darkness of his wide, deeply set eyes, and the roughly molded cheekbones. His arm loosened its grip, letting her turn to face him, their heads lying on the same pillow.

She'd never looked more beautiful to him, all tousled and drowsy, her eyes all heavy and darkly aglow, her lips soft and full in repose. It was impossible not to think of all the mornings he'd missed waking up with her beside him.

He wanted to tell her, but he didn't have the glibness of the men she must have known in Hollywood, of men like Travis. All he had were the feelings inside him and he couldn't find the words to explain them. Words weren't feelings.

"Good morning." Reaching up, she ran a forefinger over the stubble on his chin, liking the pleasant rasp of it.

"Good morning." He caught her fingers and pressed them to his lips, then lowered them and held her hand against his chest, letting her feel the solid beat of his heart. "Happy?" he asked, then felt the sudden sharp pang of fear. What would he do if she ever wasn't? He'd never be able to bear seeing her look at him with silent loathing and reproach the way Diana had.

"Mmmm, I'm somewhere between happy and delirious," she murmured. "Bordering on ecstatic."

He smiled in silent relief. "Do you know you're a very dangerous woman when you're sleeping? Your arms and legs fly all over the place."

"I have a tendency to *attack* sleep," Kit admitted.

"The same way you attack life."

"I guess." She drew back a little. "You seem to have survived the attack. I don't see any damage."

"I found a solution."

"What was that?"

"To hold you." He carried her hand to his lips again and started kissing the ends of her fingers one by one. "In the beginning, it was out of sheer self-defense, but the minute I took you in my arms, you curled against me like a snuggly kitten. You even made a little sound in your throat that sounded like a purr. Of course, you could have been snoring."

"I don't snore." She opened her eyes wide, wondering if she did.

"Then it must have been a purr." There was a twinkle in his eyes that told her he was only teasing.

She relaxed again, a smile forming on her lips. "To tell you the truth, I feel like a cat right now. I want to stretch and arch up against you—"

"Why don't you?"

She caught back a breath, a joy and a pain squeezing her heart. In the next second, their lips and tongues were meeting, her hips and stomach arching against his, her arms snaking around him.

Morning love. Before it was over, Kit discovered how much she loved the slow and lazy languor of morning love. Morning love that filled her up and emptied her out. Morning love that left the bright glow of sunshine in every corner. She lay contented in his arms, his lips idly rubbing themselves against her forehead.

"Would you believe I have to be in court today?" he murmured. "Probably all day."

She tilted her head back to look at him, cupping a hand to his face. "I guess that means we should get up."

"I guess it does."

"I could put some coffee on."

"We could take a shower." He touched his mouth to hers, then drew back when she tried to deepen it into an actual kiss. "I'll wash your back."

"I like that idea."

"I thought you might."

"But I have a better one."

"Oh?" He eyed her skeptically.

"I'll put the coffee on now so it will be done when we finish our shower."

"Efficiency. I like that in a woman."

"I have my moments, but not many," she warned, then slipped free of his arms and climbed out of bed, dragging a corner of the top sheet with her, pulling it the rest of the way loose from the foot and wrapping it around her sarong-style— not out of any desire to conceal her nudity from Bannon's eyes, but rather to ward off the room's morning chill.

When she came back upstairs a scant few minutes later,

Kit heard water gushing from the shower head in the bathroom. She followed the sound and found Bannon there, testing the temperature of the water and adjusting the taps. She paused a moment in the doorway, her gaze drifting over the rippling bronze muscles in his back, his hard lean flanks and tight bottom. The thought crossed her mind that he had a gorgeous tush. As if sensing her presence, Bannon glanced over his shoulder.

"For a minute I thought you'd started without me," Kit said as she peeled off the sheet and tossed it in a corner.

"Not a chance."

He moved to one side of the shower door, letting her be the first to step beneath the steaming spray. Following her inside, he closed the door. Water coursed over both of them. Bannon lifted her face to it as his arms curved around her and drew her back against him.

So many warm feelings flowed through her that she couldn't separate them all. For now it was enough to be close to him, to be held, to be loved.

Bannon turned her to face him, his mouth fastening on hers in a wet kiss, water streaming down their faces. She kissed him back, stunned to feel passion flaring again so quickly. She tried to check it, drawing away to rub her lips over his chest.

"I thought you were going to wash my back."

"I am," he said. "This way."

Belatedly, she felt the bar of soap in the hand he ran down her spine. She closed her eyes, hearing the spray of water striking the sides of the stall and feeling the enervating steam as it billowed around them. His soapy hands slid over her, spreading the lather, not content to wash only her back, but spreading it to the front as well, until there was soap on both of them, its scent citrusy and clean.

Kit leaned into him, her arms limply curved around his back, her hands firm on his shoulders. Water sprayed over her, gently pummeling muscle and skin, sluicing off the soap. His mouth was at her ear, his tongue exploring its shell while his hands continued their lathering journey over her body, their touch soothing and arousing at the same time.

Shifting, Bannon maneuvered both of them under the wide rush of water from the shower head, letting it stream onto them. While they stood there, hot, slick, and entangled, he slipped into her. She dug her hands into his shoulders as he took her there, amid the steam and the water and the sharp, fresh fragrance of soap.

In a sash-tied robe and with a cup of coffee in hand, Kit walked Bannon to the door. He pushed his hat on his head and turned, taking her by the shoulders.

"Don't worry about the Jeep. I'll have Hec get some gas in it and bring it back to you."

"Thanks." She rubbed her free hand up and down the front of his fleece-lined parka, feeling very wifely and liking the feeling of seeing her man off to work.

He bent his head and kissed her in a warm and amazingly tender, lip-nuzzling fashion, then straightened and reached for the doorknob. "I'll talk to you tonight."

Smiling, she echoed the promise, "Tonight." She stayed in the doorway to wave to him when he drove out.

Through a break in the cloud cover, the moon cast its pale light over the Stone Creek ranch yard, silvering the snow-draped clearing. A whispering wind went about its night's work, stirring up the crystalline powder and sculpting the snow into new drifts, playfully scattering some on the shoveled walk to the house.

It crunched softly underfoot, the stillness magnifying the sound as Bannon made his way to the stone steps. Lights glowed a warm welcome from the windows of the old log house, smoke curled from the chimney, tainting the night air with the smell of wood smoke. On the porch, Bannon stomped the snow from his boots, and hearing the bark of coyotes, threw a glance in the direction of the winter pasture. He left them to their conversation and went inside.

"Hi, Dad." Laura sat curled in a chair in front of the television set, absently playing with a lock of long dark hair. His father dozed in another chair, but snorted awake at Laura's greeting.

"Hi, yourself. Got your homework all done, I hope." He hooked his hat on a peg and shrugged out of his wool topcoat.

"All done." A commercial came on and she climbed out of the chair to wander over to him. "Did you win your case?"

"In a way." He tugged at the already-loosened knot of his striped tie and pulled it the rest of the way free, leaving the ends hanging around his neck. "The other side didn't like the testimony from some of our witnesses. They made an offer to settle. After some negotiations, our side took it."

"Is that how come you're so late?" Old Tom pushed stiffly out of his chair and went over to poke the fire.

Bannon nodded. "We had to get it all down in black and white, and it took some time to get the documents worded to the satisfaction of both sides. But it means I won't have to be back in court tomorrow."

He ran a hand tiredly through his hair. It had been a long, full day. Then he smiled to himself and corrected that thought. If he was tired it was from the wonderful night he'd had. He paused a minute and pictured Kit again, standing at the door, waving to him when he drove out in the morning, a cup of coffee in her hand, a robe tied around her, and her hair still damp from the shower they'd shared. He'd almost stopped to see her before coming home, but he hadn't made it back to the house in time to see Laura before she left for school. Another hour and it would be her bedtime.

"Have you eaten? There's some cold roast and scalloped potatoes in the refrigerator. I can warm them up for you," Laura offered, sounding remarkably like the woman of the house.

"Thanks, but we sent out for sandwiches."

"Aunt Sondra called earlier," she told him.

"Did she say what she wanted?"

"No. She said she'd talk to you tomorrow."

"Okay." He walked over to the phone to call Kit.

"If you're calling Aunt Sondra, don't bother," Laura said when he picked up the receiver. "She won't be home. She's meeting some people for dinner tonight. That's why she said she'd talk to you tomorrow."

"I'm calling Kit. I told her I'd have Hec fill the Jeep with gas and get it back to her. I want to make sure he did." He wasn't sure why he felt the need to justify to Laura his reason for calling Kit.

"When did you see her?"

"Last night." He dialed Kit's number. "She ran out of gas on her way home and I gave her a lift."

Laura frowned. "If the roads were good enough that you could drive her to Silverwood, how come you couldn't make it back home last night?"

Old Tom chortled faintly. "I'd like to hear the answer to that one myself."

"Hello, Kit," Bannon said when she answered after the first ring. Briefly he met the amused and knowing gleam in his father's eyes, then turned away to hide his own smile. "It's Bannon."

"Hi. I had a gorgeous day. Did you?"

"More or less," he replied, recalling the trouble he'd had concentrating on the court trial.

"It could be a gorgeous evening. I have a fire blazing away, a whole bag of marshmallows, and the fixings for some dangerous hot toddies. Care to join me?"

"I'm not sure." Conscious of Laura loitering nearby, he said, "Did Hec get the Jeep back to you okay?"

"Can't talk, eh?" That purr in her voice had an impish quality. Bannon instinctively braced himself.

"That's right."

"Did I mention that I'm sitting here with absolutely nothing on under this robe and I've dabbed perfume in the most unusual places. Plus, I have this marvelous scented oil and a tape on how to give a massage. Of course I need a nude male to practice on, preferably one who will stretch out on the rug in front of the fireplace while I smooth the oil all over his shoulders, chest, hips, and stomach, then glide—"

"Kit," he said thickly, feeling the vital response of his own body and the heat settling with explicit directness in his groin.

She laughed, low and soft. "Am I bothering you?"

"And then some," he admitted.

"And you accused *me* of having a vivid imagination," she

mocked, then laughed again. "All right, I'll be good. Yes, the Jeep is here, its gas tank full. And if you can't come tonight, I'll console myself with burnt marshmallows, a hot toddy, and the knowledge that I've given you cause to suffer a little, too."

"That's thoughtful of you."

"I can be wicked that way. So, tell me, how did court go today?"

Bannon repeated his earlier explanation, then added, "Since I don't have to be in court tomorrow, it means I'll have a light day."

"Light enough to slip away?"

"Maybe."

"I'm going to hold you to that definite 'maybe,' " she warned.

"Okay. Look, I'd better let you go."

"Okay." There was a slight pause before she added, "Bye. Miss you."

"Same here."

When he hung up, his glance was unexpectedly drawn to the wedding band on his finger. He touched it, not clear in his mind about the reason for his strong reluctance to take it off. It wasn't fair to Kit to wear it. Yet . . . there was that look in Diana's eyes.

Sighing inwardly, Bannon turned back to the room, to the fire blazing cheerily in the massive fireplace of river stone, his father settled back in his chair, Laura curled in front of the television again, lights gleaming on the mellow log walls, and the timbered staircase that led to the second-floor bedrooms.

With no effort at all, he could picture Kit in this setting. She'd called this house her center, a place where she felt safe and secure. But she loved laughter, excitement, and good times. In that, she was like Diana. And her life in Hollywood would only have reinforced that love. For a time she might be content here. But this ranch, this home, this life would never be enough to satisfy her. He knew that. Just as he knew he'd let her go before he'd see Kit look at him the way Diana had.

It would hurt to do it; it would hurt like hell, but it would kill him to see that reproach in Kit's eyes.

The morning sun blazed from a brilliant blue sky, turning the snow-covered landscape a dazzling white. The wind was still and the air was bracing, the jangle of harness and trace chains ringing clear and sharp across the winter pasture. The team of sorrel draft horses snorted steam as they plodded through the snow, pulling the flatbed wagon and leaving broken bales of cured hay and hungry cattle strung out in their wake.

Hec Rawlins kicked the last bale off the wagon. "That's it," he shouted to Bannon in a voice faintly breathless from the cold air and the exertion.

Bannon chirruped to the team and tapped their shaggy rumps with a slap of the reins. The pair broke into a steady trot back to the barns and their morning ration of oats.

From the day the first log was cut to build the ranch house, there had been draft horses on Stone Creek. They were as much a part of its heritage as the log house and the cattle. Once, they'd been raised to supply the demand for draft stock to pull the freight and ore wagons in the mining town of Aspen. Over the years, the size of the herd had been cut to two mares and their offspring of various ages in various stages of training, enough to meet today's limited market for well-broken teams to haul tourists around.

Even without that market, Bannon would have kept some

of training, enough to meet today's limited market for well-broken teams to haul tourists around.

Even without that market, Bannon would have kept some of the draft stock for sentimental reasons—and for the pleasure of it. A tractor might do a faster job of hauling hay to the cattle, but the chug of its engines and the smell of its exhaust couldn't compete for enjoyment with the jingle of harness and the heat smell of warm-blooded animals on a crisp winter morning.

"Whoa up, now." He pulled them up to the hay barn and jumped down to unhook the wagon.

Fifteen minutes later, the sorrel geldings were in their stalls, munching on grain, the harness was back in its proper place in the tack room, and Bannon was headed for the house.

As he climbed the stone steps, he noticed a set of skis and poles propped against the log wall by the front door. When he walked in the house, he heard the familiar sound of Kit's laugh and followed it to the kitchen.

He found her there, leaning against a counter, the jacket to her teal-and-black ski suit unzipped, both hands wrapped around a coffee cup, and her cheeks still pink from the cold. The mere sight of her warmed the morning chill from his own body.

"Good morning." Her eyes sparkled at him over the rim of her coffee cup. "The coffee's still hot if you want a cup."

"That's right, Bannon. Help yourself," Old Tom urged, an immensely pleased look on his face.

"I think I will." He peeled off his heavy work gloves as he crossed to the coffeepot on the counter and filled a cup. "I saw the skis on the porch and wondered who was here."

"It's a beautiful day, first snow of the season, the powder's fresh and deep; I thought I'd head up to the lake." Kit blew on her coffee and took a sip, still watching him. "Old Tom was just saying it had been a long time since you played hookey. Want to come along with me?"

Although definitely tempted, he hesitated. "Some calls came in while I was in court yesterday. I should return them and—"

"Listen to him," Old Tom snorted. "Wants his arm

twisted. If he hadn't settled that case last night, he'd be in court today and couldn't return those calls he's trying to make sound important.''

"Maybe he's just using them as an excuse because he's afraid he's too out of shape to make it to the lake on skis," Kit suggested to Old Tom.

Recognizing a challenge when he heard one, Bannon leaned a hip against the counter and drawled, "I can make it."

"Prove it." She took a sip of coffee.

"You're on."

Twenty minutes later, Old Tom stood at the living-room window and watched the two of them set out, all smiles and laughter, their eyes exchanging unspoken thoughts the way a man and wife did.

"That's a sight I thought these tired old eyes of mine would never see again." He turned from the window with a wondering shake of his head.

Coming out of the trees, Kit let her momentum carry her up the hillock, then carved out a stop at the crest of it. Exhilarated and winded from that last run, she planted her poles in the snow and paused to catch her breath as Bannon swooshed to a halt near her. She glanced at him, but said nothing, hushed by the awesome silence that surrounded them.

She lowered her goggles, her attention captured by the vista of far-flung mountains standing tall and proud in their white-robed majesty. Below, a small, bowl-shaped valley of whipped cream and diamonds encircled a lake that gleamed like a blue jewel. And the two of them, alone, in the midst of this lonely, powerful grandeur.

Again she was swept by a feeling of timelessness. That sun overhead had shone its light upon this land through a time that had neither beginning nor end. Her life was little more than one small beat in the never-ending pulse of the universe. What was life but a moment of happiness seized? Glory didn't last. Fame didn't last. Only one thing remained as constant through time as the sun—the love between a man and a woman.

"Incredible, isn't it?" Bannon said, leaning on his poles, his breath coming out in a vapory rush.

"Stunning," she murmured, conscious of the sudden, wonderful ache in her throat.

"Ready?"

"If you are," she said, then caught at his elbow, stopping him before he could push off. "Look. Isn't that smoke coming from that old line cabin by the lake?" She pointed with a ski pole at the faint curl of gray smoke rising from its roof.

"I think it is." Bannon frowned.

"Did you tell someone they could stay there?"

"No. Come on. We'd better check it out." He pushed off and Kit followed.

As they neared the cabin, Bannon gestured to the ski tracks in the snow. "Could be a couple of skiers making a long cross-country, stopping here for a rest."

"Maybe." It was a logical assumption.

Bannon helloed the cabin when they reached it. There was no response from inside. "Wait here," he said, taking off his skis. "I'm going to have a look inside."

"Not without me." She propped her skis next to his against the cabin and let Bannon go in first.

An old iron stove warmed the cabin's one small room. A thermos and two clean mugs sat on the wood table, its age-blackened top covered by a red wool scarf. A soft mohair afghan in shades of red, rose, and wine draped the wide cot along the wall.

"That's strange," Bannon murmured. "There aren't any packs, any gear—" He stopped and swung back to Kit, his eyes narrowing in gleaming suspicion. "You wouldn't happen to know how this happened, would you?"

"Could be some elves at work," she suggested and wandered over to the table. "I wonder what's in this?" She picked up the thermos and unscrewed the lid. "Smells like hot toddies. Do you think the elves will mind if we have a sip? Just to warm up a bit?"

"Somehow, I have the feeling the 'elves' won't mind a bit." His smile turned lazy and knowing as he advanced toward her. "Considering you're the elf responsible."

"How did you guess that?" she asked in mock demand.

"The thermos. It has your father's initials on it." He hooked an arm around her, drawing her to him.

"You are a very perceptive man, Bannon," she declared.

"No." He cupped the side of her face in his rough palm, a warmth in his eyes—and a leashed hunger, too. "I'm just a man who loves you very much."

She lost her breath at his heart-tugging words. Then his mouth was moving over hers in a light and tasting kiss. It was like falling into softness, through layer upon layer of softness, all of it closing about her, warm and painfully good. The feeling was a sustained wave that held her even after he lifted his mouth. She released a small sigh and traced the outline of his lips with the tips of her fingers, then swayed until she was against him, enfolded by his circling arms.

Slowly, his lips explored the margin between her hair and her face, traced the arch of her eyebrows, whispered over her closed eyelids, and breathed warmth onto her cheeks. Enthralled by the exquisite and unexpected tenderness of his touch, Kit couldn't move; she couldn't breathe. When his lips at last brushed her mouth, she sighed his name.

He rubbed his lips over her mouth again. Blindly, she turned her face to follow his maddening mouth when it moved away. Finding it, she stopped it and mated with it. His hands flexed, pulling her closer. She arched against him, bending to fit herself to the curve of his body, matching a woman's soft heat to a man's hard need.

Reaching up, she swept his hat from his head and dropped it to the floor, burying her fingers in his hair. She pressed close, so close she could feel every ripple of muscle, the buttons on his jacket, the metal of his belt buckle, and the larger, harder ridge in his ski pants.

He smoothed his hand inside her jacket, stopping at her breast and caressing it in hot silence. Her sweater and sheer bra were no barrier against the sensation of it—or her reaction to it. She was more than conscious of the impatient tugging of his hands as he pushed the jacket from her shoulders and arms, then pulled the sweater over her head.

He was equally quick to pull the lace bra down around her

waist without bothering to unfasten its hook, but the instant his hands touched the bareness of her breasts, their impatience was gone. Teasingly, tantalizingly, he rubbed the centers of his palms over the tips of her nipples. She pushed his jacket open, then pulled at the front of his shirt, ripping the snaps apart and sliding her hands inside to rake her nails across the muscled flatness of his chest.

Tearing his mouth from hers, he inhaled sharply, his hands closing on her breasts as she'd wanted them to do, then staying to fondle and pluck, stroke and incite, while she ran her lips over his chest. She could feel his heart, almost taste it, as its beat grew quick and heavy against her lips.

His right hand traveled down her stomach to the waistband of her ski pants, getting rid of the bra along the way. She felt them give. His hand slid onto her hipbone, onto her belly, into the pale curls of her mound, and her knees buckled. His arm was there to catch her as he turned and lowered her to the cot.

But he didn't follow her down. Instead, he rocked back, shrugged out of his jacket and shirt and grabbed hold of her ski boot, tugging first the right one off, then the left. Then he gripped the hem of her ski pants and pulled. The material caught at her hips and his tugging lifted her bottom off the cot. Kit squealed with laughter as he shook her out of her pants and dumped her onto the soft afghan.

"That was rude and unromantic," she declared with feigned indignation, wiggling out of her panties as Bannon pulled off his own boots.

"It got the job done, didn't it?" he challenged, an impish glint in his eyes as he peeled off his pants and Jockey shorts. He sank onto the cot beside her, his hand gliding onto her body, his expression growing serious, his eyes languid. "Besides—with you, I don't need a striptease to turn me on. Being near you is enough. It always will be."

"For me, too," she whispered. "Always."

He found her mouth and dived into it. She wrapped her arms around him and pulled him onto her, wanting him, needing him, loving him with a completeness that had her burning and shivering at the same time. She lifted her hips, inviting and meeting the mating plunge of his. When their passion shattered, then reformed, they were still wrapped together.

After a time, he kissed her hair. "I think the stove went out."

"I think you're right." She snuggled more closely against him, ignoring the chill.

He chuckled, his chest rumbling with the sound. "Come on. We'd better get dressed and start back."

Kit sighed because she knew he was right, and reluctantly sat up. Without the heat of his body, the room's full chill danced over her skin. She needed no second urging to don her clothes.

Sondra swung the midnight blue Range Rover into the ranch yard. As Aspen-chic as the vehicle was, she loathed driving it. She much preferred the sleek luxury of her Mercedes. But the weather and the roads in the mountains dictated otherwise in the winter.

Pulling up in front of the massive log house, she stole a glance at the dashboard clock. Her timing should be perfect. Laura wouldn't be home from school for another hour at least. Old Tom could be a problem, but he usually made himself scarce whenever she came.

She stepped out of the Range Rover and paused to scan the ranch yard. All was quiet, no sign of activity. She spotted Bannon's pickup, confirming the information she'd obtained from Agnes that he was spending the day at the ranch.

Salt crystals crunched underfoot as she climbed the stone steps to the porch. Her glance ran over the stout logs, weathered to a dark color over time. She could well understand why Diana had loathed this house. There was only so much rustic anyone could stand day after day.

Not bothering to knock, Sondra walked in. "Hello? Anyone home?" she called in a mild, questioning voice.

The thud of feet hitting the floor drew her glance to a corner of the living room as Old Tom levered himself out of a leather chair that looked as old and faded as he did.

"Sondra." He rubbed his face like a man just waking up

and crossed the room at a stiff-jointed walk. "I didn't hear you knock."

"I'm sorry if I disturbed you, Tom. I came to see Bannon."

"He isn't here."

"His truck is here. Is he with the cattle?" She half turned back toward the door. "It's important I talk to him."

"Nope. He and Kit went skiing."

She went still, the light flaring of her nostrils the only hint of the rage that swept through her at the mere mention of that name. Slowly, she turned back. "Kit Masters?" Her voice dripped ice.

"Yup. If you ask me, it's about time those two got back together again." He hooked his thumbs in the waistband of his pants. If he'd been wearing suspenders he would have snapped them, so blatant was the delight he took in telling her that.

Kit and Bannon. Back together. No. He was lying. She didn't believe him. Old Tom hated her. He'd always hated her. He'd say anything to hurt her. Two could play at that game.

"You said you needed to see Bannon about something important?"

"Yes. He's been talking to me about selling the ranch," she replied smoothly and nearly smiled when she saw the mottling in his face.

"That's a lie!"

"Why? Because he hasn't said anything to you about it?" she mocked.

"Bannon would never sell Stone Creek," he stated emphatically.

"Not while you're alive, he won't," Sondra said with sudden and absolute conviction. "You're the only thing that's stopping him. You and all your talk about your precious land. You've bound him and gagged him with it until he's sick of it."

"That's not true," he shouted. "Bannon loves this land as much as I do."

"You don't believe that, do you?" She lashed out, not bothering to hide the contempt she felt. "You stupid old man.

He hates this place. He hates this drafty old house. He always has.'' The sight of his face growing redder and redder spurred her on. ''He can hardly wait until you're dead and gone so he can sell it and move into town. He wants to practice law, not chase a bunch of stupid cattle around. That's what he's always wanted.''

''You scheming, two-faced little—'' He broke it off, his voice vibrating like the rest of him. ''Out! Get out of my house!''

''Yes, you'd like that, wouldn't you, *Old* Tom? You'd like it even better if I got out of Bannon's life, wouldn't you? You've always hated me. You've tried over and over to poison Bannon against me. But it hasn't worked, has it? It will never work. Because it's you he hates. You and this ranch, this stupid land!''

''Out! Out of my house, I tell you!'' Purpling, he took a threatening step toward her and thrust out a big hand, pointing to the door, shaking like a giant timber. ''Get out of my house before I throw you out! I—'' He gasped suddenly, his mouth and his eyes opening wide as he staggered, clutching a hand to his chest.

She saw the glazing of pain in his eyes and moved in. ''Can't your heart take the truth? Is it giving out, Old Tom? Are you finally going to die? We've been waiting for it. Waiting so we can sell this place.''

He staggered away from her, the sound of his breathing a horrible rasp. She realized he was trying to get to the phone. She made it to the table ahead of him and snatched it out of his reach. His legs buckled out from under him and he crumbled to the floor.

Sondra sat down in a chair and watched him until there was no more movement. One minute. Five minutes. She didn't know.

At last she went over to him and crouched down, touching his neck and feeling for a pulse. Nothing. She smiled.

The front door opened. Whirling to face it, she stood up, briefly panicking. But it wasn't Bannon. It was one of the ranch hands. He stood motionless for an instant, staring at Sondra and the body of Old Tom on the floor beside her.

"I found him lying on the floor," she said hurriedly. "I think he's had a heart attack. I can't find a pulse."

"Hank!" The cowboy shouted at somebody outside, then swiftly crossed to the old man. "Call an ambulance," he told Sondra.

She went to the phone and dialed the emergency number. As it rang the first time, the second cowboy burst into the house.

"Get your rifle and signal Bannon," the first one ordered. "It's Old Tom."

"Shit," the man cursed as he wheeled and went back out.

Sondra watched the first cowboy open Old Tom's shirt and start CPR. A voice came on the line. "Yes, this is Sondra Hudson. I'm at Stone Creek Ranch. The Bannon place. It's Tom Bannon. We think he's had a heart attack. We found him lying on the floor. Send an ambulance right away."

He was dead. She was sure he was dead.

A rifle cracked once, twice, three times, the loud report of it reverberating across the mountain valley.

The rifle shots, then later the wail of an ambulance siren—a thousand thoughts raced through Bannon's mind as he slithered and twisted through the trees, making a mad dash for home, with Kit right behind him. But only one surfaced when he glimpsed the ambulance parked at the house, not by the barns or corrals. His father.

When he broke out of the trees onto the level ground of the valley floor, Hank Gibbs roared out with the stock truck to meet him. Bannon threw their skis and poles in the back, pushed Kit into the cab, and climbed in after her.

"It's Old Tom, Bannon." Hank took off without waiting for him to get the door shut.

"What happened? How bad is it?" He hated the question; he hated saying it; he didn't want to hear the answer. He'd always known this day would come. His father was old; he couldn't live forever. He thought he'd prepared himself for this. He hadn't. You can't prepare for death, not your own or your loved ones'.

"It's bad. Your sister-in-law found him on the living-room

floor. Somebody said there wasn't no pulse. When I saw you coming and left to get you, them ambulance guys had zapped him, but . . . I don't know.''

Jaws clenched tight in silent protest, Bannon said nothing.

The truck pulled into the yard. Bannon was out of it before it came to a full stop. Sondra rushed toward him.

"Bannon. Thank God, you're here—''

He brushed past her, not really seeing or hearing her. His eyes were on the front door. Then Hec Rawlins was in his path, blocking him.

"They're bringing him out, Bannon.'' The front door opened, confirming his statement. He saw the ambulance medics in jacket-covered whites, the gurney, a body on it.

"Is . . . is he alive?'' He had to push the question out.

The affirming nod was hesitant. "They want to get him to the hospital where the doctors can work on him.'' Hec paused, then added, "That old man's tough, Bannon. As tough as they come. If anyone can make it, he can.''

They had the gurney down the steps. As they rolled it quickly toward the ambulance, Bannon fell in beside it, keeping pace, his gaze riveted on his father's face, seeing the closed eyes, the strange pallor beneath that seared and weathered skin, the slack muscles, the oxygen mask over the nose and mouth—the shell.

"Dad.'' It was a choked sound, barely audible.

When they reached the ambulance, Bannon stepped back, out of the way. A hand pressed on his arm, demanding his attention.

"Ride with me, Bannon,'' Sondra urged. "We'll be at the hospital when they get there.''

He shook his head. "I'm riding with Dad.''

"Then I'll meet you there.''

"No.'' He turned, some rational part of his mind finally working again, forcing back all the feelings that crowded him. "Laura. Pick Laura up from school. Take her home with you. I'll call as soon as I know anything.''

"But you'll need someone with you,'' she protested.

"Laura will need you more.''

"I'll bring her to the hospit—''

"No, I don't want to put her through that. Take her home. You got that?" he demanded harshly.

She drew her head back, her expression stiff. "Yes. I'll take her home."

They had his father loaded in the ambulance. Bannon scrambled in after them.

"Sorry," the medic said to someone behind him. "There's only room for one."

Thinking it was Sondra, Bannon looked back and saw Kit.

"I'll bring the truck," she told him as the ambulance doors closed.

~❧ 26 ❧~

Agitated, anxious, Sondra paced from the telephone in the darkened living room to the expanse of glass that gave her a view of the driveway of her Red Mountain house. Darkness. Nothing but darkness. No flash of headlights to indicate a vehicle traveling over the twisting, climbing road to her house. There was only the sprawl of Aspen's lights and the enamel black of the sky overhead aglitter with stars.

Where was he? Why didn't Bannon come?

Arms crossed, fingers digging into her flesh, she pivoted and walked back to the phone, staring at it, willing it to ring. Silence. She turned sharply and stopped.

Three hours. It had been three hours since Bannon had called. To tell her what? That there had been no change, no improvement, and—no, his father hadn't regained consciousness.

But what if he did? What if he talked? What if he told Bannon the things she'd said? If she was there, she could convince Bannon not to listen to his crazy ramblings, she could convince him he had her mixed up with Diana.

But Kit was there instead. She'd make Bannon believe anything that stupid old man said. She had to be stopped. That old bastard had to die before he ruined everything.

"Emily. Emily!" She swept through the darkened room toward the kitchen and the maid's quarters beyond it.

Sondra reached the kitchen as the Englishwoman walked out of her room, hurriedly tying the sash to her house robe. "Yes, mum. What is it?"

"I'm going to the hospital. Laura is in her room asleep. Listen for her in case she wakes up."

"Yes, mum."

As Sondra turned to leave, the phone rang. She grabbed the kitchen extension before it could ring a second time. "Hello?" she said expectantly, a tension knotting through her nerves.

"It's Bannon."

Fractionally, she tightened her grip on the receiver. "Your father?"

"He passed away ten minutes ago." The flat, emotionless tone of his voice made her pause.

"Did he—was he able to say anything at all to you?"

"No, nothing."

She closed her eyes briefly in relief. "I'm sorry, Bannon."

"How's Laura?"

"She's in bed asleep right now. Do you want me to—"

"Don't wake her. Let her sleep. I'll tell her in the morning."

"That's probably best."

"I'll see you in the morning, then."

"Aren't you coming over? I can make some fresh coffee and—"

"No, I . . . not tonight. Thanks for looking after Laura for me, Sondra. It helps knowing she's with you."

"If there's anything you need, anything I can do, call."

"Thanks."

Sondra hung up, the tiniest glint of satisfaction in her eyes. From behind her, Emily Boggs asked, "The elder Mr. Bannon, is he—"

"He's dead." Dead, and out of the way at last.

The stillness of the house hit him the minute Bannon walked in. It stopped him and held him motionless for a long second.

Slowly, he reached up and slid his hat off, lowering it to his side.

"I'll hang that up for you," Kit said quietly as she slipped the hat from the grip of his unresisting fingers.

He peeled off the ski jacket as if it might lighten the weight pressing down on him. She took that from him as well and hung it on a wall peg while he walked slowly to the table where his father had been found. He looked at the floor, then lifted his gaze to the timbered balcony and the bedroom doors leading off from it.

It hurt to breathe. Bannon caught himself listening for sounds—any sound that would indicate there was life in this house, not merely the hollow echoes of it. Its silence seemed to say more emphatically than the doctor's words that his father would never again clump down those stairs, never rear back his head and expound at length about the land, the mountains. He combed a hand through his hair, trying to rake out the knowledge that clawed at his throat and his mind.

Without saying a word, Kit moved past him to the fireplace. Kneeling on the stone hearth, she gathered kindling from the box and set about building a fire. Soon the crackle of flames curling over split logs broke the crushing silence. Bannon gravitated toward the light and the heat.

Kit watched him, his expression closed in and hard, only the stark despair in his eyes revealing any hint of the awful tension inside. She wanted to absorb some of it, draw it from him into herself. But she knew he wasn't ready to be comforted yet. He was still trying to reject the truth, still trying to deal with the helpless anger, still trying to accept this sudden hole he found in his life. She remembered that feeling of unreality she'd gone through when she learned of her father's death. So she waited.

Slowly, Bannon lowered himself into a chair in front of the fireplace and stared into the flames. A faint noise, part of the creakings and groanings of an old house, broke his absorption. He lifted his head, listening for a taut second, then closing his eyes as a sigh broke from him.

"I keep expecting him to walk in, grumping about something,'' he admitted, meeting her gaze, finally acknowledging her presence.

"I know.'' She shifted to sit on her knees by his chair, smoothing a hand over the top of his and covering it.

"He's dead.'' He rubbed a hand across his mouth. "I keep telling myself that, but I look at his chair and think to myself that he's only left the room, that he'll be back. His presence is that strong.''

"It always will be.''

His hand reached out to touch her cheek. "I can't believe he's gone, Kit.''

"He isn't gone, Bannon. He's here.'' She leaned closer and placed a hand over his heart. "He's right here where he'll always be—in your heart. Can't you feel his big hands squeezing it to tell you it's so?''

In the next second, Bannon gathered her up and pulled her over the arm of the chair, crushing her hard against him. He buried his face in her hair, the sweet, clean smell of it striking deeply into him. The shadow of death seemed all around him, but here was life. He held on to it tightly.

"Kiss me,'' he demanded in a voice that was both desperate and fierce. "Make me feel alive, Kit.''

His mouth roughly covered hers, pain, urgency, and the need for life all tangled up in the harshness of it. He felt the giving in her, the driving return of his kiss. But it wasn't enough. He needed to feel flesh against flesh, to taste the heat of bare skin, to feel the violent pound of blood through veins, to mix pain with pleasure. Nothing else would do.

Long after the need was satisfied, Kit held him in her arms, tears in her eyes and on her cheeks. His were dry. He was Old Tom Bannon's son; he cried his tears on the inside.

The glare of the morning sun bounced off the polarized lenses of the sunglasses John Travis wore. He ran up the steps to Kit's house and crossed to the front door. He knocked twice and waited, listening for footsteps inside. He tried again, this time pounding hard enough to rattle the glass panes in the door. Still there was no sound of anyone stirring.

Impatiently, he swept his glance over the ranch yard, his

unease growing. Damn it, her Jeep was here. Where the hell was she?

He hadn't realized how far the ranch house sat back from the highway, how isolated it was. Kit was so damned trusting she'd open her door to a total stranger. She probably didn't even lock her damned doors.

On that thought, he tried the front door. It swung open with a turn of the knob and a push. He walked in, half expecting to see the place ransacked. It wasn't.

"Kit!" He shouted her name and crossed to the stairs.

Five minutes later he was back in the living room. He'd checked every room in the house. There was no sign of her, and no sign of a struggle. Yet her clothes were in the closet and her makeup was strewn over the bathroom counter.

He checked the phone to make sure it was working. When he got a dial tone, he called the production number. Nolan answered. "Nolan, it's John. I'm at Kit's. Call me back. I want to make sure the phone rings in."

"Right away."

He hung up and waited. The phone rang and he picked it up. "It works."

"No sign of Kit?" Nolan asked.

"The Jeep's here, her clothes, her makeup. Nothing seems to be disturbed. Maybe she's outside somewhere." Kit lying somewhere hurt was the thought he kept to himself. "I'm going out and take a look around."

"Maybe we should call the police."

"Not yet."

As he hung up again, John heard a vehicle pull into the yard. He crossed to the door, catching a glimpse of a high-riding black pickup that belonged to the neighboring rancher. He opened the door and stopped when he saw Kit on the passenger side, relief sighing through his every muscle. They tensed up again as she leaned over and kissed the driver. Not a quick, friendly peck, but a slow and reluctant-to-let-go, morning-after kiss that followed a very satisfactory night before. John had done enough love scenes—both on camera and off—to recognize the meaning of that one.

He backed up and let the door close, then turned into the

room, fighting down the shock, the anger, the hurt. He heard the muted slam of the truck door and jerkily lit a cigarette, blowing out a quick, thin stream of smoke.

Kit walked in, saw him, hesitated, then smiled a little guardedly. "I'll bet you're looking for me." She wore a ski suit and no makeup.

"I've been calling you since ten o'clock yesterday morning. Believe it or not, by midnight I started to get a little worried when there still wasn't any answer. I don't suppose you'd care to tell me where the hell you've been," he challenged in a tightly level voice.

"With Bannon." She pulled her off ski jacket and tossed it on a chair. "His father died last night. A heart attack."

"And you spent the night with him—doing your *bit* to comfort and console him. Is that right?" He coated his rawness with sarcasm.

She was slow to meet his eyes, but when she did, her gaze was level and direct. "Maybe I deserved that, John T., but it was still a cruel thing to say."

He dropped his gaze and took a quick, deep drag on the cigarette. "You always have brought out the best, and worst, in me. It's funny, isn't it?" His twisted smile was anything but amused. "Paula told me I had competition, but I didn't believe her. How could a cowboy compete with John Travis? The old ego showing, I guess."

"I'm sorry," she said.

He glanced at the ash building up on the tip of his cigarette. "What's next, Kit? What are your plans with this Bannon?"

"I don't know," she admitted. "We haven't really talked about anything yet. And this isn't the right time, not with his father and the funeral the day after tomorrow." She knew she wouldn't see much of Bannon these next two days, not alone anyway, not with Laura, the funeral arrangements to be made, and all the friends who would be calling and dropping by. "I know where I want it to lead, but . . ." She shrugged to indicate nothing had been settled.

"That's plain enough." John stubbed his cigarette out in an ashtray. "Since I'm here, I might as well tell you that one of the reasons I wanted to talk to you was to apologize for the other night. Not for the things I said. They were true. But for the way I said them—in anger. I've been under a lot of pressure lately, my own and others'. I took it out on you.''

"You need this movie. I don't. I can afford to be idealistic about the script. You can't.'' She understood that now. "It's really that simple.''

"You can't afford to be idealistic either. You just haven't discovered that yet.''

"Maybe. Either way, it's forgotten.''

John eyed her for several seconds, then shook his head, amazed and amused. "Do you know what makes you so unusual, Kit? You actually mean that.''

"Don't tell Bannon. I don't think he'd like it coming from you.'' Her smile was back.

"A man with a jealous streak, eh? In that case, I'd better make a note to bar him from the set when we do our love scenes. I'm giving you fair warning right now that I intend to enjoy the hell out of them, and he might not like the number of takes we're doing to get it right.''

Kit laughed and pointed to the door. "Go. I have a shower to take, calls to make, and work to do.''

He moved to the door, then stopped, and sent her one of his crooked and potent smiles that could still tug. "Nobody has had a better parting line than Bogie,'' he said and Kit knew immediately he was referring to *Casablanca*. "But he could afford to be magnanimous. He had Bacall.'' He gave her a two-fingered salute in farewell and murmured, "Here's looking at you, Kit.''

He walked out, leaving Kit shaking her head, convinced anew that John Travis would have been extremely easy to fall in love with. If not for Bannon, that is.

Her smile faded when she thought of him at Sondra's now, going through the pain of telling his daughter about her grandfather. This wasn't Hollywood; no one would have the lines written out for him. He'd be on his own, never sure if he was saying the right thing or the wrong.

Dull gray clouds hung like a pall over the mountains on the day of the funeral. The canopy over the gravesite flapped noisily in the cold and bitter wind blowing off the peaks. Bannon sat with the collar of his topcoat turned up against it and his black dress hat pulled low on his head.

When Laura huddled closer to him, he glanced down and saw the simple weariness in her blank expression. She was cold and tired, wanting only to go home. He put an arm around her and hugged her to his side, recognizing she was too young to need this long ritual of saying good-bye, this attempt to reassure the living that even in death life had meaning.

Bannon glanced at the bronze-handled casket draped with a blanket of red roses, the delicate petals already showing the bruising of the cold wind. His father would have been content with a pine box and a prayer. On a bleak day like this, he would have been savoring the wind's keen edge, lifting his gaze to the far blue shadowing on the horizon and listening to the great silence of the mountains. And he would have been glad, too, to be lying next to his wife again.

His glance strayed from his father's casket to the other gravestones in the family plot—his mother's, Diana's. Over in the next section, Clint Masters was buried, too; some he had known well, others only in passing. Yet all of them had left an empty place in his life, great or small. Now his father. And with him, so many parts of the past.

Kit slid her gloved hand under his, twining fingers. He tightened on it briefly, then tried again to pay attention to the minister with no more success than before, and unaware of Sondra's cold eyes watching his every move, intercepting every glance he exchanged with Kit, observing every touch.

How could he treat her like this? She was all too hotly aware that it was obvious to everyone Kit occupied the favored spot at his side, not her. She knew they were gloating over the fact.

Briefly, Sondra glared at Kit. She had John Travis, but he wasn't enough. She had to go after Bannon, too. The bitch was just like Diana, greedy and selfish, wanting everything for herself.

The clouds lingered for two days after the funeral. Finally, on the afternoon of the second, snowflakes began to float lazily down, adding that breath of whiteness to the gray air, and lifting spirits. Humming a Christmas carol, Kit ran lightly up the steps of the old Victorian house that Bannon used for his law practice. When she entered the parlor-turned-reception area, she noticed that the door to his private office was closed.

"Hi, Agnes," she greeted the woman behind the desk. "Is Bannon busy? I was hoping I might be able to steal him away for a late lunch."

"How about a rain check?" Bannon's voice came from her right.

Turning, she found him shrugging into his parka. She didn't even try to conceal her disappointment. "You're going somewhere."

"The ranch. Sadie has a dental appointment this afternoon," he explained. "Laura insists she's too old for a babysitter. She probably is, but—I'm not comfortable leaving her home alone."

"You probably never will be." Even as she said that, Kit was thinking to herself that Laura was a problem she hadn't faced yet, one she hadn't wanted to face.

"What brings you to town?" He lifted a hand in farewell to his secretary, then took Kit by the arm and steered her back out the door.

"The heater quit working in the Jeep. The mechanic at the station said it was the thermostat. Unfortunately, it'll be a couple of hours before he can work on it."

"So you were going to use me to kill some time."

"I thought it was a good idea." She paused, fought off the nervous flutterings in her stomach, and made the plunge. "Do you mind if I go home with you? I can always pick up the Jeep tomorrow."

"Why would I mind?" The look he gave her was slightly puzzled. "You know you can come to Stone Creek anytime. Or—you should know that."

She feigned a sauciness. "I thought it was polite to ask since I'm bumming a ride to get there."

"Polite, is it?" He released a low, throaty chuckle and hugged an arm around her shoulders, walking her to his truck.

Snow fell in light, halfhearted swirls during the ride to

Stone Creek. After the first few miles they lapsed into silence. Kit found herself staring at the road, conscious of the miles falling away, each one bringing her closer to the ranch.

"I'm afraid," she murmured.

Lost in thought, Bannon didn't catch her words. "What did you say, Kit?"

"Nothing," she said with a faint shake of her head.

When they reached the ranch house, Bannon held the door open for her. Kit hesitated a split second, then walked in ahead of him, mentally bracing herself. Laura was curled up in a living-room chair, reading a book and absently tugging at a lock of dark hair. She looked up, letting the lock fall back with the rest when she saw her father and Kit.

"Hello, Laura," Kit said in a calm, quiet voice.

"Hello."

"Has Sadie left?" Bannon glanced toward the kitchen.

"About ten minutes ago," she replied, then turned cool eyes on Kit. "There's coffee in the kitchen if you want some."

The tone, the look, the texture. Bannon was sharply reminded of the cold politeness Laura had shown Kit on another occasion, virtually the only time they'd been together without other people around. She was again giving Kit the same chilly shoulder. He wanted to shake her and order her to stop treating Kit like that. Laura was too young for some things, but she was too old to be told how to think or what to feel. He had no choice but to stand by helplessly.

"No thanks. I don't think I care for any." Kit wandered over to the sofa and sat down. She glanced at her hands, then looked up, straight at Laura. "That's a pretty blouse you're wearing. I had a dress once that was almost the same color of blue. I remember it was my favorite. I wore it to a lot of parties."

Laura looked her over. "Were you my age?"

"No, I was older." The corners of her mouth softened a little. "When I was your age, I used to go to my room, shut the door, and *pretend* I was at a party. I'd put on some music and dance with myself."

"You did?" Laura sat up a little straighter. "I do that sometimes, too. How long did you have to wait before your parents let you go to parties?'' She shot a quick look at Bannon, reddening slightly as if she'd forgotten he was there.

"I thought it was forever," Kit recalled with a laugh. "It seemed that long, but it really wasn't.''

Laura shoved her book onto the table and folded her legs under her to sit cross-legged as she leaned toward Kit, a look of quickened interest on her face, that cool reserve gone. "The first party you went to—what was it like?''

It was going to be all right. Bannon was stunned by the sudden, immense relief he felt. Before Kit could answer, he said, "While you two have your girltalk, I'm going to check on that sick cow.''

"Okay, Dad.'' Laura barely glanced at him, her attention shifting immediately back to Kit. "What was it like?''

As he walked out the door, Bannon heard Kit say, "Your father took me. I wore that blue dress I told you about and . . .''

He was still smiling when he reached the barn. The cow, as expected, was doing fine. He saddled the buckskin and rode out to make a check of the herd.

Riding through the white of the snow on the ground and in the air, he started thinking about Diana. In his mind, again seeing her dark, dramatic face, the laughter that had turned to anger and resentment, hating him and hating herself for the mistake of their marriage, and dying without a kind word for him on her lips.

He thought of all those Sundays he'd stood at her grave, always silently wishing that one time he would see her in his mind smiling at him in understanding, knowing that he had tried to make her happy. He had tried.

On the heels of thought, he recalled that two days ago, when he had buried his father, he'd recognized a vital part of his past was gone. Diana was gone, too.

Bannon reined the buckskin in and sat there a minute with the snow all around him, remembering Diana as he wanted to remember her—not when she had died, but when he had first met her—her lips smiling and her eyes sparkling with laughter and promise.

That was the image he carried in his mind when he cantered

on to check the herd, the image of her death finally leaving him.

When he returned to the house an hour later, the living room was empty. Laura's book was on the table, but there was no sign of either Laura or Kit. Frowning, Bannon hung up his hat and coat, and called out a faintly worried "Hello? Where is everybody?"

"In here," Kit answered from the kitchen. He found her alone, a recipe book lying open on the table. She greeted him with a careless smile, a quick kiss, and a freshly poured cup of coffee. "I thought you might need this to thaw out."

"Thanks." He took a sip from it, too aware that Kit was very adept at hiding her feelings to accept her breezy manner at face value. "Where's Laura?"

"Upstairs, looking for her Paula Abdul tape," Kit replied, then paused, her eyes beaming. "She wants me to listen to it while we make some homemade fudge. We decided it was the perfect afternoon to do it."

"It does sound good." Bannon breathed easier again.

Kit picked up the recipe book and held it close to her for a moment. "I think she likes me, Bannon."

"I never doubted that she would."

But Kit had doubted—not Laura, but herself. Today, she'd found that she could like Laura despite her strong resemblance to Diana. For so long, she'd been bothered by that, worried that she might always resent Laura, that she might always feel awkward and uncomfortable around her. But that wasn't going to be the case. The relief she felt was almost palpable. But she didn't tell Bannon that; it was something she preferred that he didn't know.

Then she realized he was staring at her a little strangely. "Is something wrong?"

"No," he lied and focused on his coffee. There was something. Looking at Kit, remembering the way he had hurt her, he had instantly thought of Sondra.

⇜⇜⌇ 27 ⌇⇝⇝

Sondra's hand remained on the telephone even after she'd hung up. She sat motionless on the edge of her bed, the black satin sleep mask loosely gripped in her hand, the heavy drapes closed against the brightness of the morning light.

Wide awake, the last remnants of sleep gone, Sondra replayed the conversation she'd just had with Bannon. He was coming over; he wanted to see her, but he hadn't said why. What did it mean? His voice, it had sounded warm, so very sincere.

Remembering that, Sondra smiled and caressed the phone. Bannon wanted to see *her*. Everything was going to be all right. She'd been upset over Kit Masters for nothing. Grief over his father's death had blinded him, but only temporarily. He was coming back to her where he had always belonged. Her lips curved in sublime satisfaction.

There was a light rap on her bedroom door. Hearing it, Sondra pushed off the bed, suddenly conscious of all she needed to do before Bannon arrived. She barely glanced at Emily Boggs when she walked in.

"Your morning coffee and juice, mum."

"I don't have time to bother with that now." Sondra waved

off the tray the woman carried. "Set it down somewhere, then strip the bed and put on clean sheets, the Egyptian cotton ones." She crossed to the black marble bathroom. "When you finish that, go do your shopping."

"But—I did the shopping yesterday, mum," Emily reminded her.

"Then take the rest of the day off," Sondra flashed. "I don't care what you do. Just go."

The bathroom door swung shut behind her, leaving Emily Boggs standing there in startled confusion. An instant later she understood. The phone call, the fancy cotton sheets—Bannon was coming.

A few minutes past nine o'clock, the front-door chimes announced Bannon's arrival. Sondra paused in the living room and pressed a hand against the sudden flutterings in her stomach, then smoothed it over the black silk of her kimono. She wore her hair down, the way Bannon liked it, and only a hint of makeup on her face.

Aglow with anticipation, she crossed to the door and opened it wide. "Good morning," she said in a throaty voice.

"Morning." His glance skipped over her, not lingering the way she'd wanted it to, as he stepped in and swept off his hat, running ruffling fingers through his dark hair. "Sorry I'm late. I had to drop Laura off at Buffy's and I forgot how heavy the traffic can be on winter weekends."

"It's a mess, isn't it?" she commiserated and pushed the door shut. "Let me take that." She reached for his hat, moving closer and tilting her head back, expecting his kiss.

Instead he handed over his hat and proceeded to shrug out of his coat. Sondra drew back, uncertainty flickering through her and giving rise to that old suspicion. Then he gave her his coat and she saw the bareness of his ring hand.

"You're not wearing your wedding ring," she murmured, her heart, her spirits, everything soaring.

"I thought it was time I took it off," he said.

"It's long past time, Bannon. You should have done it years ago."

"Maybe. But I guess it took the death of my father to make me realize it was time to let go of the past." His sober expression stopped her from going into his arms the way she wanted to.

For now it was enough that Diana no longer had a hold on him, it was enough that he was here, with her. The celebration, like the loving, could come later when she'd made him more at ease with his decision.

Hastily Sondra hung up his hat and coat and came back, taking his arm and leading him into the living room. "This has been a difficult time for you. I know that," she said in a soothing voice. "Let me get you something. A cup of coffee, maybe."

"Coffee sounds fine."

"Sit down and make yourself comfortable while I bring the coffee in." With a graceful lift of her hand, she directed him to an overstuffed sofa, explaining, "Emily is off doing the household shopping and I'm fending for myself this morning."

But Bannon didn't take a seat. Sondra found him standing in front of the room's glass wall, staring at the mountain vista, when she came back with the serving tray. Placing it on the lacquered cocktail table, she perched on the edge of the sofa and proceeded to fill two cups with coffee.

"I take it Laura is spending the day with Buffy," she remarked as Bannon moved away from the view to join her.

"Yes. They're going skiing at Buttermilk." Taking the cup, he avoided the empty sofa cushion beside her and walked over to a gilded chair. "It worked out well considering I needed to spend some time in the office today."

"You don't usually work on Saturdays," Sondra said, then remembered. "That's right. Agnes mentioned the judge refused to grant a postponement on the Malvern case. It's on the docket for next week, isn't it?"

He nodded. "Jury selection starts Monday. The trial will probably take most of the week."

"It's being tried in Denver, isn't it? What about Laura? You know I'd love to have her stay with me while you're gone."

"Thanks, but I'll be able to make it back most nights." He seemed tense, his expression grim, not softening as it usually did when she mentioned Laura. Something was bothering him. Sondra fell.silent, confident Bannon would tell her. As expected, the lull didn't last long. "We've been friends a long time," he began.

"More than friends, Bannon," she corrected, giving him a warm and smooth smile.

"True." He looked at her. "That's what makes this so hard, I guess. But I don't want you to find out from someone else. I let that happen once before and I'm not going to do it this time."

"You sound serious." She stiffened, not liking the sound of this.

"I am. I intend to ask Kit to marry me. I love her . . ."

Sondra went to ice, freezing out the rest of his words. She'd heard all she needed to hear. After all this time—after all she'd done for him—he wanted to marry someone else.

What had ever made her think Bannon was different? He was like all men. He'd used her; he'd made a fool of her. Did he really think she was going to let him get away with that?

"Sondra? Are you all right?" His voice, heavy with concern, finally penetrated.

"As if you care." Her lips curled back on the words. She was standing, though she had no memory of rising from the sofa.

Bannon was beside her. "Damn it, I do care, Sondra," he insisted, his hand lifting toward her.

She recoiled from it. "You've said your little piece, now go." She looked at him, her eyes cold, killing.

Bannon drew back, his gaze narrowing, a frown creasing his forehead. He hesitated a moment more, then turned and walked away. Watching him, Sondra vowed he would pay for this—he and that little Hollywood slut.

She went to her room and closed the door.

Three hours and a phone call later, Sondra left the house, bundled in her full-length Canadian fisher, a matching fur turban on her head and designer glasses shielding her eyes from the glare of the sun and the snow.

Throngs of strollers roamed the bricked thoroughfares of Aspen's downtown mall, a fashion parade of high heels, furred boots, diamonds, leathers, minks, and fun furs mixing with the latest in ski togs worn by skiers and nonskiers alike. Their voices and laughter drifted through the afternoon air. Sondra ignored all of it as she waited at the appointed place near the park's timbered jungle gym.

An icy calm held her motionless. When she saw Warren Oakes moving toward her through the crowd, the corners of her mouth lifted in a small, coolly pleased smile that matched the hard gleam in her eyes.

"Beautiful day, isn't it?" he said as he joined her.

"Very." She sensed the unspoken question in his look and knew he was wondering why she had wanted to meet him here instead of the office. She also knew he had to be remembering they'd met in public places like this in the past—and the reason for it then. It was the same this time—as he'd soon find out.

"So, what's up?" he asked, falling in step when she began to wander leisurely in the direction of the real estate office.

"I find myself in an awkward position with an important client," she began carefully. "The kind of problem I had hoped was in the past."

There was a long pause before Warren nodded slowly, reading between the lines as she'd known he would. "I see. What are we talking about to solve the problem?"

"This client prefers a special kind of fastball, one that doesn't leave tracks." Sondra used their own vernacular rather than the street term of a speedball to denote the combination of cocaine and heroin. "Only the best, the highest quality, will do. Can you deliver that?"

"No tracks." He frowned. "That may take a day or two."

"That's fine."

"Who is this client?" He eyed her curiously.

Sondra smiled. "You wouldn't believe me if I told you."

"I'll have to know sooner or later."

"Not this time. The client insisted that it come from me, and only me."

"And you agreed?" Warren showed his surprise.

"As I said, this is a very important client."

"Are you sure it's safe?"

"It's the safest thing in the world. If I didn't know that, I wouldn't even consider handling it myself," she stated smoothly.

As they approached the entrance to Hudson Properties, Warren stepped ahead and held the door open for her. Sondra swept past him and proceeded directly to her private office on the second floor. Her secretary was on the phone when Sondra walked in.

"I'm sorry, Miss Hudson hasn't been in yet today," the woman said, then looked up and saw Sondra. "Excuse me, she just came in. Would you hold a moment?" She hung up her extension, informing Sondra, "Mr. Lassiter on line one for you."

"Tell him I'll be with him in a moment," Sondra replied with cool unconcern and continued straight into her office.

Warren followed. At her desk, she unsnapped her purse and took out a sealed envelope. Turning, she handed it to him. "This should handle that other business of ours."

Briefly he fingered the envelope, checking the thickness of its contents, then slipped it into his coat pocket. "It should," he agreed.

"Let me know as soon as you have it," she told him. "And close the door on your way out."

She removed her fur hat and coat, and laid them on a lacquered chair. When she heard the door shut, she picked up the phone and pushed the button on line one.

"J. D., it's Sondra. I'm glad you called. I have some good news for you."

"You do?" His reply was riddled with a mixture of surprise and skepticism.

"Yes. I met with Bannon this morning. He's decided he might be interested in selling that ridge land after all. But he wants some specifics: how much land; the exact dimensions; the price you'll pay; and when. And he wants it in writing. I told him that wouldn't be a problem."

"None at all," Lassiter assured her. "I'll have a proposal drawn up immediately. It will be on your desk no later than Tuesday."

"Bannon will be in Denver most of next week on a court

case, but I'll see that he gets it as soon as it reaches me.'' It was a promise she made without the slightest hesitation.

"Do that. And while you're at it, make sure he accepts the offer.''

"Don't worry, J. D. You will get that property. I can guarantee it.''

A smile lingered near the corners of her mouth long after Sondra hung up the phone. Lassiter would ultimately own that land, although it wouldn't happen the way he expected.

After hours, the courthouse seemed like an empty tomb. Bannon sat on the edge of the bailiff's desk, the phone to his ear, and listened to the hollow echo of footsteps in the outer hall. Absently he rubbed the stiffness in his neck and shoulders as he gazed out the window at the nightscape of Denver's skyline.

There was a click, followed by the sound of the first ring as the operator put his long distance call through. After the second ring, it was answered.

"Silverwood Ranch.''

Recognizing his daughter's voice, Bannon smiled. "Hello, Laura.''

"Hi, Dad,'' she returned brightly. "How's the trial going?''

"Slow,'' he admitted. "What have you been up to today?''

"Just everything,'' she declared. "After school, Kit and I took her old toboggan and went sledding. It was a riot, Dad. We crashed so many times we were covered with snow. We had to use the broom to brush each other off before we could come in the house. Then we made pizza for supper. Well, we made two, actually, because we burnt the first one. Cremated might be a better word. But it was okay. The second one was better anyway. And before you ask, I've only got two math problems to do and I'll be finished with my homework.''

"That's good.''

"Kit says it's remarkable,'' Laura replied. "Are you at the hotel now?''

"No, I'm still at the courthouse, so I can't talk long. Where's Kit?''

"She's standing right here. Do you want to speak to her?"

"Please."

A second later, he heard Laura's muffled voice saying, "It's Dad. He's still at the courthouse."

Kit came on the line, her voice warm and full of life. "Hi. What are you doing there so late?"

"The morning got taken up with a bunch of pretrial motions. Then the voir dires ran longer than anyone expected. The judge decided he wanted to get a jury impaneled before we quit for the day."

"That's probably good, but it makes for a long day. You must have had a premonition something like this might happen when you decided to stay in Denver tonight."

"I guess." Premonition—he wished Kit hadn't used that word. It struck too close to the nagging unease he hadn't been able to shake since he'd met with Sondra. And it was that feeling that made him ask, "Did you hear anything from Sondra today?"

"No. Why? Did you think I might?" Kit asked, her tone curious but light.

"Not really." Truthfully he wasn't sure what he thought. He just kept remembering that look in Sondra's eyes, a look that had bordered on madness. He'd expected tears, or anger, but not that. Bannon shook away the mental image. "I don't even know why I asked that question." He paused, then added, "Maybe I just miss you."

"I miss you, too. I don't know why, considering Denver isn't far away at all and you'll be back tomorrow night. Still it feels like it might as well be forever. Crazy, isn't it?"

"Not to me." The bailiff stepped in and indicated the judge was ready to see Bannon in his chambers. "I have to go, Kit. The judge has made his strikes from the list of prospective jurors. After the other side has made theirs, it'll be my turn." He glanced at his watch. Six-thirty. "With luck, we'll be out of here in an hour and I'll be at the hotel by eight. I'll call as soon as I get there."

His estimate was overly optimistic. It was after nine o'clock when Bannon finally walked through the doors of the Brown

Palace, the reigning dowager of Denver's grand hotels, showing her age in spots yet retaining her air of regal elegance.

Tired and on edge, he turned the heavy cases, bulging with trial documents, over to a waiting bellman, then checked at the desk for messages. There were three, all from Agnes, none so urgent that they couldn't wait until after he called Kit and told Laura good night. He shoved them in his suit pocket and started toward the elevator, tugging at the knot of his tie and pulling it askew.

"Bannon, this is a surprise. I didn't realize you were staying at the Brown."

Focusing on the man who had smoothly intercepted him, Bannon smiled a little grimly. "Hello, Lassiter." He went through the motions of shaking the man's hand. "How are you?"

"Fine. Just fine," he replied, a complacent gleam in the look he gave Bannon. "By the way, you should be hearing from Sondra in the next day or two."

"Sondra." Bannon frowned, the mere mention of her name making him alert. "Why?"

"We stopped over in Aspen on our way into Denver and left that written offer you requested with Sondra."

"A written offer? For what?" His frown deepened. "I'm afraid you've lost me, J. D."

Lassiter seemed amused by his reaction. "The ridge-top land you own, of course. I take it Sondra didn't tell you I was the party interested in buying it."

"No. But it wouldn't have made any difference if she had."

"I think you'll find my offer is very generous. In fact, I think you'll be very glad you changed your mind and decided to sell."

Bannon shook his head. "I don't know where you're getting your information, Lassiter, but that land isn't for sale— not to you or anyone else."

It was Lassiter's turn to frown, none too pleasantly. "According to Sondra, you met with her on Saturday and agreed to sell. I don't know what you think you'll gain by—"

"I met with Sondra on Saturday, but this subject was never part of our discussion."

"You're saying she lied. Why?"

"That's what I'd like to know," Bannon replied grimly.

Kit tiptoed down the dimly lit hall to the spare bedroom that Paula had recently occupied. The door stood ajar. Quietly and carefully, she poked her head into the room and peered through the shadows at the small body curled beneath the blankets, a tangle of long black hair framing the pale face on the pillow. Laura was sound asleep. Smiling, Kit gazed at her a moment, conscious of a warm, vaguely maternal feeling stirring within. She was glad she'd suggested that Laura stay with her while Bannon was in Denver. They had needed time to get acquainted without Bannon around. Awkward moments and all, it had turned out better than Kit had hoped.

Withdrawing, she pulled the door almost shut and retraced her steps down the hall to the stairs, avoiding the floorboards that creaked. In the living room, a cheerful blaze crackled merrily in the fireplace. Scrapbooks and photo albums lay in haphazard order on the tiled hearth, some open, some not. A giant bowl of popcorn, partially consumed, sat on the coffee table amid greasy bowls, dirty pop glasses, and wadded paper napkins. Cassette tapes littered a sofa cushion, left there after Laura had gone through them, finding most of the choices wanting.

Kit surveyed the mess, the corners of her mouth kicking up in amusement. She hadn't realized they'd had this much fun. She almost wished Bannon would call and give her a temporary reprieve from the task of cleaning all this up. Briefly she wondered why he hadn't called yet. He had said he'd phone as soon as he reached the hotel, and it was already after ten. Poor guy, she thought, hoping he'd taken time to at least grab a sandwich.

With a shake of her head, she set about straightening the living room, tackling the sofa first, gathering up all the cassettes and returning them to their slotted tape case. Turning her attention to the coffee table, Kit piled the dirty glasses and bowls atop the buttered popcorn in the big bowl and added the used napkins to the stack.

Picking it up, she wrapped both arms around the bowl's sides and turned toward the kitchen. She stopped, alarm skittering through her at the sight of a dark, slender figure in the kitchen doorway. A woman, clad in a black spandex ski suit that hugged every curve. A close-fitting knit cap covered her hair, leaving only the circle of her pale face exposed.

"Sondra," Kit murmured, almost breaking into a relieved smile; then she saw the gun in Sondra's black-gloved hand, a silencer fastened to the end of its barrel, and her heart leapt into her throat again.

"I'm surprised at you, Kit." Sondra's voice was a low, emotionless croon, its eerie cadence raising the flesh along Kit's shoulders and back. "After all those years living in Los Angeles, I thought you would have learned to keep your doors locked."

As Sondra took a slow, sinuous step into the room, Kit noticed the gleam of moisture on Sondra's black boots, the vestiges of melting snow. Too late, Kit remembered she hadn't locked the back door after she brought in that last armload of firewood.

"Why did you come here? What do you want?" Even as she asked the questions, she was afraid of the answers.

"Can't you guess?" Sondra replied in that same unnerving croon. "You had John Travis. But he wasn't enough, was he? You had to take Bannon, too. It's a shame, Kit. If you hadn't been so greedy, you wouldn't have to die."

Kit stared, hearing the words but not wanting to believe them. This couldn't be real. This couldn't be happening. This was all just some scene from a psycho-thriller. She wanted to pretend that somewhere a camera was rolling. Only there were no cameras, no lights, and no director was going to yell "Cut!" at the crucial instant.

Crazily, she remembered those low-budget horror films she'd made, the way she had always laughed and said she got the parts because she had passed the *scream* test. At this moment, she didn't think she could get a single sound to

come out of her throat. Not that it mattered. Even if she could
scream, who would hear her?

Laura.

A fresh wave of panic hit her. Laura was upstairs asleep.
If she woke up, if she heard voices, noises, she'd come down.
And if she did, Sondra would kill her, too; she'd have to; she
couldn't leave a witness behind.

Dear God, don't let her wake up, Kit prayed silently,
frightened now for Laura as well as for herself.

"Don't worry, Kit," Sondra murmured, a black leg gliding
sideways as she moved into the room, placing each foot
deliberately, then waiting a beat before taking the next crossing step, like a cat making a slow, circling stalk of its prey,
her shoulders squared toward Kit, her cold eyes never leaving
her. "I promise it will happen very quickly. You might even
like it."

Kit turned slightly to keep facing Sondra. Her mouth was
dry and her palms were wet. The woman was crazy, insane.
Stall, she thought. Keep her talking and watch for an opening.
That's the way it worked in the movies.

"You don't really think you're going to get away with
killing me, do you?" she challenged in a hoarse voice.

"Oh, but I will—the same way I got away with getting rid
of Diana."

"You . . . you killed your sister?" Kit barely managed to
get the words out, the shock of the announcement briefly
stopping her from noticing the sofa was between them.

Sondra smiled, the sight making Kit recoil. "It was so
simple. A mere matter of injecting an air bubble into her I.V.
tube. It took only seconds. No one suspected I had anything
to do with her death. No one even saw me slip into her
room—not even Bannon. He was standing at the window the
whole time. After thirty-six hours without sleep, the poor
man was nearly out on his feet. Not that it mattered. Nothing
could ever have been proved. Embolisms have been known
to occur after childbirth."

Bannon. Kit wished he would call that very second. With
the ringing of the phone to distract Sondra and the sofa between them, she might be able to reach the phone, she might

be able to warn Bannon. The telephone was useless otherwise. There would never be time to get to it, dial the emergency number, wait for an answer, and tell them what was happening. She'd be dead before the connection went through.

"How could you do it? She was your sister," Kit protested, albeit weakly.

"She made life miserable for Bannon. I rescued him from that." Her face lost its cold, expressionless mask, her lip curling back in a look of utter loathing. "I loved him, you see. But he never loved me. He only used me. He'll pay for that. Soon. Very soon."

"What do you mean?" Kit turned a little more as Sondra continued to move farther down the sofa, steadily circling to get behind her.

"I mean—Bannon will join you soon," she replied in that soft emotionless murmur again.

Kit saw the gun cabinet behind Sondra. All those rifles lined up in a row. All of them unloaded.

"You're planning to kill Bannon, too, aren't you?" Fear licked the rest of the way to the surface. Kit swore she could feel her heart hammering in her throat.

"You're trembling, Kit," Sondra observed, an avid gleam lighting her eyes. "You'd better put that bowl down before you drop it."

Trembling seemed an understatement. Her legs were quivering so badly they felt like jelly sticks. Sondra gestured with the gun, indicating to Kit to set the bowl back down on the coffee table. She wanted to throw it at her, but Sondra was too far away and the bowl was too heavy, too awkward. Reluctantly she lowered it to the table, feeling as if she'd lost her last shield.

Keep her talking, a voice in her head said. It was the only defense she had left.

"I don't blame you for wanting to get even with Bannon," she said. "He used me, too. I've waited a long time to pay him back for that. I agree with you—men like him don't deserve to live."

Sondra seemed unmoved by Kit's attempt to join sides with her. "Isn't it ironic that there is so much crime in cities like

Denver these days?'' she murmured instead. ''Street gangs,
drive-by shootings, muggings. Bannon will be just another
victim of our violent times, shot down in some parking lot or
on a dark city street. I was raised in Denver. I know them
all.''

Suddenly Kit realized how thoroughly Sondra had planned
everything. It scared her because she saw it could work.

''Such a tragic loss,'' Sondra went on, the soft croon turning Kit's stomach. ''Bannon dead, leaving his poor little girl
orphaned. As her only living relative, naturally I'll take Laura
into my home.''

''No,'' Kit murmured.

''Yes.'' Sondra smiled. ''Bannon has named me as Laura's
guardian in his will. Thoughtful of him, wasn't it? Of course
I'll sell off part of the ranch—maybe even all of it eventually.
Everyone will think it's the smart thing to do. What good is
a cattle ranch to a nine-year-old girl?''

One last step took Sondra out from behind the sofa. She
was directly in front of Kit now.

''Turn around,'' she ordered.

''Why?'' Kit glanced at the gun, weighted by the silencer
fastened to its barrel. Mentally she measured the distance,
trying to decide whether she should make a try for the gun.
The odds of success were worse than long. ''Do you intend
to shoot me in the back?''

''That would be too messy,'' Sondra declared softly.
''Now turn around like I told you.''

Slowly Kit turned until she faced away from Sondra. The
tension, the fear was almost more than her nerves could stand.

''What are you going to do?'' she asked.

''You'll find out . . . in time.''

Was it her imagination, or had Sondra moved closer? Kit
strained, trying to catch some sound, some whisper of movement, anything that might give her a clue of Sondra's inten-
tions. She caught a whiff of perfume, the fragrance cloyingly
sweet. She turned her head a fraction of an inch, trying to
see behind her. She had a glimpse of a slender black arm
swinging down.

Too late Kit tried to duck and avoid the blow. She heard the thud of impact; a split second later pain exploded through her head. Blackness swirled and thickened. She felt herself sinking into it, finding oblivion and relief from the pain.

Dimly, distantly, she felt a pair of hands tugging at her, lifting her, pulling her, dragging her out of the blackness. She didn't want to go. She didn't want to leave it. But the hands wouldn't let her stay. They insisted on saving her.

Saving her. They were trying to help. Someone had come to help. It was going to be all right. She fought to surface, struggling through the blackness and the pain.

Then she heard that crooning voice—Sondra's voice—and knew she was wrong. She wasn't safe. She tried to open her eyes, but they felt weighted, too heavy. Through a slit in her lashes, Kit hazily made out Sondra's dark shape leaning over her. She realized she was lying down—she was lying down on the sofa, a pillow propping her head up. Why? Why had Sondra done that? It didn't make sense. She struggled to focus on that voice.

"—makeup for you." Sondra was talking as if she knew Kit could hear her. "It's very special makeup, too. You're going to love what it will do for you."

Sondra was doing something with her hands. Kit heard a snapping sound, then saw Sondra fitting a pair of plastic gloves over her leather ones. The gun. She didn't have the gun. This was the chance she'd been waiting for.

"It's my own special formula," Sondra explained softly. "My own *lethal* formula combining cocaine and heroin with DMSO. That's short for dimethyl sulfoxide, a marvelous solvent that allows the cocaine and heroin to be absorbed through the skin directly into the bloodstream. It's perfect for someone in your business who doesn't want unsightly needle marks that the camera might see." She reached for something on the coffee table. "Soon you'll be high, Kit. So very high that you'll soar straight to heaven. Another actress who died from an overdose. So senseless. So tragic."

As Sondra leaned across her, a cosmetic sponge in her fingers, Kit gathered herself in one last desperate attempt to survive. With a twisting heave of her whole body, she pushed Sondra off the edge of the sofa and sent her crashing into the coffee table.

Shaking off the dizziness and the fresh waves of pain, Kit staggered to her feet. She had to get away. She had to get out of the house before Sondra found her gun. She started for the door, but something caught her ankle. She kicked out, tipping the coffee table over. The gun landed on the floor—beside Sondra's hand.

Kit saw her pick it up. Out of sheer desperation, Kit scooped a pillow off the sofa and threw it at her. With an upflung arm, Sondra swept it aside, knocking it into the fireplace, its bulk smothering the flames. In that second, Kit bolted for the front door. As she pulled it open, she heard the *splat* of a bullet striking the wood. Then she was outside, racing down the steps into the snow-covered yard.

The Jeep. If she could reach the Jeep, she could get away, she could get help. But the Jeep was in the shed next to the barn.

Kit skidded to a stop at the corner of the house, staring across that open expanse of yard, her head throbbing. There was no cover, no protection of any kind.

The front door was jerked open. Kit sank into a low crouch and scurried close to the side of the porch, letting it hide her from sight. Footsteps ran across the porch, then stopped. Kit held her breath, her heart pumping so loudly she was certain Sondra could hear it. She closed her eyes, feeling the fear creep in again, and immediately opened them, her glance flashing to the trees behind the house. She followed the march of their trunks all the way to the back of the shed.

"You stupid little bitch," Sondra crooned. "You don't really think you can get away from me, do you?"

The footsteps began a slow, steady pace toward the end of the porch where Kit hid. The trees suddenly looked very far away. But she had no choice. She took a deep, silent breath and crept forward until she reached the house proper. There she launched herself forward and sprinted for the safety of the aspen grove. Any second she expected to hear a shout of discovery, the muffled pop of the gun, feel the tear of the bullet into her flesh.

The trees closed around her. She'd made it. Sobbing with relief, she grabbed on to one of the slender white trunks and leaned weakly against it. The rush of adrenaline had blocked out all sensation, even the throbbing pain in her head.

She glanced back at the house with dread. There was Sondra, a slim black silhouette against the white snow. She was studying the tracks Kit had left, her gaze following them into the trees.

"I know where you are, Kit," she sang out softly. "You're only making it harder on yourself. You might as well come out."

Kit flattened herself against the tree trunk, unable to control the mewing sound in her throat. The fear was back, cold like the night air that penetrated the thinness of her clothes and numbed her lungs with each breath. She couldn't stay here. She had to keep moving. She pushed away from the trunk as Sondra took a step toward the grove.

Darting from tree to tree, she worked her way toward the shed, constantly looking over her shoulder, but Sondra had disappeared into the shadows. She tripped on a fallen branch hidden beneath the snow, and fell to her knees, breaking most of the fall with her hands. She scrambled upright, ignoring the stinging in her palms, and hurried on.

At last she spied the rear wall of the shed, the weathered boards rising in front of her. She stopped and scanned the shadows around it. Nothing. Where was Sondra? There was no sound except her own ragged breathing and the pounding of her heart.

Crouching low, she broke from the trees and ran across the few feet of open ground to the woodpile, then crept along it to the shed's side door. She crept inside and paused to catch her breath. There was the Jeep, the most beautiful sight she'd ever seen.

Kit scurried to the driver's side and climbed in. She groped until she found the keys where she'd left them under the seat. She was so cold and scared she was shivering, her fingers numb. She fumbled in her haste to insert the key in the ignition switch. She felt the tears rising, the fear like a sharp pain in her chest.

Suddenly the Jeep's door sprang open. A cry broke from her throat as a hand snared a fistful of hair and jerked it. Kit started to struggle, then froze when she felt the silencer's muzzle dig into her neck.

"I knew you'd try to get to the Jeep," Sondra murmured near her ear. "All I had to do was wait." Tugging on her hair, she forced Kit out of the vehicle. "If you're smart, you won't try it again. But you aren't smart, are you?"

"I won't try it again. I swear I won't," Kit lied.

Sondra kept her grip on Kit's hair and jabbed the gun into her spine. "Then let's go back to the house. You still haven't got your special makeup on." She shoved her toward the side door. When Kit stumbled, she pulled on her hair. "Walk."

"I—I hurt my ankle," Kit said, feigning a limp when Sondra pushed her forward again.

"It won't hurt for long," she crooned. "Open the door."

Outside the shed, Kit kept up the fake limp. It was a long walk between the shed and the house. If she could pretend to slip and lose her footing somewhere along it, maybe—just maybe—she'd have a chance to get her hands on the gun.

The smell of wood smoke tainted the night air. Kit glanced toward the house, trying to gauge the best place to try her stunt. An eerie yellow light danced in the living-room window. She stared at it for a long second before she realized she was looking at flames.

"My God, the house is on fire," Kit whispered, suddenly remembering the pillow that had landed in the fireplace—and the scrapbooks, photo albums, and paper napkins littering the hearth. And Laura. Dear God, was she still upstairs asleep? "Let me go."

Sondra jerked on her hair, pulling her head back. "The fire only means I'll have to alter my plans slightly."

"You don't understand. Laura's in there."

Sondra laughed at that. "You don't expect me to believe you."

"It's the truth. She's upstairs sleeping. She came over to

spend the night with me while Bannon's in Denver. You've got to let me go," Kit pleaded. "You can't mean for her to die. You can't."

The fingers loosened on her hair. "No," Sondra murmured. "She can't die. It would ruin everything. Everything." She turned on Kit, striking out. "You stupid little bitch, why didn't you tell me she was up there?"

The hard blow sent Kit sprawling in the snow. By the time she stumbled to her feet, Sondra was racing up the porch steps. Laboring for air, Kit ran after her.

Sondra charged into the house, calling Laura's name. Flames shot up, feeding on the sudden draft of oxygen that swept in with Sondra. When Kit reached the porch, flames blocked the doorway. She knew the staircase would soon be engulfed if it wasn't already.

She raced to the end of the porch and climbed and clawed her way up the metal drain spout to the porch roof. She inched her way across the snow-slick shingles to the gabled window of the spare bedroom. Crouching down, she peered through the glass. Smoke swirled thinly in the room, but she couldn't see Laura. Had she gotten out? Had Sondra found her? Kit couldn't be sure.

"Laura!" She pounded on the glass.

Something moved. It was Laura. Kit almost cried with relief when she saw the little nightgown-clad girl. Laura came to the window, coughing, her face streaked with tears. Kit pushed at the window, trying to raise it. It was stuck.

From below came a muffled burst, then another and another. The ammunition in the gun cabinet, the fire was igniting it. She had to get Laura out of there. Frantic now, Kit strained to lift the window, but her feet kept slipping on the wet shingles.

A hand grabbed her arm. She swung around, her fingers curling to form claws. But it was Bannon, not Sondra.

"I can't get the window open," she told him.

"Get back," he said and motioned for Laura to do the same. Gripping the sides of the window frame, he rammed his foot through the glass pane, then kicked out the jagged edges and reached inside, scooping Laura up.

Kit moved to the edge of the roof and swung onto the drainpipe, sliding more than climbing down it. As soon as she was on the ground, Bannon lowered Laura into her waiting arms, then climbed down himself and reclaimed Laura before guiding Kit away from the burning house, an arm firmly circling her shoulders.

A man in a chauffeur's uniform came running up. "The fire trucks and an ambulance are on the way."

Kit stared blankly at the limousine parked in the ranch yard, its lights on, its motor running. J. D. Lassiter stood outside the rear passenger door. She had no idea how Bannon came to be with Lassiter. At the moment, she was too tired, too cold, and too relieved to care.

Then she stopped, remembering. "Sondra—I think she's still inside the house." When she looked back, fire curled from every window of the first floor. She breathed in sharply, then met Bannon's gaze. She started to tell him what had happened. Instead, she simply leaned against him. She felt the brush of his lips on her hair and closed her eyes. Later. There would be time to tell him everything later. A lifetime.

Please turn the page
for a special bonus chapter
from

Janet Dailey
Tangled Vines

Coming soon

from

Little, Brown & Company

* * *

CHAPTER I

A television satellite van bearing the News Four logo of the local NBC station in New York stood at the curb a short distance from Playmates Arch in Central Park. There, along the footpath, a camera crew was busy setting up for a remote telecast for the local *Live at Five* report. Behind portable barricades erected by Park Security, a horde of onlookers watched the proceedings in the steamy heat of an August afternoon.

Old-fashioned hurdy-gurdy music from the park's carousel drifted above the drone of the van's generator as Kelly Douglas stepped out of the air-conditioned vehicle. A co-anchor on the evening newscast at KNBC for almost two years now, she was in full makeup, her auburn hair drawn back in a French braid.

"Hey, Kelly." Eddy Michels, one of the tech crew, came trotting up, slowing to a stop when he reached her. "Man, you talk about hot." He wiped a sweaty cheek on the shoulder of his tee shirt. "It must be a hundred in the shade."

"At least," Kelly agreed and lifted her hands. "Welcome to New York, nature's summertime sauna."

"You've got that right." He started to turn away, then swung back. "I meant to tell you—I loved that interview you did with that bureaucrat Blaine the other day. You really had her squirming and stammering around for an answer when you pointed out all the discrepancies in her report. You shouldn't have taken pity on her, though, and backed off."

Kelly smiled and shook her head in friendly disagreement. "I learned back in Iowa not to have a battle of wits with an opponent who has run out of ammunition. Especially an opponent with powerful friends."

He chuckled and conceded, "You have a point there."

"I know I do." Her smile widened as she warned, "Deliberately making a fool of somebody is the quickest way to make an enemy for life."

"I suppose you learned that growing up in Iowa, too," he joked.

"Naturally," Kelly replied with a straight face, then laughed and set off to join the camera crew on the footpath to the arch.

As she drew close to the crew, she was recognized and a male voice shouted from the gathering of onlookers, "Hey, Kelly, aren't you worried about coming here to Central Park?"

"Only with you," she countered quickly and smiled, automatically scanning the crowd to locate her caller.

An older man stood well apart from the others, his face turned in profile, his dark hair threaded with strands of gray. He was dressed in a plaid shirt and a faded pair of golf-green slacks, sharply creased.

The clothes, the cocky sneer of his lips . . .

Kelly went cold when she saw him, fear freezing her in place as images flashed—a hard-knuckled fist swinging with force, pain exploding in white-hot arcs, silencing a half-born cry, the jerk of brutal hands, the stench of whiskey breath, a small, frightened voice sobbing, "Don't hit me, Daddy. Don't hit me," a string of violent curses, the taste and smell of blood.

She stared, her face pale with shock, her mind racing in panic. How had he found her? How, after all these years? She had made a new life for herself. People liked her; they respected her. Dear God, she couldn't let him ruin that for her. She couldn't let him hurt her again. She couldn't.

"Kelly, what's wrong?" a voice asked. "You are white as a ghost."

She couldn't answer. She couldn't look away from him. Then the man turned, giving her a full view of his face. It wasn't him. Relief came in waves.

Finally Kelly was able to focus on the woman in front of her, one of the producer's assistants. "It's the heat," she lied, something she did with the skill of an expert. "I'll be fine."

Reassured by the color coming back to Kelly's face, the woman nodded. "Patty Cummins from the Central Park Zoo is here. I thought you might want to meet her before we go on the air."

"Of course." Kelly glanced back at the man, confirming again it wasn't him. How could it be? He was still back in California. Back in Napa Valley. She was safe. She had nothing to worry about. Nothing at all.

The vineyard baked in the heat of an August sun, its vines strung along the mountain's rugged slope in orderly rows, their roots sunk deep in the rocky soil, drawing moisture from it and the distinctive taste of the earth. The land was poor, incapable of nourishing any other crop, yet from the grapes of this vineyard had come some of the finest wines in the whole of Napa Valley—some said the world.

Rutledge wine made from Rutledge vines grown on Rutledge land.

A tan Jeep with the insignia of the Rutledge Estate winery painted on its doors sat at one end of the vineyard, parked on the grassy shoulder of a dirt road. Sam Rutledge slowly made his way back to it, pausing now and then among the vines to examine a cluster of ripening grapes.

At thirty-six, lines bracketed his mouth and fanned from the corners of his eyes in deep creases, but the years hadn't faded the faint smattering of freckles that showed beneath the dark tan of his broad, roughly planed face. He wore tan chinos and a blue chambray shirt, the cuffs rolled back exposing the corded muscles of his forearms. An old and weather-worn brown hat, the kind that had been in vogue in the Forties, shaded his eyes from the full glare of the sun.

As he neared the end of the row and the Jeep, Sam Rutledge stopped and reached down to scoop up a handful of soil, a mixture of dust and pebbles.

It was Rutledge soil, the same as the vines. His life revolved around them. It was the way he wanted it.

Still holding the dirt in his hand, Sam lifted his head and

turned to look across the narrow vineyard-strewn valley. The wild canyons and spiny ridges of the Mayacamas Mountains lay to the west, a twin to the coastal range that walled the valley on the east. The deep green of conifer and oak blanketed its slopes and contrasted sharply with the dull yellow of summer-parched pastures.

Mount St. Helena stood at the head of the valley, its rounded peak thrusting up to dominate the northern horizon. Over it all arched the blue canopy of an unclouded sky. It was a land of sparse rainfall and unrelenting sun, of cooling fogs from the Pacific and baking heat, of rock, volcanic ash and the sediment of ancient marine life. Sam saw it as nature's crucible.

His fingers curled around the rocky dirt in his palm, holding it tightly for a moment then opening it and turning his hand to let it fall back to the ground. As Sam dusted his hands off, he heard a vehicle on the road. He immediately wondered who had left the main gate open. Rutledge Estate wasn't open to the public. Tours of the winery were by appointment only, and the schedule rarely permitted that.

The sound grew into the definite rumble of a car. A green and white Buick LeSabre rounded the bend in the road, trailing a thick cloud of dust. The staccato roar from its knocking engine shattered the quiet of the vineyard.

Sam recognized the ten-year-old car even before he saw the magnetic sign on the door panel that read Rebecca's Vineyard. There was only one car like it in the entire valley and it belonged to Len Dougherty, as did the ten acres that Dougherty called Rebecca's Vineyard. The last time Sam saw it, it had looked more like a jungle than a vineyard. He hadn't been surprised by that. Len Dougherty only masqueraded as a vintner; his true career was drinking, with brawling an occasional pastime.

Sam had no use for the man and no pity for his current financial problems. It showed in his face when the Buick shuddered to an abrupt stop with a screech of grinding brake shoes. Dust enveloped the car, then swept on.

"Where is she?" Len Dougherty stuck his head out the window, his heavily lined face twisted in anger. "Dammit, I said where is she?"

"What nonsense." Her response was immediate, her voice still carrying the lilt of her European finishing school. "How could we possibly buy his grapes when we have no idea who their parents are? I planted every vine on this estate, tended them, watched them grow from cuttings into maturity. Rutledge wine is made only from Rutledge grapes. If this man should call again, inform him of that."

In full agreement, Claude Broussard nodded. "As you say, Madame."

He had always called her that, from the moment of their first meeting in France when he was a mere boy. Never Madame Rutledge. Certainly never Katherine. To him, she had been always and simply "Madame." An appellation others had picked up years ago. It was not uncommon for those in the industry to refer to wines bottled under the label of Rutledge Estate as Madame's wine. In the decade following the repeal of Prohibition, it had been used in jest, mocking her attempts to produce a red wine to rival the great bordeaux from France. When her wines began to win out in blind tastings against those from famed chateaux, it was spoken with respect and, more often, envy.

No small amount of the credit belonged to him as *maître de chai*, master of the cellar. Aware of that, Claude lifted his head a little higher. But his pleased look faded when an old Buick swung into the winery yard and stopped, the engine backfiring. A fine film of dust coated the old car's highly waxed surface, dulling its sheen. Claude cast a worried glance at Katherine.

Distaste flickered through her expression when she saw Len Dougherty pile out of the driver's side. She smoothed all trace of it from her face as he approached.

Her glance skimmed his graying hair and lined face. His olive-green trousers sported a knife-sharp crease down the legs and his striped shirt was stiffly starched. Appearance was everything to Len Dougherty, even now.

"You can't do this." He halted before her. Aqua Velva had been applied to his smoothly shaven cheeks with a heavy hand, but not heavy enough to mask the smell of whiskey. "You can't take my vineyard away. That land is mine. It belongs to me."

"If you wish to eliminate my claim to the property, Mr. Dougherty, you have only to pay me the balance you owe, and the land is yours," Katherine informed him.

"But that's more than thirty-five thousand dollars." Dougherty looked away, a watery brightness to his eyes, jaw clenched, hands trembling. "I can't get my hands on that much money before the end of October. I need more time." The protest carried a familiar wheedling note. "It hasn't been easy for me since I lost my wife—"

"She died some twenty years ago." Katherine had a voice like cut crystal, sharp enough to slice to the bone when she chose. She chose now. "You have sufficiently milked her death. Do not expect to gain any more from it."

He reddened. The infusion of color briefly eliminated the unhealthy pallor of his skin. "You are a cold and heartless old bitch. No wonder your son Gil hates you."

Pain. It struck swiftly and sharply. The kind of pain only a mother can know when she is hated by her child. A pain that hadn't diminished with the passing years, but rather deepened, just as Gilbert's hatred of her had deepened with time.

Unable to deny Dougherty's claim, Katherine stiffened, holding herself even straighter. "My relationship with Gilbert is not a subject I intend to discuss with you, Mr. Dougherty."

Dougherty had scored, and he knew it. "It must gripe the hell out of you that his winery is every bit as successful as Rutledge Estate. Who knows—in a few years The Cloisters might even be bigger."

A tan Jeep pulled into the yard and parked in the shade of the madrone trees. Out of the corner of her eye Katherine saw her grandson Sam Rutledge climb out.

"I fail to see the relevance of your remarks, Mr. Dougherty." With a lift of her cane, Katherine indicated the papers gripped in his hand. "You have been served with legal notice. Either you pay the full amount owed or you forfeit your vineyard. The choice is yours."

"Damn you," he cursed bitterly. "You think you got me beat, don't you? But you'll see. Before I let you get your hands on my place, I'll burn every inch of it."

"Do that." Sam joined them. "It will save us from bringing in a bulldozer to clear it." To Katherine he said, "I flew over his place last Saturday when I took the Cub up." The Cub was the antique two-seat biplane Sam had restored to flying condition two years ago. "From the air I could see he'd let the vineyard grow wild. It's nothing but a jungle of weeds, vines, and brush now."

"I couldn't help it," Dougherty protested quickly and defensively. "My health hasn't been good lately."

"Go," Katherine ordered abruptly, treating Dougherty to an icy glare. "I am weary of your eternal grousing and I am too old to waste more of my precious time listening to you." She turned to Sam. "Take me to the house, Jonathon."

Inadvertently she called Sam by his father's name, and Sam didn't bother to correct her. He had been a boy of fourteen when his father died some twenty-odd years ago. Ever since, Katherine would slip now and then and address him as Jonathon. Over the years, Sam had learned to ignore it.

He escorted Katherine to the Jeep and helped her into the passenger seat, then walked around to the driver's side. As he swung behind the wheel, he heard her sigh, a note of impatience in the sound.

"Thinking about Dougherty?" Sam ventured, throwing her a glance as he turned the wheel and steered the Jeep onto a tree-shaded drive. "I have the feeling he's going to cause some kind of trouble before this is over."

"Dougherty does not concern me. He can do nothing."

The crispness of her voice made it clear the subject was closed; there would be no further discussion. Her mind could shut doors like that, on things, feelings, or people. Just the way she'd shut his uncle Gilbert from her life, Sam recalled as the Jeep cruised up the narrow lane.

Sam had been away at boarding school at the time of the split. In the valley there had been a hundred versions of what happened, a hundred causes offered for it. Any of them could be true. His father had never discussed it with him, and Katherine certainly never spoke of it.

Through lawyers, she had bought out any interest that her son Gilbert had in the family business immediately following the break-up. Gil had used that money plus more from investors, bought some abandoned vineyard property not five miles from Rutledge Estate, built a monastic-style winery, dubbed it The Cloisters, and successfully launched a wine of the same name, going into direct and open competition with his mother.

More than once Sam had observed chance meetings between them at some wine function. A stranger would never suspect they were mother and son, let alone that they were estranged. No hostility or animosity was exhibited. Katherine treated him as she would any other vintner with whom she had a nodding acquaintance—when she deigned to acknowledge him at all. But the rivalry was there. It was a secret to no one.

"I spoke with Emile this morning," Katherine said. Emile was, of course, the Baron Emile Fougère, owner of Chateau Noir in France's famed Médoc region. "He will be attending the wine auction in New York next week. I have arranged to meet him there."

Her fingers closed around the cane's carved handle. Its presence was a constant reminder of her own mortality, something Katherine had been forced to acknowledge last year after she had been immobilized for two weeks from a fall that left her with a severely bruised hip and thigh.

In the time she had left, Katherine was determined to insure the future of Rutledge Estate. As painful as it was to admit, she doubted that it would be secure in the hands of her grandson.

She cast an assessing glance his way. Sam had his father's strong muscles, his height and build. There was a coolness to his light brown eyes and a hardness to his features. And yet he had never shown any pride in the wines that bore the name Rutledge Estate. And without pride there was no passion; without passion, the wine became merely a product.

Under such circumstances, she had no choice but to look outside the family. This past spring she had contacted the current baron of Chateau Noir and proposed a business arrangement that would link the two families in a venture to make one great wine at Rutledge Estate.

An agreement in principle would have been reached by now if Gil hadn't entered the picture, proposing a similar agreement to the baron. He had done it to thwart and irritate her, Katherine was sure.

"Naturally you will accompany me to New York," she told Sam when he stopped the Jeep in front of the house.

"Naturally." Sam came around to the passenger side and assisted her from the Jeep.

Katherine turned to the house and paused, her gaze running over it. An imposing structure, it had been built twenty years before the end of the century by her late husband's grandfather. Modeled after the great chateaux in France, it stood two and a half stories tall. Creeper vines crawled over its walls of old rose brick, softening their severe lines. Chimneys punctuated the steep slope of the slate roof, and the windows were mullioned, long and narrow with leaded glass panes. It spoke of old money and deep roots.

The entry door of heavy Honduran mahogany swung open and the ever vigilant housekeeper, Mrs. Vargas, stepped out. Dressed in a starched black uniform, she wore her gray hair scraped back in a chignon.

"That man Dougherty was here earlier, demanding to see you," the housekeeper stated with a sniff, indicating what she thought of his demand. "He finally left after I informed him you weren't in."

Katherine merely nodded in response as Sam walked her to the marbled steps of the front entrance. "Have Han Li fix some tea and serve it on the terrace," she ordered, then glanced at Sam. "Will you be joining me?"

"No. I have some things to do." Unlike Katherine, Sam wasn't so quick to dismiss Len Dougherty.

Sober, the man was harmless enough. But drunk, he was known to turn violent, and that violence could be unleashed on property or people. Sam intended to make sure it wasn't Rutledge.

Traffic clogged downtown St. Helena. Its postcard-perfect Main Street was lined with turn-of-the-century buildings of stone and brick, a collection of quaint shops and trendy restaurants. A Toyota with Oregon plates pulled out from its parking space, directly into the path of Len Dougherty's Buick. Cursing, he slammed on the brakes and the horn.

"Damned tourists are thick as fruit flies," he muttered. "Think they own everything, just like the Rutledges."

That thought had the panic coming back, bringing with it the tinny taste of fear to his mouth and the desperate need for a drink.

With relief Dougherty spotted the Miller beer sign in the window of a crumbling brick building. The faded lettering above the door identified the establishment as Ye Olde Tavern, but the locals who frequented the bar called it Big Eddie's.

Leaving his car parked in an empty space in front of the bar, Dougherty went inside. The air smelled of stale tobacco smoke and spilled drinks.

Big Eddie was behind the bar. He looked up when Dougherty walked in, then turned back to the television set mounted on the wall. There was a game show on. Big Eddie loved game shows.

Dougherty claimed his usual perch, the stool at the end of the bar. "I'll have a whiskey."

Big Eddie climbed off his stool, reached under the counter and set a shot glass and a bottle of whiskey in front of Dougherty, then went back to his seat and the game show.

Dougherty bolted down the first shot in one swallow, feeling little of the burn. With a steadier hand, he filled the glass again. He gulped down half of it, then lowered the glass, the whiskey flowing down his throat like lava. The foreclosure notice he'd stuffed in his shirt pocket earlier poked him in the chest.

Thirty-five thousand dollars. It might as well be three hundred thousand for all the chance he had of getting his hands on that kind of money.

Damn her eyes, he thought, remembering Katherine Rutledge's steely gaze boring into him. He threw back the rest of his drink and topped the glass again, dragging it close to him.

He lost track of time sitting there, one hand clutching the bottle and the other around the glass. More of the regulars drifted in. Dougherty noticed his bottle was half empty about the same time he noticed the level of voices rising to compete with the television. Tom Brokaw's face was on the screen.

The legs of a barstool scraped the floor near him. He glanced over as a baggy-eyed, heavy-jowled Phipps, a reporter with the local paper, sat down beside him.

"Hey, Big Eddie," a man called from one of the tables. "A couple more beers over here."

"Yeah, yeah," Big Eddie grumbled.

Dougherty cast a sneering look over his shoulder at a garage mechanic in greasy coveralls sitting with a painter in splotched whites. Common laborers all of them, he thought contemptuously. Punching time clocks, letting others tell them what to do. Not him. Nobody gave him orders; he was his own boss. Hell, he owned a vineyard. He—

He remembered the paper in his pocket and felt sick. He couldn't lose that land. It was all he had left. Without it, where would he live? What would he do?

He had to stop the Rutledges from stealing it. He had to find a way to get that money. But how? Where?

Nothing had gone right for him. Nothing. Not since Becky had died. His beautiful Rebecca. Everything had gone sour after he lost her.

Tasting it again, Dougherty tossed back the whiskey in his glass. As he did, his glance fell on the television screen.

"In a scene reminiscent of the assassination attempt on President Reagan," Tom Brokaw was saying, "New York State Senator Dan Melcher was wounded tonight and a policeman shot. Kelly Douglas has more on this late story from New York."

A woman's image flashed on the screen. Night darkened the edges of the picture, held at bay by the full illumination of a hospital's emergency entrance in the background. She stood before it, a kind of restless energy about her strong and angular features that briefly pulled his attention.

He looked down when she started to speak. "Tom, State Senator Dan Melcher has been rushed into surgery suffering from at least one gunshot wound to the chest. . . ."

That voice. His head came up fast. The low pitch of it, the smooth ring of authority in it. There was no mistaking it. He knew it. He knew it as well as his own. It had to be her.

But that woman's face was no longer on the screen, its image replaced by that of a middle-aged man coming out of a building, flashing a smile and waving at the camera, ignoring the angry shouts from picketers outside. There was only her voice—that voice—talking over the images.

"Since his election to the State Senate two years ago, Dan Melcher has been the center of controversy. His liberal stand on civil rights and pro-abortion issues has created loud opposition. Tonight, that opposition took a violent turn."

The voice stopped as a woman broke from the sign-carrying crowd. "Murderer!" she shouted and started firing.

The ensuing flurry of action was difficult to follow. An aide grabbed a slumping senator; a policeman fell; bystanders scattered amidst shouts and screams of panic; someone grabbed the woman and another policeman wrestled her to the ground. The scene was followed by a close-up of the unconscious senator, blood spreading across the white of his dress shirt. Then it cut to a shot of him being loaded into the ambulance.

It was back to the woman. "We have just received late word that the patrolman who was also shot has died of his injuries. The police have the assailant in custody. Her identity has not been released. Charges are pending." She paused a beat, then added, "Kelly Douglas, KNBC, New York."

Dougherty frowned. She didn't look the same. The coloring was right—the auburn hair, the dark green eyes. And that voice, he knew he wasn't wrong about it. She had changed a lot in ten years. She had even changed her name, took her mother's. But her voice hadn't changed. It was her. It had to be.

He stared at the television, blind to the patriotic commercial for Maxwell House coffee flickering across the screen. Beside him, Phipps groused to Big Eddie, "They call that journalism. You couldn't write lousy copy like that and get away with it in the newspaper business."

Big Eddie shrugged his disinterest. "A picture's worth a thousand words."

"Some picture," Phipps scoffed. "A pretty face in front of a camera pretending to be a reporter. Take it from me, everyone in television news is overrated and overpaid."

Len Dougherty half-listened to the exchange. He was confused, his thoughts jumbled. He started to lift his glass, then abruptly shoved it away and pushed off his stool. He needed to think.

Hello again from Branson—

By the time you read this, my husband, Bill, and I will be completely moved into our new home here on the beautiful shores of Lake Taneycomo in Branson. I know it looks very big and grand on the outside, but on the inside it's wonderfully cozy and comfortable. Believe it or not, I only have to walk *one foot* farther than I did in our old house to get Bill a fresh cup of coffee! (Yes, I still spoil Bill by bringing him his coffee after all these years. Could it be love, I wonder?)

I have to admit every time Bill and I look at our new home, we have the urge to pinch ourselves. Few people ever get the chance to build their dream home and Belle Rive is certainly ours. I don't think I'll ever forget the thrill I felt when I saw the crane lifting those towering pillars and setting them in place around the front portico.

But I guess my most vivid memory will be the pride that went into building it by everyone involved—the brick masons, the plumbers and electricians, the carpenters and cabinet makers—literally every single person who worked on it. If our home looks like a showplace, it is due to the care and the craftsmanship of those who worked on it. A public "thanks" goes out to all of them, including our son Jim who acted as the contractor, supervising every phase of it (with Bill looking over his shoulder, of course) and our daughter-in-law Mary who was our liaison with the decorator, allowing me the needed time to write another book.

Our new home was far from the only thing going on in Branson this past year. I'm proud to say Branson, Missouri, has been making news nation-wide—as many of you may know from the articles in *Time* magazine or *USA Today*, or the *60 Minutes* piece on Branson.

For several years now, Branson has been the home to such nationally known country music stars as Roy Clark, Mel Tillis, Jim Stafford, Moe Bandy, Ray Stevens, Danny Davis and the Nashville Brass, Mickey Gilley and Boxcar Willie, plus a host of fantastic local talent, all of them performing nightly in their own theaters. This year Branson adds Johnny Cash, Larry Gatlin and the Gatlin Brothers, Willie Nelson, and Andy Williams to the list of stars performing here. Not only that, the magnificent 4,000-seat Grand Palace—the Crown Jewel of country music theaters—has opened, featuring two top country stars at every performance.

You don't know what a kick this is for Bill and me. For years now every time we have told people in New York or Los Angeles that we live in Branson, Missouri, we have gotten blank looks, followed by questions like—"Where is Branson, Missouri?"—"Why on earth do you live there when you could live anywhere you wanted?"—"What is there to do in Branson?" Somehow I don't think people will be asking us those questions anymore.

Let me stop bragging about Branson for a minute and tell you about my new book that is scheduled for release in hardcover by Little Brown this coming October. *Tangled Vines* is set against the spectacular backdrop of California's Napa Valley wine country and New York City, combining the mystique of wine making and network television with the tragedies of alcoholism. Part of me wants to tell you that *Tangled Vines* is a story about Kelly Douglas, a television news personality who is forced to face unpleasant memories about her past, but—another part of me says this story is about Sam Rutledge and his grandmother Katherine Rutledge, who founded the winery of Rutledge Estate. The truth is—*Tangled Vines* is a story about all of them, "tangled" together. Watch for it.

In the meantime, if you have never been to Branson, come see us. We don't mind one bit sharing Branson with the world.

Happy Reading,

Janet Dailey

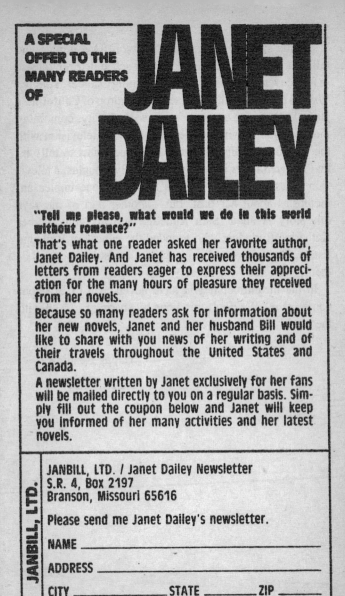